Dead in Pleasant Company
A Pennsylvania Dutch Mystery

By

Hannah Fairchild

This book is a work of fiction. Places, events, and situations in this story are purely fictional. Any resemblance to actual persons, living or dead, is coincidental.

© 2002 by Hannah Fairchild. All rights reserved.

No part of this book may be reproduced, stored in a retrieval system, or transmitted by any means, electronic, mechanical, photocopying, recording, or otherwise, without written permission from the author.

ISBN: 1-4033-0002-X (e-book)
ISBN: 1-4033-0003-8 (Paperback)

This book is printed on acid free paper.

1stBooks - rev. 10/22/02

DEDICATION

This book is dedicated to Billy…who waits.

With thanks to Betsy Zan's red pencil, to my children, for their tolerance, to John and Rose for their encouragement, to Stephen for his faith, and especially to Jen Rogers, without whose help this would have been impossible.

Thaxton Family Tree

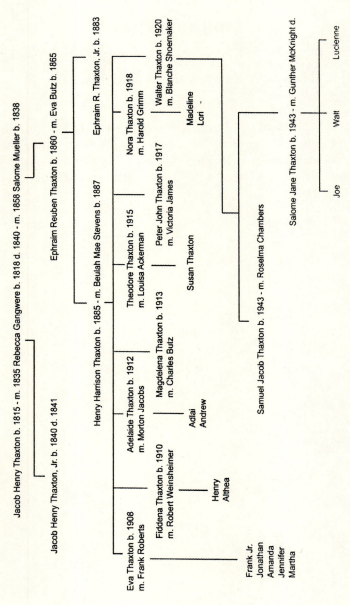

PROLOGUE

"You just left the kid on the bus? Are you nuts?"

"It's the best possible solution," the woman said calmly. "You know the damn kid! A trouble maker if I ever saw one. And that wild imagination! Nobody's gonna believe anything this kid says, believe you me."

"What the hell am I supposed to tell my sister?"

"Don't ask me! That's your problem. I told you not to bring the brat along." She looked at his face. "Well, what did ya want me to do? Adopt the kid? Bump the little monster off?"

"I don't know," he said irritably. "Could have left her with some agency or other."

"My God! Leave it to you and we'd be in the can." Her husband looked at her with varying degrees of disgust, doubt and approval. "In any case, it's done. Nothing we can do about it now."

Dead in Pleasant Company
A Pennsylvania Dutch Mystery

CHAPTER 1

Janesville Community Hospital. Janesville, Wisconsin.
They stood together looking down at the corpse. The man's worried frown touched the woman. She put her hand on his shoulder. "She's old. Old people die, Dr. Philips."

He jerked away. "Not when there's nothing wrong with them, they don't, Nurse. Not under my care, they don't."

She moved off. If he didn't want her sympathy that was all right with her. She was used to the arrogance of doctors who could not believe one of *their* patients died.

A few minutes later Phillips left too, left for home and bed. When his wife asked him for the third time to stop thrashing around, he gave up, got dressed and returned to the hospital.

At his office terminal he pulled up the woman's medical history. His patient for fourteen years, her last annual checkup showed a sudden rise in thyroid level. He'd prescribed a low dose of synthroid and told her to return in three months. Later, it had risen even further. He'd increased the dosage a cautious twenty-five milligrams. Three days later her daughter called to say her mother was complaining of headaches. He'd made an appointment to see her today. Now she was dead.

He scrolled back to the beginning of her file, studying his patient's record carefully. Yes, everything that should have been done was done. He checked the lab code to see who was on duty the last times she came in. Sometimes lab technicians made mistakes. No problem there. Marty Ackerman had been on both days and checked the results herself. Ackerman was as reliable as rain, so it was not that. What then?

He shut down his system and left. Might as well go home. If he couldn't sleep, he could always bunk down in his library and catch up on his reading.

Passing the children's ward he caught sight of his friend. He joined him at the window. "You're up late, Dan. What's up?"

His friend gave him a brief nod, then shook his head. "Had a patient die on me," he said glumly. "Five-year-old boy."

Philips heard himself saying this was a hospital and sometimes people died in hospitals, even five-year-old boys. The words floated back at him in the quiet ward, mocking him.

He heard his own angry response repeated. "Not in my care," his friend said angrily. "Not without a reason." His friend shook his head as if pushing death away. "He had a sore throat! That's all! A sore throat! Temp below a hundred. Suddenly today it pops up to a hundred and six! A hundred and six!"

"Well, that's certainly some..."

"But there's no reason for it! I've done all the tests myself and there's nothing there! This child should not have died." He looked at the other man, apparently noticing him for the first time. "What are you doing here anyway? I thought one of the perks of being Chief of Staff was you could sleep nights."

"Not when you have a patient die on you."

"You too?"

"She shouldn't have died. There was nothing..."

They looked at each other.

"Oh my God!"

"Oh no! It's not possible! Not here in Janesville!"

"Oh my God!"

They stared at each other for a moment, then Philips reached for the phone.

Dead in Pleasant Company
A Pennsylvania Dutch Mystery

* * * * *

SAM THAXTON

I sat at my sister's table and smothered a yawn. Sal glanced at me, then quickly away, pressing back a conspiratorial smile in the way she has since she—we—were seven. Our little exchange went unnoticed by her guest. No surprise there. Judd Tunnelson's name should appear in Webster opposite *self-absorbed.*

Tonight Tunnelson seemed even more full of himself than usual and there was an odd air of expectancy on the famous face. Whatever it was, it did not, naturally, keep him from jabbering. I suspected, in fact, that had thought and speech ever come to a complete confluence anywhere in the corridors of his brain, he'd not be the singularly successful tele-journalist we've all come to know.

*"Frank*ly Sal," he was saying frankly when I tuned back in, "I admit to a certain amount of fru*st*ration in getting the kind of story I came to Plainfield to *do!*" That distinctive way of punching words out at you as if they were weapons has been mimicked by everybody and his uncle, up to and including the President himself. "In fact getting *any*thing out of folks around here is like pulling *teeth*! *Hone*stly Sal, your people simply have not been as...as forth*com*ing as I like." By 'your people' he meant Plainfielders—a term which might have fit when Grandfather Henry Harrison Thaxton *was* Plainfield, but no longer. "I don't get it," the voice vibrated on, genuinely bewildered. "*Most* townsfolk are only too *hap*py to have their triumphs brought to national attention. Not that," he pointed a forked hand at us as if to ward off misunderstanding in the way of one accustomed to having

private words made public, "people have been *rude* or anything."

Honeycutt set another basket of mashed potato bread before him. "Anything else, sir?"

"My call hasn't come through yet?"

"No sir."

"And nothing new from the highway department?"

"No sir. The Interstate is still closed and more snow is expected tonight."

"Damn! Well, let me know."

"Yes sir."

Tunnelson slathered butter on a crusty slice and stuffed it in. I wondered if the anticipated phone call accounted for his edginess. "As I was saying," the newsman scarcely paused for breath, "your people are friendly enough but, well, for one thing they don't gossip—a real disadvantage in my business!" Another huge chunk followed the first. "Mmmm. Your own butter, you say? From cows right here on your place? Wonderful! Wonderful! No wonder you have trouble losing weight." This to my sister. "Not that you don't look fine *now,* but let's face it, you *were* chunking up there."

I knew it would be just a matter of time before the man's legendary fondness for the jugular asserted itself and where else could he attack my sister? Her recent struggle to bring her weight down had been damned tough. Even so, praise for the victory is not likely to be well received. Any comment about how good she looks now is likely to be greeted with, "In comparison to what?" Fact is, she resents the assumption that it's anybody's business but her own.

She was quite capable of putting him in his place. I waited for her to do so. Instead she merely replied wryly that it had been thoughtless of her to give offense to those forced to look at her. "Fortunately," she added, in rare but patently mocking tones, "I've seen the error of my ways. Do I take it I'm forgiven?"

"Hunh? Forgive?" He squinted at her. "What are you talking about? I'm trying to be nice here. I've been meaning to tell you all week how pleased I am you've finally dropped a few pounds."

A *few* pounds? Surely now she'd come out with both guns blazing, but she continued in the same vein.

"And I appreciate it. Thank you. But that's enough about me. You were saying how difficult it is for you that people here don't gossip."

"Oh yes. A real disservice in my business. And another thing," another forkful stuffed in, "they don't give a damn if they get their names on television or not." He struggled to put his finger on the Pennsylvania Dutch. I wished him luck. "They just don't seem to…respect the importance of our work as journalists." Translation: nobody here saluted his fanny.

I opened my mouth to say we are genetically incapable of bending in that position, but a warning glance from Sal kept my mouth shut. She was right of course. If the Pennsylvania Dutch *do* go to the trouble of forming an opinion, (and that's a big if), we certainly do not trot them out in public, nor do we argue with a guest at table.

Blissfully unaware of the budding atmosphere, Tunnelson yakked on. "Naturally, we in the working *press,*" here unction and virtue struggled for a foothold, "have to be able to take it as well as dish it out and yours truly is no exception, but…"

Okay. You get the idea. For twenty years that loud, highly opinionated and acid wit have lorded it over President and pauper, guest and fellow journalist alike, on the next to highest rated nationally televised news show— pardon me, news magazine in the country. I don't argue Judd Tunnelson is the country's best known investigative journalist, you might even say the father of that particular art—if art it be—but tonight, all three of his dinner companions seemed to be wishing they were somewhere else.

He'd been cluttering up Sal's gate-house close to a week now, working on a story about Plainfield's singular victory in keeping gambling out of the county. I'd been away so wasn't quite up to snuff but, guessing from my sister's untypically cool attitude to a guest in her home, his stay had not been auspicious.

Had her suspicions of his real agenda been on target? Had he been trading on the few tenuous dates they'd had when they were in London at the same time a while back to dig up something about the Thaxtons? I'd put it down to the paranoia with which my sister seems to have been born—perhaps because I beat her out of the womb by a couple of hours—yet, I have to admit this time she may have had something. *Sixty Minutes'* effort to guess at the true worth of what everyone insists on calling the 'Thaxton empire' had aired while I was gone and Tunnelson's network would certainly be looking to top it. Had Sal called him on it? Did that account for his odd expression? I looked at him more closely. No. The look was more of a cat staking-out a particularly luscious canary. What in hell had he been up to?

I turned him off to think. It is not often my sister surprises me, yet tonight she had—twice. First, when Honeycutt let me in all dolled up in white bow-tie and black suit, the most formal 'buttle' attire my sister permits him. He'd taken coat, hat and stick, directing me to the large dining room. That usually means a room full, but there was just the four of us. On top of that she'd left the conversational ball entirely to me. Now I can carry my end of jabber as well as the next guy but against Tunnelson it was hopeless. Nor was I getting any help from my nephew

Dead in Pleasant Company
A Pennsylvania Dutch Mystery

Walt, the only one of Sal's three presently at home. Walt Junior smoldered across the table from Tunnelson deep in late adolescent funk. As for Sal, her contributions were limited to small viola-like flutters of 'oh really,' and 'how interesting,' so palpably phony it wouldn't have fooled a pup. I wondered what was up. When you have shared a womb for nine months and a life for forty-odd years you'd have to be completely devoid of interest in human nature not to know that person as well as you know yourself and I know her. Like her too, come to that.

I realized I was being addressed.

"...you're here finally, Sam. I've got something to ask you."

"Eh? Ask me? Go ahead. Ask away."

"Well sir! I've decided to ask you for your sister's hand in marriage."

Sal dropped her fork. Walt's splutter sent a mouthful back on his plate and everything stopped dead. I looked at Tunnelson for some sign this was his idea of a joke. Far from it. He stayed on me, speaking as if the object of the discourse was not there. Whatever he saw on my face, he read as a need for reassurance—like I thought this was all too good to be true.

"Why yes," he said calmly. "I've been giving it serious thought all week and I think it's a workable idea. I'd be willing to take her on, even though she's no beauty and well past her prime. Naturally I don't mean to imply marriage to her would be without compensations. She's pleasant enough for the most part. Her occasional querulousness is to be expected at her age and will no doubt mitigate with marriage. On the plus side, she is rather well thought of generally, especially in Washington circles, though some do think she's a bit of a prude." He bent toward me and said confidentially, "I put that down to her not having a man. And man to man," he continued unabashed, "no doubt *your* wife would be pleased to have your sister taken off your hands. Don't mistake me, I'll derive some benefit as well. I could retire and write that book I've been wanting to write. And," the sales pitch gathered steam, "I've always wanted children and hers will do nicely. They're old enough to have passed the most tiresome aspects of rearing while still of an age that they can benefit from a man's counsel. Oh, don't worry," (he'd finally had a look at Sal's face,) "your kids will take to me all right. I know how to get 'round them. My numbers with young people don't truly reflect how well I communicate with them in person. To be honest, having a few of my own could actually help my numbers. How about it, son?"

Walt damned near choked. Tunnelson looked at each of us in turn. "I see I've surprised you all. That's understandable. My reputation as one of the country's most eligible bachelors follows me everywhere. But really Sal my dear, there's no need to thank me. Washington can use a little of the old-fashioned morality you represent. I know more than one Congressman has taken you out and can testify to your...abstemiousness. That's the kind of wife I want. I wouldn't like to be trying to do an exposé of someone in government only to discover my wife was...involved with him—or her I suppose I need to add these days. I wouldn't have to worry about that with you. So," he returned his attention to me, "what do you say?"

The three of us stared at each other. After a moment Sal tilted her head at me. "Going once? Going twice? I believe it's on you, sir."

I grinned at her, but before I could get my mouth working, Tunnelson was off again.

"Clearly you're not prepared to give me an answer at this time. That's fine. There's no urgency about it though I would like to begin looking for a more suitable residence. Do you have any objections to Georgetown or would you prefer Falls Church? I think you can trust me to find something suitable. Naturally you'll sell this place." He gave the home my sister thinks no more of than her own skin a disdainful glance. "It should bring quite enough for at least a down payment on something decent."

Surely now she would explode. The very notion of parting under any circumstances with the barn she'd converted would earn Tunnelson the put-down he deserved.

"Jump in any time, Big Brother," was all she said.

Okay, so she was giving me the pleasure. After where I'd been for a couple of weeks I could use some fun. Taking a page from her book, I said his offer was very kind "...but, naturally, I'll have to take it to the family. They'd have to approve her leaving Thaxtonville."

"Really?"

"Oh yes. I'm sure you've heard how tight the Thaxtons are."

"Yes. Yes of course," he rushed to assure me. "But surely they would like to have someone in Washington? I don't understand." And indeed, he looked bewildered. Then to her, "Is that what you want?"

"Honestly, I hardly know what to say. Such an honor! It's incredibly kind of you to ask, Judd," she said meekly, "but to be frank, you wouldn't be happy with me. I should probably put weight back on again in the future and then what would you do?" The thought jarred him. "No, no. I couldn't possibly live up to the standards expected of your wife. Please. Let's just put it aside. Why don't you tell Sam about the piece on which you're working. When do you think the Plainfield story will air?"

He looked distractedly around. "Well perhaps we *should* talk about it after you've all had a chance to think about it." He pulled himself together. "As to how the piece is going, isn't that what I've been trying to tell you? It isn't going anywhere. It just lies there! I tried to tell my producer that. I suppose he thinks I'll find a way to breathe life into it, but, except for getting to see you in your home court and having some marvelous meals, I'm just wasting my time here. As a matter of fact," the enigmatic look appeared again. "I'd be gone if I wasn't waiting for one of my...no, I promised not to say anything yet. It's too soon. I can say, however, I've got a line on...something very.... "No. No. I daren't say any more. As it stands Sal, I hope you won't be too disappointed if I push off. Fact is, I'd be gone now if the expressway wasn't snowed shut."

Surprise and relief flitted over Sal's face, but her voice reflected only genuine interest.

"Off to Philadelphia then? Have you a better story there?"

"You might say so," he said almost gleefully. "Yes, you just might say that. Can't say anything right now that might get out." He tilted his head in Walt's direction.

He may as well have poked a wasp's nest. Walt, clearly only present under protest to begin with, had been hanging on to his temper by a thread.

"Jeez! As if I cared! Gimme a break! If you'll excuse me, I'll get out of your hair and you can talk grown-up talk!" You could cut the derision with a knife. "Mom. Uncle Sam." He gave us each a nod as he rose.

"You'll be missing dessert, Son."

"I'll get something down at the 'store.'" He turned to go. "What we having anyway?"

"Scripture cake I believe."

He paused at that. "Just save me a piece then." And he was off.

The young man's departure went completely unnoticed by Tunnelson, whose mind was elsewhere. So much for his numbers with the country's youth, I thought.

With Walt gone the booming voice shrank to little more than a mumble. "Could be an incredible break for me," he

Dead in Pleasant Company
A Pennsylvania Dutch Mystery

said, absently crumpling his napkin. "Damned network's been harping at me to bring in another Pulitzer. This would do it. Why the hell doesn't he..." He looked up then, apparently rejoining us. "Get Honeycutt again, will you Sal? That call must be in by now."

"Oh? Sounds important," she said.

"The story of the century, that's all!"

"Story of the cent...You mean this Mastermind thing?" Sal glanced at me to see if I was paying attention.

I was. The old gas-bag had finally caught my attention. I drew a cigar from my case. "Sounds really important," I said casually.

He turned foxy. "Could be. Could be. Can't say for sure. Nothing official at this moment. Ah, there you are Honeycutt! What about my call?"

"I'm sorry, sir. There's been nothing."

"Damn!"

I studied him under lowered eyes. Was this legit or was he just trying to get back in the saddle? The former, I decided. For whatever reason, he'd let the cat out of the bag.

"Well, keep a sharp ear out, will you Honeycutt?"

"Yes sir."

Tunnelson turned to look at me archly, his eyes gleaming. "It wouldn't be the first time the press got there first."

True enough. Kaczynski. Watergate. Half a dozen different fill-in-the-blank 'gates.' Nope! I wasn't yawning any more!

"Think of it!" He leaned back in his chair and stretched. "The criminal of the century! Hell, this guy makes Kaczynski look like a boy scout! I was talking to the guys down at the Bureau..."

He continued to lecture 'in confidence' what the 'Bureau' thought, what they were doing, what they should do and who should do it. I listened. Somewhere in his diatribe could be something officials didn't have and it was something to add to my sub-rosa report to Cousin Andy.

Not that Andy had said just what his role in the whole thing is—Andy can make a clam look like a talk show host—but ever since the discovery of moles within the Pentagon he'd taken to calling on me occasionally for unofficial help. It seems my reputation as the Thaxton twin who got the looks while his sister got the brains is, from Andy's standpoint, a perfect cover for taking a quiet look-see into various trouble spots. Nobody takes me seriously. As it is, between the various family businesses, the friends I've made on the equestrian circuit and my old pals from my days in Air Force Intelligence, I have an unobtrusive 'in' almost anywhere. What if, after chasing halfway 'round the world, the news was here in my sister's dining room? The very idea put a burr under my saddle.

"...be surprised if this Mastermind guy isn't somebody connected to the investigation," Tunnelson was saying. "Otherwise why aren't the encryption codes working?"

I knew the answer to that, but it was not for public consumption. I tapped out t-a-l-k in Morse code on the table to get Sal's attention. She nodded imperceptibly and glanced at her guest's plate.

"Shall we have our dessert on the 'porch'?"

"My sister," I rose to push back an exuberant Thaxton chestnut curl from Sal's forehead, "wants to watch the snow."

* * * * *

Plainfield Bus Terminal.

Luke Warmkessel slogged his way up the narrow aisle of the bus, pausing briefly at each row to push the nozzle of the vacuum across the seats of No. 3134. Soda cans, coffee cups, crumpled paper bags: these he tossed into the plastic bag tied at his waist, leaving the job of vacuuming the floor between seats for the return trip.

Halfway up the aisle his eyes brightened at what he saw ahead. Someone had left a coat on the last seat. He began to calculate what it was worth, adding to his assessment as he worked his way back. Topcoat, looked like. Man's. Should he turn it in? Keep it? Sell it? He produced interior argument on all sides. Add a nice, warm coat to his wardrobe? Add, say ten, fifteen bucks to the box in his garage?

As he approached the last seat his face fell. Not worth much after all. Too dirty. Too ragged. Prob'ly somebody took it off when the bus got too warm then was lulled to sleep by the rumble of tires on uneven roads and forgot it when he got off. Somebody from where the weather was warmer. Somebody not used to wearing a coat. South of Washington, prob'ly. Worth more to him to turn it in. Look good on his record. Honest Luke. He smiled cryptically to himself.

By the time he got to the last seat he had already lost interest. He reached his hand out to throw it over his shoulder. It moved! When he saw what it was, he dropped his vacuum and went for the boss.

CHAPTER 2

SAM

I looked at my watch. Nearly eleven and we were still there: snug, warm and in my case, (there having been no further mention of either Mastermind or marriage), trying to stay awake. I'd used the phone in Sal's library for a brief call to Cousin Andy and a somewhat longer one to bid goodnight to my traveling wife.

Although there was no further actual mention of a union, Tunnelson wandered about, giving Sal's unique 'porch' the once-over, apparently estimating its sale value. He tapped the tempered glass walls, diddled with the mechanism which opens the glass roof in fine weather, expressed disbelief that Sal's home had once been the stable where we played among Uncle Charlie's prize cows. He bent to smell the roses pressing their pink, peach, red and white faces against the glass, as if they would rather be out there part of the snowy landscape than here with the man with the household name. I know I did.

As to the damned snow, I'd had enough of that too. Where my sister sees white quilted barns and churches, I see streets lined with plow-built bunkers so high you can't see around the corner. Still, stretched out here, warmed by the fireplace Grandfather built to keep his cows in a milking frame of mind through the cold winters, you could almost convince yourself winter was not too bad. Almost. It's not me. I'm a summer guy from the get-go.

Tunnelson was remarking for the umpteenth time how *lucky* we were to live in a quiet, little place like Thaxtonville. It was Sal's turn to smother a yawn.

"I'm keeping you up," Judd said, the perfunctory apology failing to mask frustrated ego.

"Sorry," Sal yawned again. "I'm on early shift this week and it's been a long day. I hope you'll excuse…"

"Okay. Okay. I must say, though, that it's just pure foolishness of you to insist on being a policeman. I don't know why…okay. I know. Look, I'll just check with the Highway Patrol once more and then I'll be off."

He picked up a phone, dialed, spoke, listened, swore, and hung up. "Still closed. Will be thirty-six hours at least 'til they open," he said glumly. "Damn!" He looked at Sal. "I don't suppose you…"

"Could fly you down? No. Not with more snow on the way."

"But you fly in the snow all the time, don't you?"

"When it's safe," she said firmly. "There's quite a wind tonight and swirling snow makes visual approaches impossible."

"Damn," he said again. "I suppose I'll have to hang around another day at least."

Sal stifled a yawn. "Fine. The gate-house is yours as long as you like. I'll be at work tomorrow and Sam at the church though, so you'll have to entertain yourself."

He looked at me. "Church?"

"Groundhog's Day," Sal said briefly.

"Oh? And what," the smile stretched, became condescension, "do the natives do on Groundhog's day? Fireworks? Dancing in the streets? It's ridiculous how much coverage it all gets—ever since that damned movie…" He stopped. "Isn't it just a joke?"

"Not to us." Sal was brusque. "Nor is there anything new about it. The Pennsylvania Dutch have given the ground-hog his due since our people came here from the Palatinate. To people whose livelihoods depend on the land, the sooner you get your crops in the ground the better."

Pressed, Sal briefly described the simple age-old activities greeting the promise of spring in a part of the world still in touch with its country roots.

"Imagine that! I had no idea it was anything more than some sort of media thing. Can I go? Maybe there's a story there."

"Good heavens no! I mean it's open to the public so there's nothing stopping you from going, but it's really just an excuse for friends and neighbors to get back together after being shut in all winter. I can't imagine that Drop the Clothespin will interest a cosmopolitan like you."

"If it interests you, it will interest me," he said coyly. "Besides, you wouldn't deny me a chance to see an honest-to-God cake-walk! I had no idea people still did such things! It's a real piece of Americana!"

Sal bristled. "I wouldn't like to think you will be rushing here and there with a camera crew, describing our friends and family as 'quaint.' Honestly, you're bound to be disappointed."

"Well, it'll give me something to do anyway." He saw her face. "Look, scout's honor! I promise no crew. One cameraman perhaps. For my personal journal? Do your people seriously consider the groundhog an accurate forecaster of weather?"

Honeycutt saved Sal from having to admit it was so. She was wanted on the phone. It would be important, otherwise the caller would have been firmly told she was not available.

"The police," he said. "Sergeant O'Connell."

Sal nodded and left the room to answer rather than taking it there as she would have had we been alone.

She was back in a moment. "I've got to go. Someone left a small child at the bus station."

I rose too. "Let me go with you." Finally we could talk.

She got my meaning. "All right." Then, offering an explanation so Tunnelson would not feel he was being given the bum's rush, "I might have my hands full if the child is difficult."

Citing the icy roads, I suggested Tunnelson let me drop him off at Sal's gate-house as well. When we reached his door a quarter of a mile down Sal's drive, he was still talking.

Once gone, she sighed and turned to me. "Finally! Glad to have you back, 'Bro. It's too darn quiet here without you." Which is her way of saying she missed me.

"So's yer Aunt Minnie," I said, meaning I'd missed her too.

"You said you wanted to talk. Good news, I hope. Your trip a success? Give!"

"Not much to give, unless you find a lot of negatives something. Cousin Andy seems to."

"Oh? It was for Andy then? Since you disappeared rather cloak-and-daggerish, I deduced it was something for him. In connection with this Internet terrorist I suppose. Am I right?"

"As rain." I gave her a rundown of the dozen or so places I'd stuck my nose in. She listened to my whole recital so carefully I could almost hear her thinking.

"So it's true then. This...unfortunately even I am beginning to refer to him as Mastermind...is home-grown, someone living but, I suppose not necessarily operating from here in the States." In spite of the cold she cracked a window open. "Did Andy really expect it?"

"An international connection? I don't think so. Just being thorough."

"As he is always. Nevertheless it was a good idea. You heard the Waters Commission charges?"

I grunted. "That 'Net users be licensed or some such thing? The man's an idiot! As to the idea it's a group of some kind, if it was they…"

"…would want to take credit, I imagine," she finished, "so they would have identified themselves by now." She paused to think. I concentrated on getting across the covered bridge connecting Thaxtonville to Plainfield. "Something Tunnelson said got me to thinking," she said slowly. "He just sort of threw out a reference to Kaczynski, but I'm wondering if he doesn't have something. There is a definite parallel between them."

"Well, they're both crazy. And both computer nuts."

"Also both using the very technology, meant to be beneficial, to do harm. In Kaczynski's case, he used science to protest against its use. In this case maybe it's hospitals which have gone high-tech: one's personal records spread all over the Internet, operations done by video, patient charts on computers rather than those old fashioned sort hung on the end of one's bed. Plenty of folks resent it. Maybe someone resents it a lot." She let me focus on navigating some icy patches before she continued. "So the question is: why *are* the encryption programs not working? I mean, they've done pretty well in keeping hackers out of other essential systems. How is it he's getting away with it?"

"Hell, Sal, figure it this way. If one guy is able to write protective software, another can figure out how to beat it. As it is, this guy gets in and out of FBI encryption files as if he developed them himself—not too big a stretch when you see how readily he gets into those labyrinthine hospital computers. Andy's had the FBI's specialists in terrorists on it and, according to them, he gets into their system by 'shadowing' the Bureau's attempts to track him. Can you imagine that? Once he's in, he enters phony clues to keep them occupied, then backs out, erasing his tracks every step of the way."

She shook her head. "He must be incredibly clever!"

"Again like Kaczynski."

"Yes," she said, musing. "And an expert in medical protocols and hospital software as well. What a lethal combination of skills!"

"The latter especially. The changes he makes on hospital charts show extensive medical knowledge. They are so clever it sometimes takes weeks before they're noticed and sometimes not even then. An increase in insulin, too little digoxin, there are dozens of ways the wrong dose of some drug can harm rather than help. The problem is complicated by the reluctance of patients to tell their doctors soon enough that they're having problems. There's no real way to tell how many people have been affected."

She stared at the mountains of plowed snow flanking the street like armed guards. After while she said, "Are Andy and his minions any closer at all to finding him? FBI profilers any help?"

"Could be if it weren't for the hospitals themselves. The Bureau is having trouble developing really good databases because medical facilities have been dragging their feet in coughing up the names of people who have a grudge of one kind or another against them."

"So they're viewing it as 'work rage'?"

"Leaning that way, yes."

Again she was quiet for a bit. "What do you think of Tunnelson's mysterious phone call?"

I grimaced. "You mean the one he didn't get? Who the hell knows? He's so full of bull it's hard to tell. Still, there could be something there. I've already told Andy about his hints. Judd'll have company when he reaches Philly." I maneuvered the car around an abandoned car stalled in the middle of the street. Sal used my phone to call it in to Traffic. "One thing in Tunnelson's favor," I said when she hung up. "Somebody, somewhere knows something—that's for sure—and they might figure the press would shell out a lot more than the ten million the government's offering."

"I suppose so. You don't think we…"

"Should get into the bidding war? No I don't." I glanced at her. "You surprise me. Have you forgotten you're a police woman now yourself?"

"No. No. I just don't like feeling helpless!"

"Don't I know it! A regular Girl Scout you are!"

"But think, Sam," she said seriously. "This Mastermind could be anyone, anywhere!" She stared out at the snow, falling again and splattering fat, wet flakes on the windshield. "I mean he could be typing away right now at a kitchen table in one of these houses we see as we drive by. He could be at the other end of the world, alone in a dark attic. Tomorrow he could just go to his job in a busy office and tap away without anyone noticing. He could work from a laptop on a plane. For pity's sake, with computers available just about everywhere, he doesn't even need to own a computer! He could simply walk into a store say, and ask to try one out, slip in his own disk and…"

I heard the tension build in her voice. She needed calming down. "It's not quite that easy. True, entering the false data could take mere seconds, but it would take some time to access the files of the targeted hospital records and still more to write the overwrite programs."

"Even so, it could be easily done on some public system—a library or university, for instance, where someone spending several hours on a computer would not be thought unusual."

She was right, of course. It was one reason the search for Mastermind, begun with such optimism, was going nowhere. It all added fuel to public hysteria. I remembered I was supposed to be cheering her up. "But," I said cheeringly, "Andy'll get him! Someone knows something and at some point they'll be more afraid of the consequences of not telling than of telling."

"Like Kaczynski's brother."

"Exactly."

We drove silently together through the slick streets. No doubt she was just leaving me to concentrate on my driving, but there was a stillness about her I did not like. Was this damned terrorist getting to her? She worried too much over things she couldn't help, however I'd been gone a while so it could be anything.

"Be not lost so poorly in thy thoughts."[1]

"What? Oh, sorry. Not very good company tonight. I'm just tired."

It was something she seldom admitted. I remembered Tunnelson's ludicrous proposal and wondered if he'd been acting up all week. Had he really upset her?

"So! Where shall we send the wedding presents? The family will want to know."

"Wedding...oh. Whatever do you suppose got into him?"

"That's what I was going to ask you."

"Your guess is as good as mine. Save for dinner and the occasional cryptic messages he left for me here, there and everywhere, I've seen little of him all week." She watched as a patrol car passed, lights flashing. "As a proposal, it certainly was unique."

"That's one word for it. The damned jack-ass! Want me to punch the creep on the nose," I asked. "Get him indicted? Fired? Shot at dawn?" I felt her relax a bit.

"No, thanks," she said. "That won't be necessary. He may need something done to his hands, though." I

---

[1] *Macbeth* William Shakespeare

remembered his grabbing at her across the table at dinner. A glance at her face in the light of a passing street lamp showed one drawn and tired.

"You okay?"

"Oh sure. I'm glad you're home though, Bro'." She threw me a brief smile, then let it slip away. "It's been a long day."

As had many days in the last couple of years. I fished around for a way to get her to talk—not an easy task for my introspective twin, but good for her when I can manage it. I remembered her promotion to Corporal, along with her first permanent assignment, was to have been announced this morning. I asked how it all went.

She rolled her eyes at the question, laying her head back against the seat. "Well, the long and short of it is, it didn't 'went'. Longnecker is on the desk this week. I guess he forgot. I'm sure it will be tomorrow though."

Damned the luck! The Longnecker-Thaxton feud goes back nearly fifty years. Naturally the current version would use his position to retaliate.

"Good thing you have Charlie there, isn't it?"

"Yes," she said frowning. "Yes."

"Well, isn't it?"

Her, 'Oh yes. He's been a god-send,' came too quick.

"But…"

"Oh it's nothing."

"Nothing? What nothing?"

"Just that he's asked me to lunch."

I could think of only one reason for the hemming and hawing. "He wants to…see you?" We'd never spoken of it, but I know, which means she knows I know, he'd spent the night a couple of years ago—that awful night when she returned home from that school[2] for the last time, shattered

---

[2] *If It's Monday, It Must Be Murder* Hannah Fairchild

Dead in Pleasant Company
A Pennsylvania Dutch Mystery

in mind and body. I'd stayed behind at police headquarters that night to make sure the murderer, who'd come within a hair of making Sal a third victim, actually got locked up. I returned in the early hours just in time to see Charlie's car drive away. I found her asleep in grandfather's enormous poster bed, her face still drawn with pain but softer.

She'd been happier at the school than I'd ever seen her. When the bottom fell out of that world, she turned her back on teaching. Looking for something new, something challenging—which to her means difficult if not impossible, O'Connell had persuaded her that meant police work. She'd protested at first. At forty-three, she was too old. She was too fat. But Plainfield was looking to beef up the number and quality of women on the force and her credentials were exceptional. They agreed to waive the age requirement if she could meet the weight proviso—meaning she had to lose forty-five pounds. She'd done so in six months. Her quick promotion seemed to promise as great a success as cop as she had as restaurateur and teacher. I got G.G.H.H.'s looks, all right, but my sister got his brain and guts.

"Do you expect things to get hairy now Charlie's your boss?"

"I don't really know. So far, he's done is hand me the open cases and tell me we'd talk later, but he was gone all day."

"Well, I'm sure you'll work it out. If he's not what you want, just tell him. He won't push, I'm sure." It was time to change the subject. "You think Longnecker will make the announcement tomorrow?"

"Have to. It's the way he'll do it that bothers me." She sighed. "Look, there's the bus station."

Later, I remembered thinking how well Sal had been looking lately. Her experiences at the school had left her clothed in a barely perceptible patina of stillness, of caution whenever people got too close. It was as if she wanted to shrink even smaller. Lately, though, she seemed relatively happy, finding satisfaction in her work. I wondered if, perhaps she was mastering the art of living peacefully.

I had no idea it was all to come to a screeching halt.

Dead in Pleasant Company
A Pennsylvania Dutch Mystery

CHAPTER 3

SAM

"Roy Leibensperger, Officer." In the murky light of the bus station, the man addressed me. We moved closer.

"I'm Officer Salome McKnight." Sal extended a hand.

"Ach oh, I didn't see...oh it's you Dr. McKnight! Oh ya, I heard tell as to how youse vas gone to a cop naw. Oh, and it's you too, vunce, Mr. Sam! Goot! Goot!" He grabbed my hand, addressing himself once more to me. The thick Pennsylvania Dutch accent sounded strange to me after a couple of weeks away. "Dankst Gott you're here! Ve chust can't vake the little fella up vunce now! Ve veshooken him up goot but he falls right back to sleep! Cum here now vunce." He turned, motioning us to follow.

"Just a minute, Mr. Liebensperger." Sal drew a small notebook from her bag. "If the child is safe where he is, I'd like..."

"Safe?" The question was put by Sal but he directed his answer to me. "Vy shuah he's safe! Dispatcher's got 'im in the nurses' station, ain't? Got six of her own, she does. He's safe enough all right, but Cowered Wagon Transit can't take responsibility..."

Sal endured. "Yes, of course Mr. Leibensperger. I just need to ask you a few questions. Who found him and exactly where?"

"Luke. Ol' Ben Fenstermacher's boy, that is. Found 'im asleep on the back seat when he was cleanin' the bus."

"What time was that?"

"Coupla hours ago. The Washington run. It's a daily. Sirty-six hours it takes for the trip. Arrived here seven-sirty six. Held off callin' it in thinkin' sompuddy's cum fer 'im vunce. Fikkered somebody chust fergot 'im. People leave behind the damn-allest things these days."

"Including children?"

"Including ennysing. Hatt a couple leave their old grandma on once." He lit a cigarette. "Cum back for her, though," he said, moderately approving.

"Can I speak to Mr. Fenstermacher? And the driver?"

"Fensternacker, ya sure, if ya can vait vunce 'til he gets done with 3025? Ve gotta keep to our schechule here and that's hard enough viss the snow and all. Ain't it awful? Vorst since I was a kitt. And the driver you say? Let's see vunce, that'd be Wally Koch. He's off 'til this after."

"This afternoon? When does he come in?"

"Two-sirty about. I don't think he'll be much help though."

"Oh? Why not?"

"Manaacher talked to 'im before he sent 'im home to sleep. Sett he didn't see the kitt get on, vas on the bus ven he took over. Got the four o'clock run. Sett he sought the kitt vas viss his family."

We made our way through the dark, cold, wet garage, searching out 3025 only to hear the same meager information repeated. Sal suggested we find the nurse's station.

The object on the cot seemed barely to fit the description of 'child:' a small, lumpy blob, face tucked into the nap of a hospital blanket. The nurse at the desk of the tiny room looked as if she'd been reprieved at the eleventh hour.

Sal indicated the blob. "This the child?"

The nurse's head bobbed vigorously. "He von't stay awake. I give 'im some cereal and milk and he et himself goot vunce, then vent right off back to sleep. I sink he's been drugged!"

"Has he told you his name?"

Dead in Pleasant Company
A Pennsylvania Dutch Mystery

"No! He ain't said nossing! That's what I'm saying! He ain't opened his mouth! He chust keeps on sleeping!"

Sal stooped to touch first the child's cheek, then forehead. "How long has he been like this?"

"Like I sett vunce! Since he come! That's about six ars now!"

"Not too long for a child to sleep if he's been traveling." She spoke more to herself than to the nurse. "Not in his own bed. Off his regular schedule. He may just now be catching up." She looked at the nurse. "He doesn't seem to be ill. I take it you found nothing with which to identify him, either on him or in the bus?"

"Ach no! Nossing! Ve prowite I D batches for small kitties and ve tell people ovah und ovah to make sure their kitty has one on him but they never listen. Always think *theirs* couldn't possibly get lost!"

"Do they? Get lost? Often, I mean?"

The nurse nodded. "Every day in the bikker cities. Evens here in Plainfield sometimes, only this is the first time in my eighteen years here nopuddy's come lookin' for 'im."

"I see."

The nurse looked at me. "I sink there's somesing really wrong viss him. Maybe he's dumb. Mental I mean. Not crazy mental, I mean, vell they call it somesing funny now but vell, retarded-like. *Versteh?*"

"*Ich versteh.*" It was Sal who responded. "Well, thank you very much for looking after the boy." She began to button up the child's coat.

"Oh, there's another sing too. The driver sett the kitty fainted when he first saw him."

"Fainted?"

"Ya." Her voice took on a funereal tone. "Maybe he's got epilepsy! Maybe that's vhy somepuddy left 'im, vunce. No insurance maybe. You'll take him then?" Again she sounded reprieved. "Gans goot! I'll get vun of the drivers to help."

I told the woman that would not be necessary. She looked at me. "Mind you don't drop him."

The kid weighed no more than a feather. He woke briefly as Sal buckled him into a seat to give each of us a calm, studied look. Sal smiled down at him in the dark and began to reassure him, explaining we were going to take him where he would be warm and safe until his family came. In answer to her question if he could tell us his name, he merely closed his eyes. By the time Sal was settled in beside me, the poor kid was asleep.

Her call in to the desk sergeant produced the information that, due to the weather, no one was available from Children's Services. She asked them to get on to whoever's name was on the list.

Five minutes later the car phone beeped. "They said to take 'im to the hospital overnight. They'll pick 'im up tomorra."

"Right," she told the phone. "I suppose that's as good a place as any," she said to me. "Better, actually. They'll see he's cleaned up and fed."

"Which one?"

"Ours."

The Thaxtonville Hospital is small but excellent and a lot less impersonal for a lost child than Plainfield General. Given that Thaxtons had built the place and still underwrite much of it, we were greeted with as much warmth and affection as the Pennsylvania Dutch have in them. Sal asked that the boy be given tests for any signs of drugs in his system, then left the still sleeping child in the hands of a motherly nurse and headed for home.

* * * * *

Dead in Pleasant Company
A Pennsylvania Dutch Mystery

It was nearly half-past three when I dropped Sal off and drove my four-by-four through the ice and snow-packed streets. I didn't go straight home but drove around a bit, checking on how well the plowing was going. In less than four hours the natives would be up and about, ready for the start of the day-long Groundhog's Day celebrations. The more sophisticated might look out on the blustery February morning and bury deeper under thick, handmade quilts, limiting celebration to the *fastnachts* someone would bring to the work-place, but the one hundred and eighty-seven residents of Thaxtonville would no sooner miss this morning than they would sleep through Christmas. Plowed or not, they would make their way from pin-neat homes to gather at the Thaxtonville church where breakfast would be dished up from dawn to ten o'clock. In addition to flapjacks and home-made sausage, scrapple, eggs and fried potatoes, home-made breads and rolls, there would be the piece-de-resistance—Elsie Coleman's hot, large, gooey, sticky buns.

Sal and I were due to take our turns at the church: me there much of the day, hauling in the nickels, dimes and quarters as they came in from the games. Sal would come in after her shift in time to serve first as one of three judges for the cake-baking contest, then to supervise the cake-walk.

I made a note or two where the wind had drifted roads shut, called them in to the street crew boss and took myself home to get a few hours sleep.

* * * * *

SAL

February 2. Ground Hog's Day. Plainfield Police Department.

"Good morning, chentlemen..." Acting Assistant Police Chief Longnecker paused, bowing first to one side of the room then the other, his accent as thick, as 'country' as the big, red hands grasping the sides of the podium. "...*and* ladies."

Rod Longnecker had been Acting Captain so long now even he did not kid himself he would ever be anything else. Acknowledging the fact had put the final crust on a personality already caustic and vindictive. Now he grinned in the general direction of the handful of women on the shift.

"If youse gals are through swapping recipes, ve'll get started vunce."

Sue Leiby started up from her chair. I touched her arm briefly.

"Pisses me off," the younger woman hissed.

"What he wants," I reminded her. "He'll just make a crack about being that time of the month."

"Yeah, I know, but still..."

Only when Longnecker was shift captain did the women officers feel the need to sit together.

"Nothing'd please the old bastard more." Rachel Green's deep voice traveled all the way up her long frame. "Gives him a reason to complain about our 'emotional instability."

Nor was the little interplay at the back of the room lost on our leader. The smirk on his face showed he scored it a victory. He gave a short laugh and went on.

"Okay, let's get to vork. Ve got a lot on our plates and ve'll be vasting enough time up there." He jerked his thumb toward the roof. "Ve'll take a look-see at the cheneral items on the log first before I giff you yer assignments." Both arms shot forward and back, signaling his readiness to get down to work.

"Numper vun is this here Mastermind fella a'course. Nacherly Washington's keepin' us up on it. Lookin' for our help a'course. FBI thinks his next target may be on the East

Dead in Pleasant Company
A Pennsylvania Dutch Mystery

coast and, since we're sitchuated in the mittle, so to speak, between Washington, Philly and New York, they 'specially vant us to keep our eyes 'n ears open. Hell, the bastard could be sitting' someplace in Plainfield right now, guzzling' coffee for all ve know. Maybe," he leered in my direction, "chowin' down on one of them famous crullers they sell arount here. Anyways," the arms shot out and back, "eversing ve know about him's in yer folders, so look it over. Ve got Marsden and Carpenter seein' to it we have guards posted round the clock at both hospitals. Nacherly this iss a purty awful thing but don't be gettin' all hysterical or nothin'. Remember, ve're professionals! You got any ideas, my door's allus open. Okay," the arms shot out and back again, "let's don't forget to check the board for details of our open cases. Make sure you're up on 'em. Pay particlar attention to them two convenience store robberies. Looks like ve got a repeater here and he's armed. It won't be long before somebuddy gets hurt."

"Naw here's numbah two. Assignments." He smirked at the group. "They're all in yer folders 'cept for Miller and Shankweiler. You lucky guys get to work up at yer ol' Alma Mammy. University Security up there asked for help. Band'll be practicin' for the Presidents Day parade, so you'll have plenty of tits to look at but keep yer peckers in yer pants." He paused to leer, man-to-man, at the male officers near him who grinned self-consciously in response. Satisfied at scoring this second point, he continued.

"Item three's the good news. We got approval for extra-duty pay on the twenty-fifth. Sign up if yer innerested. I guess that's it." He made to leave, a move that fooled no-one. They knew what was coming. "Oh, I almost forgot." He pushed an unpleasant smile at them. "Seems I neglected yestiday to announce the promotion of one of our fellow officers. Yup. Ol' man Thaxton's grandkid is now a corpral. Surprise, surprise! Ennyways, I apolochize. I suppose I simply fergot since I ain't seen any lechitimate *reason* for the appointment. But that's just me. In any case, *Corporal* McKnight has been assigned to Juvenile under Charlie O'Connell here. Under Charlie! That's a good one! Where they belong, ain' it Charlie?" I prayed Charlie's dark skin would hide the inevitable flush. "Oops! I forgot! I ain't allowed to say stuff like that no more. Better apolochize before I get my ass hauled before the Board again. Sorry everybody." His grin negated the words. For the first time he looked directly at me. "Not goin' to sic your whole *freundshaft* on me, are you Corporal? Good! Good! Now fer the rest of you guys," he paused, bowed, "and gals a'course, check the work assignments in your folders. Any questions afore youse go on up there?"

Leading the officers 'up there' for twenty minutes of exercise is the responsibility of the shift captain, one Longnecker invariably turns over to his second in command. Now he tossed his clipboard off in the general direction of his orderly, calling out with feigned briskness. "Okay, that's it then. Miller'll run you through your fun and games." Far from hiding his scorn for the required work-out, he made every effort to make his physical unfitness a virtue. "Go on naw. Yer gonna need it this morning after piggin' awt on all them crullers a certain somebody brung in," he said, pointedly ignoring me. "Easy to see," he added, lowering his voice just a hair, "haw some pipples get fat, ain't it?" Another grin, having scored one more point on a Thaxton. "Beat it naw! I got real vork to do."

* * * * *

SAM

Tuesday. February 2. Groundhog's Day. Thaxtonville Church.

Dead in Pleasant Company
A Pennsylvania Dutch Mystery

It all went on without a hitch. Naturally the Thaxtons were there in full force. Four of Henry Harrison Thaxton's five surviving children arrived en masse. Missing was Uncle Peter, now living in his wife's home in Newberry, and the three youngest of the original eight Thaxtons who'd moved Higher Up. That last group included H.H.'s youngest—our father Walter and the next youngest, Aunt Nora—as well as portly Aunt Magdalena who had raised us. Aunts Eve and Adelaide, mere kids in their late eighties and Aunt Fiddena, now ninety-something, were still very much in evidence, proof of the vigor of the Thaxton genes. I was tickled to see the traditional white cap still adorning Aunt Fiddena's snow-white hair. It meant she'd stuck to her guns over the objections of the two 'younger girls' who thought it old-fashioned, too Mennonitish.

The three grand ladies, today nobly escorted by cousin Reuben, made the rounds, greeting every man jack of the attendees by name. It was quite a crowd too, considering our church has only ninety-eight actual members of which fifty-three are Thaxtons. I was pleased to see Charlie O'Connell show up again this year. He ensured a nice profit in both the hot-dog-and-sauerkraut stand and the soft-ball toss. Anyway, I like the guy and I wanted to see if I could see any difference in the way he treated Sal.

They arrived within a few minutes of each other, shortly after five o'clock, just in time for Sal to judge the baking contests. The big surprise was Mrs. Strauch's red velvet chocolate cake coming in second to Elsie Coleman's coconut cake. If you think it silly that people line up to pay a buck to buy a chance to win Elsie's specialty, well, you 'chust don't know vat goot is!' Best Pie went to young Marilyn Bleiber and a good thing that. It should be enough to edge Jim Wheeler to the altar. Nice girl, Marilyn, one of Harry Bleiber's six daughters. Lucky guy, old Harry.

Charlie did seem to be around wherever Sal was, but that's not that unusual. Tunnelson, arriving with a man with a couple of cameras, was never too far from her either, to say nothing of the handful of other guys who have known her almost all her life. Men just like being around her, though she does nothing that I can see to encourage them.

As for Tunnelson, I had to give him credit. Once he saw that, to this crowd, fame gained neither attention or special treatment, he played along, trying his hand at 'drop-the-clothespin,' (the crowd cheered when old Mrs. Trinkle beat him) and partnering with me for the three-legged race. We were skunked by a couple of twelve-year-olds. They really should have age-groups for that, don't you think?

By evening, Tunnelson had eaten so many funnel cakes I fully expected him to bow out for dinner, which would have been fine with me, but no. About seven o'clock he searched me out and begged to be taken along to Pleasant Company for dinner. He said he was starved.

Sal, busy collecting the Schickelgrubers to play for the cake walk, Groundhog's Day's signature event, motioned us to go on, she would catch up soon. Promising to come back and take care of the day's 'take', I hustled the famous newsman out.

* * * * *

The mood at Pleasant Company was lively. The groundhog, (no respectable Pennsylvania Dutchman ever refers to him as Punxatawny Phil—he is just plain Dutch like the rest of us,) had dashed out of his hole and disappeared into the woods. That meant spring was within legitimate discussing distance, never mind the snow-packed streets. From kitchen to cashier, guests and workers alike discussed the merits of the various seed catalogs, debating the importance of planting root vegetables on the wane of the moon. The reliability of the groundhog's prediction of an early spring was referred to time and again with comparisons drawn to years past. It is one time when the young, with their pocketed cell-phones and laptops, give their seniors some credence.

Invariably patrons left Pleasant Company carrying at least one white bag of Cousin Sarah's floury, powdered sugar *fastnachts*. A tradition, originally meant as a treat reserved for Shrove Tuesday, the square doughnut had come to represent the end of winter, the beginning of spring, so naturally was now part and parcel of the Groundhog's Day festivities.

When she finally joined us at our favorite table, Sal had managed to put aside the day's frustrating search for the parents of the little boy and was relaxed and smiling. One might have thought, as I suspect the glowering Walt did, the smile was for Judd Tunnelson. I thought it more likely it was one of relief. The State Highway Patrol reported the Expressway to Philly clear and her would-be suitor had declared his intention to leave immediately after dinner.

Happily unaware of the pleasure this announcement generated, Tunnelson chattered on as we ate, pausing only to mop up the sauerbraten with home-made bread and stuff it in. Table talk that night continued to be lopsided in spite of the fact we know pretty much the same people worldwide, though from widely differing standpoints. To us they are friends or business acquaintances, occasionally enemies; to him they are 'copy.' Whereas we never discuss their personal lives, he lived for the moment, natural or contrived, when he could get behind the facade—an intolerable intrusion to us. We are, as I say, Pennsylvania Dutch.

The newsman's spirits continued to rise throughout the meal, apparently buoyed up by his carping and libelous opinion on every conceivable personality in the public eye.

He seemed to run out of gas mid-meal, once more returning to the reason for his visit.

"I know you'll be disappointed but honestly, I went over all my notes again this morning, trying to breathe life into the piece," he made it sound like he could walk on water, "but it just lies there! Your story here just doesn't meet my standards. No offense meant," he said offensively.

"None taken," we said in unison. Frankly, I was surprised to hear my vocal chords still worked.

"So, if you'll forgive me, I'll be on my way right after dinner."

"Oh? Tonight? Are you sure you want to try it in this weather?"

"Absolutely! This is something that can't wait."

"I take it you got the call you were waiting for," Sal said, possibly to check the condition of *her* vocal chords.

I said I hoped his source was reliable.

"Always has been! Just think! Tomorrow I may have a *real* story to tell! My God! I can't wait!"

In spite of his seeming impatience, he did not rush right off. Declaring he had found a gustatory Paradise, he cheerfully shelled out for *fastnachts* from each of the Scouts who stopped at our table and by nine o'clock the table was covered with white bags. Sal signaled Hal to box them up for our guest and hold them at the cashier's desk. When Judd proclaimed the sauerbraten the best he'd ever eaten, Sal again motioned to Hal, this time to bring an extra portion for our famous guest.

He was chumping down yet one more forkful when Hal approached, telephone in hand.

"Sorry Dr. McKnight. It's the police."

"Desk sergeant on middle shift," she said, hanging up. "The boy's disappeared from the hospital!"

"Oh? You mean his family..."

She shook her head. "Nobody knows. He's just disappeared." She told Judd there'd be a basket including a thermos of hot coffee and sandwiches waiting for him at the cashier's desk. Then, with the air of a woman reprieved at the eleventh hour, Sal wished him a safe trip, excused herself and went to work.

* * * * *

Half an hour later when Hal came and asked me to look over a problem in the wine cellar, the guy was still gassing on.

I asked the newsman if he would be here when I got back. When he said he wasn't sure, I pointedly reminding him that more snow was expected in a few hours which he could get ahead of if he left now. I beat it with inexcusable haste, happy to have seen the last of him.

When Hal and I surfaced some ten minutes later, we were dismayed to find the kitchen empty save for a young dishwasher, headphones clamped on his ears, swaying back and forth as he scrubbed away. Through the glass in the swinging doors we could see a crowd around the table I had so recently left. As we pushed through, someone in the front of the group stood up and moved and I heard my name. I ran to the table.

Judd Tunnelson sat in his chair, much as he had been when I left. I wondered what kind of trouble he'd made in that short time to get everybody acting so strangely.

I came around the table to face him, calling his name. He stared back at me.

"He can't answer you no more, Mr. Thaxton. He's dead!" One of the bus-boys repeated the obvious almost gleefully. "Dead as dead can be! Deader'n a door-nail!"

CHAPTER 4

SAM

The eyes were enough.

I sent Hal to call 911 then pressed the thumb nail of the still warm hand, resisting the impulse to close the man's eyes. Hal came back, gave me a nod. I looked at him, then at the on-lookers and, with a word, he got the staff back to work while I attended to one or two customers who'd wandered over to the small alcove.

"Wait a minute." I held up a palm. "Anybody see what happened?" A chorus of soft, puzzled 'nos.' "Okay. Who talked to him last? They'll want to know."

"Me, I guess, Mr. Thaxton." Annie Weaver moved reluctantly forward. I saw her give Frank Mohr a look and he disappeared back toward the kitchen.

"Okay Annie. Anyone else around?"

"Chris," she said. "He had 24, 26 and 30," she explained, indicating neighboring tables, "and Hal of course."

"Okay. Anybody else? Who was bussing?"

"That'd be me." The boy pushing forward was a carbon replica of his brother Frank. I took a second or two to guess which of the eight Mohr boys he was. I took a stab. "Jimmy? You bussed here? Good. Okay. You four stay here. The rest of you can get back to work."

I pulled out my cell-phone and tapped in Sal's code. "No." I stopped the boy's hand, reaching for the dirty dishes. "Leave it, Jimmy."

Sal did not answer, meaning she had her pocket phone turned off. I pushed a button on the watch I wore identical to hers. I'd give her two or three minutes before going to look for her—a habit born as a result of my twin's penchant for sticking her nose, and sometimes other parts of her anatomy, in danger. No response. I looked around for Walt but he was nowhere to be seen. I went in search of him.

* * * * *

SAL

The nurse, one of a handful I did not know, was defensive.

"Look, Officer, we had no reason to expect the kid would take off! Gee whillikers! He's been asleep ever since they brought him in last night! Acts like he was drugged or something! We didn't miss him right off because the shift changes at seven and the evening shift didn't realize we'd added an extra crib. They wouldn't anyway, not 'til they got through doing the evening 'meds' and with everything so full what with the flu and everything...Anyway, we've looked everywhere and there's just no sign...," she looked around as if she thought he might suddenly appear, "so that's why we called you," she said virtuously. "Must've climbed right over the side," she gave the crib a good shake. "Not that that's impossible. It's just that he was sleeping so soundly..."

I made soothing noises. "You said like he was drugged. Has he been tested?"

"We've taken blood samples but the lab reports aren't up yet. He certainly acts like it."

"Has a doctor had a chance to get a look at him?"

"Well, yes and no. The resident had a quick look last night to check for broken bones or bleeding or anything like that. He did say the boy appeared to be malnourished and ordered IV feedings to start if he didn't wake up and eat tonight. He hasn't eaten since he came in. I'd asked one of our candy-stripers to give him a bath and see if she could get him to eat." She indicated a full tray. "That's how we found he was missing."

"And that was what, eight-ish?"

She nodded. "A little after, yes. We spent a couple of hours looking for him before we called you."

"When will the lab report be up?"

"Gee whillikers! I don't know. They're usually very quick, but we're so shorthanded and we have so many people really ill with flu and pneumonia and…"

"Yes, of course," I said cheerily. "You said you were shorthanded, is that because of the flu?" In worrisome numbers, hospitals everywhere were experiencing staff shortages as nurses and technicians quit, fearful they could be blamed if their hospital was infiltrated by Mastermind and someone under their care was harmed. Only recently I'd asked our Chief of Staff if our small hospital was having such problems.

"Not yet," he'd said looking worried. "Hopefully we won't see it developing here either. Hell, here everybody knows everybody and a change in treatment would be questioned. But it is happening. There's been a lot of talk that in other places long-time staffers have either quit or taken early retirement."

"…flu mostly," the nurse was saying. "Half of the lab staff is down with it. I'll check the lab people as soon as they come in if you like."

"I'd appreciate that. Ask them to rush it, will you?" I thanked her and told her I'd look around.

I made my way quietly through the still darkened ward of sleeping children, the head nurse trailing behind. "I take it you've done a head count now."

"Yes. Of course. Look, Sergeant."

"Corporal"

Dead in Pleasant Company
A Pennsylvania Dutch Mystery

"Corporal...McKnight you said? I've...oh my God! You're the Thaxton twin! And here I am yelling at you in your own hospital! Oh my God! I'll never live it..."

"Relax," I glanced at her name-tag, "Ms. McCoy, I know how children can be. Just go on back to your work. I'll be all right on my own."

She went, muttering a jumble of apologies and self-accusations. I garnered a couple of orderlies and organized a room by room, floor by floor search.

An hour later we reassembled at the nurses' station and admitted defeat. I sent them back to work and, alone, returned to the children's ward.

I sat on the edge of an empty cot and considered the room. I moved to the wide hall outside, observing the normal activities on the floor. At this time of night there would be no volunteers, no food or game carts. If the boy disappeared just at shift time—and my estimate of his intelligence rose a notch—it could mean he had some experience with hospitals.

Nurses came and went. Orderlies came and went. One advanced now, pushing a laundry cart to the empty crib and began pulling off sheets.

I watched for a moment then approached the youth and showed my badge. "Will you answer a question or two?" The young man looked down at me and shrugged. "Were you up here earlier this evening? About seven or so? About the time the shift changed?"

He made a face. "Oh hell! I suppose them nurses complained 'cuz I didn't change all the empties! Damn bitches! Begrudge a guy his break! Anyways, my cart was full."

"Where is your cart? The full one, I mean?"

"Down to the laundry, where else?"

I asked him if he'd seen a small boy anywhere about.

"Oh." Relief flooded his face. "That's what you...you lookin' fer that kid? Well, I ain't seen 'im but I'll keep my eyes peeled."

"Thank you. That will help. Look, aren't you Fred and Martha Collins' boy?"

He smiled. "The oldest."

"Yes. Fred Junior, isn't it? I thought so. Must be well into high school by now, aren't you?"

"Yup," the grin broadened. "Senior. Graduate in May."

"Congratulations! I know your parents are really proud you've kept out of trouble. They're eager for you to do well here. Do you like your work?"

"Ts okay," he said. "Mostly the nurses are purty nice." He grinned. "Sometimes they brings me cookies and stuff."

"That's nice. I'm sure it's hard work, but there is plenty of chance to work up, even go on to school with the hospital's scholarship program if you want." I smiled and nodded, "I'm glad you're doing so well. It's not always easy to stay out of trouble. When's your next evaluation here?"

"Six weeks," he said.

I nodded, gave him a card. "Tell you what. You tell your supervisor to call me for a recommendation when the time comes. Okay?"

I could feel his eyes follow me as I moved to the bank of elevators. On my way to the basement, I wondered if my guess had been on target. He had been up to more than a break. What was it? A smoke? A girl? Or something more worrisome? I made a mental note to keep an eye out for him. His parents had fought off the 'mentally retarded' label when they married and settled in a house built by Habitat for Humanity. If he took a wrong turn now, it would give people a chance to say 'I-told-you-so' and limit the chances for others.

In the laundry room, canvas carts, some full, some empty, lined two walls, waiting the 3 a.m. shift. I slipped a

Dead in Pleasant Company
A Pennsylvania Dutch Mystery

pair of plastic gloves from my bag and, without turning on the lights, moved methodically from one cart to another, lifting out soiled garments then replacing them.

The boy lay, asleep once again, in the next to last. I did not disturb him but pushed the cart with him in it to the adjacent garage, tapping another orderly on the way to help get him to my car. The child mumbled something unintelligible as I buckled the seat belt around him, then nodded off again. I looked at my watch, then headed for home. On the way, I used my car-phone to notify the hospital I had the child.

* * * * *

"I've got a little boy here, Honeycutt," I said when he opened the door. "About thirty-five pounds I'd say. He's asleep. Will you carry him upstairs?"

If he was surprised at this request, he didn't show it. "Of course, Dr. McKnight. In the boys' room?"

"No. Better put him on the lounge in my room and have Mrs. Honey make up a cot for him there. He's not going to know where he is when he wakes and I don't want to leave him alone."

"Anyone we know, Madam?"

"No," I said, following up the stairs. "He was left on a cross-country bus last night. We don't have a name for him as yet. I've brought him...oh, hi, Mrs. Honey. Did I wake you?"

"Heart your machine, vunce. Heah." She handed me a phone. "It's your brother." She moved the blankets revealing the child's face. *"Vas gib."*

I told the phone to hang on, then told Mrs. Honey what gave. She tutt-tutted. My watch beeped.

"You mean they had him in that hospital and didn't wash him?"

Hannah Fairchild

I pressed the button on my watch. Sam on the phone *and* my watch beeping? "Just a minute," I told the phone again. "They tried some, Mrs. Honey. They're dreadfully understaffed just now and I suppose they thought they'd wait for him to wake up." She was already fussing over the child. "Oh good! He seems to be waking now. Hang on," I told the phone again. The child's eyes regarded me steadily, sizing me up first before moving on to the Honeycutts. "Hello," I said softly, doing my own assessment. "How are you feeling? Do you remember me? I picked you up from the bus station last night and took you to the hospital." I debated whether to say I was a cop. I addressed the squawking phone, "Oh, sorry Sambo. Hi!" I listened briefly. "What!" He repeated it. "But how? Never mind. I'll be right there! Don't let anybody touch anything 'til the police get there! I'll call...oh, good. All right. On my way." I stared at the waiting faces, then pulled Honeycutt aside and spoke softly. "It's Mr. Tunnelson! He's dead! At Pleasant Company! I've got to go!" I went back to the child. "Look," I told the evaluating eyes, "I've got to go out for a while son, but Mr. and Mrs. Honeycutt here will take good care of you while I'm gone. Okay?" I turned to them. "Stay with him, will you Mrs. Honey? Just go ahead sleep in my bed," I said, though I knew she wouldn't. "I'll probably be very late."

* * * * *

Sam had wasted no time getting hold of Chief Warmkessel. By the time I arrived, his official car, as well as the Crime Scene van, was already there. I passed the ME on his way out.

He nodded at me. "Mornin' Sal. Bad break, him popping off here like this. You know anything about his health? He have a bad heart?"

I said not that I knew. "He's been swimming every day and seemed to thrive on it."

He nodded. "Goes like that sometimes. Sudden. No warning. P M will tell us for sure. We'll get him out of your way here as soon as possible. Sorry," he said again. "Better get yourself in out of this cold." He hurried off.

I stood in the doorway a moment feeling almost a stranger. The warm air gathered 'round me, making my official winter coat unbearable. Shedding it gave me time to put my finger on the reason for feeling so odd in the restaurant which had been my second home since Aunt Magdalene fed our farm hands here.

It had been the most natural thing in the world to continue to feed the workers, even after mechanization took away their jobs. My aunt could not allow them to go hungry. When they found work elsewhere, they continued to come, now bringing their families, now dropping a dollar or two on the table. I was six when I began bussing tables, by ten I was scrubbing pots and making salads, at fifteen a full-fledged cook. I'd loved it and had, on our twentieth birthday, talked Sam into expanding, eventually to the international chain with which you are probably familiar. Now, standing just inside the door, I felt like an intruder.

The place was busy but we were always busy this time of night, yet this was not the excited rush of people dashing hither and yon, but hushed and...somehow menacing.

Sam caught sight of me and came to meet me.

"Mattern and his crew are here. Got things well in hand. Chief's been here too."

"What happened?"

He shook his head. "No idea. I was down in the wine cellar with Hal for a few minutes. When I came back he was slumped in his chair, dead. Doc says heart."

I nodded and moved toward the alcove I'd left a few hours ago. I stopped at the arched entrance. It was a pleasant area, converted from the original kitchen when the new one was built. A cozy place, perfect for small groups, a favorite for family reunions.

My view of the body was blocked by three men in suits and plastic gloves. They bent over, stooped, straightened, paused to speak into their hands, moved to another position, stooped, straightened, spoke into their hands, repeating this routine over and over in a bizarre business-like dance. It put me in mind of the minstrel shows put on each year by locals at the Great Plainfield Fair before political correctness took over. I felt an unwelcome giggle threaten.

Sam's eyes asked me if I was okay, if I was sure I wanted to go there. Mine said not to be silly.

I greeted each of my fellow officers in turn before looking at what remained of the man who'd been both guest and a thorn in my side. They told me "Hi," said they were just here as a formality and would make it as quick as possible.

"Don't rush," we said in unison, Sam adding that we'd finished serving those who wanted to finish and had put up the CLOSED sign.

"Oh, good, good," Mattern said absently.

"Damn muck-raker!" Sam said at my ear, his eyes on the body. "Anything for a story." I looked at my brother. "Yeah, I know," he said.

Lieutenant Peters approached and nodded. "Sal. Sorry about all this. I've had a quiet word with your patrons. Hope we don't upset them too much."

"Can't be helped, Bill" I said. "You have someone talking to the staff?"

"Harrison's doing it now."

"Good. Have they been any help?"

Peters shrugged. "Not much. Looks like he just picked your place to go. Not a bad idea at that—to die in Pleasant Company." It was a play on words the media would repeat more than once. He had the grace to look shamefaced. "Wait a minute. You can ask him. Harrison?"

Harrison, pad and pencil in hand, waved and came over.

"Lo Sal. Sorry about this. We're trying to get through before the press gets it." The press! My heart sank. I looked around for Sam. Harrison went on. "Doesn't seem to be anything unusual here though. He was waiting for your brother to come back from the wine cellar. Waiter said he suddenly gasped, felt his chest and slumped over. He, your brother I mean, called the paramedics. All of your staff have first aid training and a couple of them tried artificial respiration until the crew got here—no more than four-five minutes everybody agrees. They did everything they could, but…"

"Heart?"

"Looks like. No sign of anything else. Unless he ate something that disagreed with him." He laughed at my expression. "Oh come on, Sal. I'm kidding."

Nevertheless criminalists from the Crime Scene Unit were carefully collecting everything on the table down to the salt and pepper shakers. They were always thorough, but official procedures called for extra care in this case. Famous people attract the media and they would search every nook and cranny for an angle. Given both the Tunnelson and Thaxton names…My toes curled.

"Maybe you can help Sal. You were here tonight too?"

"Yes. Until the hospital called. I'd left an abandoned child with them last night. They called to report him missing."

"What time was that?"

"About nine, I believe."

"And then you came back here?"

"Well yes. Sam called me."

"I see. But you weren't planning to come back?"

I shook my head. "I didn't think there was much point to it. Actually, I expected Mr. Tunnelson to be gone. He was supposed to leave for Philadelphia right after dinner."

"He was? In this weather?"

I said yes. "He had planned to go and the State Police told him the Expressway was clear. He wanted to leave before it snowed again."

"Oh." Then, "Mr. Thaxton says Tunnelson's been staying with you for the past week. He say anything about having a bad ticker?"

I shook my head. "And he certainly doesn't...didn't act it. He's been swimming every day and yesterday he went cross-country skiing."

"Swimming?" I nodded. "Oh. Right. You've got a heated pool."

I nodded again. "He went along to the church today for the Groundhog's Day activities and participated in just about everything."

"Ate a lot too, I imagine."

"Everything that wasn't nailed down," Sam said. "Stuffed himself here tonight, too. I thought he'd burst."

"Well, that may be it. Overdid it maybe. No spring chicken, is he?"

No, I thought. No spring chicken. Fifty-two he'd told me. My senior by a handful of years.

Harrison thanked me and headed back to the kitchens. I searched out Peters. "What about notifying his family? He's got a sister who lives with him. His network too." My place, as hostess, or his as cop? I wondered if I would find the answer in Amy Vanderbilt. I could see it:

Dead in Pleasant Company
A Pennsylvania Dutch Mystery

PROPER NOTIFICATION OF DEATH.

1. *When the deceased is a world famous controversial figure who has been your house guest.*
2. *When the deceased drops dead dining in your restaurant.*
3. *When notification is sure to invite a media blitz. (see proper handling of the media.)*

HANDLING THE MEDIA.

1. *When someone has been...*

I pulled myself together. This was no time to indulge in quixotic behavior! Nevertheless, I could not help thinking this was just the sort of ghoulish situation in which some people would wallow. My husband would have. Indeed Gunther would have demurred, put on a long, grave face and relished every minute of it.

Peters was saying something about checking with the Chief.

"Yes. Yes. Good idea," I said, relieved. I began to turn away. "Ask him about the press too."

"The press? Oh. Of course. Will do. Look Sal," he said, "you look bushed. You may as well go. There's nothing you can do here. We have permission to keep the restaurant closed until we're finished?"

"Of course. Just tell Hal."

The lieutenant nodded and left me with the body.

I found my brother in the kitchen, getting the staff settled down, telling them we'd be closed the next day. I nodded at the door to let him know I was leaving and happily left him to it.

CHAPTER 5

SAM

Sal was making her way across the parking lot through four inches of new snow when I caught up with her. It was still coming down—the thick, wet flakes of early spring. I pulled the hood of her coat up over her head.

"Catch your death," I scolded. The lights on the lot shone down on her face. She looked as if she could use a laugh. I searched for a topic. "Tough on you. Good we didn't put out the two bucks for a license though."

"Very funny," she said.

Humor not welcome, I settled for something upbeat. "Good thing he didn't get started. Imagine if he'd been driving when it happened."

"Yes. That's something at least." She did not sound cheered.

Okay. She wanted to be serious. "Did you have any idea he was in poor health?"

"No. And he certainly didn't act like a man with a bad heart. You saw him eat," she said resentfully. "And he swam every morning. Complained the pool was too warm."

"My God! You keep that pool like a polar lake!" She ignored me, having heard my complaint often enough. We concentrated on not falling for a bit. "Chief still looks done in, don't you think?" At the car she struggled to get the key to turn in the door lock, already freezing. "Isn't there anything we can do for him?"

She said she was trying. "I've been working on him quietly to get some help."

"Who?"

Dead in Pleasant Company
A Pennsylvania Dutch Mystery

"Oh, Dr. West, I think. He's not always on target with kids outside the mainstream, but I think he's pretty good with men. He's been a help to Pete anyway."

I couldn't see her face, buried as it was in a search for a windshield brush.

"Oh? Is Pete seeing him?"

"I don't know if he is still. He was when I...when we...when I left." She handed me a brush and took her own to the other side of the car. "Probably though. They're good friends you know."

The business of brushing snow off windows occupied us for a few minutes, then I held the passenger side door open, motioning her to enter. "You're bushed and have to go to work in a few hours," I said firmly. "I'll be going back so I have to stay awake."

She gave me a brief look, then got in. Not for the first time I marveled at the grace with which she moved her short body.

"I'm glad," she said to my decision to return to the restaurant. "Find out for sure who's going to notify Tunnelson's people, will you? I guess I..."

"Taken care of. Chief's going to call the sister—they found her number in the little black book in his pocket—and he wants the police commissioner to call his producer. I told them I'd call Tom at the network." I've been friends with the network CEO for years. "Anybody else we ought to call? He have any other family?"

She shook her head. "Not as far as I know. Sister, producer and network. Should do it. Except...what about the press?"

"Tom'll want to do that. Wouldn't do to have another network scoop him! Chief'll get a press release ready too."

"Not a bad idea for us, either. Will you tell Mrs. Sweeney?"

Hannah Fairchild

* * * * *

The kid, now pinkly clean, was fast asleep on a cot in Sal's bedroom. Late as it was, Mrs. Honey was waiting. She brushed aside the news about Tunnelson, took one quick glance at my sister and took her firmly by the arm. "Youse chust get yerself into the shar naw vunce Missy. Mister'll get a hot water bottle in yer bed and I'll be right back up with a pot of hot chocolate."

"Gosh, you've already done so much tonight, Mrs. Honey. I didn't mean for you to have to stay up so late."

"Neffer you mind naw. Chust get yourself to bett before you catch yer death and I have to stay up nursin' you. Yer no sprink chicken no more. And you," she said, shoving me out the door, "get yerself home so's she can get some sleep."

Sal obediently began to undress. "How is the boy? Did he give you trouble?"

"Depends on vat you call trouble." Mrs. Honeycutt nodded at the child on the bed.

Sal looked up from removing her shoes. "Meaning?"

"Meaning, that boy you brung home's no boy."

Sal looked up. "What did you say?"

Mrs. Honey shook her head. "I sett that there boy's no boy. He's a girl!"

* * * * *

I left Sal to deal with yet one more shock, wanting to waste no more time getting back to Pleasant Company. I was surprised to hear Walt on the phone as I passed his rooms on the way down and out. The door was open just enough to let spikes of one-ended conversation float through. The words 'progeny sales,' 'win streak', 'classic' floated past the open door.

I stuck my head in. "You hear what happened?"

He told the phone he'd call back and came to the door. "What's up? Ladies have a fist fight over who got first prize in the pie-baking contest?"

I told him about Tunnelson, trying not to let his manner get under my skin. I've always gotten on well with Sal's kids and even better since their father did everybody an enormous favor by bumping himself off. I told myself Walt's present behavior was just a necessary part of growing up and finding his niche—not easy in a family like ours. He was the only one of Sal's three to get my goat. Not for the first time I thought my sister hadn't warmed his pants often enough while he was still small enough to do it, but Sal disagrees and they are her kids. Several times he'd hovered on the brink of trouble and I suspected some day he would not just hover. What, for instance, did the phone conversation mean? What was he up to? I decided to check with Cousin Susan who manages the Thaxton stables to see if she had any idea.

He pulled on boots as I talked. "Tell Mom I'm going over there," he said bossily. "Never mind. I'll tell her myself."

"Good. I'll go with you."

He stopped. "Why?"

"Well, for one thing, my car's there."

He seemed about to object, then shrugged. "Oh hell! Why not?"

I thought he could come up with a number of reasons why not. I followed him back to Sal's suite. We found her just climbing into bed, one eye on the television news.

"*...the latest in the investigation into the activities of Mastermind, the Internet terrorist. FBI director Roscoe Alvarez said, in an exclusive interview you saw here just about an hour ago, 'they are proceeding as rapidly as possible. He called on the American people to come* *forward with any knowledge they might have concerning this man at whose hands many innocent people have suffered. The President spoke again tonight from the Oval Office, urging calm, although he admits, under the circumstances, that is not easy. In other news..."*

She touched the button, the face disappeared and the doors of the cherry cabinet slid shut. "Any bets," she asked softly with a glance at the child on the cot, "who they'll be talking about tomorrow?"

We both muttered soothing, superior male sounds, kissed the tired face and left her to a few hours rest.

* * * * *

Wednesday: about 2 A.M.

Walt drove through the starless night with an adolescent disregard for either icy roads or motor vehicle code; not, I felt sure, his usual driving style, but rather a comment on the forced inclusion of his passenger.

Once through the covered bridge linking Thaxtonville to Plainfield proper, I'd expected to talk to him, try to get a bead on the reason for his sudden interest in the restaurant, say a few encouraging words, but, once across the wood plank floor of the bridge, he punched it up even further, driving far too fast, veering dangerously around snow plows and giving stop signs only a token application of foot to brake.

The young man was due a lecture, but not now and not from me. For one thing, I did not think he would get too wild. He knew he would be held accountable, not only for his own car and expenses, but for my welfare as well. Nevertheless, I was grateful when we reached Pleasant Company in one piece.

Dead in Pleasant Company
A Pennsylvania Dutch Mystery

The place was still brightly lit, the CLOSED sign clearly visible from the street. Inside, a handful of co-workers hung around, keeping themselves busy scrubbing tables and chairs, these up-ended so they could scrub the underside as well. I smiled at them, thinking how different they are from workers at restaurants in other parts of the country. Only here, among the step-scrubbing Pennsylvania Dutch, had they, as co-owners, granted themselves four days unpaid leave a year to do their own spring and fall house-cleaning.

A single exception to this frenzy of tidiness was the table at which the three of us had sat, it seemed an age ago. Except that the chairs were now empty, the alcove looked much as it had when I left.

One or two other tables held cups and saucers in use, along with plates of the last of Elsie's sticky buns and fastnachts. To these, both workers and police would go, take a sip and a bite and return to their quite different tasks. Captain Shoemaker, head of PPD's Serious Crimes Division and a life-long friend, came to greet me.

"We're just about done here, Sam. The Chief asked me to hang around a bit in case the press gets wind of it, but there's been no need really."

"Anything new?"

He shook his head. "Strauch's going to cut him up first thing in the morning but we don't expect any surprises."

"Definitely a heart attack then?"

"Looks like." He unwrapped a stick of gum, grimaced at it, stuck it in his mouth. "Supposed to take the place of cigarettes. Right."

I told him I'd been there. "How are they doing?" I nodded at the men still working at the table.

"Just finishing up," he said laconically. Close up I could see they were boxing up each of the items they'd bagged and marked earlier. "You know these guys. Mattern keeps 'em on their toes. Deihl's doing prints. Bill Peters's crew's doing scene-of-crime stuff. We're just playing it extra safe as we do these days."

I nodded and said I'd try to stay out of their way. In the small office at the back I found Walt on the phone canceling the produce and bakery orders for the coming day. I would have liked to say something nice, show I was pleased with what he was doing, but he would only resent it. What right had I to approve or disapprove anything he did?

"Where's the chef?"

"Sent him home," he said shortly. "I can handle things."

"Naturally. I wasn't...I just wondered where he was. Look, will I be in the way if I use the phone here?"

Without a word, he picked up his order books. "Knock yourself out," he said tersely as he left. "Let me know when you're done."

I punched in the home number for Tom Halloran, United Broadcasting Company's CEO and gave my friend the bad news.

"Oh my God no! There go our numbers! Damn!" Then, "At your place you say?"

"At our 'store' here in Plainfield, yes. The ME here says heart attack. Did you know he had a problem there?"

"First I heard of it," he said. "Not that they tell me anything worthwhile. Complaints. Requests for more money. Union problems. Sponsor gripes. *That* they tell me, but that our star on-air personality has a bad ticker? No, that's not important," he said sarcastically. "*You're* in good health I hope Sam. Not going to drop over on me too, are you Sammy my boy?"

I assured him I was in fine health.

"Good. Good. Okay, well, I'll get our 'suits' down there pronto. Maybe we can find something to sue you for," he chortled. "Recoup some of the millions I've lost in suits because of him!"

Dead in Pleasant Company
A Pennsylvania Dutch Mystery

A peculiar sense of humor, my friend has.

* * * * *

Walt, cigarette in hand, was still working, now at a corner table with a lap-top. I debated whether to ask him how the new computerized perpetual inventory was working. Shoemaker approached and asked if I would take care of the press beginning to trickle in. I looked at Walt.

"Be my guest," he said and departed again, taking cigarettes, ash-tray and lap-top with him. It was another clear message, daring me, I suppose, to tell his mother he was smoking. He still has a lot to learn about me, as I suppose I have about him.

* * * * *

SAL

I opened my eyes to find the child (I was having a hard time thinking of her as a girl,) sitting up on her cot, looking around my room. Moses, the stray grey cat my daughter had dragged home one day, lay nestled up against her. I lay quietly, watching, deciding what approach to take.

The girl's eyes were moving slowly around the room, pausing first at Grandfather's long, oak mirror, then at my rose-splashed lounge, next at the glass-doored bookcases. Her small face bore the same expression of knowing appraisal as an auctioneer at an estate sale. What experiences in that young life could produce such a look?

When they came to the row of long windows, the eyes stopped to stare at the huge maple just outside, its bare branches thick with snow. That longing look wrung my heart and suddenly the child was more than just another case. The eyes moved on finally, back to the interior and the huge four-poster that had been my parents'. I waited until they came to rest on me.

"Good morning," I said softly. "Did you sleep well?" The girl eyed me steadily for a moment. I was surprised how pleasant it was to have a child around in the morning again. "How are you feeling this morning? We were a bit worried about you yesterday." How much of the last few days did she remember? How much did she understand? Did she even remember me?

She did not seem to be frightened, merely waiting. What for, I wondered? What had greeted her as she woke up before this? I debated whether to go on asking questions. I tossed a mental coin.

"Do you remember me?" I paused briefly. "My name's Salome McKnight." I smiled at her. "I took you from the bus station to the hospital and then later from the hospital here. It would be nice to know what your name is." She continued her steady examination of my face, saying nothing. "I must get up now." It seemed advisable to warn the girl, as if she were a fawn. I looked at my watch. "I must go to work." Hoping it would not alarm my small guest, I added, "I'm a policewoman." Then the memory of last night's events returned and it was no longer so pleasant.

I touched the bell to let the kitchen know I was up, then turned to the girl, still watching my every move. "I'm going to have to go to work soon," I said again. "I'm afraid we're in for a hectic...oh, good morning, Mrs. Honeycutt."

Mrs. Honey, not one to waste perfectly good breath on useless words, reported the day was not so good, the phone was ringing off the hook. "Them teewee pipples again. I called Mrs. Sweeney."

I thanked her and, against the good lady's objections, ordered toast and coffee only. Mrs. Honey did not hold with 'diets.' If you were fat you were fat. Period.

To forestall the usual lecture on that subject, I turned to my small guest. "You remember Mrs. Honeycutt? She gave you a bath last night and put you to bed. She will take care of you for a while. *Gut genuk* Mrs. Honey? Bathroom first I imagine. Do we have something she can wear?"

"I got somethin' reaty already, never you mind, en it won't be them raxs she had on venn she cum vunce."

The odd couple left hand in hand, passing Mrs. Sweeney at the door. I wished my right hand good morning, trying not to sound too cynical, told her she was early and asked her if she'd heard.

"Yes. Your brother asked me to get in as soon as possible this morning, so here I am. We'll need a statement."

"Yes. Will you do that? The usual I think. Hearts go out to family and co-workers."

"Sorely missed? Sincerely regret the loss of one of the country's leading journalists?"

"The latter yes. Better not go so far as the former."

"Okay. Any mention of Pleasant Company?"

I thought. "Let's not." Thought again. "Or perhaps we'd better." Thought some more. "Look, just be prepared in case they bring it up. You can say the Hamilton Street 'store' will be closed today in his memory."

"Okay. I'll get right on it. The phone was ringing non-stop as I came in."

I thanked her again, donned a swimsuit, forsook the elevator to the ground floor (burning twenty-five calories, half of one slice of toast,) and did my thirty-six laps.

* * * * *

SAM

Wednesday, 6:30 A.M.

Dog-tired as I was, Sal needed to be brought up to date. The smell of coffee lured my sleep-starved body to the kitchen. I reached for the coffeepot and got my hand slapped.

"You chust vait naw, yunk man. It vants to sett vunce. You chust go in an' sett vunce en' I'll brink it in ven it's goot."

"Okay, okay boss," I grinned at her. "Where's my gal Sal?"

Hands deep in batter, she pointed her shoulder upstairs. "Talkin' to the little kitty vunce I imachine."

Sal appeared on cue, the child clinging tightly to her with one hand and clutching an upended Moses to her small chest with the other. The cat did not seem perturbed in the least.

Sal asked the girl if she remembered me. The child merely clung more closely to my sister. Sal went on speaking quietly, reminding the child who I was. The kid ignored me completely, her whole small being focused on Honeycutt as he opened the hot servers and dished up my breakfast: scrapple, Gold Yukons fried with eggs and a dollop of onion, toast and jam.

I looked at my sister. "Be good for you to have some of this today. You'll need it."

She shook her head. She would put on a pound just looking at it. Honeycutt asked if the ladies were ready, the kid's nod was tiny but eager.

"That's a definite yes, Honeycutt."

Sal let the kid decide where she wanted 'her' chair— one of a pair made for us forty-odd years ago, child-size with longer legs, but otherwise an exact match of those in

Dead in Pleasant Company
A Pennsylvania Dutch Mystery

Aunt Magdalene's formal dining room. The question was put to the child with the same regard for personal choice as it had been yesterday to Judd Tunnelson. Or would be for me, for that matter. That's how my twin is. You have to have a fairly healthy ego to put up with it.

The kid looked from the youth chair to Sal before scrambling up on a regular model and settling back. When Mrs. Honeycutt brought her fare, it was not as hearty as mine, but plenty for her size: hot oatmeal, toast with peanut butter, a scrambled egg nestling in the hollow of a small, familiar blue bowl, hot chocolate in a matching pot. The kid dug right in. She was so intent on getting her breakfast down I could see it was no use asking the usual kid-type questions.

"She's not quite ready to tell us her name," Sal said, reading my mind. "She will when she's ready." Then, giving her guest time to settle in, "How about you? You've not been to bed?"

I gave her the gist of the past hours, leaving off any mention of Walt but to say he was at the 'store' and working. She said it was good to see him finally focus on something. "What about the press? Were they awful?"

For us, for any Thaxton, the press looms vulture-like, just off the horizon in a perpetual state of readiness, waiting to swoop down at the slightest opportunity. That we've given them so little to write about seems only to pique their interest. It's tough for all of us but especially for Sal whose need for privacy is intense. "Not bad, considering. Mrs. Sweeney will take them now." Sal nodded. "You planning to go in?"

"You mean because I'm not in uniform? Oh yes. I just thought it might be better today if I weren't." Better for the kid that meant. A police uniform might intimidate the kid in this vulnerable state. That, too, is how she is. "I'll change down there after our workout. Why do you ask? You expecting a fuss about Tunnelson's death?"

"No, but the press'll be all over down there for one thing. They'll especially be looking for you. They know you work there now. The man was your guest and bought the bullet at our store." I munched away. She sipped her coffee. "I suppose you realize," I said morosely, "the Hamilton store will forever be known as the place where 'that newspaper fella' died. They'll remember that long after they've forgotten his name."

"You think so?" She frowned at me. "I suppose it will. Dear heaven! There really is never an end to it..." She stopped.

"What?"

Dismay flooded her face. "Thank God it was a natural death! Otherwise people might be wondering if his Plainfield story had something to do with it."

"Or that it was something he ate."

"Don't *say* that!"

"You know they're likely to say it anyway. All it needs is for one of Tunnelson's brother journalists, looking for a new angle, to speculate out loud."

"Or need to fill in a few seconds of air time." She stared at me. "Or make points with his boss."

"Or get his own name out there."

She paled and said 'dear heaven' again. She looked beyond me into the past. "Twenty years of building a good business and all...for what?"

I damned the press, not for the first, nor, I felt certain, the last time. I looked at her. "You know, there's one good thing about what happened last night."

"There is? I wish you'd tell me what."

"At least," I said, studying her face, "he wasn't here to do a story on us for a change." I put another forkful of crisp potatoes where they belonged. "Of course that doesn't mean we're out of it completely. Speaking of which, do we know what's happened to his notes on the story he did come here to do? Did he send it in? Have you seen any of it?"

"He showed me a few video clips early on. Wanted a pat on the head for his 'hard-hitting' criticism of CRE's tactics I suppose but, if you recall, he told us just last night he wasn't going to use it."

"So, where is it then? Still at the gate-house?"

"I imagine so. Unless he went ahead and sent it in."

"I think I'll take a look-see. And Sal, sorry if I got you worked up. You know how I like to hear myself jabber. So," I tried to change the subject. "What are you going to do about your current guest?"

She accepted my effort with a docility that wouldn't fool a nit. Me and my big mouth!

She said she was anticipating a call from the child's family at any moment. "I've notified Missing Persons and disseminated her vitals to all other related services, so I don't think it will be too long. I've been on the phone to Social Services as well. They're reluctant to let her stay with me for another day, but the Health Department has prohibited foster home placements during this flu epidemic. At least," Sal sounded defensive, "she eats here and the doctors did say she was seriously malnourished. Mrs. Honey's fixed up the old nursery for her. Have you talked with Roselma?"

I played along as if it were business as usual, saying I planned to call my wife (and her best friend) later when I thought she'd be up and around. "I'll suggest she stay on with her mother a few days more until this blows over."

"Good. Good," she said absently. "In answer to your question, yes, I've a full day ahead. Two court hearings this morning, a couple of parents coming in and Charlie's asked me to take Career Day at the high school."

Honeycutt put a plate of wheat and amaranth toast before her, adding a carousel of fruit spreads. "How 'bout you?"

"I'm home to bed," I mopped the last of my eggs with toast and gave the offer of more coffee the okay. "I'll probably be somewhere around the stable this afternoon if you want me."

"Will Mountain King be ready do you think?"

"I think so. Benjam's not so sure, but I think so. We've got three months before we run again."

Again she nodded approval but we both knew the effort to make the day appear normal was a sham. Damn the press!

A few minutes later she picked up her uniform bag, tossed us a wave and dashed off to the car Honeycutt had heated and waiting. My watch buzzed. "Miss me already?"

"Yes," she said simply. "Look Sam. Let's let the police look for Tunnelson's story. I'll tell them about it and give them permission to search the gate-house. Okay?"

I said it was and went home to get some shut-eye.

Dead in Pleasant Company
A Pennsylvania Dutch Mystery

CHAPTER 6

I woke myself two hours later to let my wife fuss over me a bit before assuring her all was fine and she need not spoil her visit. I hung up, shut off my phone extension as both wife and sister had my private cell-phone number, and dropped back to sleep briefly, this time to be called to the phone by our housekeeper with the first sign of the trouble to come. It came, not from the press, but from a Thaxton.

"Sammy my boy! What's going on over there?" Cousin Reuben's voice, thin and reedy like the rest of him, had a tendency to rise stridently when under stress. "I don't want to upset you, son, but I've had everybody and his brother on the line here this mornin'."

I kicked myself. I should have at least notified Reuben, who is, after all, the titular head of the Thaxton *freundshaft*. I played dumb. "Really? Why? Who?"

"Why this business with that reporter friend of yours. They said he 'passed' at your place last night." I'd given up ragging him about his old-fashioned reference to death. "What happened? He et something that didn't agree with him?"

"Oh jeez, Reuben! For God's sake be careful where you say that!" I rubbed my eyes, then my head. It did not seem to help. "The man had a heart attack after dinner is all." I wanted to say he'd stuffed himself like a pig all day and it was a wonder he didn't explode. "Who did you say called?"

"Freddie Frey called me, as he should under the circumstances." Naturally. As Police Commissioner, Frey would want to know how Mayor Reuben Thaxton was involved. "There a question about the cause of death?"

"Hell no! The guy'd been eating all day at the church and then stuffed himself at dinner and…"

"The church? What was he doing there?"

"He wanted to see what Ground Hog's Day was like. He stuffed..."

He was not interested. "What makes you think it was a heart attack?"

"Hal Strauch says so. He was there."

"What was he doing there?"

"He's the Medical Examiner, remember. Look Cousin Reuben, Tunnelson spent the afternoon at the church then had dinner with us at the Hamilton Street store. He dropped dead after dinner. Suddenly. Naturally we called the police."

Thaxton-like, he would be mentally jogging back and forth between doing the right thing and a passionate wish to avoid the press. Thaxton-like, the right thing won.

"I see. Well, you best be getting yourself over there. Talk to Freddie. Wouldn't hurt to talk to the chief too, although I don't know..." Whether Warmkessel was up to it. Whether our formerly stellar chief would ever be the man he once was. It was the sixty-four thousand dollar question.

The tone of my cousin's 'good-bye' was so 'be a good boy and run along and play,' I was tempted to say, "Yes, Cousin Reuben" and do just the opposite. For a moment I felt much in league with Walt. But the call had the desired effect and by the time I was ready to leave, I was feeling guilty that I had dropped the ball. Anything even remotely newsworthy about the Thaxtons is cause for public speculation and the sudden death of the country's most loved and hated investigative journalist in a Thaxton-owned restaurant while a guest of the Thaxton twins, could not, even by me, be considered remote.

* * * * *

An hour later I was in sight of the sparkling white facade of the unique octagon-shaped building the Thaxtons

Dead in Pleasant Company
A Pennsylvania Dutch Mystery

had built for the county. Quite a flurry of cars and one or two mobile media units bearing their station's call letters were squirreling their way into Thaxton Park just across the street. As I drew nearer, I could see the police already had a traffic unit in place and were shouting orders through a bull horn.

As I was here on my own, I parked in the visitors lot closest to the General Public section, one of a half dozen ways to enter the building. Although the architects had designed this, the General Public Entrance, they had left it to each of the tenants: state, county and local governments and Judiciary, to design its own.

I ignored the bronze map in the center foyer, flicked a salute to the statue of G.G.H.H. just above it and considered where to start. I had a lot from which to choose since just about any one of the eight sections would take me to a Thaxton or next to.

For the real skinny on what was going on behind the scenes, official or otherwise, Judiciary was the place to go. Cousin Maddie Grim was certain to be there, hustling her way up the ladder on the DA's staff and, though there'd never been any love lost between us, we had a quasi-bond born of the closeness of our ages. She was a little too bent for me, having too keen an interest in other people's affairs, but if there was anything to know in that building, she would know it.

Sooner or later I would have to stick my nose in the Public wedge where the rent from private businesses pretty much paid for the upkeep of the building. Among the rent-payers, Stephens, Jacobs, Weinsheimer and Butz, the law firm of assorted Thaxton uncles, cousins and in-laws, pretty much takes up one whole floor. They would have heard the news by now and were doubtless expecting a clarifying visit. I decided to save them for last. They could be relied on to get the accurate story of what happened to the rest of the family.

I considered each of the other wedges. Nobody much in the Schools section anymore since Sal quit teaching, so I could skip them. Not the Fire department. Which then? Police where Sal was? City with Cousin Rueben? State?

Still undecided, I headed for the center of the building and took one of the bank of mostly glass elevators which had given the building its nickname, "The Apple," a term coined by Phyll Dayly of the *Morning Times* who said riding up and down in them was like coring an apple. I flipped a coin as I rose soundlessly. Heads. Cops.

I was directed to a pair of swinging doors through which officers came and went, mostly in conferring pairs. You might have expected to find cops grouped in knots jabbering away about the big news, but everybody seemed to be going about business pretty much as usual. Naturally, I thought. They'd have asked one another if they'd heard the news and gone back to work. As Tunnelson said, we are not a gossipy people. One of the officers pointed to my sister's desk but she was nowhere in sight. Plan B. I headed for Chief Warmkessel's office.

In spite of the natural cheer given each office by the airiness and daylight pouring in through floor to ceiling windows, Warmkessel was anything but cheery. Like any Pennsylvania Dutchman, the big man was no good at equivocation and the heartiness with which he greeted me was both palpably false and typical of him. I asked him if there was anything new.

He hemmed and hawed around trying not to say anything that might offend. "New? No. Oh! You mean with that reporter fella? No. Not really. In the morgue. They're working on him now I believe. Family coming up. Sister I believe and," he referred to a memo on his desk, "someone from his insurance company name of Fowler."

Dead in Pleasant Company
A Pennsylvania Dutch Mystery

I spent a few minutes trying to cheer the old guy up, then headed up a few floors to Police Commissioner Frey's office. I stopped to banter with Lainie, the commissioner's right and left hands for nearly twenty years. Frey greeted me with the same long face he had ever since our father (and his friend), crashed his plane with our mother aboard nearly forty years ago. He patted me on the shoulder, assured me he would do everything he could to keep things quiet.

I did not like the tone of that. There was nothing to be kept quiet. I told him so. He said he was preparing a statement for the press and asked me if I'd like to look it over. I did, suggesting a few changes which he penciled in. I said I'd appreciate if he kept me up to date and departed, back to the elevators, this time to City section.

In the mayor's suite, I stopped again to chat with the woman who'd followed cousin Reuben from law office to mayor's office and would doubtless follow him back to private practice when the time came. Like Lainie, she was as much a part of the Thaxtons as anyone. She ushered me into His Honor's office.

Cousin Reuben stood at the bank of windows looking out across Thaxton Circle to Thaxton Park. Soon the flower beds would bust out with yellow aconite, muscari and early tulips; clumps of daffodils would emerge beneath the white and pink crabapples, peach and dogwood. Next the white birch, weeping willow and mountain ash would leaf out, each adding distinctive shape and color to the fountains and ponds in the hot summers. Still it is awesome in autumn with the riotous yellow, gold, orange and red of the native oaks and sugar maples that got to me. Chokes me up. However, there was none of that now.

I joined him. We had a bird's eye view of traffic cops directing yet more network vans where to go—which, I am going to do myself one of these days. You watch me.

"Glad you made it in, Sammy. Have you seen Sal? Is she okay? I'm wondering if she shouldn't stay home for a bit. What do you think?"

I thought him cute. Archaic but cute. Naturally I didn't say that. "My God! Do you have a derrick? That's what it would take to keep her away. She works here now, remember? Besides," I said firmly to close off further discussion, "we certainly wouldn't want people to think she's being given special treatment because she's a Thaxton, would we?"

"Well, no, but..."

"Relax, Reuben. I've conferred with Frey over a statement for the press. We've nothing to do but answer their questions. It will all be over by tomorrow. Don't worry."

All of which shows to go you how much I know.

* * * * *

This time when I stuck my head in the squad room, Sal was behind a file-strews desk, just one among many in the central squad room. The reward for achieving her new rank and assignment as Juvenile Officer did not, it seemed, include anything approaching privacy.

Even from the far side of the room I could see she was oblivious to the chatter of voices, the clatter of electronic equipment, the incessant ringing of phones. A youth and a worried looking couple dressed in work clothes sat facing her. The little group seemed to be set off by itself, an island, isolated by a sea of noise. I was gratified to see that today, befitting the uniform, the Thaxton chestnut curls, which usually felt free to roam at will, were neatly in place. She looked completely at home in her new job and every bit a cop.

Dead in Pleasant Company
A Pennsylvania Dutch Mystery

I remained out of sight, waiting for her to finish. From my vantage point I could see her look steadily first at the boy, then at each parent in turn, then back to the boy. I know what it's like to face those intelligent, shy eyes, compassionate but without a hint of sentiment. They pierce your carefully acquired armor, take a good look at who you are and let you know you'll do, despite your particular warts. Quite a person, my sister. If you're beginning to get the idea I think she's the bee's knees, well, I told you from the get-go, I like her.

As for the trio before her, their body language spoke for them: the boy slumped down in his chair as far as he could, the parents facing away, not only from their son, but each other as well.

It took about fifteen minutes for the eyes and matter-of-fact, confident voice to do the job. As I watched, the boy slowly straightened into his chair. The couple began to cast quick glances at each other, gradually shifting position until they were side by side. Finally, all three rose, shook Sal's firm hand, nodded and departed. As they passed me, still oblivious to their surroundings, the man reached, first for his wife's hand, then to put an arm around his son.

I wormed my way past a bunch of desks to hers. "Witchcraft," I said, by way of greeting.

She looked from me to the departing family. "What? Oh. Don't be silly." She made some notes on the computer. "You slumming or did you come to take me away from all this?"

"Yes and yes. Are you free for lunch? It's sunny out there."

"I was going to brown-bag it so I could stay on the search for the girl's family. She has me flummoxed! Can you believe there's not been a single inquiry about her? It's worrisome." She looked up. "I can go if you need me though, assuming we make it quick."

"Quick it is then." I pointed to a pile of papers a couple of inches high. "What's all this?"

"Results of my search for the child's family! Printouts from various sources: the Center for Missing and Abused Children, Child Find, the Association for Children in Crisis and half a dozen other databases," she said glumly. "Can you believe it? Even after removing the duplicates there are seven hundred and four children, no, not children, girls under the age of six reported missing within the last three months! I know! I know," she said before I could respond. "I shouldn't be surprised after all the years I've been working with children but…"

"…it's different when one of those numbers is someone for whom you're responsible. Natch." I took her arm. "Come on. Let's go. The sooner you go the sooner you get back."

For my part, lunch was a miss. She'd brightened at my suggestion of a winter picnic and we stopped at the nearest PC Junior. (Two turkey barbecue and fries for me, chicken pot pie for her.) Then on to the spot on Thaxtonville Road where, snow or no, the creek rushes over a low wall of rock before sliding smoothly under the red covered bridge.

Today I might as well have eaten alone. I'd expected to engage her mind by a recounting of my earlier visits to one and all with the combined banter and wit that is the meat of our usual discourse. She listened all right, or at least I think she did, but when I asked her what she thought, she just said I'd gotten more done than she.

"Okay, Princess Pea," I said finally. "What's going on in your head that's more important than me? Something to do with that kid, I bet." It was a sucker's bet. Only kids come before me with Sal.

She admitted she could not get the girl out of her mind. "I was certain that knowing she was a girl would help, but all I have to show for it is a daunting list of families who

Dead in Pleasant Company
A Pennsylvania Dutch Mystery

seem to have misplaced their small daughters." She stared out at the running water. "It's awesome." I did not think she was talking about Ma Nature. Yup. Her mind was engaged all right but not on me.

I asked her how long she was going to keep the girl at her home.

"Up to Children's Services," she said glumly. "I hope at least until we get the test results from the hospital. If she's ill, we'll admit her." She shivered. "Let's go. I'm getting cold."

We cleared the remains of our meal from the back of my station wagon which had provided both seat and table for our picnic. I looked at her face. "You'll want to check up on her before we go back, I assume?"

"If you don't mind," she said, and took a last, long look at the creek, blabbering away, defying the cold.

* * * * *

Naturally, everyone was in the kitchen. The kid was propped up on a high stool at one end of cook's work-table, being instructed in the art of shelling peas. The sight brought with it a kaleidoscope of memories as I watched, the picture subtly shifting with each turn of the glass. First the teacher, no more than a sixteen-year-old cook's helper, the youthful learners my sister and I, the task the same. Turn the glass and the teacher's face bears the confident look of the mistress of the kitchen, engaging in giving Sal's three the same precise instructions. Turn once more and see the slim form spreading, the fair hair graying, only the directions—now to this strange silent child—remain unchanged. It was as if the learner in the scene remained constant over generations while the teacher gradually aged. Shades of Dorian Gray, I thought! When the picture shot ahead to the time when the teacher would be gone, I quit the mind game. Kid stuff anyway.

The forehead of today's student was creased with the effort to concentrate on her task, but when she saw us she popped up, staggered around in a circle, swayed back and forth a bit and, without uttering so much as a syllable, fell to the floor.

We all dashed to the rescue, fussing over her, checking for broken bones and bruises. The ladies took turns feeling her forehead. The child seemed not to give a hang for the fuss she'd caused. She treated our worry with superior disdain, climbed back up on her stool and returned to her task. A piece of work, that one!

The women continued their fugue-like questioning until the soft chime of the half-hour drifted in from G.G.H.H.'s hall clock. I reminded my sister of the time.

"Okay," Sal said, frowning at her charge. "I'm coming. Perhaps," this to Mrs. Honeycutt "you would see to it that our guest gets a good nap." To the child's raised protest she added, "then she might like to see the horses. *After* her nap," Sal said firmly. "Call Benjam to come for her though. I don't want you walking around in that snow. There's still ice under it."

* * * * *

I eased off the gas as we approached the covered bridge, the snow packed ramp my excuse.

"Give," I said.

"What? Oh." I pulled her hood up around her head. "I was just thinking about that little drama we just saw. What in the world was that all about, do you suppose? Some kind of brain damage? Perhaps connected with her not speaking? Darn! I wish I'd asked the resident to give her an EEG. I missed the boat there. I suppose it's too late…look, Sam.

*Dead in Pleasant Company
A Pennsylvania Dutch Mystery*

I'd better get back to work before I goof up anything else. See you tonight?"

I said "Yop" and buzzed off.

* * * * *

I did not make it back to bed. My car phone rang before I was halfway home.

"Sammy, my boy."

"Reuben, my man."

He would be pulling a long face at my levity. "Sorry to bother you like this again Son, but it can't be helped. You better get down here. There's trouble."

That was at ten past two. I turned around and headed back downtown. My watch said quarter to three when, this time on official business so to speak, I pushed my ID into the slot at the underground parking lot and pulled into one of the official spaces. A minute later I was being ushered into the mayor's office for the second time that day.

"...nip this thing in the bud," His Honor was saying as I entered.

Police Commissioner Frey stood at the window with cousin Reuben. They turned to nod at me, then resumed their oversight of the park. I joined them. The number of media vans and trucks had multiplied like...well...rabbits. Now they were circling the park, jockeying for position like settlers preparing for an attack—the difference being that it would be they who were doing the attacking.

"Sorry about draggin' you down here again, my boy," Reuben said, "but we don't want to let things get out of hand."

"What's going on?"

"Well Son, we're gettin' a lot of calls askin' a lot of questions we can't really answer."

"Questions? Like what?" I didn't have to ask from whom.

"Like how sure are we this fella's death was a natural death. Like which of the Thaxton restaurants did he die in. Like is it true the Thaxton twins were actually with him at the time. Like what was he doing in Plainfield. Like is it true that Salome Thaxton is on the Plainfield Police force. Like is she investigating the death. Hell, son, look at 'em out there! CBS. Tom Halloran's people. NBC. ABC. CNN. Rupert's gang. Hell, that means we'll be international! And every local station within forty miles has a crew here already and New York and Philly on the way. We gave them a statement, but..."

A tap on his door and his secretary slipped through the skimpiest of openings, apologized for the interruption and addressed the police commissioner. "The man from Mr. Tunnelson's insurance company has arrived, sir. He says he has to attend the autopsy before he signs off on the insurance." She handed Frey a card.

The commissioner's eyebrows rose. "The autopsy? I think that's all done, isn't...?" He studied the card, then dropped it on the mayor's desk. "Where is he?" She nodded toward the outer office. "Okay. Just give us a moment...oh, never mind. Go ahead and send 'im in." He muttered to us, "Let 'im know we run a clean ship here. Get things cleared up in a hurry."

I took an instant dislike to the man. He was just a shade shorter than I, putting him at about an even six feet and exuded the polish and shine which telegraphs health club, personal trainer, golf and tennis. His grey suit, no doubt meant to make a lot of his eyes (a shade of blue I've never liked), was tailored to camouflage the fact that he had no hips to speak of. A sandy tooth-brush mustache dragged your eye immediately to the guy's mouth, no doubt to enhance the value of his words—of which he had plenty.

Dead in Pleasant Company
A Pennsylvania Dutch Mystery

"Ken Fowler. Horizon Insurance. New York office." He made it sound like Nirvana. "I won't keep you. Do my best to not get in your way."

Reuben took his hand and gestured. "This is Fred Frey, Commissioner of Police. I'm the mayor, Reuben Thaxton."

"Thaxton? Oh? Of the famous Thaxtons, eh? I see." Yeah, he saw, all right. "A pleasure sir, a very great pleasure. I've heard so much about you. And this?" He turned toward me.

"Mr. Sam Thaxton. Mr. Tunnelson was his guest at table when he had his heart attack."

"*Apparent* heart attack, not so? I'm certain we would not wish to be accused of a rush to judgment, would we?" His tone did exactly that. He spread a thin, confident smile on each of us. "Of course not! You know what happens when the press gets *that* idea." He turned back to me. "Well! So! This is Sam Thaxton! One of the notorious Thaxton twins, isn't it? Yes. I had the very great privilege of watching you take the gold at our last two Olympics! Wonderful, really! I been hoping I'd run into you while I was here. Tried to talk insurance with you and your sister once or twice. We specialize in working with persons of high risk," he turned to explain to the others, "but couldn't get past your secretary." I made a note to give her a raise. He pumped my hand and pointed to my suit. "Like your tailor," he smiled. "Markham's eh? Work with Ralph there?"

I said something like 'meetcha'. I can't stand name-droppers. Still, I had to admit I worked with Ralph at Markhams. I took another look at the grey suit. The insurance business must be good, I thought.

"Like your stick too. Ash, is it? Quite a fashion statement. Known for it, aren't you?"

I wanted to fashion statement him. "Good of you to approve," I said sarcastically. "Otherwise I don't know what

I'd do." The intended insult flew right by him. Thick skinned I thought, no doubt used to it. He went right on with a salesman's enthusiasm.

"Well! And your sister's on the Plainfield Police force, isn't she? And, correct me if I'm wrong, but I believe she was also present at Mr. Tunnelson's last supper." He looked from one to another, still smiling. His wit unacknowledged, he went blithely on. "Well, well! Isn't this cozy! It's true then. Thaxtons everywhere. What they say, I mean. Just one big happy family."

The door opened and the secretary begged to be excused. "Sorry for the interruption sir, but they're waiting for Mr. Fowler."

Fowler smiled at us. "Asked them to let me have a look at the body. Nothing here to worry you though. Just a formality. Company policy for our larger policy-holders." He shook hands with each of us again. To me he said, "Really would like to talk with you before I leave, Mr. Thaxton. Your sister too."

"Oh? Officially?"

"Oh no," the smile beamed apologetic, "let's not say that. I'm sure your police have been very thorough in their investigation into the death of our insured. No, let's just say as one of Markham's clients to another." He started toward the door, then turned back to me. "You don't have any objection to talking with me, do you, Mr. Thaxton?"

I looked him in the eye. "None that you haven't heard before, I'm sure, Mr. Fowler." I turned to go. "You'll need to call my office if you want to see my sister and me together. You have the number, I take it" I turned to bow slightly to the others. "Commissioner Frey. Cousin Reuben. Thanks for the chat. We'll stay in touch." I brushed past him and beat it.

* * * * *

Dead in Pleasant Company
A Pennsylvania Dutch Mystery

Sal was back at her desk in the squad room, engrossed in her computer search. The atmosphere in the large room was subtly different. Now officers who had treated Tunnelson's death with the detached air of professionals looked up each time the door opened. This time only one or two nodded at me when I came in.

One look at Sal's face and it was obvious she'd already heard the news. I told her about Ken Fowler's request, if you can call it that, to meet with us. "Look out for him, Sal. The man's a barracuda."

She raised her eyebrows at me and shrugged. I knew what was going through her head. Here we go again. What else is new?

I used her phone to call the ME. Dr. Strauch was defensive and reluctant to talk, but he'd brought us into the world. He assured me his autopsy had found no indications of anything other than that the man's heart stopped supplying blood to the rest of his body. "Nothing to worry about Sam, I'm...hello? Who? Oh." Then speaking to someone else, trying to rein in his exasperation, "Come in, come in. It's all done, but you're welcome to take a look." He returned to the phone. "Guy from the insurance company's here. Wants to see everything. Gotta go."

When I hung up Sal was back at work facing a handful of young males, so I threw her a wave and beat it.

I had a couple of hours of sleep to catch up on and did so. When I woke I got into warm riding clothes, told Annie I'd beg dinner from my sister, and though it was early, got Nimbus saddled for our usual sunset ride.

The old fella was eager too, and, as I was early, I decided to ride him an extra hour or so. I chose the north trail between the Thaxton compound and Elk Run. Chilly gusts of wind pushed at both man and beast from time to time and dropped sizable drifts back on the paths, neatly plowed just a few hours earlier. It was hard to say which of us got a bigger kick out of charging through them. It wasn't long before we were both huffing and puffing and ready to join the world.

I was doubly glad we'd gone off on our own when I got to Sal's. The kid, wrapped snugly in a basket a-top gentle, old WonTon, would be tagging along. That meant taking one of the easier trails, following the creek from Sal's home, past the cattle farm, through the woodland trail which, protected by evergreens, remained fairly drift free.

Sal and I blabbed on as usual, the kid between us. She did not speak but her eyes, made wet and glowing by the cold air, took in everything.

We all ate voraciously at dinner, the kid still not talking, and by the time we pushed our plates away her eyes had resumed their watchful look. Nevertheless she went willingly enough to bed, again clutching tightly to my sister's hand.

I had the news on when Sal returned.

"...at least two more deaths in County Hospital in Janesville, Wisconsin, are believed to be the work of Mastermind. The President, speaking today at the University of California's Berkeley campus, is asking for calm heads."

"Finally, this network wishes to mark the death last night of one of the country's legendary journalists, Judd Tunnelson. Often considered the father of investigative journalism, CBS News joins FBC in mourning his passing. Tunnelson died suddenly on assignment in Plainfield, after dining in one of the Pleasant Company restaurants owned by the famed Thaxton twins. Tunnelson was believed to have just completed his work there and was preparing to leave for Philadelphia when he died of an apparent heart attack. An inquest is scheduled for tomorrow at noon. We

*Dead in Pleasant Company
A Pennsylvania Dutch Mystery*

go to Bob Crowley in Plainfield with our affiliate there. Bob?"

The scene shifted to one all too familiar.

"Thanks Fred. I'm standing just outside the Plainfield Community Building, a state-of-the-art structure the Thaxton family built a few years ago to house Plainfield's city and county offices. I've just spoken to Eileen Tunnelson, the sister of the newsman, who has flown from her home in Georgetown to take custody of her brother's body. Let me switch you to Harold Long who is at the scene of death. Hal?"

"Thanks Bob and Fred. Judd Tunnelson died last night in this," the scene shifted to one even more familiar, "Pleasant Company restaurant in downtown Plainfield. This is the original of the family-style sit-down restaurants in the vast Pleasant Company chain now numbering nearly four hundred. I venture to say, Bob, you'd be hard put to find anyone who has not stopped at the familiar sign of the friendly, old couple huddled over a hot cup of tea," (here the camera focused on the company logo towering over the restaurant) "or one of the hundreds of PC Juniors throughout the country."

"We hope to have Ms. Tunnelson on camera later, but in an interview today she was raising questions about her brother's death. Stating that her brother was in excellent health, Ms. Tunnelson and her attorneys are questioning the Plainfield ME's verdict of natural death. The dead man's sister feels the ME may have rushed to call the death natural because it occurred in a restaurant owned by the Thaxton twins to whom the city here owes so much. Back to you, Bob.

The scene switched back to the Community building.

Thanks, Hal. I have Acting Captain Rod Longnecker here who's in charge of the case. Chief Longnecker, how do you respond to Ms. Tunnelson's charges that your ME may have rushed to judgment in determining the cause of Mr. Tunnelson's death?"

The ruddy face appeared close up.

"Vell naw vunce...," he stared at the cameras, his self-consciousness intensifying his accent to the point of satire, *"youse pipple shout be careful of vat you say. Ve gott a goot police department here und ve know our chops."*

"Yes, I'm sure, but sir, didn't you tell me earlier that, what with all the Thaxtons involved, you wouldn't be surprised..."

"Hold it buster! I was chust tellin' you how things are here. I didn't say nothin'..."

"But isn't it true that you've got a Thaxton serving as mayor and there are Thaxtons both on the police force and in the DA's office?" Longnecker's face reddened visibly, but he said nothing. *"Captain, isn't there a possibility there could be an effort to, well, let's say, smooth things over?"*

"Naw you're chust puttin' worts in my mouth! As far as ve know there is nossing in that lady's charges. Chust so you know though, the Plainfield police don't play favorites en if evidence is uncowered that the Thaxtons were in it, the law in Plainfield will make no exceptions."

With that, he turned on his heels and stalked away.

The reporter, listening to someone speaking in his ear, called after the departing policeman. *"One more thing sir. Isn't it true that the coroner's jury has just been moved ahead to Friday? Can you tell us why..."*

Longnecker pushed a palm at him. *"That's chust to giff us time to do the chob right. That's all now!"*

"Thank you, sir." The reporter faced the camera triumphantly. *"That was Acting Captain Rodney Longnecker of the Plainfield Police Department who is in charge of the case. Fred, the Thaxtons could not be reached for..."*

Sal clicked off the set and went off mumbling something about a bath. I restrained myself from putting my foot through the damned set.

CHAPTER 7

SAL

Thursday.

It was still dark when I coaxed Benjam's old station wagon to life and left for work. After a long night spent in a futile attempt to sleep, it was a relief to be doing something, anything, and I looked forward to the twenty minute drive ahead. With the child moved to the nursery next door, my room had been quiet and dark, an irresistibly fertile environment for the day's unfinished business to float to the surface in search of resolution. Excited by the challenge of my new responsibilities for Plainfield's youth, I'd lain awake, wondering if my luck with young people would hold. Had I finally bitten off more than I could chew? Then too. bits of last night's news report persisted in complicating my attempts to sleep. Longnecker's vengeful inferences about Tunnelson's death were dangerously misleading. How much trouble would come as a result? It seemed now that his hatred for me would stay with him always. Had I done the right thing a few years ago when, as a volunteer youth counselor, I'd warned him to back off his harsh treatment of his ten-year-old son before it was too late? It was, he'd shouted, none of my damned business, nor was it. Not officially, anyway. When the boy hung himself by his belt from his bedroom window a few months later, he had found one more reason to hate the Thaxtons, me in particular. How much would that effect my work now that he was my senior officer?

Certainly my first official day at the job did not bode well. Unable to get anywhere in my search for the

Dead in Pleasant Company
A Pennsylvania Dutch Mystery

antecedents of the odd little girl now in my care, I appeared to be failing to solve my very first case.

Leaving aside the question of whether or not I had what it takes, I'd begun to worry what effect the press might have on my efforts to do this very public job—an ancillary of police work I'd not considered when I decided to join the force.

Would the press be sniffing around at every turn? It would be an unacceptable invasion, not only of my privacy, but that of the young people with whom I would be dealing, to say nothing of the PPD in general.

Forgetting to figure the press into the mix before I took the job was no small omission. Ever since our parents' death, the media has kept a rather proprietary eye on the 'poor little rich Thaxton twins.' I'd learned to expect the decades old photo of the two of us to be produced anytime our names were mentioned: my eyes barely peering over our mother's casket, Sam, already several inches taller than I, thrusting a small, angry fist at the photographer.

Until recently the attention, though unwanted, had been fairly benign. Perhaps because the Thaxton clan is close-mouthed, even those events, such as the sudden, unexplained death of our young cousin a while back, had been handled with restraint. Then my husband's suicide, followed a few years later by my involvement in the murder of a fellow teacher,[3] turned the spotlight on my private life. And now this. Still, I couldn't honestly blame the press. Obviously the unexpected death of one as well-known as Judd Tunnelson is news: that he died in a Pleasant Company restaurant only added a sense of familiarity to the story. Since journalists abhor a vacuum as much as does Nature, I could anticipate that, lacking anything of substance about which to write, all sorts of stories about me

---

[3] *If It's Monday, It Must Be Murder* Hannah Fairchild

and mine would be subject to distortion, half-truths and conjectures and all reported as titillating fact.

Nevertheless, I had no intention of letting the press keep me from my job, so when my watch indicated it was five o'clock, an hour at which I could reasonably be up and about, I had risen, done my laps by rote, downed toast and coffee in minutes and, with the child still asleep, grabbed my uniform bag and headed down and out. A brief stop in the mud-room to grab one of the nondescript parkas hanging there and shove my tell-tale Thaxton hair up under an old Phillies cap and I was ready.

In the still gray morning, I tipped said cap in the general direction of the gathering hordes of cameras and the concomitant concabula of the trade as I passed and slid, unnoticed, into the underground entrance tagged OFFICIAL USE ONLY.

As I approached my assigned space, I spied O'Connell waiting for me and I knew the news was not going to be good. I pulled up and parked. He came and held my door open. I wished him a good morning. "You're early. How come?"

"Hope you've had your Wheaties," he said, grimacing. "You wouldn't believe what Longnecker's up to now."

I would believe. "I know. I caught him last night on the tube."

"Yeah, well, he did a lot more shootin' off his mouth before he realized he was going to be quoted."

I looked at him. "And what is he saying that is so quotable?"

"Oh, just that the Chief is white-washing the investigation into Tunnelson's death because of his feelings for you and your family."

"White-washing? How? What's to white-wash? The man had a heart attack. The ME says so."

"For all that may mean. They've been after him too."

Dead in Pleasant Company
A Pennsylvania Dutch Mystery

"They? Who they?"

"Tunnelson's sister and that gang from New York. That Fowler guy's insisting on a full autopsy—blood and tissue samples—the works. Naturally Strauch told 'em it wasn't necessary. Then they asked if he thought to check for echoli! When Hal asked him what the hell that meant, the sister said she'd heard her brother had died in one of the Pleasant Company restaurants, probably from that echoli thing.."

Echoli? My God! I tried to remain calm. "Such rot! We have the highest possible standards for our…"

"Hey!" He threw up both hands. "I'm not the one that needs convincing. I'm just telling you what they're saying, not what anybody here believes."

But they could begin to if 'they' made enough noise and the press caught wind of it. And they wouldn't have to prove it: just the question raised could prove fatal for our restaurant chain and the men and women whose livelihoods depend on it.

At the elevator, he held the door open again. I asked, "Is he getting away with this? Longnecker I mean."

The massive shoulders shrugged. "Hard to tell. The Chief's had him in his office for an hour now, hopefully gettin' the riot act read to him. I'm damned if I know why the Chief puts up with it."

Because, I thought, they went all through school together, joined the force together; because the Chief feels guilty that he moved up passed his mate in the ranks; because he feels sorry that the world had changed and Longnecker had not changed with it; because, since the Chief lost his son two years ago and wife a year later, he had lost his spark.

"Have you heard about the coroner's jury being moved to Friday?"

I said I had. "On the news last night."

"This morning too. Coupla stations led with it."

We were silent the rest of the way. When he pushed open the huge, double doors to the squad room, it seemed to be in its usual early morning end-of-the-shift hub-bub. I thought my fellow officers, though still friendly, greeted me with a bit more caution than usual. A rookie needing direction stopped O'Connell and I went on to my desk.

Three tags, one red and two yellow, meant new cases had come in over night. The early hour gave me time to take a look at them before the morning work-out. O'Connell caught up with me afterward.

"You get a chance to look over the new cases?" I said I had. "That Leiby kid's been an on-going problem," he said. "I hope you can do something with him. Let me know if you need anything. By the way, have you had any new ideas in your search for the kid's family?"

I told him no. "I'm open to suggestions."

He shook his head. "I read your dailies. Can't think of anything you've missed. Look Sal," his voice dropped, "I don't know what you can do about Longnecker and that mob but there must be a Thaxton somewhere who can rein them in."

"More than one, I imagine. I must admit it's tempting. The family seems always to just tap-dance around him."

"Why? That's the question lots of people here are asking." He nodded toward the busy squad room. "No smoke without fire's what some of them think."

"You know the Thaxtons. They don't make waves." Though there was more to it than that, especially for me. "I suppose we think we're being kind. I suspect it will all come to a screeching halt some day."

"Well, I hope it's soon. Anyway, good luck with your search. Let me know when you get anything."

When O'Connell appeared a third time, it was to say the Chief wanted me in his office. I wondered why Warmkessel

Dead in Pleasant Company
A Pennsylvania Dutch Mystery

had not buzzed me himself in the usual way. I tapped at his door and entered when told to do so.

The police chief's ruddy face flushed a deep red at my "Good morning, sir."

He cleared his throat. "Oh. Yeah. Mornin' Sal. Sorry to drag you away from your work, my dear. Hope all this is not too hard on you. I guess you know the coroner's jury's been moved up to tomorrow afternoon." I refrained from replying irritably that apparently everybody on the seven continents knew that by now. "I think your brother should be there. As mayor, Reuben will be, of course, but Sam's more…"

Was he going to say intelligent? Whatever he was going to say, I agreed. Sam was more of it. I wondered, fleetingly, what it would be like to have a twin of whom I could not be proud.

Warmkessel fiddled around with his pen before starting again. "I've got something else to ask you and I hope you won't take it the wrong way." He gave me a sharp look. I kept my face blank. We'd been friends since his rookie days when he was charged with protecting us against a kidnap threat. Later, as detective, he'd been assigned to look into the accidental death of our small cousin. As adults we'd worked together on many civic activities. When I joined the force and he became my boss we knew the time could come when our long friendship could make a working relationship difficult. I hadn't expected it would come so soon.

He, too, seemed to be thinking of our joint past. I took a chair across from him and spoke softly. "Chief?"

"Well," he said, letting it hang.

"Let's have it, sir." I tried not to sound impatient. "What's up?"

"Everything! God! I feel like this place is fallin' apart! Strauch is fit to be tied and threatening to quit. An' Roddy's actin' like a horse's…Look Sal," he swiveled his chair to face me, "I've had a long heart-to-heart with Rod Longnecker and set him straight. Told him that, whatever his personal feelings toward your family, we've seen nothing but the best from the Thaxtons and he could damn well get his mouth under control. Hell, I'd bring him before the board if it wouldn't just give the press another bone to chew on! Damn it! I've known you and your brother all your lives and there's not an unkind..." Again he slid into the past. When he spoke again, it was with despair. "I don't know, Sal! I've just lost it! I can't seem to..." His eyes began to tear. "I've about decided it's time to step aside. I just don't have it anymore."

It was to be expected. When things get painful, I, too had run away. "And leave Longnecker as Chief?"

He looked up. "Oh God! Is that..." He put his head in his hands. "That would be worse. What am I to do?"

"Look Chief, you've been sick at heart since Annie and Tom Junior died," I replied, saying their names deliberately, "and that's no different than any physical sickness. You need help and, more to the point, Plainfield needs you. You've made this force one of the best in the country and without you it's going to fall apart."

"I've tried. Don't you think I've tried? I just don't know what to do."

"Sir, nobody could deal with what you've had to deal with alone and come out whole. You've been mourning your losses and that's all to the good, but you're still here and we need you. If I may repeat your own words back to you sir, why not take advantage of the system. When you don't know what to do, find someone who does and get help."

"Help? You mean a shrink?" His eyebrow squinted, forming a deep bushy Vee. It was as if I'd suggested he talk to the tooth-fairy. He might as well have said it out loud—

real Pennsylvania Dutch don't need no shrinks. "Jeez Sal! I...I just can't face talking to a stranger."

"It doesn't have to be a stranger."

"You mean...you? I don't..."

Good Lord! Did he think I was suggesting he unload personal troubles to me? Even if I had such an interest, which I don't, I'd be drummed out of the clan. "Not me, sir. I was thinking of Ron West."

"West? Oh." A faint smile tilted his lips. "I thought you didn't think much of him."

"We have crossed swords over the treatment of street kids, yes, but outside that he's sound. He's been very helpful to...others." I let him think it over, using the time to consider how best to handle the immediate problems he, we faced. "As far as your suggestion that Sam be at the inquest, I agree, but I think you wanted something else, didn't you?"

"Well uh..." Here it comes, I thought. "...uh, we'd like to have a look at Tunnelson's quarters."

I breathed again. I thought he was going to ask me to resign. "Fine. I'd planned to suggest that yesterday and forgot. I'll call and have Honeycutt make a key available."

"Good. Thanks." Clearly he was not finished.

I prodded. "What else, Chief?"

"Well...uh...we'd like to have a look at the restaurant's security tapes from Tuesday night. You keep them, don't you?"

I'd given up telling people it was 'they,' not 'we' who ran the Pleasant Company restaurants now. "I think they do. I'm not sure how long though. I'm sure you're welcome to them. Shall I call?"

Some of the red drained from his face. The call took only a moment. "Someone will bring them right over." I looked at him. "Anything else, sir?"

"Look, Sal. I've checked your personnel file. You've got quite a few days coming. Don't you think it would be better if you took leave 'til this all blows over?"

Leave? Better than a resignation request at least. I told him thanks, but no. "I've a full docket of my own and I've got this child to get back to her parents."

"Okay. Okay. I didn't think you would. I've never known you to run from anything, even as a kid. You were always such a tough little kid. People always wanted to be hugging you but you always held back, studying everybody with those eyes." Yes, because even at three I knew most huggers wanted something from you. People who really cared about you did not try to hug you right off, but waited until your hearts and minds had touched. "I still remember how good I felt when you came and took my hand finally."

"I trusted you, Chief. I still do."

"Oh?" He spoke absently, again in the past. Then, more briskly. "Well, that's something anyway. Thanks. By the way, how's the search for the kid's family going?"

I told him it wasn't going anywhere. "I've searched all the databases for missing children and have been on the phone to my counterpart in all the districts within a three hundred mile radius. I've listed her in Child Find, so perhaps I'll hear something today. I've got her at my place for the moment. Children Services has given me temporary custody until this flu thing breaks and they can place her."

"Oh, good. Good. Yes. Keep in touch with them. Don't want them complaining we're trying to do their job, do we?" He waved me out, then called out as I closed his door. "Did you say her? A boy, I thought the report said."

"It did. That was before Mrs. Honey gave her a bath."

"Oh? Well, keep me posted." But his mind was already gone back to pick away at the boil of his pain.

* * * * *

Dead in Pleasant Company
A Pennsylvania Dutch Mystery

I stopped off at Hal Strauch's office. He was sitting at his desk, the pencil in his hand beating a rapid tattoo on the ancient surface. I wished him a good morning.

"What's good about it," he asked sourly.

"I just wanted to see how you are doing."

He grunted. "About the way you'd expect! You met this Fowler character yet?"

I said I hadn't.

"The damned pip-squeak! I wish he'd take his fancy shmancy ass out of here! I been sittin' here prayin' the good Lord lets me do *his* autopsy next!" He glanced at me. "Whatdy'a think old H. H.'d say if he was still around?"

I had an idea things wouldn't have gotten so far out of hand had Henry Harrison Thaxton been around. I did not say so. "Probably nothing printable," I said instead. "I understand you sent blood and tissue samples to Atlanta for analysis. How soon do you expect to hear something?"

"Who the hell knows? If they're anything like they were when I was in the Army it'll be a case of hurry up and wait!"

I debated whether to offer to speed things up. It would take no more than a phone call, but knowing the press would find out, decided against it.

I turned to go. "I suppose," he spoke morosely to my back, "you want to know the results when I get them. I'd say I'll call you, but I'm sure you'll hear as soon as I do."

Implying, I suppose, that with so many Thaxtons around..."I'd appreciate it, if you have the time. Hang in there, Hal."

At my desk I found one more case added to my docket. A check of voice, e-mail and fax for replies to yesterday's inquiries about the child turned up naught but blanks. Stymied for the moment, I pulled up the new case for review. After a while O'Connell wandered by to ask if there was anything new on the 'kid.'

"I wish!"

He grunted. "You got any theories on why?" I shook my head. "Hell Sal, she's got to have people somewhere. She didn't just appear out of nowhere."

I thought how apt his remark seemed. The child had an 'other world' look about her. I told O'Connell what I thought.

He grinned. "Maybe she's an alien!"

I gave him a smile I did not feel. "Perhaps not quite *that* other-worldly—although she is a puzzle." I told him about the fainting episode, adding, "And here's another strange thing. Sometimes she eats everything that's not nailed down and other times she eats nothing. Mrs. Honey's about wild. And she still hasn't said a word!"

"Maybe she can't. Talk I mean."

"Some sort of aphasia? It's possible but I don't think it's that. The nurses at the hospital," I said reflectively, "think she's retarded. I could have her tested but I don't like to do that without consent from her parents."

"But you don't."

"Don't...oh, think she's retarded?" I shook my head. "No. I get the impression she just feels her words are her own and she's not going to part with them until she's good and ready. So far I have more questions than answers."

"Like what?"

"Like how long has she been away from home? Like why has no one called to claim her? Like why was she left on the bus? Was it deliberate or mere carelessness?"

"I see what you mean." He frowned in thought. "Maybe her parents can't claim her for some reason."

"I'm considering that. Perhaps no one knows she's missing." I inhaled and sighed. "You've worked in Juvenile for years. Have you come across anything like it before?"

Dead in Pleasant Company
A Pennsylvania Dutch Mystery

"Not with a kid that's still alive, no. You're doing everything possible as far as I can see. Don't be neglecting your other cases for her though, Sal. What's next on your agenda?"

I looked at the clock. "What's next is my appearance in court on the Trumble and Jackson cases." I piled files in my briefcase and ran.

* * * * *

I slipped into courtroom #3 just one step ahead of the judge. The courtroom was about half full. I looked around for Cousin Madeline, newly appointed Assistant District Attorney. Although closest to us in age of all our cousins, I saw her the least. She was caustic in the way people with superior intellects often are and I'm afraid a mutual dislike as kids had continued into adulthood. Still, I was proud of her. When her parents died some ten years ago, she'd gone ahead and gotten the law degree her father had forbidden and was now said to be the up-and-coming star of the DA's office. Recently, rumors began to spread that, after years of celibacy, Maddie and the DA had moved in together. I was curious to see if it had sweetened her disposition any.

But the People were being represented this morning by a pair of young men barely dry behind the ears. Were they really that young or was it more the excess of my own years rather than the absence of them in theirs?

Neither the two Trumble boys nor their parents put in an appearance. I kicked myself. I should have anticipated that. Charged with truancy, obviously they were even less likely to show up in court. On the other hand, the young Jackson girl, there to answer to two counts of shop-lifting, sat right up front between mother and father. I went to sit with them, shaking hands with all three, each hand-clasp more limp than the one before. When I said we were tenth on the docket, the girl wanted to leave until her case was called, but I shook my head. To hear the judge mete out sentences to others couldn't hurt.

I studied the girl's sullen face. Was she salvable? What had put those stains on her heart—a temporary breakdown in the family, normal to adolescents, or a permanent scar? All I knew about her was what was here on a few sheets of paper. Whatever it was, I was not likely to find it in her file.

I opened my briefcase and began to review the remaining new cases. Leafing through the police reports, I let my imagination loose, reading between the lines and concocting scenarios which might have brought these young people to the attention of the police. When I finished my cursory study, I closed the files and added one little lost girl. Which was most important, most urgent?

The bailiff called the next case. The sitting judge was new to me so I returned my attention to the court to get a feel for his approach to youthful offenders. The current case was all too common: two boys, already on probation, stopped for speeding, caught with open cans of beer on the seat between them.

A rustling of voices behind us: young voices, protesting voices, voices complaining about life's unfairness, and a group of late arrivals caught a reprimand from the judge.

I was surprised when one broke away from the group and slid in next to me. "Good morning Officer McKnight."

The voice no more than a husky whisper, the merest touch of massive shoulder against my small one, the scent of after-shave and cigarette floating over me, and I stopped breathing. I could not, however, stop the grin starting somewhere around my shoes from rising up and spilling over my face.

"Pete!" My voice echoed in the suddenly quiet court and I got a look from the judge.

Peter Hammond grinned, his eyes on the judge. "Still making trouble I see."

"Your influence, you notice," I whispered, trying to squeeze the ever-spreading grin back into place. "What brings you to these parts, Stranger?"

"Varmints, ma'am," he gestured at the young men behind us. "We're next," he said and moved up to the bench, ushering his charges ahead of him.

I sat through their cases, only half hearing, any prospect of reasonable thought gone. I had not seen him for more than two years and I was grateful he was up there where I had time to look at him unseen. Was it my imagination or were the broad shoulders a bit more stooped, the hair a touch grayer? Those sloping shoulders. That's what has me hooked, I thought.

He was called on to speak twice: once, in response to the judge's question, he acknowledged he was acting *in loco parentis* for two of the lads, later declaring himself witness to the erratic behavior of a third. Although his voice was quite capable of filling an auditorium with ease, today he spoke with the soft rumble that did odd things to my stomach and I had to strain to hear. Not the shoulders, I thought, it's his voice.

I've no idea what the judge said. Though they were boys I did not know, Pete's charges kept turning to cast surreptitious looks in my direction. I suppose they wondered how a middle-aged cop could, in an instant, slither into blushing girl-hood.

I stared at my uniform sleeve in a desperate effort to regain control. There was one more case between his and mine. Trying not to be obvious about it, I watched him thank the judge and, without so much as a glance in my direction, lead his little group out of the courtroom. Two of his charges insisted on waving madly at me as they went by, limited to mumbling ecstatic, 'Hi, Teech,' by the authoritative pull toward the door.

Had a tidal wave sucked him out to sea leaving me spent on the shore, I could not have felt more desolate.

I told myself that was that. I told myself that though my feelings for him remained steadfast, his had not. Perhaps I'd imagined it. Perhaps he'd never cared for me at all. No doubt he'd found someone else in my absence: someone younger, prettier, more...more available. I told myself to grow up. I forced my mind back to my job and when we were called, I almost ran to the front.

Dead in Pleasant Company
A Pennsylvania Dutch Mystery

CHAPTER 8

When I left the courtroom an hour later, he was waiting.
"Are you, by any miracle, free for lunch?"

I thought of the pile of work on my desk, thought of a small child lost and not eating, thought of the cloud over our restaurants, but I'm only human.

Ask me why I suggested the Dorchester on Thaxton Circle just across from the Community building rather than the building's own rooftop restaurant and I'll say it was merely quieter. The truth is, Plainfield's elegant landmark hostelry with its crystal chandeliers and thick white table linens just seemed appropriate.

Pete could not keep his eyes on his menu and I couldn't take mine off mine. We stalled, asking inane questions about our jobs, our families, assured each we were well. Without asking, he ordered coffee for two.

"Well!" he said at last. "So I finally got you to have lunch with me! I take it that means you haven't forgotten me."

Ha! I said merely, "No. I haven't forgotten you."

"That's something anyway." A look, both pained and familiar, glinted from his eyes for a moment and was gone. After a bit, he cleared his throat. "I take it you like your work?"

"Oh yes. It's both interesting and frustrating—much like teaching." I smiled. His face flushed.

"Yes," he said, agreeable as always. "I suppose it is. We sure do miss you though." Again there was a silence to bridge.

"How is my...the class? I often wonder how they're doing without Theodore. Who's taken over as leader since he graduated? Is Tommy Mudra hanging in there?"

"Your class, and they will always be your class, has its ups and downs but yes, pretty much they're all hanging in. Robey graduates this year if he can keep out of trouble: Kit, Shari, Bronson Matthews and Tommy next year as things stand so far. Believe it or not, it's Kit Gaumer who's emerged the leader and she keeps them in line by quoting you at every turn. Not very amusing for your replacement as you might imagine, but there it is. I've always said you are irreplaceable."

The waiter hovered. I again picked up the menu I knew by heart and studied it as if I'd never seen it. I did not want to think about how much I missed my class of 'incorrigibles.' Pete ordered something. I said I'd have the same.

"You saw by the reaction of my young friends today how excited they were just to see you. Those boys weren't even your students, but your class has made you a legend in the school. Why don't you come to visit," he asked gently, as if coaxing a wounded bird to come and eat. "I'm sure they'd love it."

"To what end? They need to forget me." I need to forget them. "I do hear from Main Duke from time to time." I grinned. "He says he's doing so well at his job he's practically running the school." I did not say he always adds, 'I'm looking after Mr. H. for you, Tee—Miz McKnight!" I said merely, "Is he? Doing well at his job?"

"Yes indeed. I've asked the board to move him up when old Saul retires at the end of this year."

"Good. I'm glad." Sad too.

"As for forgetting you," he shook his head, "it's not going to happen, my dear S. J." His voice grew husky. I wanted to tell him to stop it, to say more. "I'll tell them you asked about them. They'll be overjoyed." I looked at him and our eyes locked. "No one up there is ever going to forget you, starting and ending with me." My eyes dropped first and there was another awkward bridge to cross.

I groped for a change of subject. "Tell me about the troubled young man you had with you today. I don't think I've seen him before. Stewart, I think they said his name is." I have no idea where the name came from. I wasn't even aware I'd heard it.

"Lew Stewart. Yes. One of those inexplicable tragedies we come across all too often."

"What's wrong with him?"

He shook his head as if to say this is not what he wanted to talk about, but he did. "A tragic case. Star of the football team at West Cedar. Quarterback. Offered a contract with the Eagles minor league team. All sorts of college scholarships. Good grades. Popular. Then he began to become a discipline problem. Temper tantrums—real doozies. Teachers, parents, nobody could handle him. Two months ago his folks couldn't take it anymore and turned him over to the court. Naturally we got him. West's working with him but so far..." He shrugged. "He's not on drugs. Give anything if I knew what to do with him." He stabbed at his lunch. "Any ideas?"

"What does West say?"

Pete lifted his shoulders. I wanted to tell him not to do that, to do it again. Yup. Definitely the shoulders. I stirred my broccoli. "You say these outbursts are recent? Not part of his normal personality?"

Pete nodded. "What they tell me. We've only had him a short while."

"What sets them off?"

"Anything and nothing as far as we can tell."

"I see." I thought a moment. "Has he been checked for steroids?"

"Steroids?" He looked surprised. "I don't think so. There's been no hint of...I don't think high school athletes do that sort of thing anymore." He looked at me. "You think that's worth looking into?"

"Possibly. Has he complained of pain in his kidneys, do you know? Or stomach ache?"

Pete frowned. "He has been down in the nurse's station several times. I think they did say he had belly ache."

"Kidney infection is one of the signs of steroid use—as are sudden rages. Also I noticed the acne on the back of his neck. Do you have the authority to make him give you a urine sample?"

"A urine...no. Not in his case. He's not on parole or anything. If you think it's pertinent, I'll ask the judge while I'm down here. May I use you as a reference?"

"If you think it will help."

He shook his head at me. "You amaze me. You still have no idea what kind of weight your name carries. I mean, not just because you're a Thaxton, although God knows that doesn't hurt, but you, personally. People hold you in such high regard." Pure projection, I thought. I had plenty of reason to think so. "Okay, okay. I know you don't like...I'll ask. Can we change the subject?" He stirred his coffee, searched, found another topic. "You on this Tunnelson thing?"

I shook my head. "Not *on* it. *In* it possibly." His eyebrows asked a question. "He was my guest and he died at Pleasant Company while dining with Sam and me, though neither of us was at the table at the time. So yes, it involves me to that extent, but I'm not working the case. Actually, I've just been assigned to Juvenile."

"Naturally. That would follow, wouldn't it?"

"I suppose so."

He must have heard something in my voice of which even I was not aware. "You don't like Juvenile?"

"Oh yes. For now anyway. Just not forever." I hadn't realized I felt like that until I said it, but unacknowledged

Dead in Pleasant Company
A Pennsylvania Dutch Mystery

truths frequently found their way out of my mouth when we talked—what had drawn us together in the first place. I did not want to think how good he had been for me. I chattered on. "I loved my first year on the force. After formal training at the academy we get assigned to each department for a month, then we're on street patrol for the rest of the year. I liked that very much. You know how I like variety."

"Yes." A small word, speaking volumes.

Unbidden, a picture of the apartment the family keeps on the Dorchester's twelfth floor flashed through my mind. Was anyone staying there now? We all use it on a first come, first served basis. Was that behind my suggesting the Dorchester? Did my subconscious plan an invitation to an afternoon of lust? If so, I thought Freud had outsmarted himself this time. Much as I'd wanted that, our relationship had not gotten that far as yet and it never would.

He was asking what I liked best. It took a second to realize he was talking about police work. I reined myself in.

"Oh, street patrol so far I think. I asked to be assigned to it, but I suppose they think I'm too old." I continued on. I needed to keep talking. I did not want to hear myself think. "I'd like to take a crack at Fraud Division some time as well, but Juvenile is interesting too. Right now, for instance..." I went on to tell him about the lost child. He was interested, asking what I'd done so far to find her. I told him.

"I suppose you've considered looking at court records for kids going through the system—kids awarded in custody cases for instance?" I said I hadn't. "It's easy for kids to fall through the cracks where custody is shared, don't you think?" I did think. It is what keeps us apart.

I thanked him for the suggestions, said I'd certainly follow through. I asked about his new staff. Two deaths, two firings and one other besides me leaving voluntarily would certainly change his small twelve member faculty.

"As good as we have a right to expect. I've promoted Liz Pealing to your place as Master Teacher. She's ten times as good as we have a right to expect in our salary range and about half as good as you. We sure do miss you."

"I'm sure you're exaggerating. Liz is particularly good."

"A pale substitute at best." His throat needed clearing again. "Yes," he said, now more matter-of-fact, "Liz is great, just not in your class—but then, who is?"

"Hordes, I imagine. You're just..."

"...prejudiced. I admit it. The question is why, isn't it? Just look what you did today! That young man has gone from a popular, happy lad facing a bright future to next thing to a commitment. He's been examined by all kinds of experts look at him in two counties, yet you take one look and you know what his problem is. Do you realize that, once again, you may have affected a person's whole life?"

"If I'm right. I'm just guessing, you know. Even if I'm right, you make too much of it," I said, somewhat crossly. "I just happened to notice..."

"Bull! Today was nothing unusual for you. The way you turned an entire class of misfits around is legend up there. Hell, that whole gang'd either be here in jail or the booby hatch or dead but for you."

"For us." I said and wished I hadn't. In it now, I had to finish. "I could not have gotten to step one with them had it not been for you." I searched for other things to say, but what was there? Did either of us want to bring back the bittersweet years I'd spent up at Hawk County, years that ended in murder? There, in the midst of territorial, arrogant, ill-prepared teachers fighting tooth and nail to stay that way, we'd looked up and found each other. Fairy tale stuff sans the happy ending. More like Greek comedy. Or soap opera, I told myself sternly.

I wanted to study his face, judge for myself how he was doing, yet I had no doubt he'd read mine as well, see how I still felt about him. I told myself to grow up. I looked up.

"Sal." He reached for my hand and I watched helplessly as he took it and held it, in that familiar way, against his breast.

"No, Pete." It was barely audible. I retrieved my hand. "Please. Don't let's spoil it. It's so good just..." Being near you, I wanted to say. Hearing your voice. Smelling you. That's what it is, I decided. His particular combination of cigarettes and aftershave. "...seeing you again," I finished inanely. "How...how's your family?"

"The boys are fine," emphasizing 'boys,' perhaps, to assure me his wife had not changed. "Growing like weeds. We get along though, which kind of surprises me." Because they were adolescents now. Because his wife had done everything possible to alienate them from him. I knew what he meant. "That's thanks to you too."

"Oh please, Pete. You'd think I was the..."

His look stopped me. "You are."

I could think of nothing to say. We poked at our food silently for a few moments. His voice was husky when he spoke again. "You've not eaten much."

"I'll live."

"I hope so," he said fervently, "I hope to God so!" We were quiet again, then, his voice more normal now, "I hope this Tunnelson thing gets cleared up in a hurry. It's amazing really. Here's a guy who, even dead, causes controversy." His eyes took him far away for a bit. "On the other hand," he said briskly, "at least people knew he was alive."

"Don't be ridiculous, Pete. You're worth a hundred of him. You know that."

It was another of the bonds between us—the freedom to admit to the self-doubts which creep up on risk-takers, knowing the other would be there with the right words.

He shrugged. "Whatever. To be perfectly honest, my job is no fun anymore." He reached for my hand again. "I'm afraid you took the sun with you when you left."

The waiter moved between us, took our plates. "Something wrong with your meals sir? Dr. McKnight? You've hardly eaten…"

"No, no," I pulled my hand back and rushed to assure him. "We've just been too busy talking. Everything was fine, thanks. No, no more coffee for me," I said to the lifted pot, "I've got to go. Perhaps my friend…?"

But Pete declined as well. He stood and reached for my coat, held it for me, held it around me for a moment. "Love the way you smell," he said, not for the first time, "among other things."

My arms in the sleeves, I buttoned up. "Well, thanks for lunch."

He dropped bills on the table. "I'll walk back with you. My car's over there anyway," he added, forestalling objections. "Besides, I want to stop and talk to the judge."

Icy streets were a quasi-legitimate reason for his firm hold on me as we crossed the Circle. From the far side of the community building we could hear the racket made by the press at work, but here it was quietly normal. At the door we told each other how great it was to see each other again, shook gloved hands and parted.

* * * * *

The elevator rose to my floor and stopped. The door slid open, but I did not get out. The door closed and began automatically to rise. Fourth floor. Fifth. I had made no conscious decision to do anything in particular, I only knew I could not possibly go directly back to work. For one thing, I could not stop smiling, unseemly for one who has just had

Dead in Pleasant Company
A Pennsylvania Dutch Mystery

a guest die at her table. For another, I was not willing to unwrap myself from the glow surrounding me just yet.

At the roof the elevator stopped and waited. I stepped out and considered my options. The building's octagonal identity was obvious even here, offering an array of choices: restaurant, coffee bar, day care facilities, two after-school clubs, a sound-proof 'green' room, the gym we used for daily workouts and a greenhouse. I started for the green room but decided stretching out on a slant board or sitting on a yoga rug would probably cause me to implode. I needed somewhere to hug this bit of private joy as close and as long as possible.

The greenhouse was empty save for one of the young high school work-study students who comes in daily to water plants. I chose a bench where I could look into the faces of peach, apricot and red begonias and feel my happiness reflected back.

One by one, like cellophane-wrapped Belgian chocolates, I pulled selected memories from my teaching days: of his thunderous roar directed at rule-breaking students in the hall outside my classroom; sprigs of Queen's Anne's lace or yellow clover left behind on my desk; of strong arms catching me the morning I found the dead body of a fellow teacher in my closet; of waking in the hospital to find my hand clasped firmly to his breast; of the intoxicating scent of him.

I stopped. Even with prized Belgian chocolates one can have too much of a good thing. I reminded myself I was nearer fifty than forty and it was time to grow up. I reminded myself he was married, although I did not need to be reminded. I asked myself why we continued to fight an attraction so powerful. Why not just 'do it?' Everybody does. Or, if not happy with an affair, why not a divorce?

The questions were not new. My brother has put it to me at least a hundred times and the answer has as much to do with common sense as anything. Simply put, if he could forget his marriage vows with me, how could I expect him to remember them with me? On the other hand, imagine how wonderful it would be to know the person to whom you have committed the best you have can be trusted to withstand the inevitable temptations always at hand?

I'm not sure how it works for others, but for me, if I wish to keep conversant with my soul, sharing my body goes well beyond the desires of the moment.

I sighed regretfully, checked my face in the ladies room mirror, a bit surprised to see it looked much the same as it had this morning, then, heartened by the notion he'd given me an idea which might help find the child's family, once more took one of the glass elevators down to my floor.

CHAPTER 9

SAL

Pete's suggestion made sense. The detritus of custody battles, often as bitter and prolonged as an ethnic war, sometimes resulted in the most innocent becoming the greater victim. If the child in my temporary care was part of a contentious divorce case or a ward of the court, perhaps placed in foster care, her absence might go unreported to the usual authorities.

I worked quickly through my other cases, then, with time to spare before my next appointment and energized by the feeling I was again working with Pete, I returned to my search. I faxed the child's photo and description, along with a request for information, to all agencies serving children through the court system. Recalling the girl's clever hospital escape, which I thought spoke of familiarity with similar institutions, I obtained a list of Head Pediatric Nurses and faxed each a letter with a request for help.

I spent some little while pouring over the existing databases of missing children—a distressing task. In a better world, I thought, people would be required to take an oath during pregnancy.

> *I, therefore, do promise under penalty of law to give my child the same care, respect and attention I would like for myself, whether I had it or not. If a situation arises when we can no longer do this, I agree to find someone else willing to do so without any recompense or let the state find such a person for me.*

It couldn't happen of course. People would consider it an invasion of their rights. Rag dolls, I thought, are treated better.

* * * * *

"Still at it?" I jumped at O'Connell's voice. He looked at me curiously. "Sorry if I startled you. Everything okay? You look...funny."

"I'm fine." I tapped away, my eyes on my monitor.

"Anything new on Orphan Annie?" I brought him up to date. "Good work," he said, pulling up a chair. "I wouldn't have thought of that myself. Going beyond the usual pipelines I mean."

"I didn't either. Someone suggested it."

"Oh?"

It was a question requiring an answer. I told myself to act natural. "Yes. Pete Hammond actually. You remember him?"

As if he was ever likely to forget. "Pete? Hammond? Yeah sure. I didn't realize you'd kept in touch."

"We haven't. I ran into him at court today."

"Oh yeah?" It was half request, half demand for further information.

"We had lunch," I said flatly.

"Oh. I see," he said, seeing. "In any case, it was a good idea." He tapped a file in his hand. "What I came to talk to you about is your report here. What conclusions have you drawn about the kid?"

I told him what I'd learned or guessed about the lost child. He listened carefully. "You don't think she was abused?"

"She may have been, but I don't think so."

Dead in Pleasant Company
A Pennsylvania Dutch Mystery

"But she was left on a bus, for God's sake Sal! And wasn't she drugged and uncooperative when she was found?"

"Yes, but I've been on to the doctor about that. They found traces of marijuana, but he thinks the drugs were recent. She shows no signs of withdrawal. As for physical abuse, there are no traces of broken bones or old bruises as there would be if that had been the case."

"What of sexual abuse?"

"No evidence of that either. As for emotional abuse, I've worked with more than my share of such children and they don't survive with the expression I've seen in her eyes. I think it's more likely she's been neglected. She does fit *that* pattern."

He nodded, told me to let him know if he could help and left me to it.

Throughout the afternoon shards of conversation filtered through the incessant clatter of the squad room. One officer, coming on duty, described the mounting hordes of media as 'swarming 'round like bees servicing a queen.' Later Rachel Greene passed through with the news that Tunnelson's sister was huddled in Commissioner Frey's office. Then came a report that they'd been joined by network 'suits' and the insurance investigator.

In spite of the buzz of activity in my periphery, I stuck to my work until my two o'clock appointment arrived at three-thirty, citing the impossible task of getting past the press. Like a recurring nightmare, a persistent memory came flooding back: anonymous figures bending over me to thrust microphones in our five-year-old faces; voices asking unfathomable questions. I still feel the fury at this intrusion and the intolerable outrage at seeing our mother lying asleep, with all her clothes on, right there in the church where people kept coming to look at her. What right had they to see her like that? Why did she look so stiff and scared? And why was our father just lying there beside her instead of taking care of her? I was sure it was the fault of the microphone holders, the picture takers. No wonder they lay there so still, much as they'd taught us to do when playing hide and seek.

It was an introduction to the press not likely to ameliorate the natural mistrust which is a Thaxton characteristic. The price of fame and fortune you say? Perhaps if those twin devils are something you sought, but what if the more you avoid the spotlight the more it seeks you out? I prayed it was not all going to happen again.

I managed to return my full attention to my parent interviews but my glow had faded to the merest glimmer. By late afternoon, when the grapevine reported Chief Warmkessel's appointment of a Press Officer to play ringmaster to the rapidly developing media circus, it had disappeared completely.

Finally, my last set of parents had come and gone and I began gathering signed forms to take to the court. Sam appeared, as if out of nowhere.

"You off somewhere?" No kidding. No teasing. His voice telegraphed the dramatic change in the atmosphere since my return from lunch. He gave my shoulder an even more telling squeeze, his voice unusually affectionate.

"To the court," I told him. "What's up?"

"Just came from Warmkessels's office. They got the videotapes from Tuesday night all right, but they were blank. Apparently the cameras weren't on. I checked with Hal. He says when they were re-loaded somebody simply forgot to turn it on."

"I see." I continued putting files in my briefcase. "I hope Warmkessel doesn't see anything ominous in that. It's not the first time it's happened."

"So I told him. Reminded him that Groundhog's Day is always a hassle because we've got people waiting in line all day and the staff likes to volunteer to help out at the church."

"And?"

"Wants the staff brought in. Those involved anyway."

"Involved?"

"Anyone around there at the time who might have seen something—servers, bus staff—you know."

I knew all too well. "Hal, too, I imagine." I looked at him. "Why the face? Are you expecting trouble? Is there something…"

"It's certainly not going to do the restaurant any good—bringing our people in I mean. Not with the vultures out there."

"But there's absolutely nothing that can…"

"Doesn't have to be anything for them. You know that as well as I do," he said angrily. "Besides, are you remembering Barney Schantz?"

I said "Oh?" Then, "Oh. The trouble between Schantz and Tunnelson?" He nodded. I said I'd forgotten. "Anyway, that was years ago and it's all been settled."

"Mach's nicht aus. They'll dredge it all up again." He sank into a chair and stared at me. "Do you think we should advise Barney to tell the cops about it right off?"

"I don't know what to say. It was all too awful at the time and It would be the worst kind of tragedy to make him go through it again. I think," I added, thinking, "it would be best to get the 'Firm' in on this."

"Reading my mind," he said. "Matter of fact I'm on the way there now. Then I'm off to round up the restaurant people they want. Probably go in with them too."

We walked to the elevators together. At the seventh floor we parted, me to one of four courtrooms, him to the opposite side of the building to the law offices of Stephens, Jacobs, Weinsheimer and Butz.

"Hang in there," I said in parting.

"So's yer ol' man," he replied glumly.

* * * * *

Promptly at five, I flipped off my computer and chalked out for the day. I would have been surprised had I been able to get out without incident and I did not. Waiting for an elevator, I heard my name called from somewhere down the hall.

I told myself I was an idiot for not taking the stairs to avoid the press. What could be worse? Too late, I looked around for an escape.

"Dr. McKnight! You *are* Dr. McKnight, are you not?" The man approaching wore no press badge. Not a network then. "Great," he waxed enthusiastic. "So happy I caught you. Good afternoon. I'm Ken Fowler."

The insurance investigator. An answer to my 'what could be worse' query. I nodded, not wanting to agree even on the goodness of the afternoon. "Yes, Mr. Fowler. What can I do for you?"

"Have dinner with me if by some miracle you're free."

My, my! Two miracles in a day! The comparison to the earlier questioner was unfortunate, putting me off this one immediately. "I'm sorry. It's not a very good day, Mr. Fowler. I'm up to my ears…"

"Oh yes! I believe that, but you *do* eat dinner, don't you?"

Ouch! The very mention of food and I feel guilty. Naturally, I got defensive. "I should think that was obvious," I said wryly, "but I…"

He hurried to interrupt me. "Look, Dr. McKnight. I realize you don't know me from Adam and I'm imposing on your precious free time, but I know what you're going through, really I do and I would like to help. I don't approve of all this fuss the Tunnelson woman is making. No sir, I don't at all! I was hoping we could get my part of it over and done with as quickly as possible before things escalate unnecessarily. Does that sound do-able?" He did not overdo it, putting his request reasonably, much, I thought arrogantly, the way I would have done. He saw me hesitate and moved in. "I suggested dinner only because I thought that would be the least imposition on your time. I'd planned to catch you for lunch but you were nowhere to be found." Another stab of guilt. "If," he examined my face, "tonight is not good, I'd happily settle for any time that suits."

I sighed. "All right, Mr. Fowler. I appreciate your thoughtfulness. Would you object to dining at my home? I've got some obligations there..." I left it hang.

"Object? To dine at...good heavens, woman! I'd be honored! When and where?" I said we dined at seven and I'd send a car about half-past six.

"I'm at the Dorchester." Naturally, I thought. "I can't tell you how much I appreciate your offer. Good afternoon, Dr. McKnight and thanks."

I left him standing there, taking the POLICE ONLY stairway to the garage. There I donned my disguise and flew past the gathering crush of press. Several networks had already constructed scaffolds on which cameras perched, ready for that Pulitzer Prize winning, income earning, photo or interview. I congratulated myself on my forethought in this at least and wondered how long I could expect to get away with it.

* * * * *

The child was with Benjam giving the horses their evening feed. There was no need to ask if she liked the horses. Her eyes told the story. I asked her if she would like to ride again. The nod was the first uninhibited act I'd seen. I told Benjam to forget the basket and saddle up my daughter's old pony, then took her inside to find suitable riding clothes.

I told Honeycutt about the guest coming for dinner. He said my brother had called to say not to expect him tonight as he would be staying with the staff as long as they were at headquarters. "In the formal dining room, I assume?"

I took that as a statement. "All right if that's what you think." Honeycutt has rules tattooed somewhere inside him. Mostly I go along.

The child and I rode alone, taking an easy, short trail slowly. On our way back, snow began to fall: huge, soft flakes falling silently. My companion giggled. Before long pony and rider looked like they were dressed from head to tail in dotted swiss. From time to time the little girl stuck out her tongue to catch a flake or two, laughing out loud as they landed. The happy face demanded an answer to the mystery surrounding her. Why did she not speak? Why had I not found even the slightest trace of her family?

When we returned, Mrs. Honeycutt, possessing rules of her own, took one look at the snow-covered child and took her away for a warm bath, flannel pajamas and supper in bed. I left the child in her hands and went to change for dinner.

* * * * *

I diddled so long over what to wear that by the time I got one guest settled, I was late for the other. I expected to find the insurance man on the 'porch' where we usually had a pre-dinner glass of wine when the occasion calls for it and he was. He rose and turned as I entered.

"Ah! There you are!" I apologized for being late. "Please! Don't apologize!" He came toward me, hand extended. It was a salesman's handshake, firm but not intrusive. "I thought you might have changed your mind and would send me pack..." He whistled softly.

"Oh." I followed his gaze. "I hope that means it's all right." I brushed at the folds of the simple, soft, rosy wool. "It just came today and I've barely had time to look at it. It just seems after twelve days straight on duty and this weather, it was the right thing. It is a nice color, though, isn't it?"

"Nice color, indeed, and perfect for you, if I may say so. Is it from Markham's as well?"

He couldn't have surprise me more. "Markham? Uh, yes, as a matter of fact." I looked at him sharply. "You know them?" I reflected the insurance business was more profitable than I thought.

"I'm glad you don't object to my comment. It certainly put your brother right off. Yes, I know them. I work with Ralph there."

"Really?" I hurried to collect myself. "Gosh, I don't know what I'd do without Markham. He's so good with difficult figures."

"Difficult?" He paused, looking me over. "I wouldn't say difficult in your case. Disturbing perhaps."

Caution flags rose to full mast and Sam's warning, on hearing I'd invited Fowler for dinner, to 'watch my back teeth,' floated back. He'd added an injunction to count the silver when my guest had gone, ending, "The man's up to something, Sis."

To be always on guard against the hidden agenda of those seeking any relationship is part and parcel of being born both Pennsylvania Dutch and rich, yet here I was, gurgling because someone had complimented both dress and figure within seconds of meeting. I stifled the impulse to check my back teeth.

Fowler was going on. "I know what you mean though, because he does the same for me. I'm not at all good looking really," he said mildly, "but folks often think I am, thanks to him."

"I see." A simple frank statement or intended to disarm? *Was* I being disarmed? "You say you think your comment about Markham bothered my brother?"

He shrugged. "Something did. It's the only thing I can think of. I'd sure like to know though."

I ignored the hint to explain my brother's behavior, instead saying I liked Markham because he saves me the bother of shopping. "Unfeminine of me you may think, but there it is. I just tell him what I need and he sends me something."

"Really? You leave it all to him?"

I nodded. "Other than dropping in when I'm in London for him to take my current measurement, yes."

"Remarkable!" He followed me to the comfortable chairs facing the long window wall. "I must say though, a dislike of shopping must be the only unfeminine thing about you. You're not at all what I expected." I debated whether to bite or not. I needn't have bothered. He went on, settling back in his chair. "I admit I expected someone...well, all business I guess. I mean, *Business Today*'s named you Businessperson of the Year, haven't they? Twice, if I'm not mistaken. Yet here you are, all rosy and warm, looking more like someone's well-loved pet than a tycoon!" He smiled.

The face of my lunch companion popped up out of nowhere. I turned away to hide the incipient flush. Was this man psychic? He was staying at the Dorchester, had he seen us? Would our treasured private lunch be all over the news tomorrow? I tried to think of something clever to say and failed.

He seemed not to notice. "Dr. McKnight, it's incredibly good of you to admit me to your home when you know nothing about me." My God! Apparently I was as transparent as cellophane to him! My guard went up another notch. "I've so looked forward to meeting you."

That was better, the sort of perfunctory charm to which I was accustomed. I strove to keep the conversation on less personal subjects. "I see Honeycutt has kept you from dying of thirst at any rate. Have you been enjoying the view? Have you had enough of our snow?"

He laughed. "Yes, yes and yes, I suppose I have had enough of the snow, although the covered bridge just south of your home is so incredibly beautiful one can't help wishing it would last forever! And your home too! Frankly, Dr. McKnight, I've heard so much about your converted barn I was fully prepared to think people were exaggerating, but I'm utterly delighted! This room is perfect," he gestured in the general direction of the roses. "I can't imagine a better one. One feels immediately relaxed."

Indeed, he seemed right at home. "I suppose," I said, trying to keep it all business, "you'll be at the inquest tomorrow."

He nodded. "Part of my job, unfortunately."

Honeycutt entered with my drink. Fowler eyed my glass. "Champagne?"

"White burgundy," I said. One hundred and twenty calories. "Are you ready for a refill?" I eyed his glass. "Glen Fiddich is it?"

"Yes," he said, "and no. That is, it is Fiddich and this will do me for now. I'm not much of a drinker though I admit to an addiction to this particular scotch." He leveled his glass at the windows. "Are those crabapples?"

"Yes," I said, surprised. "Not many people recognize them, especially in the dormant state." I wondered if he'd gone to the trouble of priming himself before he came. Curiosity got the better of me. "How is it you know?"

He turned to smile at me. "A city slicker like me, you mean?" He rose again and moved closer to the snowy view.

"I wasn't born in the city. Fact is, I'm inordinately fond of trees. I hope you won't find that too difficult to believe." The thought seemed to amuse him.

I conceded it was possible. "As am I. I just can't decide when I like them best. Right now I'm opting for winter."

"Oh? The contest is usually between Spring and Fall, isn't it? They're just bare now."

"*Just*? Heavens!" I went to stand beside him. "Look at those velvet branches silhouetted against the dark grey sky! It lets one see clearly how unique each is, as identifiable as people. When they're leafed out I think of the Biblical injunction against hiding one's light under a bushel."

He studied the half dozen or so trees within our view. "Yes. I see that now. I never thought of it that way."

Honeycutt coughed.

"Oh, sorry Honeycutt. We'll come." We moved to the table in the adjoining room. "I hope dinner is not too early for you. I'm afraid we still have a lot of country in us. We always fed our hands at six and ourselves at seven and now we just get too hungry to eat later, much to Honeycutt's distress."

Of course, Honeycutt had him at my right. Only my oldest son or Sam would be seated across from me. Honeycutt held my chair, then rolled in the trolley. "Corn Soup with Rivels today, Madam," he said, ladling the pale golden soup into blue and white bowls. Half a bowl—forty calories—and three rivels—twenty each—for me. Add twenty-five for one of Mrs. Honey's home-made crackers. One hundred twenty-five.

"We've a very 'down-home' menu tonight, Mr. Fowler—not the sort of thing we usually have for novices. Wiener Schniztel, a Pennsylvania Dutch favorite, is the entree. If you prefer to not eat veal, Honeycutt is always looking for an excuse to make an omelette.

"No, no, not at all. This soup smells marvelous." And Fowler dug in, neat but enthusiastic. He declared the soup excellent, the crackers stellar. "This is incredible." He slurped away at the soup. "Who is your chef?"

I tried not to smile. "My 'chef' is Ariadne Honeycutt although you would hear some harsh words from her if she heard you refer to her that way."

"Oh?" He worked on the last bit of soup. "Absolutely the best soup I've ever had. My compliments to her." Honeycutt took his plate.

"You'll pass that on to your lady, won't you Honeycutt?" Honeycutt acknowledged he would, bowed and departed.

"Husband and wife team, eh? How fortunate! Where did you find them?"

I said I didn't. "I inherited Mrs. Honey from the aunt who raised us. It was she who found Honeycutt when we were in England for Uncle Peter's wedding. He was working for Uncle Peter's best man. Mrs. H gave us a choice between losing her or hiring him. Naturally we..." What was I doing? This man was a potential pain in the neck, if not dangerous to me and mine and I was chattering away as if we were bosom buddies. "...hired him." I shut my mouth determinedly.

"I see. The case of the purloined butler." He laughed.

"Footman actually. His former employer thought his blindness too much a handicap for butling."

"Did you say blind? Oh, you mean partially."

"No, completely."

"Good heavens! You'd never know it! I've been envying you the quality of service he gives you. That makes it even more remarkable."

The arrival of the man himself halted whatever he was going to say next, but he watched as Honeycutt served the Wiener Schnitzel: a half portion to me-three hundred calories and the noodle pudding, a smidgen for me—one hundred more. Five hundred and twenty-five. My dinner allotment.

Honeycutt turned to me. "Shall I?"

"You'd better," I said. Then to Fowler, "In Aunt Magdalene's time we kept up with the tradition of seven sweets and seven sours with dinner. I managed to persuade Mrs. Honey to cut back *some*." Honeycutt set the lazy susan between us. "What do we have tonight Honeycutt?"

"Starting in front of Mr. Fowler and going clockwise: the sours: pickled red beets, corn chow, sweet and sour tomatoes, hot cabbage slaw. The sweets: buttered baby carrots, apple butter and roasted Brussels sprouts."

"Not quite the tradition but we're not feeding dozens of farm hands either. Rolls tonight Honeycutt?"

"Corn meal muffins and pumpernickel rolls. Can I get you anything else?"

"Let's give this a try, Honeycutt. I'll ring if we're missing anything."

Fowler shook his head. "Incredible! I must say I am impressed!" He frowned at me. "You said he was a footman. What made you think he could butle if his former boss didn't?"

"I didn't," I said. "He did. I just agreed to let him try." I added Brussels sprouts and carrots to my plate. Eighty five calories. Extra laps tomorrow morning.

"Incredible," he said again.

Two bites of the schnitzel promoted questions regarding its preparation. The man seemed genuinely interested and before long we were knee deep into Pennsylvania Dutch cuisine. I could hear how Aunt Maggie would have snorted at the high sounding label given her humble cooking. Before long we'd moved on to the source of all this food, the network of farms and cattle ranches which service our restaurants.

He smiled. "Yes. The best outcome starts with the best ingredients. Your slogan, isn't it? I'm ashamed to admit," and indeed he sounded ashamed, "I've never eaten at any of your restaurants. The Red Goose in New York is a favorite of my Mum's but I've steadfastly refused to dine there with her. I'll be eating crow when I tell her what a fool I've been."

"Why?" I wondered how many calories were in crow.

"Why? Why wh...oh, why did I refuse to dine at the Red Goose? Oh, I've got this miserable idiosyncrasy. I hate to go to places that everybody raves about. Been disappointed too often."

I nodded understanding. "Yes. I'm like that too, especially with books. Nothing keeps me from reading a book as readily as being told it's a best-seller."

"Really? Me too! Worst thing a person can say to me is to say..."

"...you'll just *love* it!" We both laughed. "How nice! You really do understand. I must confess though, I cheat a bit. Sam reads everything and usually gives me the gist of it. He's got a real talent for it—can summarize a three hundred page book in a few minutes and not leave out anything important. Except the language of course."

"Ah yes. Why I won't read abridged versions."

"Really?" I could not help but smile again. "Me, too."

"Kindred spirits," he said, smiling back.

"Perhaps so."

His eyes stayed on mine for a moment, then dropped to focus on his food. My attention was on the sweet-and-sour compote. A few slices of tomato perhaps? I reminded myself I'd not eaten much lunch, took a generous helping and a corn muffin. Two hundred and twenty five calories.

"I suppose," he said without looking up, "you've heard this before, but you've got one honey of a smile. Lights you up like a Christmas tree. Shows off those eyes of yours."

I had heard it before. Or something like it. "I think you're supposed to add something like I should try using it more often," I said, feeling childishly demure.

"It wouldn't hurt," he said. He put another forkful in his mouth. "On the other hand, why should you waste a smile like that on a bunch of boobs?" Another forkful gone. "I'm sure I should not say this, but..." He looked steadily at me again for a moment, then his eyes dropped to his plate. "Forgive me," he said apologetically, "I am being much too...intrusive. I shall confine myself to praising your food. Surely that," he glanced up with a smile, "is safe enough. And I hope you'll forgive me for this," he said, breaking off a piece of roll and using it to mop up gravy. "Most people would think me a pig," he stuffed it in his mouth, "but not one who appreciates good food as you do. This is just too good to waste." He mopped and ate again. "Nobody knows how to make gravy anymore." He swallowed. It looked wonderful. "Salsas, coolies, chutneys—those they make but not honest-to-God gravy. That was superb! Tell me, is your brother likely to show up later this evening?"

I blinked at the abrupt change of subject. It was as if he'd come close to a precipice then backed off. I said I didn't know. "He's still down at headquarters with the staff." I realized, once again, I was verging on what was for me garrulousness. My reputation as a clam would be ruined.

"At headquarters? I thought all your people were crossed off the suspect list."

"Suspect list? What suspect list?"

"Sorry. I should have said witness list." He looked at me. "Better yet, I should have kept my mouth shut. I see I've upset you."

"Do you know something I don't?"

"No. No I don't. I suppose I just took it for granted that with all the death threats Tunnelson's had they'd want to…Look Dr. McKnight. Let's just say I misspoke. Call it a consequence of my job."

"Which is?"

"Verifying the cause of death. Being suspicious. When the insured carries the kind of policy Tunnelson did, it's my job to see the correct amount gets paid out."

I hadn't thought about that either. "You may be right. Maybe there is a list. To tell the truth, I'm pretty much out of the loop on this." I rang for Honeycutt.

"Oh? Well, I suppose they are bending over backward to keep any hint of favoritism out of it."

"I suppose so."

"Yes. You know, I hate when people say this to me but I think I honestly *do* know how you feel. My family's Fowler Industries and, as you doubtless know, we've had our share of fish-bowl living."

I was tempted to emulate Johnny Carson's 'I did not know that' but the occasion did not seem to call for levity. I did know about Fowler Industries. Everyone did. Arthur Fowler had been accused of insider trading when his company was about to be acquired by a competitor. In a case that had been a media event for more than two years, he'd been indicted, tried and acquitted. "Yes, perhaps you do know."

He nodded. "Yes." He smiled sardonically. "Afraid I'm the Fowler family's purple sheep. They turned on me when I changed my major to Chem from Law. Couldn't understand why I did not want to join the family business. They actually would have preferred I didn't work at all! But I don't have to explain that to you." He didn't. I wondered how he knew. I was beginning to feel as though he'd read my diary had I kept one. He was staring down at his plate reflectively, his hands motionless. "You get a place on the team, it's your family's money. You get honors at college, it's your family's money. Prettiest girl on campus falls for you and even your friends tell you she's after the family dough." He stabbed a pickled beet and forked it in. "Gets to the point where you doubt yourself." Stabbed another. Down it went. It looked delicious. I took a couple too. Sixty five calories. "I hated it. I just felt I had to see if I really had anything of my own to offer." The smile came and went. "So I went off on my own. It didn't help much though. They still say it's the family name that got me this job. It wasn't. I knew I could sell and when I went to Horizon it was as myself, plain old Ken Fowler."

"'I am the author of myself.'" I thought out loud.

"Yes. Yes. I suppose so," he said. "You do understand."

I tried not to watch as he took another muffin. One hundred calories. I debated. He spread it open and tucked butter inside. Another hundred. I hung tough. "Amazing how often one thinks one's come up with an original thought, only to find the Bard's said it already—only better." I settled for another pickled beet. Thirty-two more.

"The essence of good fiction, isn't it? Write characters and situations so true they are universal and forever."

He asked what I thought about the current dispute over certain works generally attributed to Shakespeare. I accepted the change of subject gratefully. Shakespeare was a lot safer than introspective analysis. I wondered if he felt the same.

"...the possibility that such a fraud could be perpetrated on the public for so long titillates the policeman in me. How was it done? When? By whom? And why? On the other..." I stopped, again puzzled by my gregariousness. Was I being mesmerized by the thoughtful way he listened? Genuine interest in one's rambling can be intoxicating. I expounded further. I was startled when Honeycutt began to clear away. How long had we, mostly I, been talking?

He was too quick to miss the surreptitious look at my watch. He sighed. "Well," he said conclusively, "this has been utterly delightful! You've given me so much to think about. I suppose I should go and let you get some rest."

"I've enjoyed the evening too, Mr. Fowler. Will you be staying in Plainfield long?"

He shrugged. "I can't say at this point. Only as long as it takes certainly. I'm meeting again tomorrow with your Chief and your ME. He gave me an odd look. "They all seem to think a lot of you down there."

"Not all," I said.

He laughed again. "Ah yes! Your assistant chief. Longnecker is it? What's his problem?"

I found myself wanting to tell him but I didn't. Be telling him your favorite color next, I warned myself. I shrugged. "Who knows?"

"Well, Chief Warmkessel seems able to handle him and that's all to the good." He folded his napkin neatly. "I must say this though, I am a bit surprised that your ME has not done a really thorough autopsy."

"He hasn't? I don't..."

"Blood. Tissue. Organ samples—like that. I had to request he do them. Got to be sure we have the reason a man, apparently in perfect health, died so suddenly, don't you agree? I think we both know these things can leave a cloud hanging over people's heads and I'd hate to see that happen here. I know what that could do to the fine reputation of your family. I would especially hate to see a cloud over your head."

"Why especially me? We barely know each other."

"An omission I hope it's not too late to correct. Is it? I mean, are you committed elsewhere?"

I had an impulse to run. Or count the silver. Still, it was no more than a normal request to get together again from one with whom one had gotten along well. And we *had* gotten along well.

"Yes, I mean no. I'm not committed I mean." I was beginning to think I should be. "I must tell you frankly I'm not very good at making friends. I just seem to lack the knack."

He looked at me, perhaps deciding how much of what I said I meant. Then, "Well, what do you say we leave the future of our relationship to happen or not as it will." His smile was almost shy. "For now, perhaps we can settle to be, if not friends, at least friendly. Okay?"

I felt I'd been rude, arming myself against a summer breeze. "It's my turn to apologize Mr. Fowler."

"Ken."

"Ken, then. I do so."

"Forget it Dr. McKnight. As I said, I understand. Only a fool does not feel the need to protect oneself."

I gave in. "Make it Sal then. Can you do with more coffee? Or perhaps you're ready for brandy?"

"Brandy would be fine Doc...Sal. Unless you happen to have more Glen Fiddich."

I said we did and touched the bell. We returned to my 'porch.'

"Sal," he said thoughtfully. "Short for..."

"Salome. Two syllables. Accent on the second. Rhymes with home."

"Not as in the dancer?" He smiled.

"No. The oldest fashioned of names I'm afraid. My mother's name."

"Salome," he said thoughtfully. "It's right for you. Unique and elegant."

I sought for a less personal topic. "I've been wondering what the network will do now without Tunnelson. He was so much the heart and soul of the show."

"Interesting you should be thinking about that because I've been wondering if they'll use the piece he was working on here. Did he finish it, do you know?"

Dead in Pleasant Company
A Pennsylvania Dutch Mystery

"I believe it was finished, yes. I know he'd spent some time editing it. He planned to leave that night for Philadelphia."

"Oh? Do the police know that? I imagine it would be of interest to them. Perhaps there's a connection there." I said they did. When he asked what I thought of 'this Mastermind business,' it seemed again he was reading my mind as I'd deliberately left out the purpose behind Tunnelson's wish to leave that night.

We chatted on pleasantly enough, but I found myself yawning anyway. "I'm sorry," I said for the third time. "I've a true lark. Up with the sun, down with the sun."

He laughed. "Days a bit short in the winter then, aren't they?" He rose. "Well, it's been a delightful evening. I'll be on my way. I hope I may call you some time."

I said that would be fine, walked with him to the waiting car, bid him good night at the door, told him to watch his step, thanked the Honeycutts and took myself off to bed.

* * * * *

The child was sound asleep when I got upstairs. I dawdled over my preparations for bed, waiting to hear from Sam regarding how the questioning of the restaurant staff was progressing.

I decided to skip the news as it might wake the child, instead propping myself up in bed to retreat into the newest Simon Brett, but after I'd turned yet one more page without having any idea what Charles Paris was up to, I put the book down and thought.

I realized I'd been unconsciously drawing a comparison between my lunch and dinner companions. I told myself I should stick to the latter. "Just the kind of man you need, my girl. Intelligent. Fun. Doesn't need your money. Comfortable. And unmarried."

"Yeah," I thought falling to sleep, "you're talking but nobody's listening."

* * * * *

About midnight I woke suddenly to find a small shape standing across the room, barely visible in the dark.

"Hi," I said softly when my heart returned to normal.

"Janus Morgan Alexander."

My heart stopped again. "What?"

"Janus Morgan Alexander." Nearly a shout this time. She ran across the room and dove on my bed. "That's my name. Janus Morgan Alexander!"

Dead in Pleasant Company
A Pennsylvania Dutch Mystery

CHAPTER 10

SAM

Friday.

When I finally pulled up at Sal's that never-to-be-forgotten morning, I brought dawn with me—a cold, grey February dawn to be sure, but dawn. Barely half-past five, yet off to the east a faint grey crack between earth and sky offered proof the days were getting longer.

I parked and jogged the hundred yards or so to her back door just to prove I could still do it, even after having been up all night for the second time in a row. I'd managed to keep my cool, too, in spite of the police insisting on holding Barney Schantz until the wee hours. When they finally let him go, it was with a warning not to leave town.

I'd dropped our chef off at his place before heading here to bring my sister up to date and deliver a message from Schantz to Walt. The breakfast room empty, I invaded the kitchen to beg Mrs. H. for a 'morsel'. Asked, I said waffles, sausage and eggs would do for a start.

"It chust wonders me haw you can et yerself like a pik and stay skinny vile your sister chust looks at it and gets fat," she muttered, adding with unconscious aptness, "Makes a body sink!"

"I take it your boss is having her swim. Is Walt up?"

"He's et himself already and gone vunce."

My eyebrows rose of their own accord. "Up, eaten *and* gone? Walt? *Our* Walt?" Any one of those was a record.

"Only Valt ve haff now since your Dad vent over," she said with asperity.

I resisted the temptation to ask 'over where?' "What d'you suppose is going on with him? He growing up at last?"

"He's chust tventy-vun naw, Mr. Sam. I rememper you at that ache and folks who liff in glass hawses shouldn't throw stones."

"Are you alluding to my own stellar youth? Why I was the…"

"Lazy is vat you ver. If it varant for your sister you…"

"Yeah, yeah. I know," I admitted it. "She worked me like a dog." The voice of my slave-driver came faintly from somewhere in the house. I followed the sound of soft voices.

They were halfway down the stairs, one of the child's hands holding fast to Sal's, a doll gripped firmly in the other. Moses wound in and out between their legs. Sal flung me a sisterly wave, told me "hi," then to the child, "Would you like to tell Mr. Thaxton what you told me?" The kid shrank closer to her, whispering something.

"All right," she said, then to me, "Sam, I'd like you to meet Miss Janus Alexander Morgan."

So! The kid had finally talked! I said I was delighted to meet her.

"But you already did meet me already," she said primly.

First words out of her mouth and they were to put me in my place—another case of being careful what you wish for. I told Sal we needed to talk.

She gave me a swift appraisal, then turned the girl over to Honeycutt. "Let her have breakfast on the porch. She can watch the men bringing in a load of hay." She turned to me. "You look remarkably chipper for having spent the night being grilled." She accepted coffee from Mrs. Honey, took it into the breakfast room and sat. "Give."

I gave, describing the previous fourteen hours. "They asked a lot of questions, first with everybody together, then taking each one alone. I think they would have liked to let us go much sooner, but they couldn't, what with the press there and Barney Schantz's history with Tunnelson and, frankly, I wouldn't have thought them doing their job if they had."

"Oh? How did Barney's past come up?"

"One of the network 'suits' recognized the name."

"Did Barney tell the police the whole story?"

"His version of it, yes."

She looked at me, worry etching tiny lines on her face. "More ammunition for Miss Tunnelson's charges if they think Barney still has it in for him. Do they?"

"They're trying not to. Unfortunately, it seems Schantz made some rather nasty comments about Tunnelson in the kitchen that night."

"Really? Such as..."

"Such as calling Tunnelson some rather unprintable names. Such as saying the world would be a better place if he dropped dead."

"Good grief!"

"Indeed." I thought about the interview. "I guess I should say Warmkessel's trying not to."

"Trying not to...oh...make something of Barney's history with Judd. Right." I didn't have to say who'd give his eye-teeth to put Barney in it.

"Difference being Longnecker's got allies this time, what with Tunnelson's sister and her retinue and this Fowler guy."

"Ken? Oh, I doubt Ken's part of it. He seems to be being reasonably reasonable about the whole thing."

"He does?" Bowl me over with a feather, why don't you. I studied her. She looked innocent enough, sipping away at black coffee. I said snidely, "I take it your dinner went well."

"Satisfactorily." She took a bite of toast.

Satisfactorily? Good God! Worse than I'd figured! "Counted the silver this morning, have you?"

"Yup," she said uncharacteristically foxy. "Back teeth too."

"Good golly Molly. Let's hope he didn't get as far as that. Not with you."

"Oh," she snapped, "the original ice-maiden you mean. No chance of a quick one for old Sal, that it?"

"No," I said confidently. "None."

"Don't be silly." She threw her napkin down and got up. "It's already..."

"With a man you knew well and trusted, yes. When you were physically and mentally smashed, yes. Not with a man you just met."

"Well, don't be so darn sure it couldn't happen." She rose, picked up her bag and turned to leave. "I'm going to be late."

She was going to be no such thing and we both knew it. I also knew I'd gone too far. I retreated. As I said, I like my sister. "So what's on for today?"

She took a second or two, then sat back down. "Well, among my other cases, I'll be reworking my search for Janus' family, now that I know her name. It shouldn't take long to find them now. You, I trust, shall be getting some sleep before attending the inquest."

"Soon as I stop in at the restaurant. Have a message for Walt." At the door I helped her into her coat. "You think this Schantz thing could mean trouble?"

She reminded me that anything could mean trouble in a situation like this. "Look Sambo, I hate to leave you still eating, but I really must go. Have a good rest, will you?"

"Yup. Take care yourself," I told her back.

I went to find a couple of ropes—one for my tongue and one for the first person to cause cross words between us since she met and married Gunther McKnight. The

Dead in Pleasant Company
A Pennsylvania Dutch Mystery

reference bothered me even more. I had warned her against him too and he wound up coming within an inch of destroying her before doing us all a favor by bumping himself off.

Forsaken by my twin, I headed to Pleasant Company, there to find the kitchen in the Pennsylvania Dutch equivalent of a tizzy over the absence of their chef. Schantz had neither shown up for his shift nor answered his phone. Walt had gone to look for him. Now, who was to decide on the day's specials? My culinary talents are limited to the production of scrapple and sausage, but I chipped in and helped for a while until they decided I was more a hindrance than a help, finally bluntly suggesting I leave.

I hung around until Walt returned with the news that Barney had packed up and left town. Walt's attitude was pretty cavalier about it. I reminded him Schantz was specifically told to stick around and that his mother was a policewoman.

"At the moment anyhow," he said. I looked at him. "Who knows what she'll be next week?" He straightened the already neat stacks of dinner menus. "I just wish to hell she'd stay at home like a normal mother." Normal' mothers these days, I reminded him, went to work. "Not when they don't have to."

"Well, there's have to because you have to and then there's have to because you have to."

"I know. That's the problem."

I wanted to ask him in what possible way he'd been short on mothering. I didn't bother. Some people just like to complain. "In any case, the sooner Barney gets back here the better. For one thing, he's got a good job here that will not be easy to replace. For another, what with the publicity this case is generating, wherever he's gone, I'm sure it won't take the cops long to find him. The press too."

"Oh, hell! He's a dead duck anyway. He'll fry."

"Fry? For what? The guy had a heart attack! You don't fry for that!"

"Yeah? So why did they hold him all night?"

"They're just doing their job. You know how quick the press is to claim we're getting special treatment. Everybody knows Barney's innocent of any..."

"Right. And we never convict innocent people in this country, do we?"

I held my temper. "You watch *American Justice* too much. Not all courts are like those they portray. Ours is pretty decent. Look Walt, you can believe what you want but we've got to get Schantz back and pronto. Your mother will never forgive us if we don't." To say nothing of how the rest of the family would react. "Can't you see his going off will just keep the spotlight on us, give people a reason to ask questions? And," I sought for a point that might carry some weight with him, "it's not you they'll focus on, you know. It'll be the family, or the restaurant and your mother. If they mention you at all, it will be to say your mother spoiled you. They may even suspect you of protecting Schantz and her of protecting you and wonder why." He looked about to throw a punch at me, but I was saved by the bell. I flipped on my cell-phone.

It was Chief Warmkessel, warning me that Tunnelson's sister was on her way to the restaurant. "Got 'er lawyer with 'er. They're openly accusing you two of having something to do with Judd's death."

"Oh?"

"Yup. Say he'd just had a physical and was healthy when he left Washington. Think it's funny both of you left the table when you did. Talking wrongful death suit against everybody—you, Sal, Pleasant Company and the PPD."

I swore under my breath, made an effort not to confuse the messenger with the message. Damn Judd Tunnelson for sticking his damned newspaperman's nose into our lives.

Damn litigious attorneys. Damn the voracious appetite of the press in general and investigative journalists in particular.

It was going to hit the fan all right!

* * * * *

Fowler fingered the object in his pocket. Was he really going to use it?

He had not counted on meeting the perfect woman. He had not even believed there was such a thing for him and if there was, he would certainly never have expected it to be her. But meet her he had. There was no doubt about that. And she seemed quite taken with him as well.

He was sorry now he had not called his boss. In a sense that tied his hands, yet he had always acted on impulse and things had worked out for him so far. Would his luck hold?

He thought of wonderful days and nights when they could share their mutual interests. Fair, genuine, warm. When he said at lunch he enjoyed the old fashioned dances best, her face lit up with pleasure. Another shared interest. He could not wait to take her in his arms and whirl her around the dance floor.

He would have to make peace with his family if he were to continue seeing her. She was not the kind of woman one took to the justice of the peace.

He saw her face before him and heard her laugh. He couldn't wait to see her again. He had his hand on the phone to call her when his boss arrived. He put the phone down, indicated the way to the morgue and they went in together.

* * * * *

Hannah Fairchild

SAM

From my car phone I got hold of Mrs. Sweeney, asking her to get down to the restaurant and deal with the Tunnelson woman's entourage, then headed for home. Halfway there I called her a second time, advising her to ask the family when they would be coming to pick up her brother's belongings, still in Sal's gate-house. She wanted to know if one of the family, meaning one of the lawyers in the family, should not be present. I said that would just make it look like we had something to worry about.

I thought about Judd's sister as I drove. She must be quite a piece of work to use her brother's death to make a quick buck. I reminded myself she had, after all, lost a brother. I wondered if they'd been close. What would it be like if sudden death came between Sal and me? The early death of our parents and my twin's propensity for stepping on rat's nests kept the possibility in the back of our minds.

I told myself to can it. I was tired. I did what I was told a couple of hours ago and went home to get some shut-eye.

An excited Annie met me at the door. "Your sister wants you to call," she said, taking coat, hat and stick. "Important she says."

I punched Sal's number on my cell-phone.

"You had your phone turned off," she said rather crisply. "Is something going on there?"

"Barney's gone," I said.

"Oh?" Meaning why didn't you call.

"We're taking care of it here," I said, hoping that was not a lie. "I was going to try to get a few hours sleep. What's up there?"

"It looks like Tunnelson *was* murdered after all! The people from his insurance company found it. Two tiny pin-pricks at the base of his hairline."

Dead in Pleasant Company
A Pennsylvania Dutch Mystery

"Pin pricks? At the base of his hairline?" You could blow me over with a feather.

"Word is the ME missed it because Judd's hair is so thick."

"By insurance company you mean Fowler? How did that happen?"

When her voice came, it sounded odd. "It is part of his job to attend the autopsy on a large claim like this. I imagine Horizon will be shelling out a pretty penny. In any case, it was his boss who actually found them."

"His boss?"

She was being patient. "Yes. Ken sent for him."

"Oh?"

"I suppose it's something they do in the case of someone as famous as Judd. Anyway, I think it advisable that whoever is 'taking care of it,' as far as Barney is concerned hops to it. The chief has appointed a Special Investigating Team to take over. I'm sure they'll want Schantz back in again. Look," she said, ending it. "I've got to go." She was silent for a moment then, "You'll be in for the inquest then?" I said of course. "Good. I assume you'll stop at the 'Firm?'"

I said 'natch', adding I'd stop to see her after the inquest if she was around and hung up.

Bad as the news was, I knew I'd be useless without at least a few hours sleep, so I told Annie to wake me at one o'clock. I dropped off as soon as my head hit the pillow.

* * * * *

I was several blocks away when I got caught in the midst of a bunch of media vehicles inching their way onto Thaxton Circle. I recognized a few faces as I drove by and quite a few more apparently recognized me for, as I passed, microphones were grabbed and a reporter would begin to babble into it. I kept just far enough ahead of them to avoid having to comment on anything. As it was I was late, slipping in the back just as the coroner's jury was being seated.

It was quick, cut and dried. With Tunnelson's own medic there to testify Tunnelson had not, to his knowledge, had a heart condition and with no reasonable explanation as to how, when, why or by whom the pin-pricks might have been induced, the jury, most of whom are friends of the family, cast an apologetic glance in my direction and brought in a verdict of death by person or persons unknown.

* * * * *

My stop at Stephens, Jacobs, Weinsheimer and Butz was, if not sweet, at least short. I put them wise to the Tunnelson woman's threatened lawsuit, asked them to be prepared to send someone to protect Barney Schantz's interests then headed for Sal to give her the bad news.

Mine would not, apparently, be the first. If looks could kill, her computer would be lying there in a heap. To avoid having the look turned on me, I waved a white handkerchief at her from the doorway.

"Oh," she said unenthusiastically as I approached. "Hi." Her desk was covered with printouts and marking pencils, the clutter an odd contrast to the small, neat nosegay of delicate pink rosebuds, each perfect in form, perched on one corner.

She saw me glance at them. "Ken," she said offhandedly. "We had lunch." Like it was nothing. She had her 'no trespassing' sign up so I kept off it. "So, give! Tell me how it all went."

I told her how it all went, adding that I'd brought the lawyering Thaxtons up to speed. "For Barney too, when he gets back."

Dead in Pleasant Company
A Pennsylvania Dutch Mystery

"Assuming he gets back."

"He will. Walt will find him."

"Walt? Why Walt?"

I remembered I'd yet to tell her what I'd learned of the budding friendship between the two. I made it casual.

"And Walt is out looking for him now?"

"I think so."

She sighed. "What the devil is going on, do you suppose? Could we be wrong about Barney? Could he have tried to play some kind of joke on Judd that went wrong? Because if so..."

Because if so her son could be in danger. I said quickly, "I don't think so, but somebody killed Tunnelson. Cousin Reuben wants the police to leave it for the FBI."

She swiveled to look at me. "The FBI? Surely we can trust Warmkessel to handle this."

"The old Warmkessel, yes."

"Good heaven! You think..."

"...that with him off his feed these days, this thing could drag on and on. That will keep the damned press here increasing the possibility we'll be involved one way or another and in that case..."

"...we better not stand around watching the grass grow."

I nodded.

She stared away in the distance. "Well, if it's not us, that leaves Judd's family, business associates and..."

"...the public at large I'd guess. I imagine the list of enemies he's made could dwarf your list of missing kids. Schantz is not the only one he's injured."

"Yes. That's what Ken says too. I think that's the best place to start then, don't you?"

"I do." I wanted to tell her to ask Ken.

"Look, Sam, I've got to stick to my work here. Can you..."

"...get to it? Sure thing. I imagine a good place to start is with Tunnelson's enemies—people he's injured. I'm sure the cops are on it too, but it won't hurt to give my friend at the network a call." I gave it more thought. "Or maybe I'll just buzz up there. It'll be harder for him to say no to my face. I'll soften him up with dinner at the club first."

I used Sal's phone, making it short, casual, and charging the cost to our office. "So what is it you're so busy doing here," I asked, gesturing to the mess on her desk.

She made a face. "Exercises in futility, it would seem. It was bad enough when the girl's prints and description turned up nothing, but even the addition of her name hasn't helped! Can you believe that? I was so sure that would get me...It's as though the child doesn't exist." She stared resentfully at the screen. "O'Connell wants me to give it to the press—ask for help in locating her family but..."

"You think they'll think you're using the kid to take the spotlight off us in this other thing."

"Partly, yes, and partly because you know how I feel about putting a small child in the spotlight. Besides, there are aspects of this case that just don't...feel right."

"Such as?"

"Such as why nobody is looking for her. She's been gone five days now! I've heard back from just about everybody and there's not even a peep!" She glowered at the stacks of names. "Do you think it's possible her family doesn't know she's missing?"

"Maybe they know and don't care."

"Yes. I suppose that's possible," she snapped irritably. She hates to think such a thing can happen, but it's my job to make her think about things she doesn't want to think about. "I know parents can get overwhelmed at times," she admitted reluctantly. "Sometimes it takes all one has to just keep one's own head above water."

"That could account for her being left so unceremoniously on a cross-country bus I suppose."

"But, if that were the case, I imagine they would come forward eventually, if only because they were concerned with how it looks. I mean, wouldn't family and friends ask questions if your family was suddenly short one child?"

We stared at each other. "Maybe they don't want to call attention to themselves," I said. She looked at me. "Especially if they themselves are wanted by the police."

She nodded. "Possible, though I think in that case the child would have been made a ward of the court and I've checked that already."

I shrugged. "Maybe they just plain don't want her found."

She made a face. "I've considered that too, but why, for heaven's sake?" Her frown deepened. "They could be dead. Or," she turned back to the computer, "maybe they're separated and each one thinks the other has her."

I said that, too, was possible. "Has she told you anything about herself now that she's started talking? Does her speech suggest what part of the country she's from?"

Sal shook her head. "No, but that itself could be some help if it weren't for the ease with which people move from one part of the country to another. I've talked to the bus people again, but they were little help. She came in on one of the regular runs originating in DC on a run that connects to travelers from every nook and cranny in the country. That particular bus makes eleven stops between Washington and here. It's a regular daily run and is usually full. Theoretically, she could have gotten on at any of those stops. I'm requesting help from police departments within fifty miles of each of those stops. Some of the stops are little more than a convenience store or gas station, but somewhere this child either wandered on to the bus

143

unnoticed or was brought on and deliberately left. If she was alone, surely someone will have noticed her."

"What do you expect the local cops to do?"

"I'm asking the police at each stop to meet the bus tomorrow and interview the regular passengers on that run. Riders don't have to give their names when they buy a ticket, but there are some who travel every day and they might remember something. I should have done that right away, but it never occurred to me I'd have so much trouble identifying the child…"

"Doesn't the driver make a head count at each stop?"

"Supposed to, but I gather sometimes it's just a quick look to the back to see if anything's different. Then, too, she's so small she would be easy to miss."

"You leaning toward thinking it more likely she was deliberately left there?"

"I'm beginning to, yes, because otherwise someone would have come looking by this time. The bus people say it is not unusual for a child to be left behind, especially at night, but someone comes back for them, usually within an hour or so."

"Have you considered what you'll do if you find the family and they don't want her back?"

"No," she snapped, "and I don't intend to." She cooled down after a bit and apologized for her outburst. "Be up to Children's Services, if that happens. They'll place her, probably in a foster home." Her phone rang. "I've got to get back to work."

"Meaning I should beat it. Okay." I pushed her hair back out of her eye, saying for the thousandth time, "I don't see how you can see."

"I can't. Not with you bothering me."

"Okay, okay. I'm outta here."

"Thanks for stopping though, Sam. See you later?"

Dead in Pleasant Company
A Pennsylvania Dutch Mystery

I gave her shoulder a squeeze. "Me and my Aunt Tillie." With which time-honored affectionate Thaxton rejoinder, I finally went.

CHAPTER 11

As it turned out, no pressure was needed. At the United Broadcasting Company I was greeted by Tom Halloran with open arms. I wondered if my welcome said anything about what it had been like to work with Tunnelson or if this was just an example of any news being good news. In the offices of UBC, there was a noticeable lack of crepe-hanging.

I gave Halloran the gist of what I wanted, not bothering to sugar-coat it. He rang for a body.

"I don't have to tell you how many people Tunnelson got to," he said. "He was good for ratings, no doubt about it, but we keep…kept an entire staff of attorneys just for him." An aide tapped and entered. "Run up to Legal and get me the files on Tunnelson disputes."

"Paper or disk?"

Tom looked at me. "Whichever is easier. A disk is fine if you can manage it."

While we waited I said I knew something of the tussles Tunnelson had with people and companies who'd been the focus of one of his 'investigations' as I know how to read, but how had he been to work with.

"Work for, you mean. Actually, though, I guess I've known worse, once you got past his ego."

I nodded. "How would you characterize the lawsuits filed against him? People looking to make a few bucks or legit?"

"Both. Mostly the former. Quite a few were disposed of with a letter, some with a check, only a handful actually filed suit and of those, few got to court—as you probably know since those make headlines. Actually they're the best from our standpoint, believe it or not."

I raised eyebrows at him. "Really? Why was…oh, of course. You're in the news business and lawsuits are news."

Dead in Pleasant Company
A Pennsylvania Dutch Mystery

"The bigger the better."

It was an alien thought to me, but one must allow for differences. I considered it from his angle. "Of those that went to trial, did you lose many?"

He shrugged. "Please! Never say 'lose!' We settled three or four I guess. Like I said, it's free publicity. When you think what a fifteen second spot in prime time costs, bottom line, you could say we never really lost any. The bigger the award, the more coverage. And his public loves...loved it! Thought it was proof he was looking out for John Q. Public."

I said I saw. The aide tapped and entered carrying two zip disks and a carton. "These," pointing to it, "go with the files. Anything else?"

Halloran said no thanks and the aide trotted off, no doubt to help with the ever-ringing phones.

I looked at the young man's retreating back. "What about co-workers? If he was so difficult to work with, there may be more than one who'd like to see him out of the way."

Halloran shook his head. "I don't think so. The network is well aware of the difficulties his crew has and we make sure they're taken care of. Let's see what we have here."

He called for a laptop and inserted one of the disks while I sorted through the box. The contents appeared to be objects sent in the mail or hurled at the newscaster.

They'd done a good job with the records. Each file included a copy of the original threat or complaint, usually in the form of a letter or letters, sometimes transcripts of phone calls. Handwritten letters were followed with typed copies of the contents, presumably to resolve questions about penmanship. Copies of responses, in most cases written, in most cases from one of the legal staff, but sometimes from other experts in a particular field followed next. A comprehensive log of communications, including mail, fax, e-mail and phone calls was included along with a chronological narrative describing the events in each case, a numbered reference to the show which had generated the complaint, a video of the same, the disposition and any final comments. A surprising number of people had walked quietly away with healthy chunks of dough.

Halloran stopped and indicated the file on the screen. "Here's one I felt really bad about. We were only too happy to pay him off."

I looked. It was the file on Barney Schantz.

Halloran grimaced. "Aired while I was on vacation otherwise I would never have let him use it. Accusing a man of being a child molester is pretty devastating. I agreed with the poor guy's attorney it would severely damage the man's ability to make a living, no matter how innocent he was. Often wonder what happened to him."

I debated telling him what happened to the maligned man: to do so would get it out in the open which none of us wanted, yet not to do so would mean every time my friend and I had a serious sit-down he'd wonder what I was holding back.

"Matter of fact, he's working for Pleasant Company."

"Really? Oh. Well that's all to the good then."

"Good man too. We're happy to have him." I decided not to say exactly where Schantz was working. There was no point really. I was here to get information, not give it.

We separated out those cases which seemed most promising. In a short time we had about eight tagged for further study, cases which he said had ended in acrimony or threats.

A loud skirmish at his door preceded the aide whose entrance was buffeted by a wall of sound. A young man squeezed through and pressed his back firmly against the door.

Dead in Pleasant Company
A Pennsylvania Dutch Mystery

"Sorry sir," he panted. "A crew from *The Star's* out there. Won't take no for an answer." He stopped to catch his breath. "They're convinced one of the Thaxtons is here. I tried to tell them…" He saw me for the first time. "Oh. You *are* here! And I've been insisting…"

Halloran moved to the door. "It's all right Hendricks. I'll take it. Excuse me a minute." This last to me.

He disappeared and I could hear him being firm and resolute to the interlopers. Gradually the racket trailed away, his voice with it.

While I waited I used my cell-phone to buzz Sal. She suggested I ask Halloran what he knew about the lead Tunnelson was planning to pursue in Philadelphia and whether it had anything to do with Mastermind. I'd forgotten all about that.

It was ten minutes or so before Halloran returned, apologizing for the intrusion. "They keep somebody in our lobby at all times. I guess they saw you come in." He grinned. "I told them you'd gone out the back."

I thanked him and said I'd used the time to look over the cases he'd left and had some questions ready. "Can we start with Providence Insurance?"

Halloran surprised me with the grip he had on each of the cases. We made short work of my list.

"I don't know how much of any of this will help," Halloran said as we repacked the boxes an hour later, "but you're welcome to it all. What will you do with it?"

"Hand it over to our researchers I guess. Find out if any of these people still held a grudge and, if they did, were they in Plainfield at the time—that sort of thing." I pocketed the disks, then remembered Sal's suggestion. "One of the last things Tunnelson talked about that night was a lead he was most anxious to follow up. Somewhere in Philly, he said. We got the impression it was something to do with Mastermind. Do you know what it was?"

"Mastermind? First I've heard of it, but my God! What a coup that would have been! Wait! You don't suppose that had anything to do with his death?"

I shrugged. "Could be." I thought it a lot more likely than thinking Barney Schantz had anything to do with it. "Are you saying he didn't tell you about it?"

"Hell no. I had no idea! Perhaps his assistant..." He pushed a button and spoke to someone in another office. In a moment, yet one more young man appeared, asked if he could help. Halloran repeated my question.

The young man nodded. "Yes," he said. "I've been wondering why nobody's asked about it."

"This is the first I've heard of it! What kind of a lead did he have?"

"I've no idea. I only know he got a couple of phone calls from one of his sources, one before he left for Plainfield and one or two down there. Asked me to arrange the payment."

"Which source? Do you know?"

He shook his head. "Not one of his regular 'snoops,' I don't think. He asked me to request a cash payment to be sent to our affiliate in Philadelphia."

Halloran said, "Philadelphia? Payment?"

"Yes sir. Twenty-five thousand dollars."

The amount surprised me. "In cash?"

"Yes sir."

Halloran frowned. "Well, there's nothing really unusual about that. We keep...kept an account for Tunnelson to pay his sources. Naturally we don't know who they are."

"Naturally," I said. "That fits with what he told my sister. He was getting ready to drive down there when he died. One of us should tell the cops. I'm sure they'd be interested. He also told my sister he wasn't going to use the story he came to Plainfield to do. Did he tell you that?"

Halloran said no. He looked at the young man.

"Nor me, sir. I put a memo on your desk this morning to the effect that we needed to do something about whatever notes and tapes he left there. They would belong to UBC."

"Of course! I never even thought about it. What about it, Sam?"

"The Plainfield police may want to look them over, but certainly you can have them. Perhaps you should contact the Chief personally." He took the name down. "One more thing, Tom. What about his private life. Anything there?"

Halloran said he thought not. The young man agreed. A youthful marriage had ended some years back in an amicable divorce. There were no children. Since then, there had been brief trysts with different women, nothing serious though. I reflected if the proposal to my sister was typical of him, there was good reason he'd remained single.

I rose, thanked them both, said I'd be waiting for the promised updates, told Tom I owed him a dinner and flew back home. A bit of hustling on my part and I'd make it in time for our usual sunset ride.

* * * * *

I tracked them down in my sister's enormous attic where they were pulling riding clothes from the trunk Mrs. Honey kept anticipating grandchildren. Sal was waiting patiently for young Janus to decide between the worn jeans and tee tops Lucy had favored and a new-looking riding habit in Thaxton indigo blue and silver—a gift from me to my niece. She'd worn it once.

For the kid, it was no contest. She turned up her nose at the tatty jeans and donned the Thaxton cap with a cocky tilt of the head. If Sal was right, (and I've never known her to be wrong about such things), the child had been neglected, so what right did she have to have this air of self-confidence?

The question irritated me. Was my sister's penchant for always looking for reasons, for connections, rubbing off at last? I told myself one of us was enough. Some things just *are*.

So there were three for the ride tonight: the kid resplendent in my nieces' riding habit and astride her pony. We took the long trail, past the still frozen acres of farm land between our two homes. I gave Sal a thumbnail sketch of each of the possible candidates for 'X' I'd gotten from Halloran.

"As we thought," I said by way of introduction, "there are plenty from which to choose, but Halloran picked out those he thought most likely to harbor ill feelings."

"Such as?"

"Well, you remember Tunnelson was the first to charge State-wide Insurance with sinking their clients retirement funds into junk bonds."

"Which then went bust. I remember, yes. Tens of thousands of policy-holders lost everything, didn't they? It was a major shock. Nobody wanted to believe one of the country's oldest and most revered insurance companies could be so duplicitous. Misrepresented their retirement plans as federally insured as well, didn't they?"

"That's them. The government got after them after Tunnelson's story aired. Settled out of court. Cost 'em billions, one of the largest settlements on record. Heads rolled. Art Presly was summarily fired, remember and I've heard he's having a hard time of it still. Wouldn't be surprised if he bears a grudge against the guy who started it all."

"State-wide is not taking care of him?"

"Nope. Halloran said they're a cold bunch."

"Any other individuals there in particular? Management? Board members? Large stock-holders?"

Dead in Pleasant Company
A Pennsylvania Dutch Mystery

"I asked the same thing. Halloran didn't know but I've got our research staff on it. Another even worse outfit was Madison and Madison. Halloran said that outfit scared the day-lights out of him. Judd had a series of near misses at the time that story broke. Network called in the FBI. Said we could use his name if we wanted to talk to them."

"That was the Wall Street firm accused of burying excessive charges and permitting clients to exceed their account limits. The government has proceeded against them as well, hasn't it?"

"In the works, I gather. Halloran's getting that file up-to-date too. The last entry in the file was dated some nine months ago. Then there was Watson Medi-Group. Tunnelson charged them with defrauding Medicare. That one netted him last year's Press Club Award."

"Yes, I remember."

"You'll remember this too because we talked about it. Some woman sent him a video showing street workers in some town in Texas dumping barrel after barrel of unused cleaning fluid down the sewer. Judd investigated and learned the stuff had been purchased from a company owned by a member of the city council.

"Oh yes. The woman was out taping her grandchildren in a park when she saw the men and thought it was odd. She didn't know what it meant, but her husband thought it fishy and called the local UBC affiliate. Several people doing jail time as a result, aren't they?"

"Far as we know, yes. That's on the list to check too. Then there's California's major lettuce growers. He accused them of 'dumping' to push up prices. Halloran thinks they're capable of just about anything. And, let's see. Oh yeah. Took on the whole exercise equipment community, charging their infomercials contained unverifiable claims about the efficacy of their products. Said their 'life-time guarantees' were merely intents to defraud."

"Oh yes. They go out of business before claims can be made, file for bankruptcy and come back under a different name with a slightly different product. Tunnellson's investigation virtually put an end to that whole industry."

"Right. There were more than a few other big stories he'd broken as well, but Halloran thinks these the most likely to be what we're looking for."

We rode silently for a few minutes. Then she said, "I feel as though I've misjudged him. He's certainly been a friend to the consumer."

"To himself too, of course. Made a bundle doing it."

"Yes, well, there's nothing wrong with that, is there? Was he working on anything else currently? Besides the one here, I mean."

"Apparently he had two stories in the works. He was looking into one about produce distributors. Someone in the industry wrote him charging that the reason produce companies wet down fresh produce before shipping was not, as they claimed to keep them fresh, but to add to the weight, thus the price. What made this of interest to me was the rumor circulating that the mob had moved into the produce business. The other concerned a militia group charged with voter fraud. According to reports of police in one midwest town, armed members had hung around the polls, handing out literature about the man they supported."

"What about this Mastermind thing?"

"What indeed? Halloran hadn't heard a thing about it. Tunnelson's assistant did though. Said they'd sent twenty-five thousand dollars to Philly for Judd to pay the guy."

"And nobody knows who it was?"

"Nope. I thought it damned odd, so did Halloran. Naturally Tunnelson liked to keep his sources well protected, but for a story of that magnitude he would certainly have expected Tunnelson to let him know it was in the offing."

"I wonder," she said thoughtfully. "Maybe there is someone in Halloran's office he didn't trust."

"Or Halloran himself?"

"You know him better than I."

"I could swear not, but most heinous crimes are committed by people beyond suspicion, aren't they?"

"Yes. Why they get away with it." She thought again. "I wonder if Andy has gotten anywhere following up on it. The so-called 'lead' he was supposed to have in Philly. I mean. It would be awful it we lost an opportunity to get him."

"Don't worry. If Andy's on it, we'll get him. Eventually. Anyway, I turned all this info over to Mrs. Sweeney. She'll get our researchers on it, checking the current whereabouts and status of the major players in each case. We'll take it from there."

"Good," she said absently.

"That's about it for me. What's new with you?"

"New? Not much. I've had a chat with Walt for one thing," she said, "strongly suggesting if he and Barney were such good friends he get him back to work before the police get any ideas."

"Yeah? I bet that went over big."

"He reminded me he was not a child and insisted Schantz had nothing to do with Tunnelson's death. I think he'll do it though. He seems really interested in the restaurant business lately. I hope so. I hate to see him just floating."

We rode in relaxed silence for some minutes. Making the last turn on the way back I got a good look at her face.

"What's bothering you?"

"I was thinking about your list of potential villains."

"And?"

"Aren't you leaving someone out?"

"I don't...oh, you mean Cedar River Gambling?"

She nodded gloomily. "And the 'major players,' as you called them, in that case."

"Meaning us." I mulled it over. "I don't see what bumping off Tunnelson would get either them or us. He wasn't even going to use the story."

"Yes, but there's no proof that we knew that and certainly CRG didn't. Their defeat here was a huge financial setback after the money they'd invested. And since our fight with them was successful, at least one other county is planning to boot them out and sue them for fraud. Who knows how many more municipalities might do the same once the story aired?"

"And a lawsuit would almost certainly blow the syndicates' cover..."

"...to say nothing of encouraging more litigation."

"Yeah! I see what you mean."

"We know they still have people in the area working to get the issue on the ballot again. It was public knowledge that Tunnelson was here. It wouldn't have been difficult to track him down. They might even have been at Pleasant Company and seen him there. Perhaps they couldn't pass up the chance to make Tunnelson an example of what can happen to people who can't keep their mouths shut..."

"...and, since we pretty much started it all, get back at us as well. You have a point there, Sal. If someone from CRG did decide to bump him off," I said grimly, "Pleasant Company would be the perfect spot to do it. Kill two birds with one stone!"

"Yes." She gave it some thought. "It would help if we knew what actually killed him."

"Nothing on that yet?"

"No. Or at least not that they're telling me." Suddenly she swiveled around on her horse. "Oh-oh. Where's our companion?" Both said companion and the sun had completely disappeared from sight. It was a hairy ten minutes before Nimbus, told to find Ske-daddle, Lucienne's pony, took us back to the stable where we found Janus already helping to brush down her ride.

"I was hungry," she said to Sal's anxious questions. "You two could talk forever so I just go-ed home."

"I suppose the ride in the cold air made her hungry," I said. "God knows, I could eat a horse."

As, apparently, could the kid. She dug into Mrs. Honey's crab patties and corn oysters with the determination of Cal Ripken, Jr. showing up for a game. Sal eyed her curiously. "Miss Morgan. We are not going to run out of food. Please take your time! Your body needs time..."

"I'm glad we had this *today*," she said, shutting out the lecture with the same full concentration she was giving her food. "I hope she's got more of this stuff out there."

"Those are corn oysters and I think you've had enough. You've put away more than half the..."

"I'll bet I missed something really good yestiday. That lady sure does know how to cook!"

No argument there.

"Yesterday? It *was* good," Sal said. "Mrs. Honey's dumplings are the best in the world. Why didn't you eat some yes...?"

"Next time I'll tell her to save me some. What was that black, sticky stuff she made yestiday?"

"Shoofly pie," Sal said.

"Hunh?" Sal repeated it. "Shoe pie? Pretty dumb name for a pie."

"Shoo-fly pie. You don't think much of the name?"

"Is it made out of shoes?"

"No. It's called that because cooks used to set them on the far side of the kitchen on baking day to attract the flies and keep them off the other food."

"That's dumb," she pronounced. "What's a fly anyway?"

The question was as transparent a challenge to duel as a glove slap in the face. Sal did not bite.

"Why doesn't she still do that?"

"Because now we have refrigerators, which keep food away from insects."

I decided a rescue was in order. "I imagine by now you miss your family. My sister's knocking herself out trying to find them for you."

"Don't care if she does," she said, still spoiling for a fight. "I'll just run away agian anyway soon's I get back."

"Oh?" Sal looked up. "You ran away?" The child just chomped away. "That's interesting," she said mildly. "You don't want to go home? That's the first I heard of it. I didn't know that. I don't suppose you want to tell me why."

"They're boring."

If she'd expected the usual complaints about the unreasonable expectations of parents, once again the child surprised her. Sal sought for facts. "Boring? Who's boring? Your parents?"

"All of them. Ever-body." She looked longingly at the last of the corn oysters.

Sal found it impossible to deny food to anyone. "Go ahead. Might as well finish them. Honeycutt?" Honeycutt put the last two on the child's plate. They went down in half a dozen gulps. "Mrs. Honey says you didn't eat all day yesterday. Want to tell me why? You wouldn't be so hun…"

"Be*cause*," the kid snapped, apparently irritated beyond reason.

I bit. "Because why?"

She ignored me. Feigning disinterest, Sal turned her attention to me, suggesting we take coffee in the library as we had mail to go through yet tonight.

Dead in Pleasant Company
A Pennsylvania Dutch Mystery

The kid tagged along. In the library she stood at Sal's desk, watching as we sorted through the usual stack of letters and messages Mrs. Sweeney left for us. Before long the kid graduated to my lap, pestering me for a sip of my wine, trying to braid my hair, which, other than being shorter, is the same curly, chestnut variety as my sister's.

I put up with it for a while. I'm used to it. Kids take to me like, well, like a Dutch uncle. I kid around with them, generally remember which name goes with which kid and otherwise pretty well ignore them—which they seem to eat up. This one, though, was beginning to bug me, calling me 'Daddy.' 'Can I have some of your wine, Daddy?' 'Throw me up in the air Daddy,' and the like. An abstemious man in such things and childless, the appellation continued to make me wince until I heard her call Honeycutt 'Daddy' as well.

"If you want to know," the kid said out of the blue, "I'm not allowed to eat every day."

Sal looked up from the mail. "What did you say?" The girl repeated it. "Not eat every day? Is that what you said?"

"Sure! Are you deaf?"

"Not noticeably, 'though there are times when it would come in handy," Sal said dryly. She looked at me. "By golly, that fits though. She ate Monday night at the bus station, did not eat Tuesday in the hospital, ate Wednesday, did not all day yesterday, did today." She turned to the child, now engaged in pushing buttons on the television.

"Don't push the buttons." The order was matter-of-fact but firm. "Use the remote control there if you want it on. Bring it here and I'll show you how."

The kid did as she was told for once and the television blared on.

"Janus, why don't you eat every day?" Sal asked. "Didn't your family have enough…"

The small eyes were giving Daffy Duck full attention. "Cuz that's how girls get fat," she said. "Like you."

Hannah Fairchild

I sputtered. It was, for Sal, the most unkindest cut of all. I tried to make a joke of it. "That's a new one! I thought we heard them all—the cabbage soup diet, the fruit juice diet, the milk-shake diet, the all-carbohydrate diet, the no-carbohydrate diet to name a few! My personal favorite was the whiskey diet." But I could see years of reassurance going down the drain. I wanted to choke the little brat, biting the hand that not only fed her, but treated her like one of her own.

"Lots of people, that is, almost everyone eats every day," Sal said, managing to sound reasonably reasonable. "I mean, they might skip a meal or so but..." Her argument was going nowhere. She switched to another. "Children especially need to eat regularly. Your body is growing very rapidly and food is the fuel that..."

But the kid knew what she knew and the subject was closed. She hopped over to the window. "Where's the horses? I want to see the horses."

"They're sleeping."

"I want to watch them sleep."

Sal sighed in defeat. "Go ahead then. Stay with Benjam though. Turn the television off first."

We stared after her, Sal deep in thought, my rescue unheard.

"Well, that explains the malnutrition anyway. But who told her that and why?"

"*If* they did. Maybe she made it all up."

"She's inventive enough, that's true, but it's an odd thing to...No, I don't think so. She believes it. Another thing. Notice how fast she eats? That suggests hunger or perhaps fear of not getting enough to eat. One might hypothesize that supports my neglect theory. Yes, Honeycutt?"

"Telephone Madam. Mr. Fowler."

She took it without looking at me. She wished the creep a good evening, then listened. "Fine, thank you." Again she listened. "Oh well, you know how it is. One plunges on." I cringed. He knew how it was? "...new with you? Oh?" Whatever his response was, it was unexpected. She turned away. "I ah...I don't know...well no, not really. What time? Yes, I think that would be fine. Thank you. See you then." I looked at her.

"Dinner tomorrow," she tacked a firm period on that one and returned briskly to our discussion. "Let's see. Where were we? Oh yes. Janus. No. She'd have to be either a psychopath or sociopath to pull off that piece of acting and, having seen more than my share of both, I just don't..." Her frown deepened. "What did I just say? I feel as though I just said something import...Well, it's gone." Her voice changed. "Sam, you don't suppose..."

Sal's eyes said she was off somewhere, giving me time to pat myself on the back for not letting the occasional appeal of a smiling child's face con me into producing any of them myself. Honeycutt came, announcing the arrival of Charlie O'Connell.

Sal said to bring him in. "He may be hungry, Honeycutt."

Charlie's normally sanguine face was creased with frowns. Seeing it, Sal skipped the preliminaries. "What's up, Charlie?"

He nodded at me but spoke to her. "Thought I ought to tell you." He looked like something was giving him indigestion. "They've put out an order to pick up Barney Schantz."

"They have?" Sal sounded shocked.

Charlie said he was sorry, shifted from one foot to the other, his eyes not on her now, but on me.

Sal looked at him. "Yes, Sergeant?" The use of his rank seemed to get him off the dime. "I've been told to ask you to take leave for a few days. Paid of course. I mean...we know you don't need the money, but we...that is they...want it clear this is not in any way..."

"Disciplinary?"

"Yeah. Damn! I hate this!"

"Come, Charlie. I understand. I do. And it's no problem really. I can continue to work at home, unless you think..."

"No. Oh no! I'm sure they don't care about that. It's just that, with that bastard's sister and her gang of lawyers all over the place, they, well, the chief, that is, thought it best if we kept you out of the line of fire."

Sal nodded. "I see. Of course. Thoughtful of them."

"Also..."

Benjam's timid cough came from the doorway. He had the child in tow, her clothes spattered with dirt, her face alight.

"Here she is vunce." Benjam thrust the child forward. "Chust hasta get inta everysing. Got herself goot an' *shmutzig* vunce. Nothin' that von't come off in the vash though, *nicht vahr*?"

Before Sal could say anything, the child took one look at Charlie, clutched her chest, staggered and fell to the floor.

Charlie's mouth dropped. He ran to pick her up. Sal intervened. "I'm quite sure our young friend will get up when she's ready."

"He's *supposed* to help," the young friend protested from the floor.

O'Connell fussed, gave her a hand up. She peered up at him. "I remember you, don't I, Daddy?"

Charlie's eyebrows shot straight up. "Jeez, no! I don't think so." Sal touched the bell. "Sergeant O'Connell, I'd like you to meet Miss Janus Morgan Alexander. Miss Alexander, Sergeant O'Connell."

"You're black," she said to him.

"I know," he said.

Dead in Pleasant Company
A Pennsylvania Dutch Mystery

"Honeycutt, I believe Miss Morgan is getting tired. Will you ask Mrs. Honey to help her get ready for bed?"

"Can I come back and say good night?"

Granted permission, the girl bounced away, clearly none the worse for her fall.

The room was quiet with the kid gone. I joined the two police officers, now discussing the developing atmosphere at work. Honeycutt brought Charlie a tray of sandwiches and beer. Gradually the deep folds in Charlie's forehead began to smooth out and eventually talk turned to the search for the child's parents. Sal invited him to join her at her computer to review the summary of her work to date. He was bending over Sal, pointing to something when the kid came bouncing noisily in from the hall. She saw them and stopped dead, the disgusted look returning.

"Sumuvapeach," she said with vigor. "I hope *you're* not going to do that 'ohraymond ohraymond' thing!"

Startled, they both looked up. Sal found her voice. "What did you say?"

"I said I hope you're not going to do that ohraymond…"

"Not that. The other thing.".

"What other thing. Oh. You mean sumuvapeach."

"Yes. Where did you…never mind. What do you mean that ohraymond thing?"

"Oh. That." She was being patient, a parent explaining something basic to a rather slow child. "You know. What they always do back there in the corner."

"They?"

"A'course they. Raymond and Dumbdonna."

"Raymond and Dumb…?"

The kid was impatient. "Dumbdonna! *You* know. The two of 'em. What they always do."

"Do?"

"Gee you're dumb! That 'ohraymond, ohraymond' thing! Back there in the corner," she insisted.

"Back there in the..." Sal looked at me. "I seem to be becoming echolalic!" Nonetheless, she trod determinedly on. "What is it they do back in the corner?"

"How should I know? It's dark. I can't see. They think I'm asleep. All I know is it's very hard work."

"Hard...How do you know that?"

"Cuz of the way they huff and puff. Then Dumbdonna groans a lot and that's when she says it."

"Says it?"

"Oh boy you're dumb! 'Oh raymond oh raymond!'" The kid came to her typically abrupt stop. We stared at each other in disbelief. There could only be one explanation. Raymond and Donna, whoever they were, thought it would be all right to make love with the small, supposedly sleeping, girl in the darkened room. Both Sal and Charlie flushed beet red.

Charlie grabbed his cap and mumbled something about having to leave. Sal could not look at him so it was I who saw him to the door. When I returned the child was gabbing away, struggling to force Moses into a doll's dress. Sal, somewhat recovered, was asking if Raymond was her Daddy.

"No," the child said, pure disgust dripping from every pore. "I *told* you."

"Oh, did you? I don't remember. An uncle then?"

"What's an uncle?"

Refusing this tempting offer to do battle, Sal moved to the flank. "So you lived with Raymond and Donna?"

"A'course! What d'ya think?"

"I see. Was your Daddy there as well?"

"Which one?"

"Your re…" She stopped. "Did you have a lot of mommies too?" She looked at me. "A commune! That would explain…"

"No, a' course not! I just only has one. She's at home."

"I see." Shot down again! But there is nothing faint hearted about my twin. She persisted. "Where's that? Where is your home?"

She shrugged. "Where Mommy is."

"Oh. Of course. Is your Daddy there too?"

"Sometimes. When he's not away." Faultless logic. He was there when he wasn't away.

Sal muttered. "Down through the looking glass. Why do I bother?" Nevertheless, she geared up for another attack. "So Mommy and Daddy were at home but not Raymond and Donna. They were at a different place and you were with them?" The child, engaged in trying to get Moses to bite her own tail, ignored her inquisitor. "Does somebody else live at home besides Mommy and Daddy?"

"A'course. All the others."

"The others?" Sal took another stab. "You mean brothers and sisters?"

The kid jumped up. "Sure. I want to go to bed. Can I have the television on?"

Sal tried to press on, but the kid was having none of it. Even a deal to watch television in exchange for a few more questions fell through. "All right. Go to bed. Ask Mrs. Honey if you may watch television. I'll leave it to her," Sal said, touching the bell.

Passing the buck was a clear indication my sister's head was elsewhere. Personally, I was glad to see the kid go. She was wearing me out.

"Curiouser and curiouser," Sal said from far away. "I need to think."

* * * * *

Deserted, I read for a while. At eleven o'clock, I turned on the television news. I did not expect it to be good and I wanted to be with her when she heard it.

The Internet terrorists was no longer the lead story.

"...coroner's jury today returned a verdict in the death of Judd Tunnelson, one of the nation's foremost news journalists. We take you to Plainfield where Roger Gerber is following this story for us."

"Thanks, Dan. It was just a few days ago that the biggest news here in Plainfield was the ground-hog's emergence from his hole. That was supposed to predict the end of winter but you couldn't prove it by me. It's bitter cold here in this corner of the state and more snow is predicted on top of the fifty-two inches they've already had this winter. It's also pretty chilly inside the Plainfield County Courthouse where the verdict of 'death by person or persons unknown' was handed down this afternoon by a coroner's jury of two men and three women. We've had a chance to speak with Police Commissioner Frey who is with us now. Commissioner Frey, are you any closer to determining the exact cause of Judd Tunnelson's death?"

"No. We're working on it."

"Sir, has it been established that the two pin-pricks found on the back of Tunnelson neck indicate Tunnelson was poisoned?"

"No, that has not been established at all. So far, all the tests are coming back negative. All we know right now is that whatever caused Mr. Tunnelson's death, it is something which appears like a heart attack."

"Do you have any leads as to who might have done it?"

"No. That field is still wide open."

"I understand that many people have made threats against Mr. Tunnelson. Are you..."

Dead in Pleasant Company
A Pennsylvania Dutch Mystery

"*The FBI is looking into all that. Perhaps Mr. Fielding, here, can help you.*"

The Commissioner pushed another man forward and turned to leave. A reporter called after him. "*Sir? Does that mean you have cleared all the locals as possible suspects?*"

"*No. Oh no. No, we have not as yet ruled out anyone.*"

"*Even those close to the Plainfield Police Department?*"

"*Yes. Here's Mr. Fielding.*" With that, Frey disappeared from camera range.

Fielding jabbered a lot of FBI-speak, skillfully avoiding answering any of the reporter's questions. It was, I thought, a tale told by an idiot, signifying nothing. I looked at Sal. "Not too bad, though, eh?"

"It could, God help us, be worse. They don't seem to know about the Mastermind connection, assuming there is one. I wonder how they've managed to keep that quiet."

The news turned to the wildly fluctuating stock market and I clicked off the set and told her to go to bed.

"Right," she said absently. "I wonder what else Charlie was going to say." I walked with her to the bottom of the stairs. "Oh well, I guess it'll wait until tomorrow. 'Nite Samuel."

Samuel? Samuel? I couldn't remember when she last called me that. She had to be either worried or scared, but which? I buttoned up, climbed into my car and headed home.

CHAPTER 12

SAL

Saturday.

As I could just as readily work at home, Chief Warmkessel's 'request' to take leave was no excuse to dawdle and I was already on-line in my library by the time Sam, ubiquitous cup in hand, arrived early next morning.

"Told Roselma you wouldn't leave a little thing like being told to stay home keep you from working," he said by way of greeting. I wished him good morning and asked how my favorite sister-in-law was feeling. "*She*," he said pointedly, "is fine. Wanted to know if I thought she should come home and hold your hand."

"Nice of her."

"Yep. Nice person all 'round, my wife. *You*, on the other hand, are being a pain. Got Mrs. Honey mumbling to herself out in the kitchen. Hope you're proud of yourself." He dropped into the chair across from me and settled back. "What'd she do to you?"

"Nothing," I said irritably. "I just skipped breakfast."

"Skipped....*Just* you say? What's up? You join the eat-every-other-day bunch?"

I'd already been grilled at length on that point by the Honeycutts and I snapped. "Good heavens! From the fuss you're all making anyone would think..." I was about to say I couldn't live without eating, but thought better of it. My fondness for food, breakfast in particular, was no secret. For me, the very word, 'breakfast' conjures up an irresistible feast for the senses: long tables bearing heaping platters of pancakes and sausages, gleaming compotes keeping hot eggs and bacon, fried potatoes and scrapple, baskets of toast lathered with butter, blue and white stoneware jugs keeping cool the milk, fresh from the morning's milking, the sound of the hand's good-natured prattle, and everywhere the air redolent with the enticing aroma of coffee. It is a far cry from the three hundred calories that break my fast these days.

Sam was contrite. "Sorry. I just wondered if..."

"...I am giving credence to my young friend's weight stabilization theory. Of course not!" I said it firmly as I'd been doing just that. Knowing Sam would see through me, I hurried on. "It's just that I've got an idea." That, at least, was true. "I'll have something later if I feel faint," adding "and speaking of fainting—I think I'm on to something." I continued to pull up files on my computer as we talked.

It took only a second for him to follow me. "That fainting business with Janus?"

"Exactly. We both felt the act was phony, didn't we? Last night I began to wonder what precipitated the act. This morning it occurred to me she always 'swoons' in the presence of someone in uniform. Remember? The other day when I came home at lunch I was in uniform, then Charlie last night. *Nicht wahr?*" He admitted it was so. "Also, I checked with the Covered Wagon people again. Remember they reported she'd fainted there as well? Well, that was in front of the bus driver who, of course, was in uniform. It all fits."

"Feinting the faint, as it were."

I ignored that. "So, the question is," I typed a response to the question on my screen, "under what circumstances would a person (it helps to forget she's just a rather small child) pull a stunt like that and the answer is obvious. Uniforms generally mean some sort of officialdom, n'cest pa?"

"If you mean com esta," he said, returning my serve, "Si, Señora."

"Further, we have Janus' own words to support the hypothesis that it is done, not only on cue, but deliberately. Remember? She said Charlie was *supposed* to pick her up." He nodded. "The implication being that she has been taught to do it to draw attention to her and, one assumes, away from something else. Argument?"

"You're saying she's been taught to play a part in some sort of scam."

"Exactly. Which, if you think about it, could account for why no one has shown up to claim her."

"I see where you're going. If they've been involved in some sort of crime, they would obviously be reluctant to come forward. By George, I think you've got it!"

"Yes, I think so too, but," I said dryly *"what* is the question."

I continued calling up official police files, typing in official access and security codes when asked for. Finally I got to the screen I wanted.

The screen glittered. 'Which agency files?'

I typed, "Federal Bureau of Investigation."

'Which department' it queried.

"Major Crimes," I told it.

It told me to wait. Waiting, I asked Sam what he was up to.

"Got a Track Association meeting later. Right now I'm waiting to hear from Mrs. Sweeney."

"About candidates for 'X'?" My screen cleared, blinked and asked, "Classification? I told it "Fraud. Bunko. Scams. Con games." I told Sam "You know, I've been thinking about that. Perhaps knowing which persons holding a grudge against Tunnelson had been in the vicinity at the time of his death might well be moot."

He frowned. "Moot? Why moot?"

"Because we don't really know what killed him, therefore we have no way of knowing when whatever it was might have been introduced into his system. If, for instance, it was a slow-acting substance or one that required a trigger, the murderer wouldn't necessarily have had to be anywhere near Judd that night." I watched the screen flicker in silence. "I imagine that may be why they haven't charged Barney Schantz."

"You think that's the reason?"

"It makes sense, doesn't it? On the other hand, if it was something reacting instantaneously, it would have to be someone nearer and that means..."

"...someone at the restaurant."

"Including us. Or someone we know. I don't recall seeing any strangers around that night, do you?" I turned to look at him. "Things are heating up entirely too quickly, Bro'. I'm beginning to wonder just how innocent was the request for me to take leave. It's getting worrisome."

"It is for a fact." He sat on the edge of my desk and looked down at me. "It's a damned mess! It's bad enough we haven't a clue as to who did it or why or what killed him but I thought we at least knew when and where!" He stared at my screen, still blinking away in search mode. "Damn him! The guys' dead and he's still making trouble!

I asked if he could stand more bad news.

"Sure! Why not? Misery loves company! What else is there?"

"I talked to Bill Peters a while ago. He's got half the PPD out interviewing everybody Tunnelson saw that day." I looked at him. "You realize that means..."

"...everybody at the church for Groundhog's day. Neighbors. People we've known all our lives. Pastor Wert. Restaurant patrons too. Damn!"

"And the entire family. Including the aunts."

He chortled. "Like to be there when they get to the aunts!"

"I suppose we should have expected it but..." I reflected it was heating up indeed.

He was looking over my shoulder. "Doesn't look like your search here is going anywhere either. Isn't it easier just to check VICAP?"

"I have. Nothing there, but that's not too surprising. VICAP only works if local officials enter the data into the system."

"Which also means the scam or whatever has to have been discovered."

"Discovered, reported and recorded. Right."

"But you're pretty well convinced she's part of a scam?"

"Oh yes. I think so."

"A violent crime you think?"

"No-o. Not necessarily. If fact I doubt it. More like a game." I lowered my voice. "She'd behave quite differently if she'd been subjected to violence of any kind."

"I see." Then, with an abrupt change of subject, "So, what about it? Can you spare an hour or so later?"

"To go over Mrs. Sweeney's findings? Glad to though I don't see what I can add to what you all are doing."

"Just the same. You might see something simple that we don't. You know how your head works."

"Master of the simple thought? Yes. Perhaps that is me!" I knew what he meant. "Okay, but I need to have a chat with our young friend this morning and then," I'd been tapping in answers to requests for badge number, official status, base unit, security clearance and the like, "even though I feel certain these fainting spells are not genuine, nevertheless she needs to have an electroencephalogram and whatever other tests might account for them. I really should run her in to the hospital and get those done first."

He took the hint, bless him, offering to take the child in and let me continue my search. When I rang for Honeycutt to get the child ready, Sam told him to bring our breakfast trays to the library.

The screen blinked twice and began to tick away, providing official records of reported scams, frauds and con games. I scrolled through them first, familiarizing myself with the format and current codes. These data bases changed so rapidly that even small police departments found it advisable to assign at least one officer as 'tech' just to keep them up to date. PPD had such a one, a young man with an attitude. I was not ready to trust him with my investigation so I scrolled and read and typed and, when it came, worked on toast and coffee.

I was not even aware Janus had joined us until she suddenly jumped up and pointed to the television. "I was on that!"

"What?"

"That."

I looked. "The train? You were on that train?"

She nodded solemnly. "It was fun! I even slept on it!"

So much, I thought, for my search of neighboring towns. "You did? When was that?" She did not answer. "Was it before you got on the bus?"

She lifted one shoulder at me. "No," she said with disgust. "It was on another different day."

I felt my toes curl. Was I going to learn something at last? The child had an incredible knack for playing 'gotcha!' I kept my eyes on my work, effecting only nominal interest. "How did you get on the train?"

"How do you think? I just walked on."

"Oh?" I kept my tone casual. "Where did you get the ticket?"

"Ticket?" She frowned. "What's a ticket?"

"Didn't a man come along asking people for tickets?"

"Oh, him!" She dismissed him. "He just asked the lady how many were in her party."

"The lady? Oh. A lady took you on."

"A'course not!" She was indignant. "The lady keeping care of the other children, Potato Head."

"Oh." I flashed back to my teaching days. I took a stab. "The teacher with all the school boys and girls."

"Sure. A'course."

"I see. So you took a train trip with your school friends?"

"Not *my* school, Dummy! I *told* you a hunnert times I'm too little to go to school!"

I did not remind her she'd already given as many accounts of her age as an aging beauty queen, though in the reverse direction of the truth. "Oh. I see. So who was with you when you got on?"

"Nobody! I told you! I was all by myself!"

"So you did." I waited a bit, then said with as much disinterest as I could manage, "You were on the train a long time then, weren't you? How did you know when to get off?"

"Oh, that! It was the lady's fault! She told the man I didn't belong to her. Told him I was lost! Boy, that was dumb! I was *not* lost! I knew *ezzackly* where I was!"

"But you got off then?"

"Sure! I heard them sayin' a policeman was coming for me so I just snuck off while the guy was talkin' to somebuddy else."

"Then what did you do?"

Tiny shoulders moved up and down. "I don't know. I just ran 'til they couldn't see me no more."

I thought a minute. Most train stations are located in the same downtown area as are bus depots. "Did you see buses then? Did you decide that was a good place to hide?"

"A'course! It was easy! I seen all them busses was all just standing there and I wanted to see what they were like, so while the man wasn't looking, I just got on and looked.

Dead in Pleasant Company
A Pennsylvania Dutch Mystery

There was a lot of people sitting around and eating and one of 'em offered me a sammich so I sat down and ate it and then another guy gimme a brownie. It was good. Then I fell asleep."

Made sense. She would have been tired, perhaps cold. I remembered the hospital report. Had someone thought it funny to feed a pot-laced brownie to a child? Did people still make pot-laced brownies? It was something a juvenile officer ought to know. "And when you woke up you were here? In Plainfield?"

She said nothing but pulled a sour cherry fritter from her pocket.

"I take it you're eating today," I said dryly.

She threw me a contemptuous look. "I'm just lookin' at it. Keeping it for tomorrow." She thrust it back into her pocket and went to the windowed wall, studiously examining the scene before her.

"Tell me," I said mildly, "did you like sleeping on the train?" I might as well have been talking to the wall. Abrupt as always, she required a change of tactic. I considered my next move. "Janus, I want to ask you something." She pretended not to hear me, but I plodded on. But her attention was fixed past the snowy lawn to the track where the horses were being exercised. "That's quite a funny game you play—that business of staggering around and falling. Matter of fact, you do it very well." I took a shot. "I hope 'Ohraymon' appreciates how well you do it."

The child turned to roll her eyes at me in hopeless disgust.

"*Raymond*', you silly. Not *oh*raymon'! Oh boy!"

I accepted the correction with patent humility. "Raymond. Of course. All right then, why did Raymond want you to do it?"

"Why do the horses make all that smoke when they run?"

"Answer my question first."

"Humph! I don't have to. I can just ask Benjam." I waited. Finally, "Anyway, it was so he could give me a present, Silly."

"A present?" Again she'd surprised me. "You got a present when you did it?"

"Sure! A'course! Ever'time. At the party."

"Every time? The party?" Echolalia once more reared its head. The small head bobbed up and down. "What party was that?"

"Oh boy, you're du…" Apparently she remembered she, too, wanted something. She spoke with exaggerated patience. "We always had a party when I did it. Until I got here." This with devastating angst. "I guess I won't be getting any more presents."

It was too much for my childless twin who'd been observing this tête-à-tête and trying not to laugh. He reminded her she'd already had quite a few presents from me.

I tried to steer the conversation away from a potential battleground. "You are certainly a lucky young lady, aren't you? Where were you when you played the game?"

"There they go! There they go!" She ran back to the glass wall, her back to me. "Look at 'em!"

I went to stand beside her as she watched the activity on the exercise ring for a few moments. "Yes. They do make a lovely sight, don't they? Do you know their names?"

"A'course! What d'ya think? The big one's Nimbus and the middle-size one's Twilight and the white one's Wackadoo. Where's the rest of 'em?"

"In the stables. They'll come out later."

"Why can't they come out now?"

"Because we exercise them three at a time. Janus I…"

"Why?"

"Why what?"

"Do you only essercise them three at a time?"

"Because I only have three lads. Janus I want..."

She yanked at my arm, fixing pleading eyes on me. "I can be a lad! Then you could essercise another one. I could do two! They just take 'em 'round that circle. I can do that." She went for the door.

I caught her arm. "Hang on Sugar Plum. There's a lot more to it than that. I'm sure you can learn to do it but not right now. Now I want to talk to you."

"I don't have to talk if I don't want to."

"And I don't have to let you ride any more if I don't want to."

"I'll tell the cops if you don't."

"Go ahead. I am a cop, remember?" High noon at the OK Corral! We glared at each other. "You answer my questions," I said calmly, "and I'll speak to Benjam about teaching you to help out with the horses. Now, why don't you tell me about these presents. How many did you get so far?"

"A lot."

I considered my adversary. "Never mind." I turned back to my computer as if done with her. "Probably weren't very good ones anyway. You can go. I'll call..."

"Were too, good ones! Better'n any your Lucienne ever got I bet."

"I gave Lucienne a pony when she was about your age." About the age I was acting I told myself. What was it about this child that brought me down to her level? I told myself to grow up. "Did Raymond give you a pony?"

"No," she exhaled disgust.

"See! I thought so. I'm going..."

"They gimme a Barbie on roller skates one time and a Barbie house another time and a Barbie car too, so there!" She eyed me speculatively. "Why doesn't Lucienne ride the pony?"

"She's gotten too big." We went on like a couple of backwoods traders. "Where is your Barbie? Wouldn't you like to play with it?"

"Sure but I had to leave them at the 'partment. They're gonna send 'em to my house. Where is the pony? He's not in the barn anymore."

"Back in cousin Susan's stables. I'm glad your presents are safe. Is your Barbie house there too?"

"Sure, what do you think?"

"I imagine you would like to go and get them, wouldn't you?" No answer. "We can go now if you can tell me where they are. Can you?" No answer. "Are they in the same place where you eat every other day?" No answer. I decided to try going around the roadblock. "Do your brothers and sisters eat every other day too?"

That got her. She spoke with extreme disdain. "A'course! The boys eat one day and the girls the other."

She had taken to galloping around the room, shouting 'yippee' so loudly I wondered if I'd heard her correctly. Sam raised his eyebrows at me. I decided not to push my luck. I had to raise my voice to be heard. "Do you still want me to answer your question?"

Janus stopped dead in her tracks and returned to me. "What question?"

"About the smoke the horses make when they run."

"Oh that. Can I go out and play with them now?"

"Not this morning. This afternoon perhaps. Mr. Thaxton is going to take you to the hospital first. No," I said to the look I was getting, "not to stay. I just want you to talk to the doctor for a bit. Let him take a picture of your head." Make a great medical study, I thought. "Mr. Thaxton will wait for you and bring you right back. All right?"

In answer she took Sam's hand. "Okay then Daddy. Let's go."

I tried again. "Just a minute. Is Raymond a friend of your parents?"

"I don't know. Maybe."

"Did your Mommy and Daddy know you were with Raymond?"

"My Mommy and Daddy are dead," she said, transparently glib. I played along. "Is that why you went to stay with Raymond?"

"I guess. He just aksed 'em if I could stay with him for a while."

"Asked your parents?" Once again the child was mute. "So your parents said you could go and stay with Raymond so he could teach you this game and you could have parties and presents. Is that it?" Still nothing. "I bet your parents liked the party. Did they play the game too?" Were the parents in on it? Perhaps the entire family was involved. I thought of Ma Barker.

"Heck no! They just wanted to get rid of me. They didn't know what to do with me when the new baby came. They tried to get me in school like the others but I wasn't old enough."

"I see. By 'others' you mean your brothers and sisters?" She nodded, showing signs of incipient boredom. "How many brothers and sisters do you have?"

The shoulders rose and fell. "I don't know. Lots." She was busy yanking Moses by the leg in an effort to pull him down from the library shelf. "I don't want to talk anymore."

"All right. Go ahead with Mr. Thaxton then."

She began to move away, then turned to eye me narrowly. "If Lucienne's too big, why can't I have the pony?"

"It's still belongs to Lucienne. You'll have to ask her. We'll have to ask your mother first, though. Where does she live?"

"At home, Silly. With the baby."

"Oh? Tell you what. I'll talk to your mother and ask her if it's all right. What's your phone number?"

But my subtle flank attack failed. Her face brightened for a few seconds, then fell. "Never mind. She'll say no. She never lets me have anything."

Including regular meals, I thought. Honeycutt appeared to tell Sam Mrs. Sweeney was on the phone.

While Sam talked, I began to tally up what I now knew about this strange child. I'd learned a lot in the past hour but there was a lot more I needed to know. Two solo sallies, one on an overnight train, another on a long distance bus, would be considered a challenge by any one, much less a small child, yet her tales had the ring of truth and I could see it all happening much as she said it did.

I felt quite certain the conclusions I'd drawn were on the money. Based on her behavior, her character and the snippets of information with which she'd parted over the past two days, the child most likely was, technically, a criminal, part of a three party 'scam.' She'd been handled carefully by someone intelligent. It was not mere serendipity that she did not know the names of places she'd been. That information had been carefully kept from her. Had she been picked deliberately because she could not read? I thought so.

I still needed to know where and when these events took place. I considered how to go about pin-pointing the location. Would it help to try distinguishing one geographical location from another? A bright child would notice her surroundings but how much of what she knew was she willing to tell me?

I knew the going would be rough, but I might not have another chance. I debated how to start. "Janus, do you have a lot of snow where you live? Like we do here?"

"Sure. Ever-body has snow. Boy, you don't know anything."

"Thank goodness I have you around to tell me things then." Even to my own ears, I sounded petty. I tried again. "Let me ask you another question."

But I had lost her. Declaring she wanted to see what Mrs. Honey was making, the girl took Honeycutt's hand and went off in the direction of the kitchen, reminding me to not forget about the pony. It would be useless to call her back.

* * * * *

"Why the face?"

I jumped! I'd not even heard them return, yet Janus was already ensconced before the television, eyes glued to the antics of Daffy Duck.

"Sorry I startled you."

"Back already? What time...good heavens! I had no idea..." I realized Sam had asked me a question. I pointed to the message blinking on the screen.

ACCESS DENIED

"Denied from what? What are you trying to get into?"

"FBI files for juveniles involved in scams."

He whistled. "Hold on! You got this in response to your search for the kid?"

I nodded. "I was doing fine until I narrowed it down to scams or con games involving small children. Now every time I seem to be getting somewhere this screen comes up! I've been trying to get around it."

"Damned odd, isn't it? If it's an investigation involving a kid, you have a right, don't you? As juvenile officer..."

"So one would think, especially if it's an open case. Certainly any with which the department has been asked to help. I called down there and O'Connell said there was nothing on our wire."

"Can't they get clearance for you?"

"Tried that. O'Connell said he'd request it but it could take a while."

"And naturally, you don't want to wait." I did not answer. He knows well waiting is not my strong suit. He looked at me. "Andy would know."

"Yes. I thought of that." I considered that small face. "Problem is, I may not be able to un-involve him once I got what I need."

"How about Jacob Junior?"

"Thought of him too, but I can hardly ask him to break the law when it is to my advantage and follow it other…Besides, what if he got caught? Henry Harrison Thaxton's great grandson arrested by the Feds! It is, after, all, a federal crime. That would be media fodder for months." He did not try to sway me. "Truthfully, I suppose the chances of anything there being relevant to Janus is minimal. I just wish I knew why I'm being shut out." I gave it up with a sigh, then turned to face him, remembered his errand. "How about you two? Everything go all right at the hospital?"

"Fine. EEG is clean. Took blood samples again. Said they'd let you know if there's anything. I also stopped by Mrs. Sweeney's office. She gave me these." He dropped a stack of memos on me. "All but the top one are requests for interviews. She wants to know what we want to do about them."

"Oh, all right. Give me a minute." He remained there, staring down at me. I looked up. "You off for your date with the steeplechase people?"

"Yes, but…"

I felt a pang of guilt. "Oh yes. I said I'd give your names some thought. I'm sorry. I've been so focused on this child I just didn't…"

"Yeah, I know. As always. Always with you it's children first." He eyed me keenly. "You try to paint in the missing spaces in your own childhood by meeting the needs of other kids."

"What?" He sounded exasperated with me, but when I looked at him I saw only affection there. "Where did that come from?"

"Forget it. I'm just being a piss-head. How's it going anyway?"

"I'm being thoughtless. I'm sorry, Sam. If I didn't ask about your lists it's because I figured if you were taking care of it…"

"You have too much faith in me. I've told you before. One of these days you're going to be disappointed."

I shook my head. "Not going to happen. Anyway, here I am. Let's have a look at your list."

"Never mind the list for the moment. That's not what I wanted to tell you. There's been another development."

I turned. "For heaven's sake, what now?"

"Better look. From Mrs. Sweeney. Top memo."

I took it. "It's from Ron at the bank. For Walt. Marked urgent."

"Right. Questioning a deposit Walt made a couple days ago. Wants to know what account he wants it in."

"Deposit?" Sam nodded. Walt was better known for his withdrawals. "I don't see…" I examined the note from the banker. "What's the problem? Why didn't they just put it where they always do? I admit Walt's been making a lot more withdrawals the last couple of years than deposits but still…"

"Look at the amount, Sis."

"The amount?" I turned the memo over. "Oh my God!" I stared at him, aghast. "But this is for…"

"Twenty five thousand dollars. Right."

CHAPTER 13

Saturday.

It had been the most frustrating of mornings. The possibility of making real progress for the first time in my search for Janus Morgan's family had evaporated into the rarefied air of the Internet and I had no idea where next to turn. My attempts to make contact with my remaining juvenile cases had met with a continuous round of invitations to leave a message at the beep. On the domestic scene, Walt's absence was making me feel increasingly uneasy as the morning passed. The bank was not the only one wanting an answer regarding his latest deposit. At the other extreme, Janus was all too visible—well, audible actually, now loudly blaming me for the scratches on her tiny arms—the consequences of her experiment to see just how far she could torment Moses before he fought back. With Sam gone to his meeting and no one to whom to complain, I was about to explode.

"Telephone madam. Mr. Fowler."

I took the phone, praying this did not mean more trouble, told him 'hi.'

"Hi yourself! Looked for you at work this morning and was told you were at home. You AWOL?"

"Oh no. No. It's just..." I wanted to tell him I'd been officially confined to quarters, "...a regular day off."

"I see," he said, obviously seeing. "You okay though?"

"Oh yes. Fine."

"You don't sound fine."

I grimaced. This man was entirely too perceptive. I took a deep breath. "I am though. Really. How are you?" Turn the question back on to the questioner. I've never known it to fail.

"Good. Good. Look, I was hoping I could entice you out for a bit. It's a beautiful day and I'd bet dollars to doughnuts somewhere on the Thaxton estate there's a pond."

"Ice skating? Gosh, it's been a while..."

"Me too. We can stagger around together. What say? The fresh air will be good for you."

It was just what I needed. A complete change of scene often generates new ideas. I looked at the time. "When?"

"Anytime. Now if you're free."

"About half an hour then?"

* * * * *

"This all your property?"

I nodded into the cold wind. We were warm enough, tucked into a two-seated snowmobile. We'd had a half hour or so on the ice, (and I mean that literally), then, given a choice, Ken had passed up cross-country skies, opting, to my relief, for this less rigorous form of travel.

We drove past stables and sheds, across the fields that would shortly be wheat and oats, amaranth and corn and acre after acre of wild flowers.

"There's a setup I could go for!" He pointed across the way. "Nice barns, good stand of trees and the house is great! Think they'd sell?"

"I doubt it," I said, hoping the question was rhetorical. "Most properties here in Thaxtonville are kept in the family. Actually that one is Sam's. We've been on his property for the past ten minutes or so."

"Oh." He sounded disappointed.

"Actually, that's the house in which we grew up. Most of the stone and clapboard homes you see here belong to Thaxtons. Turn left at that next stand of trees," I shouted in his ear. "I'll introduce you to downtown Thaxtonville."

Dead in Pleasant Company
A Pennsylvania Dutch Mystery

We went right down Main Street where all but a few of the town's businesses were: gas station, barber shop, corner bar, police station and post office. Residents going about their business waved at us as we scooted by. I thanked God silently for the incurious Pennsylvania Dutch who would not read too much into seeing me with a stranger. The trip down the whole length of Main took no more than three minutes. I motioned him to pull up at the end of the street in front of a small square building marked Schneck's.

"Let's go in," I said, removing helmet and gloves. "I want a red licorice whip."

Inside, the store was much the same as it had been in Grandfather's time. Just about everything one might need was for sale here: sewing scissors or power saw, nails or nail polish, penny candy or rib roast. One wall held racks of books and magazines, another an astonishing array of clothing. In the back three scarred, wooden tables with unmatched chairs provided space for customers to sit with coffee and doughnuts and read one of several newspapers lying about. It was not unusual to see a high level business meeting among the shoppers or sales 'reps' taking advantage of the wonderful soups and sandwiches from the tiny deli. Today a trio of seniors played pinochle at one table while at another a shopper read and rested, her boots slipped off for comfort.

I like to bring newcomers here. I like to think I can read a lot into the variety and depth of interest they show as they pass through. Some, my husband was one, feel uncomfortable with the clutter, the crowded aisles, the informality of the staff, the occasional fly. Ken, however, did not disappoint. He spent delighted minutes sorting through bins of screws and nails, asked about the genesis of the cigar store Indian, sniffed the air at the tiny deli trying to guess at the ingredients in Granny Schneck's potato salad. He even plowed through piles of jeans for a pair in his size.

I introduced him to Granny Schneck and her grandson. He produced a giggle from the former by kissing her dry, wrinkled hand and a grin from the latter, today doing duty as stock cum delivery boy, by noting he had the physique of a football player.

He reciprocated my invitation to join me in a thick red licorice "whip," ordering hot chocolate for two, then wandered around with his cup like a kid at the North Pole. From time to time he'd call out his discoveries in delight. "Good grief! You even have electric train supplies!" "My God! Computer paper and floppy disks!"

After a bit I said we'd better leave or we'd lose the sun and we did so reluctantly. Back aboard, I directed him westward. "We'll cut through these fields. It's more private and there's no speed limit." Or press, I told myself.

He steered us in the designated direction. "Nice barns around here. So well cared for. Haven't seen a single one in need of paint or repair."

"Nor are you likely to. We treat our barns the same as our homes."

"Look there! I bet those are 'distelfinks' aren't they? I had no idea they were relevant anywhere but in Trivial Pursuit."

I confirmed the round signs with the stylized blue, yellow and red painted birds and flowers were indeed 'distelfinks.'

"Meant to bring good luck, aren't they?" I said they were. "Do people around here really believe that?"

"Most people say not, but they go to quite a lot of trouble to keep them up and painted. We'll need to turn up ahead. If we continue on another mile or so we'd be in Elk Run. There is a road there still, but it's rather too wooded to drive through anymore. Besides it disturbs the deer."

"How far back do these woods go?" he shouted back.

"A couple of miles or so. We used to ski through them all the time when we were young. It's actually quicker than driving during the winter months, but then the woods were young too. We've all spread out some since then."

"What's Elk Run got to offer?"

"Not much. Movie theater. A smallish strip mall. Gas station that doubles as restaurant and bus terminal. That's about it. Bigger than Thaxtonville, of course, but a lot smaller than Plainfield." I said I ought to be getting back and he turned around neatly and retraced our steps.

I felt certain he expected an invitation to dinner, but, as with most pleasures, once satisfied, I felt increasingly guilty about my abdication from duty. I'd work to do. I had family responsibilities. Joe and Lucienne were due rather long e-mails if I was to keep them from worrying unnecessarily and as for Walt, I was beginning to feel I needed to do some serious tracking down of that young man. Sam would expect me for our usual ride and I had yet to look at his lists of prospects for 'X' as promised.

But, when, after parking the snowmobile neatly in its slot, Ken turned to me and said he guessed he should 'get out of my hair before I got sick of him,' I heard myself telling him not to be silly.

When the message came from Sam that he could not get home for our ride, I was relieved. I would not have to listen to him trying to be polite to a man he did not like. Anyway, tonight I had better use for the time. I asked Benjam to have the lads exercise the horses and told the Honeycutts we had a guest for dinner. I introduced Ken to Janus, offered the hope my disparate guests could amuse each other and went, ostensibly to shower and change. In need of some time alone, I took my time, first sending e-mails to Lucienne and Joe, then putting in a call to the restaurant in search of my middle offspring.

They were just about to call me. Walt was due to go on duty at three and had not shown up. I remembered I'd not returned the call from the bank, thinking to ask him about it first. Now, unable to reach him, I felt a stab of guilt. Where had he gotten that kind of money? Certainly not for his work at Pleasant Company. I realized I knew next to nothing about what he was doing at the restaurant. They said he'd not shown as scheduled, meaning he wasn't merely popping in and out. Whatever the basis of his association, the twenty-five thousand dollars could not possibly be part of it. It would be easy enough to find out. A phone call to Hal would do it, but that was not my way.

I buzzed Walt's rooms, then, getting no response, padded barefoot across to the children's wing. At his door I tapped and called his name. No answer. I felt uneasy, a state not unfamiliar where he was concerned.

Back in my rooms, I considered various alternatives to flush out Walt but discarded all of them. I reminded myself, not for the first time, I'd chosen to raise my children with an eye to their being autonomous and responsible adults, which meant allowing them to make their own decisions, including wrong ones. I reminded myself Walt is a risk-taker. I reminded myself I'd learned long ago the futility of worrying about him. He would turn up somewhere, unexpectedly, doing something unexpected. I prayed his predilection for the unusual did not extend to getting involved in murder.

In the shower I returned my thoughts to Janus. My optimistic belief that the startling revelations concerning her curious life-style would get me a step further in finding her family had vanished. Where in God's name had these rather odd circumstances taken place? Who taught her to play this game and why? Who was Ohramond? Where was he? And why had my search for answers led me to secure FBI files to which even I was not privy, even with my clearance?

Dead in Pleasant Company
A Pennsylvania Dutch Mystery

It seemed less likely now that someone would claim her, meaning I had probably no more than a day, at the most two, before having to turn her over to Children's Services. I retraced my efforts to date. What had I missed? The usual search tools: city directories, tax roles and the like were useless without more specific information. The family name may not even be the same as the child's, given the plethora of 'Daddys.' And now, knowing my success would lead to her return home, she'd dug in her heels, telling me nothing more that could help.

I turned my shower to full force. Maybe if I could get my blood circulating…The girl reminded me of someone, but who? The water stung my skin. Then I had it! Theodore Reinhard! The Main Duke! A sixteen-year-old truant who held the school district hostage for years, rendering opposers unconscious by pressing firmly on the vagus nerve until the unfortunate foe passed out. In my class he'd given the term 'street-wise' new meaning.

But what did that adolescent non-reader with limited intelligence have in common with this very bright, little girl?

For one, that calm self-assurance, that confidence in one's own rights. Add an instinct for self-protection. They could be neither bullied nor threatened.

Still, I reminded myself I had achieved a workable dialogue with the boy. How? I'd never given much thought to it before. In the faint hope it would help me now, I tried to analyze how this amicable relationship had come about.

With the Main Duke, it had, in the beginning, been a case of if-you-can't-lick-'em-join-'em. His peers had already anointed him leader, I merely let him lead. My acceptance of him, warts and all, seemed to open a crack allowing for me to help him see that what he really wanted was the same respect from the adults in his life as he had from his gang and that the path of petty crime on which he'd embarked was not the best way to achieve that. Bit by bit, he had permitted me to show him that learning to read, take care of his check-book, arbitrate disputes with dialogue and generally follow school rules could get him respect from all quarters. Had a more adequate intellect come with it, who knows what pinnacle could have been his? Success in business or politics certainly. We were a great team. I missed him.

So what was the connection between the two? Something in their past? In The Main Duke's case, I had the school's permanent file to reveal the unimaginable treatment he'd had to survive, but, except for the crumbs she'd scattered so enticingly before me, I had no such help with this child.

So, from what was Janus Morgan protecting herself? Abuse? I thought about the abused children with whom I'd worked in one way or another over twenty-odd years. In the case of sexual abuse, the child's own ego shrinks away and she becomes either flat and emotionless, sexually provocative, or compliant, anxious to please the abuser. Too often suicide seems the only recourse. There was none of that with Janus. A physically abused child usually becomes abusive too, either to himself or others. Again, not Janus.

No. I was increasingly certain her behavior was more symptomatic of those who've been left to raise themselves—a condition much less accessible to amelioration. Sensitive, intelligent children, deprived of core needs for identity and a sense of worth born of the knowledge one is wanted, spend their lives getting someone to pay attention. Rock star or writer, comedian or criminal, he will find a way to ease his pain. If his need is to "even the score," you have the makings of a killer. Neglect produces children who surprise everyone by shooting their parents, their fellow students and sometimes total strangers. The message is clear—someone must pay for my pain.

Dead in Pleasant Company
A Pennsylvania Dutch Mystery

Janus was not at that point now, but she could get there some day without help.

By this time I'd brushed my skin to the point that it actually hurt. I turned the water off and grabbed a towel, the need for a way to help the child now even more urgent. Back to square one. What did she have I could work with? A keen intelligence. Okay. For that, give her something to feed the ever-hungry brain. What else? A strong sense of self—that was paramount. Perhaps, I thought with a pang, she needed to know she mattered. On that subject, I could write a book.

One thing was certain. She knew more than she was telling. The problem was how to get her to talk again?

Give her something she wants. The pony perhaps. No. that was out of the question. It was not mine to give. Food? No. What I wanted was something to get a bead on her home town, but what?

Descending the stairs, a germ of an idea presented itself. Janus had been begging to know what was up the cantilevered staircase beyond my porch, permission denied because it led to a part of the house I hold most private. What if I let her go up? Would she accept that as the rare privilege it was?

Up there, in addition to two generations childhood treasures, was a complete replication of Thaxtonville. Always reluctant to put away the traditional Pennsylvania Dutch 'Putz' from under the Christmas tree when the holidays were over, we'd decide it need a permanent home. We'd delighted in adding to it from time to time so by now we had complete replicas of most of the Thaxton businesses. Would the model trains, puffing over, under and around mountain and valley, the working lumber mill, the Thaxton stables, evince a comment, a remark, a memory, anything remotely helpful in narrowing down the little girl's origins?

With time to spare before dinner, I decided to give it a shot.

The trip up to the tower room produced the desired reaction all right, but not from Janus. It was Ken who was awe-struck, Ken who watched with delight as, one by one, I slid large trays out until they formed a huge flat, waist-high surface, Ken who asked the questions.

"Each is an exact replica of what it represents," I explained. "Here's my home and farms. There's Sam's place." I pulled out a second tray. "This is downtown Thaxtonville."

"Hang on. Isn't that the little store where we got the licorice whips?"

I said it was. "And there's cousin Sarah's tea shop. Here the Thaxton stables" A third tray came up and level. "There's Thaxtonville Lumber Company. Cousin Henry runs it now for his grandmother, Aunt Adelaide. Over there's Thaxton Publishing, Uncle Peter's business."

Ken was almost speechless. "Good Lord! I'm looking at the Thaxton Empire! I can't believe it! I've seen bits and pieces of it often from time to time," he said, clearly impressed, "but never this! Is it true these were all originally the old man's businesses? And he left them to his kids? Is this what Tunnelson was here for? To tell this story?"

"Good heavens no! I would never show any of this to anyone in the media. As to how they came about, it's quite simple really."

He seemed determined to have the full story; how Grandfather passed his various businesses along to his eight children, each of whom did the same when the time came. "Take his first child, Aunt Fiddena. She'd managed grandfather's real estate properties so she inherited the real estate business. As a young girl she also made superior baked goods, so grandfather encouraged her to open a stand

Dead in Pleasant Company
A Pennsylvania Dutch Mystery

at the farmer's market. After all, she had evenings and week-ends when the office wasn't open. Technically anyway. Fiddena had five children. One of them, Amanda, loved to help her bake, so Aunt Fiddena let her take over her stall at the market when she got old enough. Then we asked Amanda to bake the bread and rolls for our first restaurant and, as we grew, she grew. She now has a bakery within a few hours of every one of our restaurants. Her sister, Jennifer, couldn't decide if she wanted to teach or bake, so she runs a school to train Amanda's bakers. See. Here," pulling out yet another tray, "is the Plainfield Bakery. Amanda's daughter, Jennifer, has just started up a little cafe inside where she sells homemade carrot chips and yogurt drinks."

"Incredible! An enviable family, the Thaxtons! How did you two get hold of your restaurants then?"

"I inherited our father's dairy farms," I said. "Sam got the hog farms from Uncle Charlie and Aunt Magdalene, who had no children of their own and raised us." I laughed. "Actually, initially we were looking for a place to sell our farm products. When people kept after us to keep Aunt Maggie's restaurant open the two seemed to work together. We were young, just twenty and had just finished college and liked the restaurant business. It wasn't long before we opened a second store and one thing led to another."

"Incredible," he said again. "I can't thank you enough for showing it to me." He continued to examine the buildings. "Do the trains work?"

"Of course. Everything works. The trains. The Lumber Mill. Everything." I realized Janus had yet to show the slightest interest. "Come Janus. Look!" One by one, I turned on the trains but even the smoke-puffing engines and the descending crossing gates failed to draw Janus from the tiny horses and sulkies which had claimed her attention from the beginning.

I joined her. "That's cousin Susan's stables," I said. "She takes care…"

"I know! I know! Where my pony's kept."

"That's right. See? The jockeys are wearing outfits just like…"

"Hey! This one here looks 'zacky like Nimbus! Where…Oh! Oh! Here's my pony!" She grabbed the tiny miniature and stuck it in her pocket. I made her put it back. The bell for dinner provided a welcome distraction. "Let's go. It's time to eat," I said, hoping to prevent another confrontation.

She gave me a look that could fell a tree. To make her point, she insisted on being taken to have her supper with Benjam who, she said, 'really liked her."

So again I had failed. Far from making her feel wanted, I had done just the opposite. There was nothing more for me to do. All that was left was to turn her over to Children's Services as soon as possible.

* * * * *

SAM

Daylight had shriveled away to next to nothing when I set the 'copter down on Sal's frozen lawn. The meet with the steeplechase people had gone well, meaning I got my way with both the site for the new course and the date to begin construction. Heading for Sal's, I felt pleased. We'd have something pleasant to talk about for a change.

Or not. I switched to the police band on my car radio just in time to hear an APB being broadcast for my nephew.

I was relieved when the Chief took my call. He reported that Walt, whom the police apparently had been tailing hoping he'd lead them to Barney, had managed to give them the slip. The APB, Warmkessel insisted, was merely for his protection as they feared he'd been drawn in by Barney Schantz, perhaps against his will.

Asked, the Chief admitted he had not notified Sal as yet. He did not want to worry her and, as they thought they would pick him up shortly, there was no need. I told him I'd take care of it and pushed down on the gas. I thought Chief Warmkessel was being inordinately naive. If it was on the police band, it would be on the news and Sal would want to rush off looking for him and would need to be dissuaded and if not dissuaded, accompanied.

My rescue efforts imploded, however, when I learned she'd again invited Fowler for dinner. I got it from Honeycutt who, taking my sheepskin-lined jacket and headgear, said they were in the library.

"They?"

"Mr. Fowler, sir."

"Oh? When did he get here?"

"He's been here all afternoon. Had the grand tour, sir."

"The tower?"

"Yes sir."

I was floored. That was serious. We rarely took anyone up there other than family. What in the hell was this guy after? "Do you, by chance, know where Walt is? Has he been around today?"

"No to both sir. Are we in trouble?" If it was trouble for Sal or hers it would be trouble for Honeycutt and his.

"Nothing really serious, I think, Honeycutt. The police have an APB out on him. Does Sal know?"

"She knows he didn't show up for work as expected. They called here asking for him. I believe that may be why she's dining in, in case he calls, sir." He paused a moment. "She seems rather...cheerful today."

"Tell me about it! Let's hope it's because the kid's finally talking. I hope she's not blabbing it all to Fowler."

Especially, I thought, without blabbing it to me first. "I don't like him Honeycutt. What's your assessment of him?"

"The same, sir, though I can't say why."

"Gotcha," I said. "I'm checking on him."

"Yes sir. I knew we could rely on you, sir."

* * * * *

They were having drinks (it would be something non-alcoholic for my twin) in front of a blazing fire. Outside, thick flakes once again draped everything in sight. My sister was looking pretty good, every hair in place and all dolled up in a close-fitting blue wool I'd not seen before. I wondered when she'd found time to shop. And why.

My quarry seemed perfectly at home, rising easily to greet me as if he'd done it a thousand times. "So pleased you could make it, Mr. Thaxton," he said, making me sound the intruder. "Sal was just telling me how you fell at the Rider's Cup last year. Lucky you weren't hurt."

"It was the horse that fell," I felt compelled to say. "Had a dickey knee." Honeycutt appeared with my drink. "Nice dress," I said, pointing my glass to my sister. "Been to WalMart?" It was nasty and we both knew it, yet it seemed necessary to establish contact, as if she'd been far away.

"No," she said mildly, letting her eyebrows ask what my problem was. "It came with those things from Markham the other day. You don't like it?"

She knew damned well I'd like it. I am forever trying to get her to wear more blue. "Seen worse." With my eyes I told her we needed to talk. She nodded imperceptibly.

I told Fowler I needed to borrow my sister for a moment and went to the library, closing the door firmly behind her. I gave her the news about Walt, not cushioning it as I might have done otherwise. I admit to being pleased to see I'd put a dent in the god-awful cheer I'd sensed in the other room.

Asked, I said, "Of course I talked to the Chief. I told her what he said.

"Well! That's all to the good then, isn't it? I'm certain he would not mislead us, don't you agree? If he says they're primarily concerned for Walt's safety then that's what it is. A pre-emptive strike I think Sambo. From the police point of view, Barney's disappearance makes him look guilty. Walt, as his best friend, knows or guesses where he is, therefore he could be in danger and since we know Barney's not guilty. I think it's safe to say that, whatever Walt's up to, he is not in danger. Or have you had second thoughts about Barney's involvement?" I told her no. She took my arm as we walked to the door. "Let's not worry then. You know Walt. He marches to his own drummer. He will come back when he's ready."

So much for needing dissuading from rushing off. Apparently she had more important things to do.

So my good news, not asked about, went untold. My own words echoed in the empty room. Maybe my motives needed looking at. I wanted her to be happy and she looked happy. Was I just not willing to lose her company as I would if she married again? I told myself that was crap. I would be perfectly happy to lose her to the right guy. Pete, for instance. The echo said yeah, it's easy to say that when you know it ain't gonna happen. I told myself to shut up and, feeling every inch a jerk, went to join them at the table.

I listened to the two of them jabber all through dinner. Suddenly I was lonely for the nice, sensible, uncomplicated woman I married. I decided to phone Roselma and suggest it was time for her to come home.

My suggestion was received with gratifying enthusiasm. I had plenty to do before my wife returned. I went to bed at a reasonable hour and by the time sleep came, I'd a mental list of what I needed to do.

CHAPTER 14

Sunday. Thaxtonville Church

We'd agreed to ride together to church and we did so, the kid between us. Today, in testimony to the four generations inside, a couple of snowmobiles rimmed the parking lot and several pairs of skis amicably rested against the self-same rail on which we, along with Cousin Susan, had tethered our horses. In the spot nearest the door, unofficially reserved for it, the ancient Packard which provides transportation for Aunt Fiddena and the two 'younger girls,' stood chauffeur-less, gleaming in the sun. (He would be in church). Its owner, along with Aunts Eva and Louise, would have been the earliest to arrive taking their place in H. H.'s pew which, much like his politics, was up front and to the right. Fiddena's husband, Uncle Theodore, a sprightly ninety three, would have scoffed at riding with his wife. He would have walked the mile and a half or so with Uncle Morton, the original Jacobs of the family law firm, presently 'batching' it these days while his wife, as you know, is wowing them on Broadway. A handful of other cars indicated the small church would be more full than usual.

Spared from the glare of the media by its location on private property, even the most publicity-shy Thaxton could kill two birds with one stone, fulfilling obligation to God and family in one fell swoop. Naturally, being Thaxtons, they would want to know how Sal and I were coming through all this. Naturally, being human, they would want the inside scoop on the death of the famous newscaster. Naturally, being Pennsylvania Dutch, they would not ask outright.

Dead in Pleasant Company
A Pennsylvania Dutch Mystery

Throughout the service, members of the congregation stole judicious peeks in our direction until Pastor Wert prefaced his homily with words to the effect that it was gratifying to welcome *all* the Thaxtons today, offering the hope it wasn't only trouble that brought them—this, no doubt, directed at Sal who is wont to play hooky.

Afterward we were collared by Aunt Fiddena and taken off to 'coffee' at her home, along with the pastor and a couple of dozen others, each of whom wanted a personal accounting of the Tunnelson matter. Janus was accepted without question as any other guest would be and she (apparently it was an eating day) permitted herself to be fed and fussed over.

At noon, I pried myself away from Eva's aunter-ly grasp to rescue Sal from a knot of cousins in vigorous discussion, not, as I'd assumed, looking for the real skinny in the death of the famous man, but the ideal conditions for skiing and plans for an afternoon trip to our lodge in the Poconos.

As usual, it was left to Cousin Peggy, Aunt Adelaide's granddaughter and Sal's personal attorney, to be the organizing force.

"...Mary can take care of her," she was telling Sal. "You know how good she is with kids." Meaning, I suppose, Sal had cited her responsibilities to the child precluded her going along. "It'll be good for you."

Told to ask her mother's approval, ten-year-old Mary dashed off to beg permission from mother Catherine, which meant getting permission from grandmother Eva. It was she who posed the critical questions.

As to who was going, it seemed Catherine and her three girls, cousins Jake Junior and Jake III, cousin Peggy, Sal and young Janus.

As to how long would they stay, Sal chimed in. For the afternoon only. They would be home by dark as Jake Junior, with the 'firm,' and Peggy, an attorney on her own, would be expected at work Monday morning and the children at school.

It was Sal again who answered the 'how' of the trip. She would fly them up in the helicopter if I would go along as co-pilot. I said I could fly up with them but couldn't stay...Jack Jr. offered to go in my place so it was all settled.

Departure time was set and the Thaxton *freundshaft* dispersed. Since I was not going, they left it to me to call the lodge asking our caretaker to plow a space for the 'copter to set down and give Cook time to prepare lunch for the gang.

Frankly, I was a little surprised that my sister accepted the invitation to join the outing. She's the nose-to-the-grindstone type and can't relax until the job is done. Riding back I offered that observation.

"Oh, I've given up on finding Janus' family. I'll be turning her over to Children's Services tomorrow. She may as well have some fun today. Besides, I thought it just possible Walt might be up there."

She had a reason. I should have known.

I decided it was all to the good. Perhaps a Ken-less morning freed her to remember she had a family. As for me, I had a date with my computer.

* * * * *

SAL

I had hoped to persuade Jake III, my co-pilot for the forty-five minute trip to the lodge to put his inquiring mind to use in a hunt for signs that Walt might have been there. Once airborne, however, I changed my mind. The cousins were of the age when loyalty to peers still holds sway.

Dead in Pleasant Company
A Pennsylvania Dutch Mystery

As promised, young Mary took charge of Janus, assessing her interests and skills with the expertise of a camp counselor. In a twinkling Janus was fitted with boots and skis, shown the basic steps, then turned over to a younger sister to be led down the 'baby slope.' Hoping I would not be missed, I took a few runs down one of the more challenging runs myself. It is a great way to burn calories.

Far from missing me, I returned to the lodge to find Janus paired up with Mary against her sisters for a snow-fort building contest. I took advantage of the freedom to look around. Certainly Walt would have scattered when he heard a ski-party was on the way up, but it was worth a look.

I began with the half dozen or so bedrooms spread above the main floor. All were neat and orderly, beds stripped and ready, cupboards stacked with clean bed linens and pillows, the air redolent with the smoky smell of cold fires and timbered walls typical of mountain cabins.

I sought out the care-taker.

"Nope. I ain't seen 'em. Not Walt I ain't. Not since the holidays. Nope. Not since the holidays."

I thanked him and continued my search. The main room, now with today's ski party wandering in and out helping themselves to waiting refreshments or warming up at the open fireplace, was not likely to yield any clear evidence my son and his friend had been there. I tried the equipment room. Here things looked pretty much as usual until I noticed Walt's favorite skies were missing. Perhaps someone had borrowed them. I checked among those propped up outside, waiting for users to return for a second run, but they were not there either. I hunted out the care-taker again.

"Could be anywheres," he said. "Down at the shop to be waxed, maybe. Maybe somebuddy's usin' 'em today."

I thanked him again and went in search of the cook. She, too, said she'd not seen Walt 'fer a whiles naw.' I asked her to let me know if he should come around, adding innocently, "I've got a message for him from his bank."

I joined the rest, by this time back under Peggy's benign rule, announcing it was time to leave. They moaned and groaned but soon began moving toward the 'copter. Waiting for the last one to leave, something caught my eye, something familiar, yet out of place on the bookshelf next to the door. It took a second to identify it: a lap-top computer, barely distinguishable from the odd assortment of books left behind by one family member or another, easily forgotten in the rush. Peggy's no doubt. I waved it in her direction letting her know I had it and ran to join them.

I was relieved to see that Janus, though ignoring me with lordly disdain, was permitting herself to be buckled into a seat beside Mary. She seemed well at home among the noisy, chatting group and I wondered if that could be taken as confirmation of her own large family.

I handed the laptop to my cousin. She said it was not hers. Whose then? Obviously a Thaxton's, one of dozens purchased together, ease of inter-communication the justification cloaking pure honest-to-God Pennsylvania Dutch thrift.

I shut the 'copter engine off and returned to the lodge. Once again I sought out the care-taker.

He paused in his task of storing skies and equipment. "*Ich weiss nicht*," he said. "Lotsa them up here from time to time. All look the same to me."

I did not believe him. That he may not be able to tell one lap-top from another might be true, but he knew to whom this one belonged. It had to be Walt's—always the care-taker's favorite.

I asked when he'd last seen my son.

"Not for a whiles naw," he said, turning too quickly away. "Been really busy up here ya know, what wis all this here snow."

"Look, I appreciate your loyalty to Walt, but this is different. Walt may be in serious trouble. The police are looking for him and you know that's beyond the bonds of loyalty. You can certainly trust me not to do anything that would harm him."

The admission came reluctantly. Walt *had* been up at the lodge with a friend. When they heard we were coming up, they'd taken off.

"I see. What were they doing, do you know?"

He shrugged. "Stuck inside mostly. Made a bunch of phone calls. Fiddled around on that thing." He pointed to the lap-top.

"Phone calls?" I did not want to ask him anything further. He would not admit he'd listened. "All right then, thanks for your help. I'll leave this where I found it. Walt will be back for it."

I took my place behind the stick, thinking the only good derived from my grand plans to make the afternoon pay off was that I'd burned enough extra calories to forget them for once. I called Mrs. Honey on the way home with a request for spareribs and sauerkraut tonight, a meal normally outside my five hundred calorie limit. Well, perhaps more goal than limit. To one raised in a culture which prizes good eating somewhere between God and cleanliness, five hundred calories does not go far.

* * * * *

With an exhausted Janus gone early to bed, I looked forward to dinner in blissful solitude. Later, armed with a small vase of geranium blooms cut from pots on my 'porch,' I made my way to Walt's rooms. I do not like to enter my children's rooms unless invited, but I reserve the right to do so when necessary, so when my tap got no response, I called out and entered.

His sitting room looked normal for him, that is, cluttered with the detritus of the electronic age. By contrast his bedroom and bath seemed unusually tidy, almost sterile. Only the faint tell-tale scent of cigarettes hung in the air. I left the geraniums, Walt's inexplicable favorite since he was three, on his bed stand where he could not miss them if...when he came in. I hoped he would read their message: remember you are important to me. I'm here if you need me.

Back in my own bed, I tossed and turned all of three minutes before the day's trip brought sleep.

* * * * *

Monday.

Morning brought no news of Walt nor did I see anything of Sam all day Monday. A telephone call from Bill Peters capped an uneasy breakfast. The Special Investigation Team would like to ask me a few questions if it would not be too inconvenient. Could I see them, say at eight o'clock?

"This morning? Here?"

"Yes, if you don't mind. The press is all over the place down here."

"You know the way in?"

"The way...I know where your gate is."

"Better ask the gate-keeper to direct you. You can get lost on that drive."

I notified the gate to lead him through.

* * * * *

They arrived about ten minutes late. I was surprised to see Hal Strauch with them.

"Sorry we're late," Peters began. "I didn't realize your driveway is so long. A person could get lost in there. Great natural security." He looked at me. "But then I guess that's the point."

"Pretty much," I admitted.

Peters swept a hand in the general direction of his companions. "You know Harrison here and Rachel Greene. And Hal of course. This here's Sergeant Rick Masters." He indicated a tall, blond young man. "From Los Angeles. Their 'tech' jock." I shook hands all around. "Says he's been sent to check out our Personal Identification System. I say he really wanted to see how a good police force operates."

The banter drew a grin from Masters. He stretched it to me.

"I understand the PIS was a gift from the Thaxton Foundation. Want to buy one for LAPD?"

I smiled back. "Perhaps. Someone at the Foundation would certainly discuss it with you—as long as you realize it's a two way street."

"Meaning?"

"Meaning LA would have to meet..." I saw Peter's face. "Tell you what. I'll have a proposal sent to you." I motioned to chairs round a table. "Honeycutt's bringing coffee but can I offer you something to eat? Toast? Muffins? Eggs? A sandwich?" I smiled at them. "Doughnuts?"

They said no thanks, but when Honeycutt arrived with coffee, Janus trailing behind with a basket of breakfast goodies, Peters looked at the others and said, "Well..."

Rachel Greene threw officialdom aside and examined the offerings.

Hannah Fairchild

"Them's the best," Janus pointed. "Sour Cherry Critters."

"Fritters," I said. "Go ahead," I smiled wryly. "I acknowledge your presence here is an official one. I'm not offering you a bribe. I just know how difficult it is to get time to eat during an investigation, especially with the press on you every minute. Besides, you'll make Mrs. Honeycutt's day if you send the basket back empty. She's having a difficult time with no one to feed but me." Rachel Greene loomed over me, one fritter already gone. "That's what I like about you, Sal. Sensible. I told these guys I was not going to let them rag on you."

Masters poked at the long, powdered variety. "What are these?"

"Crullers," I said. "Like a doughnut but, I think, better. More body. Let me know what you think. Now, is there anything new you can tell me and how can I help?"

Peters drained his cup and pulled out a small notebook. "Well, I'm sure you understand we can't really talk about the case since you are involved—as a witness at least."

Rachel spoke up. "If there was anything new to tell, which there isn't. Don't be ridiculous, Bill. This is Sal we're talking to."

I nodded at Peters. "So, how can I help?"

"We'll take Hal first," Peters nodded at the older man.

"Just want to check one or two things." The ME said. "Did Tunnelson ever talk to you about his health? Ever mention anything about heart trouble?"

I shook my head. "And it's surprising, come to think of it. He talked about everything else."

"Talked a lot, did he?"

"Incessantly."

Hal frowned. "Did he seem to be avoiding the subject then?"

I considered it. "No-o. It was more as if health never concerned him—the way people in good health do."

Hal nodded to himself. "The kind it hits, often enough. Don't pay attention to their bodies until it quits. Sometimes first time is the last time." Then to me. "It would help if I could get a bead on Tunnelson's behavior that day. I know something stopped his heart from beating but so far, but for those two tiny holes, we found nothing that accounts for his dropping like that. I'm hoping we can find something, anything, in his behavior that day that might help." So much, I thought, for not telling me anything. I said I understood. "Knew you would. I heard he'd been swimming that morning, that true?"

I nodded. "Yes."

"How long? Do you know?"

"No. I was at work at the time. Honeycutt might though."

Rung for and asked, Honeycutt said he thought Tunnelson had been down in the pool area for about an hour, but there was no way of telling if he'd been swimming the whole time.

"We've phones and a television and the like down there," I said.

Hal said he'd like to see it sometime. I responded as expected, not necessarily truthfully, he was welcome any time.

"Was that unusual? Did he swim every day?"

Honeycutt and I both said yes. "He likes...liked...the water even colder than I, if that means anything," I volunteered.

Peters looked up. "Oh? Is that why you didn't' swim together?"

"Not really. I swim early, somewhere between five and six—a bit too early for him."

"Every day?"

"Just about." He blinked at me.

Hal resumed. "Then he went to the Groundhog's Day thing at the church here. Stuffed himself all day I believe you told us."

"Going by what I've been told, yes. I didn't get there until my shift was over and I was pretty busy when I did."

"Where were you?"

"Judging the cake baking contest. It can get a bit hairy. A few of the ladies take it rather seriously. Get their feelings hurt. I had just time to grab a hot dog before supervising the cake walk. It always draws a crowd and some of the teen-agers can get out of hand if we're not there to keep an eye on the trouble makers."

"So you don't know where he was during that period? Did he come over and talk to you, for instance?"

I nodded. "Oh yes. Matter of fact he took part in the cake walk."

"And that was pretty late in the day, wasn't it?"

"Yes. Right around six o'clock. We like to schedule it when working people can get there."

"And Tunnelson was in it. How did he look then? Did he hold his left side, for instance? Was he short of breath? Did he seem tired?"

"Certainly he seemed somewhat fatigued. Frankly, we expected him to beg off dinner, but he insisted he wanted to dine at Pleasant Company one last time." Which, I told myself grimly, is what he did.

"I see." The ME paused to think. "How did he seem at dinner?"

"He seemed fine by then, at his most…" I wanted to say irritating. "…lively. Gregarious. Seemed to have gotten his second wind." Should I tell them of his bizarre proposal? It pointed to an expectation of living a long time.

Peters nodded. "What your staff says, too." He looked at Hal. "Anything else?"

The doctor shook his head. "Not for me."

"I don't suppose I've been any help," I said regretfully. "Is there anything else I can do? I know I needn't tell you we're rather anxious to get this all straightened out."

"What we want, too. Get the damn press out of here, for one. Okay, thanks Sal. Do you know, by chance, where Sam is?"

I said I wasn't sure, that he'd be picking up his wife at some point, just when I did not know. "I can let him know you want to speak with him if that helps."

They said it would, thanked me again and departed.

In a moment Peters came back alone. "Sal, I know I don't need to say this but it's part of the job and I think you'll accept it as that. I'm assuming if you've heard from your son you would have let us know."

"Yes, Bill. Hopefully you would hear from him first."

He nodded, no longer smiling. "Thing is, Sal, we're being pressured to bring Barney in and what with Walt gone too, well…"

"Bring Barney in? On what charge? Do you have something?" I wanted to ask if Barney's disappearance was all they had. If so, it seemed precious little. It had, after all, been a week since Tunnelson died.

This time the nod was grim. "Might as well tell you, if they haven't already. A couple of your kitchen staff on that night say that when he heard Tunnelson was out front he said something like, "Give me his order. I have a little surprise for him." And later added that somebody should put him out of his misery."

"Oh?" I was stunned. "But that's just the way people talk. I'm sure he didn't mean…"

"Yeah. I know. Anyway, you see what we're up against. We've got to find them."

"Yes. Of course." He was waiting for me to say something. What could I say without actually lying? I thought again of Tunnelson's absurd proposal, but how could it possibly help? I equivocated. "Look, I honestly haven't seen hide nor hair of my son in the last several days." This, at least, was so. I hadn't seen him. I hoped he would not ask if I knew where he was.

"He wasn't at the Ground Hog day thing?"

"No, but that wasn't too unusual."

"Not home for meals? Didn't that worry you?"

I shook my head. "Not at all. Really Bill. He's seldom home for meals these days."

"Yeah. At the age when parents are to be avoided as much as possible. I got one like that too."

"Yes. Then, too, he's been working at the restaurant and I assume he's having his meals there."

Peters nodded. "Know how it is. Nevertheless Sal, we've seen first hand what happens when parents put themselves outside the law." He looked at me again. "Well, do your best, eh?"

I told him he could count on me and offered up a prayer that, when and if the time came, he could.

* * * * *

In spite of my conviction that it was useless, I spent the rest of the morning stubbornly re-checking every database which might conceivably lead to a usable clue to Janus's past, finally returning to the official website I'd been warned off. I tried one thing after another, searching for an unofficial way in. I was frankly relieved when, several hours later, Honeycutt said Ken was on the phone.

"You busy for dinner?"

"No. What do you have in mind?"

"That bird of yours know its way to Manhattan?"

"Like a homing pigeon."

"Good! I have the urge to confess my sins of omissions and remedy them. Want to aid in my enlightenment?"

"Oh. The Red Goose?"

"Yes. What say? Want a convert?"

"Always. About seven then?"

Once again the man I'd determined to keep at arm's length had made the perfect suggestion. Manhattan seldom fails to cheer me and tonight, the combination of cold air and cloudless sky would make the view of the New York skyline from above more than usually exciting. I warned him to dress warmly.

CHAPTER 15

SAM

You're wondering about my failure to show up at Sal's for dinner Monday night. Okay, so maybe my nose was a little out of joint! Hell, I'm only human. But I wasn't just playing hooky. I had legitimate work to do.

I'd never trusted the smooth-talking Fowler any farther than I can throw a freight train. For one thing, why was he still hanging around? The coroner's jury verdict was out so what excuse did he have? I didn't need a crystal ball to figure out a couple of good ones—the least damning of which was to sell us another insurance policy. Worse, it was himself he was selling. I figured I'd better hop to it before things between them got out of hand—if they hadn't already. Besides, it would do Sal good to miss me for once.

I'd hauled the president of my own insurance company out of bed that morning. He let out a snort when I invited him to lunch at his own club. My stated excuse—to discuss Tunnelson's sister's threat to sue—obviously could have been done by phone, but I had another purpose in mind.

We dispatched with the threatened lawsuit over the first drink so the path was clear to go to Plan B. I asked, casually, what he knew of a hotshot agent from Horizon.

"Ken Fowler you say? Hmmm. Nothing about him in particular, but Horizon has been making a name for itself lately." My host paused to light a cigar. "A small company, comparatively speaking, but solid. Used to confine itself pretty much to 'second' work. Then a couple of years ago they began to specialize in large policies for high risk clients and people otherwise hard to insure. It was a waiting market—folks who, either for health reasons or the dangers of their jobs, have trouble getting enough insurance and they've had commendable growth since. Last I read they'd a twelve share in that market nationwide. I know we've lost a couple to them."

"Pretty remarkable, isn't it? How're they doing it?"

"Follow basic rules for successful business really. Find a need and fill it. See, as you well know, most high-profile, high-risk clients—Tunnelson is a good example—are insured by their place of business. The policies cost a mint and, naturally, the company is also the beneficiary."

"Have to be. The company may be left holding the bag when the insured bites the dust and they have to replace him."

"Right. Also there could be a lot of things left dangling: unresolved lawsuits or contracts which might be cancelled if the point man dies. That's all well and good for the insured's employer, but it does not really take the families into consideration. Oh, the company may take out a policy for the family, but it's not nearly enough to replace the income they're used to."

"And Horizon?"

"Sells policies to this high-risk market with the family as beneficiary. Frankly, I'm surprised they haven't tapped you as yet."

"Don't be. So they go against the actuarial tables. Something like Lloyds?"

"In a way, yes."

"And you say their bottom line is looking good?"

"You bet," he puffed, filling the air with smoke. "Why do you ask?"

I said we'd been approached. While he smoked away, I digested this new information. I began to see why Fowler called his boss to Plainfield. If they were going to shell out big bucks for the claim he'd want support. Had the claim already been paid? Surely they didn't have to hold off until the murder was solved. Could it be the creep had a legit reason for hanging around after all?

What if it was never solved? A permanently unsolved murder might work in Fowler's favor, but it was certainly not good for the family. We were already beginning to see signs of tarnish on the Thaxton name. Damn! There was no way around it now. I'd have to really dig into Tunnelson's death and that meant solving the mystery of the damned pin-pricks.

I was trying to figure out how I could bring up the subject in a natural way when my friend gave me an opening.

"Your cousin Andy on this Mastermind thing?"

"Jeez, I don't know. Don't see him much," I lied.

"Like that, these big families. Spread out these days. Saw his mother's show the other night. Damned good! Hear she's up for a Tony."

"So I hear."

"Too bad this Tunnelson thing is being such a bother. They getting anywhere?"

I said I didn't know. I asked if he'd heard how Tunnelson died.

"Poison, not? In the neck?"

I said they'd found no traces of poison, at least not yet. "Just those two tiny pin-pricks. Odd way to bump a guy off, don't you think? Ever heard anything like it before? Any of your policy-holders maybe?"

My companion squinted into the winter sun. "None of mine, I don't think. I've a vague memory of such a death but I'm not sure how it's come to my attention. On the news maybe. Why do you ask?"

"Just that it seems to be at the heart of the thing. We'll need to know if Miss Tunnelson goes ahead with the suit. The guy from Horizon told my sister he'd heard of it before. I thought since you're in the same business..."

Dead in Pleasant Company
A Pennsylvania Dutch Mystery

"Hold on, I'll check." He produced a phone, dialed, explained, hung up. "Where will you be? I'll call you if I get something."

I told him I didn't know where I'd be and gave him a number. "That will find me wherever I am." I thanked him for breakfast and toddled off.

Things were getting hot and the was no time to waste. That meant staying in the city, which meant avoiding the Red Goose and the Thaxton Building on fifty-seventh, both of which would be staked out by the press.

I was sure the president of our New York bank would be at his desk, Monday or no. He's very much a 'hands-on' CEO—the reason we bank there.

He was. I had a chat with him, then borrowed an empty desk and used my lap-top to access university records. Next I stopped at my club, donned a gray wig, eyeglasses and a somewhat worn professorial looking jacket I keep in my locker. I hailed a cab and paid a visit to a couple of mid-level editors at the *Times* and the *Star*. Last but not least, I flew upstate to pick up my wife. We dined with her mother before heading for home.

Naturally, Rose insisted on calling Sal as soon as we hit the doorstep. They jabbered away for a while before hanging up.

"She says to say good night to you. She's off to bed. Wants to get an early start in the morning."

Snuggled up against her, I told her what I'd been up to. She was quiet for a moment then, "Sam. Have you ever considered this man could be good for Sal? You said she seems happy when he's around."

I told her a little of what I'd already learned. "I've got more stuff coming in tomorrow."

She said she saw. "All right then. Just make sure you're being fair. Sal will jump on you in a second if you aren't."

A fact I knew all too well. I promised I'd be careful and, with her delighted responses, went on to more interesting things.

* * * * *

Tuesday.
I dragged myself out of bed before the cock (early for Sal means early), pulled on wool pants, shirt, sweater and sheepskin, then, ready for whatever the day might bring, took the Merc down the back road between our homes.

You might have guessed. She was already at the computer, coffee and toast cooling off beside her. She'd apparently come up with some sort of search plan for as each new screen came up, she referred to notes and typed again. I squeezed her shoulder in greeting, then stayed put where I could see what she was up to.

She said merely for me to hang on. "I think I've got something! I'll know in a minute."

I watched as the FBI logo came up. She spent perhaps half a minute searching their website before sighing approval. To me the information appeared cryptic.

FILENAME: CRISS CROSS.
LEGEND. QVT1-QVT2-QVT3
STATUS: SECURITY CODE: IA999
NOTICE: THESE ARE OFFICIAL Federal Bureau of Investigation FILES
UNAUTHORIZED PERSONS MUST EXIT NOW!!
FAILURE TO DO SO MAY RESULT IN CHARGES OF TREASON.

She said "What?"

That screen cleared and another appeared. I told her to hold it. "Did that say *treason*? What the hell…!"

Dead in Pleasant Company
A Pennsylvania Dutch Mystery

To my astonishment, she typed again.

"I know! I know!" she said. "I'm a little surprised at me myself. I'm behaving badly, but I'm not just curious. I'm too darned worried."

The next screen followed:

WARNING!
SECURE FILES!!
ACCESS TO THESE FILES BY
UNAUTHORIZED PERSONS IS A FEDERAL CRIME!
PERPETRATORS ARE SUBJECT TO
LOSS OF BIOS FILES, FINES AND/OR IMPRISONMENT

LAST WARNING.
ENTER YOUR SECURITY CODE OR EXIT NOW!

Her eyes shot up at me. "Can you believe this? This all came up as a result of my search for Janus' family."

"Then the fact that you are merely ignoring a threat to be hung for treason is not that surprising. How did you..."

"I had help—a visiting policeman from LA named Rick Masters—one of their 'tech' support people. He was here yesterday with Bill Peters. I called him later. Very nice about it." She frowned at the screen as she talked, then hit the scroll button.

The next screen read:

FEDERAL BUREAU OF INVESTIGATION
Related files:
ICF; 400 320 303 740 555
ENTER YOUR VAC DATA NOW!

She uttered a rare "Damn!" Surely, I thought, she would have to quit now. Barring the right voice, there was no way around voice activated commands. I thought this a damned odd place to require them. Andy had mentioned the Feds used VAC to keep certain files out of the hands of an ever invasive media, but how did my sister's work enter into it? I told her to hold on and went to sit across from her where I could see her face. "Maybe you better tell me exactly how you got here. I know you said it had to do with the kid but…"

"I'm cross-referencing cases of scams involving young children," she said angrily.

"And you got into these secure files?"

"Yes."

I looked at the screen again. I pointed to the codes named. "Which codes are they? You know?"

"They're new. Most of them are not even in the code book as yet, but hanks to Rick Masters, I've got some of them. Wait." She flipped through her pad. "Here it is. Four hundred is Public Health and Safety. Three hundred twenty? Hmmm. Can't find that. Three hundred and three, that's an older one. Wait." She referred to a book. "No. I don't see it here. I wonder if…" She stared ahead, caught up in thought.

"And seven hundred and forty?"

She again referred to her pad. "What the…I don't believe it! That code's for crimes involving Internet Access!"

"What the hell! Internet access. What was the other? Oh yeah. Public health."

"And don't forget these came up in my search for scams involving children." We stared at the screen together in disconcerted silence. "Kiddie porn you suppose?"

"That fits," I said. "Can you think of anything else?"

She shook her head. "I can't imagine…" She stopped.

I looked at her face. "Andy?"

"Andy," she said.

CHAPTER 16

SAM

Sal's decision to break down and consult Cousin Andy was a break for me. I'd learned enough yesterday to confirm my suspicions that Sal had called more than one con artist 'guest' in the past few days. But that was me. I needed a lot more to convince my sister. I reasoned that since Fowler was the one who had mentioned hearing of other pin-prick deaths, chances were it was in connection with his job. Could be someone else there had knowledge of them as well. A friendly visit to the Washington offices of Horizon, just a hop and skip from the Pentagon, could furnish the last nails I needed.

Having called ahead for clearance, I dropped us neatly on helipad #5PWD atop the Pentagon. We'd been here often, mostly as quasi-official consultants or advocates of one cause or another but, not surprising to anyone familiar with that labyrinthine structure, never to the section in which Cousin Andy kept an office. I was more than curious to see it.

What Andy actually does for the government and for whom depends on which family member is doing the talking. According to Aunt Adelaide, her son had run a 'missions impossible' kind of covert operation for some years, had retired and returned here as a dollar-a-year consultant. All I know is that from time to time he'll turn up, all very casual and innocent as he had a couple of weeks ago, to 'suggest' something I might want to look into on the 'q.t.' He never says why or for whom it needs doing and I never ask.

Today it was to be a case of hurry-up-and-wait. A young agent in a dark suit came and said Mr. Andrew Thaxton had been delayed. Could we meet him at ten?

It was a perfect opporchancity and I grabbed it. "We've got nearly two hours," I said, aping disgust. "You got any...hey, I've got an idea. Horizon has offices here. What say we drop in. I'd like to..."

"Horizon? Horizon Insurance? Whatever for?"

"Well," I said, keeping it casual, "you said Ken said he'd heard of other pin-prick deaths but couldn't remember when or where. If it was connected with Horizon, which seems likely, they may have talked about it there and somebody else there would remember. Give us something to do while we wait for Andy." Good supporting argument, I thought. She hates to sit around and wait. "Unless," I added cunningly, "you'd rather go get something to eat."

She gave me the look I deserved. "Oh I doubt if it had anything to do with Horizon or he would have remembered. He only mentioned it in passing, you know."

"Yeah, I know. While you were skating, hand in hand, off into the clouds."

"What *is* your problem, Sam?"

"No problem," I said innocently. "We've got time to kill and I just figured you'd be hot to do something toward bringing an end to this thing. If you don't want to, just say so." We waited for an elevator in silence. When the door opened I tried to move the discussion along. "You know who Horizon's CEO is by chance?"

"Should I?"

"No. I just thought his name might have cropped up. You said he was with Ken when they found the pin-pricks, didn't you?"

"So I've been told."

"You and Ken didn't discuss it."

"No. Ken and I did not discuss it."

Dead in Pleasant Company
A Pennsylvania Dutch Mystery

Obviously, I thought kicking myself, they had more interesting things to discuss. "Well, it's no big deal. I admitted there's only an outside chance anybody there will know anything. Besides, I'm pretty sure their main offices are in New York so probably his boss won't even be here. Let's forget it," I said, making it sound reasonable. "Come on! We'll get some breakfast, check out this Chanterelle place everybody's talking about. Got to keep an eye on the competition. What say?"

"No Sam. It's a good idea. As you said, it's something to do while we wait."

"You wouldn't rather eat?"

"Of course I would rather eat!" Her voice took on a familiar tone, a blend of anger, fear and desperation. It meant only one thing.

"Uh-oh," I said, carefully not teasing. "How much?"

"Five pounds in the past ten days!"

I told her it didn't show and that it didn't matter anyway. She scowled at me. I hailed a cab and we headed for Horizon Inc. without further discussion.

Traffic was light for a change and we got a driver who actually admitted knowing the way, so before long we were being ushered into a large, cheery corner office, splattered with some half-dozen photos of wife and kiddies.

Luck was with us. Roland Finch professed himself glad to meet 'the famous Thaxton twins,' regretted having missed us when he was in Plainfield and asked how he could help.

"We're in town on other business and I got the cockeyed idea you might help us with our little mystery. It's a long shot I know, so if we're dragging you from something important say so and we'll go quietly."

He said no, adding it was too bad about 'that reporter fella's death. "But if it's hands-on you're wanting, you'll want to talk to our man in the field. He'll be on top of everything. On top of everything."

"Yes. Ken Fowler," I said agreeably. "Yes. Yes, we've met him. In fact my sister is quite taken with him," I added, moving imperceptibly out of target range.

"First of all, let me assure you Ken Fowler is not *my* man, Mr. Thaxton. Oh no! Definitely not! He's his own man. Definitely his own man," he repeated again, putting me in mind of Rain Man.

I jumped on what I saw as implied criticism. "Difficult to work with, is he?"

"Good heavens no! Nicest fella imaginable! Nicest fella. Like a son to me. Why the man has almost single-handedly saved this company! Fact is, he's been a god-send to Horizon. God-send."

"Your best investigator then, would you say?"

"More than that. Come through in the Marketing department too. Developed a whole new market for us. Sales too. Knows quite a few people in the high-income, high-risk market personally, what with his background...excuse me. Yes?" This last in response to the buzz of the phone at his desk.

"Oh yes. All right. No, tell her I've not forgotten. What shall I get?" He scribbled a few notes on a pad at his desk. "Cake at the baker. Candles. Pink. Okay. Got it. Yes, I'll be home on time." He hung up. "Sorry. Daughter's sixteenth birthday. Wife all a-flutter. Needs a few last minute...Well Mr. Thaxton, you sound like you have a complaint about Mr. Fowler."

Yeah, I thought. Tell him to buzz off. "No sir,' I said, "Not at all. We just wondered if we could tap your memory. You probably are aware that Judd Tunnelson's death has us quite worried, in particular the method by which he died."

He nodded. "Poison, not so? It's not really that unus..."

"Oh? You think he was poisoned?"

"Well, yes. What else could it be? Poison. Yes. Somebody injected him with something, probably while standing behind him, leaning over him probably."

Like a waiter, I thought. Or a host. "Trouble is sir, there doesn't seem to be any evidence of poison in his body. Forensics is completely mystified at this point."

"Oh? Missed it I guess. Small town coroners aren't always up on such things. They will find it in time. In time. It's not as though it's never been done before."

It was a perfect place to jump in, but I did not want to alarm him. I played it cool. "Oh yes. I remember. Sal, didn't Mr. Fowler tell you the same thing?"

She glared at me. "He said he'd heard of murder done this way before, but couldn't recall any specific case."

"That's right! That's right! Is it possible you remember something more Mr. Finch?"

"For the police, isn't it? Forensics? Got some kinda database that has all that sort of thing on it now. They'll tell you about other similar cases. Piece of cake."

I nodded. "Oh yes. The Victim Identification and Classification Profile. Naturally PPD's checked that. Trouble is, VICAP has to rely on local police to input the data and they don't always do that. I mean," I said to his look of apprehension, "pin-pricks by themselves are not going to kill anybody. We just thought, that is, I thought…"

"Surely a man with your connections doesn't have to come to me for that. Surely somebody…"

I shook my head. "No sir. So far we're drawing a blank on this. That's why we came to you. We need a place to start. If you could remember the situation in which you heard of the prior pin-prick deaths it would help. Naturally, we'll keep anything you tell us to ourselves and I hope we can expect the same from you."

"Of course! Of course," clearly irritated now. "I'm not a blabber! Not a blabber."

"Naturally not! Naturally not!" I seemed to be catching whatever he had. I labored on. "Sorry, sir. We just thought, that is to say," my twin's eyes were burning a hole in my back, "I thought that perhaps, since both you and Mr. Fowler heard of this method before, maybe it was, say, discussed at a staff meeting for instance or perhaps your company had another claim…"

"Really, Mr. Thaxton! I don't know what you're implying but if you think we're holding something back from the police…"

"No sir! Not at all! That was the furthest thing from my mind!" I grabbed a handful of sugar. "Your company has an unparalleled reputation for integrity." I kicked myself for bungling things and searched for a way out. My eyes fell on a framed photo of a smiling family. "It's just that, unless the real culprit is found, our family stands to be implicated by default. Think of it! My sister and I can take it, we're tough, but my sister's two boys and sixteen year-old daughter could have this follow them all their lives!" A quick mental inventory of the photos in the room. I recalled one of Finch in Air Force officer's regalia. "And Joe, her eldest boy's in the Air Force you know. I imagine it could follow him there! So you see, I'm just trying to help, looking in every possible corner. The family relies on me you see. You know what that's like." I gave him what I hoped was a meaningful man-to-man look.

That helped. He looked somewhat mollified. "Just what is it you want from me, Mr. Thaxton?"

"As I said, Mr. Finch, I was hoping you or someone on your staff just might remember something about these other pin-prick deaths." I looked for a go ahead sign and got a shake of the head.

"I'm sorry Mr. Thaxton. I have a vague memory of a similar death, but that's about all. It seems to me…no, I won't speculate. Is that it?"

"Well sir, if you can't remember, you can't. I wonder sir, if it would be possible if we, that is I, could have a look at your claim records. There might be a mention of it somewhere. I would be enormously grateful."

"Claim records?"

It was hard to say which of the two was more surprised. Hell, I surprised myself! How far would I go to show the guy up?

"Yes sir. If we'd not be in your way. As I say, I'm concerned that unless the person responsible for Mr. Tunnelson's death is found, our family and our business as well could be unfairly touched with the brush of suspicion. I can't afford to leave any stone, however small, unturned." Sal was rising, preparing to leave. "Being a business man, I'm sure you understand that."

He rose too. "I understand all right! What I understand is, it's time for you to get the hell out of here! Hell out! Find some other rock to look under." He bowed to Sal, impatient to be gone. "You seem sensible enough. Take your brother home. My secretary will show you out."

He stalked out, cutting a wide path to avoid any contact with us, papers falling from his desk in his wake. Sal picked them up, stacking them neatly before returning them to his desk. Then she picked up one of them.

"Look, he's forgotten his list."

I was more than surprised to see her reading it. I got sarcastic. "Something interesting?"

"Oh." Her cheeks flushed. "I...I'll just give this to his secretary. Maybe she can get it to him."

I hustled out, waiting for her at the elevator. I'd intended to bring Fowler down in my sister's eyes, but it was me at whom she glowered. This was, I reflected, another fine mess I'd gotten myself into.

* * * * *

Andy's reference to his office as a 'hole' did not prepare us for the large, sunny, corner suite on the top floor, to which a young FBI-clone in a dark suit ushered us. The room was furnished sparsely but with pieces of the best quality. Other than a couple of largish paintings hung where they could be seen by the man at the desk, there were no photos, no awards, no talismans pointing to world travel, yet, get him in conversation and you'd soon learn there wasn't a corner of the world with which he did not have first hand knowledge.

He rose from behind a nameplate-less desk with the easy grace of a man whose body has been tested and found lacking nothing: tall, silver-haired, handsome, Thaxton blood at its best. At six-foot three he has me beat by two inches, but towers over Sal. Although his body looked lean and tough as always, I thought his face seemed sharper somehow, with worry lines firmly entrenched. His eyes, the same clear grey as my sister's, lit up at the sight of us and he threw us the same quick smile, so puzzling in its sweetness, he shares with Sal.

He gripped my hand but hugged my sister, one of the few, besides me, who get that privilege. Hell, I've known since we were all kids together how he feels about her and it's only their cousinship that keeps him away. I suppose by this time you're thinking I'm prejudiced where my twin is concerned. You may even go so far as to suggest I'm projecting when I tell you how men fall for her, but it's just plain fact. She neither flirts nor teases, nor does she, as far as I can see, treat them in anyway special, yet around her men seem to feel it is good to be male. She won't believe me when I tell her a sizable lot of guys, young and old, look at her as if she were a chocolate fudge sundae and I've made it a point not to tell her Cousin Andy is one of them. As I say, she wouldn't believe me anyway and it would just force her to keep her distance from one of the few people she genuinely likes.

A little flushed from the hug, Sal sat as suggested and looked around. "Perhaps," she said smiling, "you need to look up the definition of 'hole."

He had no trouble picking up the reference, ancient as it was. That quick intelligence too, he shares with Sal.

He laughed. "Just didn't want to get you taxpayers in a tizzy. Actually," he included me in his smile briefly, "with all the personnel cutbacks, we have more offices like this available than 'holes.' I guess they decided to treat the old man to one of them." He smiled at us again. "I'm delighted to see you both," he said, carefully including me. "Sorry I missed Groundhog's Day this year. Did you see me Mum there?"

Sal shook her head. "I didn't. Ray drove her down for the lunch crowd then right back to New York for the eight o'clock curtain. I was on duty so I missed her, but I'm told she wowed all as usual. They appreciate that she doesn't forget her roots."

"Yes, yes," another smile darted out and back. "Mustn't forget the little people. Dines out on it for weeks, I'm sure. Gave me an earful though when I didn't show. Well," he said, brushing both mother and Groundhog's Day aside, "you've made yourself rather popular around here— bumping off our nation's chief pain-in-the-rump. How'd you do it? Arsenic in the shoo-fly pie? My boss said to ask." He laughed.

I told him it warn't funny. "Thur's them as would like to put it on us."

"You're not serious?"

"I am."

"I've heard things of course. You're saying there's something to them then? I figured if it was true you'd get in touch with me. So it's not just media hype?"

I shrugged. "Unfortunately, in this case, the media has plenty to 'hype' about."

"Meaning?"

"Meaning the deceased met his Maker in one of our stores, and was our dinner guest that night, yet both of us were away from the table at the crucial moment—a fact which seems to have piqued the imagination of more than one idiot. At the moment, however, one completely groundless guess which has grown from theory to possibility to probability, is that he was there to write the long-awaited exposé of the Thaxtons." I muttered under my breath. "One of these days the Thaxtons will have to do something awful just to make ourselves believable."

Sal threw me an undecipherable look. "You must admit though, Sam, there is a genuine mystery there."

"There is? Oh. You mean the how of the thing. Yes, that is strange." I looked at Andy. "What do you know of this peculiar method of killing someone? It's new to us."

"Two pin-pricks at the base of the hairline?" He shook his head. "There has been nothing in our pipe-line here. If it was two bullet holes now, we'd know where to look, but pin-pricks? VICAP should have something."

"Doesn't though. Sal's checked that herself."

Andy looked from one to the other. "What is the official line?"

I shook my head. "Officially they're mystified. They're waiting on blood and tissue samples sent to Atlanta."

Andy frowned. "Be interesting to hear what they say. I'll see what I can find on this end. What's the unofficial version?"

I brushed at the crease in my trousers. "Ya puts down yer money an' ya takes yer choice. Tunnelson's sister is busily suggesting a variety of motives, all attributable to us and/or the restaurant. She's suing us. Then there's our chef, Barney Schantz. You remember that situation. Anyway,

Schantz has put himself and us in it by disappearing, apparently taking Walt with him. There's an APB out for both of them."

"For Walt too?" He looked at Sal. "You should have called…"

Sal said it was for his own protection. "According to Warmkessel anyway." To Andy's questioning look she added, "Walt and Barney have become very friendly lately."

I went on. "Officially they're keeping Walt's possible involvement quiet for now but when it gets out, they may not be able to. Then too, Sal's position on the force makes the word 'cover-up' inevitable. Add fuel to the ever present suggestion that the cops are playing favorites because we're Thaxtons."

"Not too much we can do about that," he said. "It's one of those when-did-you-stop-beating-your-wife things. Why are they looking for your chef? After all, that was all in the forgotten past."

"Not any more," I said. "I'm afraid Barney himself resurrected it by shooting off his mouth when he learned Tunnelson was in the restaurant that night. Said something that could be taken as threatening."

"Not very smart of him," Andy said mildly. "I hope that's all."

"Not quite." I grimaced. "We're wondering if perhaps Tunnelson and we have a mutual enemy, someone who decided to kill two birds with one stone by killing him in our store."

He swept us again with a quick glance. "Cedar River Gambling for instance."

I nodded. "For one, yes."

"I don't imagine," he grunted, "there is any dearth of others who are just as glad Tunnelson's no longer around. Is the PPD looking into that possibilty? I don't think they've called on us for help or I would've heard. Somebody ought to…"

Sal said, "What Uncle Reuben thinks too. In the meanwhile, we've been working on it ourselves. At least Sam has. He's had a look at the network records of people who've had it in for Tunnelson over the past few years. It's an incredible list! I'm surprised Tunnelson got around without a bodyguard!" Andy nodded, said he knew. "We have, of course, our fair share of people who don't think much of us. I seem to tick people off in particular."

Andy grinned. "Old man Longnecker being a problem again? According to me Mum, he's had it in for the Thaxtons since H.H. bought the Longnecker farm when they went bankrupt."

"Good heavens! That's ancient history! Besides, Grandfather let them stay there and keep their home and all their crops. He kept them from being homeless!"

Andy nodded. "I suspect they've put their own spin on the story. That's Mum's theory anyway. Jealousy, that's what it is," Andy smiled at her. "That's nothing new for you. You're just too good at too many things. If I didn't like you so much I'd find you a pain-in-the-neck myself." The smile stretched to a grin. "In any case, I'm assuming you think I can help. What do you want me to do?"

"About Tunnelson, nothing. At least not now. Actually we were just telling you how things are at home. We're here, that is Sal is, on something else entirely."

My sister took the cue and got down to business, reporting in her crisp and thorough way how the abandoned child came to her attention and the frustrating search for the child's family. "It's curious enough that I can find no reference to her in any of the usual data-bases. As a last resort, I accessed FBI files on scams and finally seemed to be getting somewhere when darned if I didn't get shut out just when it looked hopeful…"

Dead in Pleasant Company
A Pennsylvania Dutch Mystery

Andy studied her face. "You must be pretty good to have accessed that particular section. I won't ask how you did it. Yes, I'm familiar with it. To say it's top secret is putting it mildly."

Sal kept her eyes on him and waited. He got up to close the door, pushed a button on his desk and came to face her, sitting on the edge of his desk (another habit shared with Sal). "Look, it's no mystery really. Both of you know what a problem we've had with security on the Internet. I emphasize what I'm going to tell you now is, literally, just between us." He gave us a second to underscore the point, then went on, his eyes on Sal's. "The code, ICN900, stands for International Crime Network. It's assigned only rarely and then to cases in which there are multiple investigations being run simultaneously across borders, either state or international. You can imagine what that's like: multiple teams, each with a support staff, each having access to the intimate details of an investigation. Add access to the 'Net from every Tom, Dick and Harry from any remote outpost in the globe and leaks are inevitable. Not only is it possible that a criminal knows as much about his case as we, but it encourages 'copycats.' Hell, it's an open invitation to folks with an ax to grind, to say nothing of would-be Woodward and Bernsteins. In cases where rewards are offered you can add to that 'hackers' eager to help finger the guilty. Unfortunately, bad guys know how to use the 'Net too. Any one of these can really throw a monkey wrench in an investigation. So now we're playing hard ball. To begin with we've gone back to using voice activation to access the system, adding a couple of new wrinkles, one of which would have given you seven seconds to exit the program. Failing that, your hard drive would have crashed and your BIOS files erased without which, as you no doubt know, you would not be able to even turn your computer on." He flicked a glance at me and went back to her. "We've tried to keep quiet about it of course. No sense telling John Q. not to put the beans up his nose, eh?"

"I see," Sal said, thinking. "Which is why local police have not been alerted."

"Yes. It's always a tough decision who should know what." He shifted his weight and bent closer to her. "We've learned some hard lessons lately about whom to trust. In addition to all the possible invaders outside the investigation, there's always the possibility of another Nicholson or Hanson right among us. Do a lot of damage. What we've done is to limit access to just three people, world-wide, in each case. It's only in a trial period right now and we'll have to see how..."

But he had lost Sal. She sat, staring into the space above his head, oblivious to all around her. I love to see her like that. It meant she had hold of something big.

For the next few moments I engaged Andy in chit-chat, giving her time to work it out. Then her eyes dropped, she drew in a breath and I knew she was done. She rose abruptly and offered Andy her hand.

"Andy, it's been fun to see you again! Sorry if we got into something we shouldn't. Come on Sambo. Let's let the man get back to work."

"Just a minute! I want to know more about your young friend."

"Of course. I'll call you," she said.

I followed my departing sister, nearly colliding with her when she stopped at the door and turned. "Thanks again Andy. I'm glad you're working on it. I'm confident if anybody can stop him it's you." She looked at him. "I assume the child was used as a decoy?" She nodded at his expression. "I know. You can't tell me. Okay. Thanks Andy. Let's go Sammy me boy."

"Sal! Wait! If you've any information at all..."

"Don't worry cousin. You shall be the first, well, the second, to know." She tossed him a salute and turned to go.

His voice followed through the closing door. "For God's sake, Sal! Keep out…"

We fled.

* * * * *

The trip home was eerily quiet. My sister had that closed-in expression which made conversation futile. She'd even foregone our usual you-fly-one-way-I-fly-the-other rule. I dropped her off at home, gassed up and took off once more. I, too, had a lot to do.

CHAPTER 17

SAL

The flap, flap, flap of 'copter blades provided a screen of noise against which my brain seemed free to bring order to chaos. There was nothing nebulous now about the signals emanating from my personal early warning system. What was fact? What was logical? What was possible? And above all, to what conclusion had my damned toes jumped?

I've always 'read' cousin Andy well and was certain I'd done so again. For the Pennsylvania Dutch euphemism, 'helping out,' read he was in the Mastermind case up to his silver eyebrows—most likely Washington's point man and he had, unwittingly, given me the answer I wanted.

I no longer resented getting shut out of the FBI files. There were, I now conceded, plenty of good reasons to limit access to them. More than one criminal had eluded capture recently, thanks to premature leaks to the press. And there was one further inference to be drawn. Unbelievable as it all was, in the most shocking and terrifying of home-grown terrorist crimes ever—a child was involved—alarming enough, but add Andy's reaction to something I said about my charge and it was at least possible the child's description fit Janus. It was the only reasonable conclusion to draw and my toes had gotten there ahead of me.

But what had I said?

Had I remained a moment longer, Andy would have had to warn me to keep out of it and that was out of the question, but neither could I blithely ignore him as I might have a few years ago. Now his order would be, not from cousin to cousin, but from one law officer to another, so a direct request for clarification was out and I was left to work out on my own what, if any, connection existed between Mastermind, the Internet terrorist and Janus Morgan Alexander.

I dug out my small notebook and forced myself to set down in chronological order what I knew of the exploits of Mastermind. I worked steadily on, ignoring the pleas to be 'let in on it' I was getting from my brother. As soon as we touched down at my place, I waved at Sam, told him 'later' and hurried home. The chronology had been very helpful and, based on it, I'd quite a list of questions to be put to the child, the answers to which could confirm or obviate her involvement.

* * * * *

The black car in my drive was nothing special to look at but it gave me a jolt. I swore under my breath. I should have anticipated it. I was not the only Thaxton who knew how to put two and two together and, if my guess was solid, every moment counted.

Andy rose from the depths of a chair. At the sight of me, his companion turned and scooted from the room, mumbling something about having to help with the horses. He made no move to stop her, nor did he show any signs of the urgency he must be feeling. Had I been wrong?

"I've been chatting with your friend," he said innocently. "Quite a delightful package to be left at a bus station."

It was as if he'd come to tea: no annoyance at my abrupt exit from his office, no effort to regain the upper hand. I was not surprised. He was a gentleman and no erratic behavior on my part would change his.

I tried to respond in kind. "Yes she is. I assume your presence here means I have guessed correctly, that a child is involved with Mastermind and my charge may fit the description of the child."

He grinned again, much as he does when we play chess. "I may or may not respond to that, but first I need a full report."

It was a request from one professional to another. "Yes sir. I suppose you want everything."

"If you don't mind."

I told it again, succinctly, but leaving nothing out: how Janus Morgan Alexander had come into our hands, what I'd learned of the couple with whom she'd been permitted to stay and the 'game' she'd been taught to play. When I told him of our initial belief she was a boy, his eyes flickered.

"And this 'fainting' game made you connect her with Mastermind?"

"Not directly. It just seemed to indicate she'd been part of a scam. It's just a hunch really."

"A hunch?"

"Well, perhaps more reason actually. The only reasonable reason," I said redundantly, "for the phony fainting is misdirection—to draw someone's attention away from something or someone else. That she is taught to do it before someone in uniform points to something criminal. It was being shut out of FBI files to which I would normally have access that got me thinking." I looked at him. "I take it you're on the case?"

He smiled again. "I help out when I can. I'm just the Pentagon's general dog's body you know. Odd jobs and all that."

I pleaded foul, reminded him I'd come clean with him.

"Okay Sal. I forgot you know how to keep your mouth shut. Our professional interests may, and I stress may, cross here. Yes, I'm on it as of the last couple of weeks. Now back to you. You've told me the facts about how she came into your hands, now tell me about her."

"Well," I hesitated, sorting through all I had gathered or guessed over the past days, "about all I actually *know* about her is her name, which" the thought struck me, "she *says* is Janus Morgan Alexander. She's a very imaginative child."

"Meaning she makes things up?"

I nodded. "For instance, she claims to be six years old but I believe she's more like between half-past four and five. She had all the bus people convinced she was mute, possibly retarded. Obviously she's not but it may mean something to your investigation that people thought so. It may be part of the act she's been taught. In addition, she's bright enough to tell us her parents names and address, but either she can't or won't. She does not seem in any hurry to go home."

"If she's living with you, I can see why. Incidentally, why is that? I thought your experience with the Rotters had cured you of taking in strays."

I flinched. In more innocent times my home, much to the dismay of Sam and the rest of the family, had always been open to anyone needing shelter. When the Rotters, parents of one of Joe's friends, lost their home in the turbulent '80's, I'd offered them the use of my gate-house until they found something. They stayed for months, living, as it turned out, off the family treasures they'd lifted from it. I'd been forced to throw them out when Honeycutt caught them looting the house. They'd gone, taking Joe's new truck with them. The episode had become a great source of family amusement.

I explained the joint circumstances of flu epidemic and weather. "She's just here until the county can go ahead with foster placements."

"I see," he said, looking around. "Where is she now? Can we get her back again?"

I wanted to say no and wondered why the urge to shield her from this very fine man. "Because he's with the FBI," I told myself. I told myself to lighten up. I rang for Honeycutt.

"Can you find our guest and bring her here?"

"Yes, Madam. She's with the horses."

Andy told me to go on.

"That's all there is. What else do you want?"

He gave me a look. "Don't dawdle Amaryllis."

I sighed. "Anything else I can tell you is pure guesswork. That what you want?" He nodded again. "All right then. She speaks of two sets of 'theys', from which I deduce she's spent some considerable time in at least two different homes. One, it seems logical to assume, being her family and the other the couple with whom she was left. It's difficult to say which experience is the more odd."

He nodded me forward. "Explain."

"Well, she says she's one of a rather large family, one which may have been more than her mother could handle—her eagerness to get the child in school, her apparent willingness to permit Janus to go off with someone else."

"You think the mother just let her go? She wasn't kidnapped for instance? Didn't run away?"

I shook my head. "No. Otherwise…"

"Of course. She would have been reported missing. Okay. Go on."

"It is somewhat curious that she's not been to school. She says she was too young, but preschool programs of one kind or another, even for infants, are pretty widely available these days."

"They're not always free though. Perhaps they were too poor."

"Good heavens! There are 'Headstart' type programs available for low-income families just about everywhere." I frowned. "It could be their family finances fall somewhere in between—too much money to be eligible for public program and not enough for private. It is also possible," I said reflectively, "they don't believe in preschool education."

"Doesn't everybody?"

"No," I said, still thinking. "Also, most schools require parents be actively involved in the school program, particularly at the preschool level. Her parents could object to that."

"Yes. Especially if they did not want any interest shown them. That would fit with their reluctance to report her disappearance. Good. Anything else?"

"I can think of one circumstance under which her parents may not know she's missing."

"That being?"

"Well," I imagined a scenario, "suppose they let her go stay with this couple—I'm assuming one of them is either family or otherwise known to them—and the child got lost. It could be they are not telling the parents the child's gone missing."

"You say parents. What makes you think she has both? You told me earlier she has a habit of referring to all males as 'Daddy.' Doesn't that indicate a certain transience in that position?"

"Ye-es," I said. "But somehow...I don't know. It's difficult you know. One can't tell how much, if anything, she says is true."

"I see. Anything else?"

"Let me think. I'm really tired..."

"What of this other life?"

"Oh, yes. Her other life. What I can't help but think of as her 'professional' one in which she plays this 'game,' staggers around and faints when she sees someone in uniform and gets 'paid' for it in the form of presents."

"Which, as you said, is what led you to the secure files. I see. So easy when you know how." He smiled fondly at me. "And you think she's at least four years old. Closer to five?"

"I do. Size-wise she's more like a four-year-old but her pattern of thinking puts her older."

Honeycutt appeared, the subject of discussion in tow. Clearly the delay was due to a visit to Mrs. Honey for cleaning up. She was scowling again.

"Janus, this is Mr. Jacobs, my cousin," I explained. "He's come to help us find your family."

The scowl deepened. "I was busy," she said firmly. "Benjam's lettin' me comb Rhubarb."

"Oh? Well, that's good then, isn't it? Look Janus, Mr. Jacobs may be able to help find..."

"I *told* you I don't want to go home!"

I did not look at Andy. I got tough. "That may well be, young lady, but the law requires us to find your parents. When..."

"Then it's a dumb law."

"Possibly, but, as I was saying, when we find them, we can discuss whether or not you should return to them."

"You can ussuss all you want," her nose pointed upward, "but if you send me back, I'll just run away again."

Andy leapt in. "Oh, so you ran away? That was clever of you. You know," he bent closer to her, his tone conspiratorial, "I tried to run away once when I was your age, but they caught me right away. How did you do it? You must be awfully smart!"

It was a perfect tactic, one I should have thought of. I had only a moment to wonder at the effect this child was having on me.

"I didn't run away *that* time," she said, unabashed, "but now I know how so I can!"

"Why don't you tell Mr. Jacobs how you got on the bus? That was pretty clever I thought."

"Oh that! That was nothing," she said, disdain dripping from the tiny face.

Andy conveyed astonishment. "Really? Well, I must say I'm impressed! I'm sure *I* couldn't have done it. Got on a bus all by yourself?"

"Well of course, Dummy. It was standing right there near the train!"

He looked at me. "Oh yes, Mr. Jacobs. I forgot. I told you I was tired and it all seems so...Anyway, Janus had quite a wonderful ride on a train as well, didn't you?" She looked at me suspiciously. "And there were a lot of other children on the train too, weren't there? Tell Mr. Jacobs about them."

"Oh them," she cast them aside. "They were just a bunch of babies. Had to have their mothers with them." She seemed to be reflecting on the experience. "Had good lunches, though."

"Oh?" Andy said. "Did they share them with you?"

"Sure. A'course." She paused, apparently thinking back, adding with arare bit of honest, "Well, sort of. When the man came around with the lunches he just gimme one." A cunning look replaced the reflective one. "Thought I was with them, I guess."

"Lucky that was an eating day," I said, trying not to sound petty.

The child gave me the look I deserved. Really, I thought, what is with you? I felt obliged to address Andy's questioning eyebrows. "Miss Alexander only eats every other day."

Andy's ears picked up. "What's that?"

"Sorry. I forgot that too. Miss Morgan is only allowed to eat every other day. It seems she doesn't want to get fat."

Andy almost choked. "Oh?" Then recovering, "My goodness! That's a new one on me. We all eat every day and *we're* not fat."

"*You're* not," she said pointedly.

My cousin leapt again, this time to my defense. "Neither is Dr. McKnight. She's beautiful. And besides, even if a person is fat, that doesn't mean that they're not perfectly wonderful people."

"They don't *look* wonnerful," she said crossly.

My cousin has always known when to concede a point. "Well then, Miss Alexander, tell me about your train ride. Where did it begin?"

"Where I got on," she said reasonably. "At the train station." She turned the look on me. "Boy, is he stupid!"

"No. He's really quite smart, you know. There are a lot of different train stations and he wants to know which one you were in. Do you know? Did the station have a name?"

I had put my foot in it again. "How would I know," she asked, throwing up her hands. "What d'you 'spect? I *tol'* you I can't read! I'm just learning."

"You're learning to read? That's great." Andy applied grease to the wheels. "You look awfully young to be learning to read though. How old are you?"

"Seven," she said promptly.

I bit. "Seven? You told me you were six."

"That was when I came here," she explained impatiently. "I got older since then."

"God knows *I* have," I couldn't help saying.

A grin escaped Andy and was immediately retrieved. "I see," he said to her. "I guess you go to school then."

"A'course not! I ain't goin' to school anyway. Ever."

I didn't bite at that, trying to stick to the business at hand. "Tell Mr. Jacobs about the game you play. The falling down game, I mean."

"Okay," she said with alacrity. "Want me to show him?"

I pretended indifference. "If you'd like."

She did so, swaggering about a bit before falling to the floor. Andy's face was a mask. I said, "She's good, isn't she Mr. Jacobs? Her friend Raymond taught it to her."

I thought Andy had stopped breathing. "Raymond?" He looked at her closely. "Raymond..." He looked at me then, his expression demanding details. I tried to help.

"Yes. Raymond and Donna. The couple with whom she's been staying. They tell Miss Alexander when and where to play the game. Then when she's done it, they have a party."

"Don't forget the presents," she said, now coming to me to put her hand confidently in mine.

"Right. She gets a present each time she plays it. Isn't that nice?"

"Oh yes. Very nice. Very nice indeed," he said from a distance. "Yes, you are certainly a lucky girl. Miss Alexander," he returned to us. "Now this is a very hard question and I'm not sure you're old enough to answer it. What do you think, Dr. McKnight? You know her pretty well."

"I don't know," I said doubtfully. "She forgets a lot of things."

"I don't either forget! Aks and you'll see."

"Okay. Okay. Now, how many times did you play the game.?"

She leaned closer to me, hoping, I thought, to get a clue as to how she might answer. "I told you! Ever time I got a present."

I said, "Tell Mr. Jacobs about the presents you got."

"Oh, sure," she said, confidence returning. "Let's see." She ticked off on her fingers the gifts she'd described earlier, but her interest seemed to be waning fast.

"Three then." Andy nodded as if she'd given the right answer. "Three times you played the game."

"Oh and a bed for my Barbie."

"Four," I said, looking at him.

"Where?"

The question was to me. I felt certain we'd reached her limit but sought for one more prise. "Did you always play the game at the same place?"

"A'course not," she said.

Andy pressed it. "In different cities then?"

Too abstract, I thought. I said, "Did you live in different houses when you got the presents?"

"No, Silly."

Energized by this new information, I decided to try for one more bit of information. "Janus, let's talk about the places where you played this game. Did it take a long time to get there? Did you go by car or did you go on a plane or a train or perhaps…?"

But we had lost her completely. As she had before, she just came to a full stop. "I'm hungry," she told me.

I resisted reminding her this was not an eating day. Or at least it hadn't been this morning. I rang for Honeycutt and turned her over.

CHAPTER 18

The child swept out like the tide, leaving an awkward silence between us. When it came, Andy's voice held a tone I'd not heard before.

"Sal, I want to take her with me."

"Why?" It was a transparent stall.

"Look Sal, I'm going to put you in the 'need to know' category, but it's absolutely got to stay with you. Okay? I mean, I know you'll tell Sam, but the two of you have got to keep this wrapped." He studied my face a moment, then went on. "Here's what we've learned to date about Mastermind." His voice dropped and I had to lean closer to hear. "As you may have heard, our first real break came when we got hospitals to keep their access code off-line on a disk. It meant anyone wishing to tamper with their system would have to get hold of the disk—meaning Mastermind would have to choose between maintaining the anonymity the Internet accorded him, in which case he'd have to quit, or come out of hiding and we'd have a shot at him."

"Yes. The idea of a bookkeeper in Janesville, wasn't it?"

He nodded. "It increased the chances that the other systems we had in place would produce something. We'd already had all medical facilities add video cameras in the areas we considered most vulnerable: entries, elevators and their main computer room for example."

"I know. Our hospital got the directives as well." I studied his face. His eyes fairly glittered with excitement. "So did that help?"

"To a fair-thee-well. As soon as the Janesville people called us, we set up a review of their videotapes and spent hours with hospital staff identifying the people on the tapes and eventually put it together." He looked at me. "Sal this won't be easy for you."

"Come on 'Cuz'. Now who's stalling. How…"

"How did the 'criminal of the century' get by with his crimes? You said it yourself earlier. Misdirection," he said angrily. "The oldest weapon in a criminal's arsenal. It was a cunning and carefully designed scenario. It went like this."

The tale he told was awesome in its simplicity.

"Just as shift changes at eleven p.m., an unfamiliar doctor appears at the receptionist's desk, identifying himself as Dr. Milliken. He says he is substituting for one of their staff physicians, a Dr. Singh, now on vacation in India—which, incidentally, he was. None of this is surprising, as it is a common practice. For the first two nights he asks for the list of Dr. Singh's patients, and makes the rounds with the head nurse along.

"The third night he insists on going on his own, claiming none of the patients is critical and the nursing staff is already overworked; both of which are true.

"He chats for a moment with a receptionist as she prepares to go off duty, then heads to the elevator. At the same time, a woman and a small child come running in the Emergency entrance, the woman, on the verge of hysterics, claiming she's been ordered to bring the child to the boy's mother on the sixth floor without delay. The doctor offers to see they get there safely. The shift is changing and they are glad for the help.

"They ride up together. At the sixth floor, the elevator doors open, revealing a guard in uniform on duty. The child staggers and falls." He threw a confirming look at me. "All three rush to help. The doctor orders the guard to go for a gurney for the child. As soon as the guard is out of sight, man, woman and child all step calmly back into the elevator, continuing on to the seventh floor, where Patients Records are kept. There the 'doctor' proceeds without obvious haste to a computer, locates the access disk, which, oddly enough, is in a box labeled *Keep Out*, inserts the hospital disk, removes another from his pocket, inserts his own, taps a few words replacing the original disk in its place, returns to the elevator and pushes the button for the main floor, with the woman and child in tow.

"Less than three minutes for the whole thing! He looked at me again before going on. At the main floor, he waves to the now replaced receptionist, calling out to her he will see to it that the child gets safely home." Andy stopped.

I was speechless. Had I heard this tale from anyone but Andy, I would have dismissed the whole thing as impossible.

"...no excuse," I heard him mutter.

"You're quite sure this 'doctor' is Mastermind?"

"We weren't at the time, of course. It was several days later we got called because there were the two otherwise unexplainable deaths there. When we checked with Dr. Singh, for whom he claimed to be filling in, we learned Singh had made no such arrangements. Then we ran the name he gave through the AMA Register, along with every other database of medical practitioners and came up blank. No. There's no question."

"But we at least know what he looks like."

He shook his head. "Unfortunately, he was ready for us there too. A slight limp, a goatee, eye glasses. loose fitting clothes left little to see." He got up to pace. "Only thing that's gone right so far is we've manage to keep it all quiet.

"A miracle in itself, isn't it, what with all those who know about it? How..."

"Naturally no one at the hospital wants the story to get out. They've threatened to fire anyone who talks. Nevertheless, we're keeping a close eye on all the involved staff in case they are tempted to run to the press with it."

"Oh? Surveillance? Phone-taps?"

He nodded grimly. "Something like that."

"I see." I considered the can of worms that could lead to if…when it got out.

"I know," he said, not for the first time reading my mind. "We'd have a time doing it if it weren't for the 9-11 Terrorist Act." He stopped to face me, his face bearing an expression I never thought I'd see there. Behind the determination, anger and urgency, lay fear. In all the years I've known him, I'd never seen him frightened and I, too, was suddenly afraid.

"And all for…what, revenge, I imagine. There's no profit in this, is there?"

"Not unless he's in the insurance business," he said dryly. "Sales of medical and life insurance are up seventy-two per cent nationwide." Like for Horizon, I thought. And Ken.

"Anyway, it could all blow up in our faces any minute, which accounts for my urgency. I hate to think what our chances of getting to the bottom will be if, or should I say when, these details are made public."

"Hold it Andy. What about the other hospital, the one in…"

"Dundale." He sat down and again took my hand. "I'm coming to that Sal and I'm telling you this for a reason. In Dundale things were a little different. Bear in mind that, at the time, the problem in Janesville had not yet been reported to us so it is left to us, once again, to read the main events courtesy of hospital surveillance tapes." He got up and began to pace. "The story in Dundale is much the same, a woman enters late at night with a child who suddenly falls to the ground. The guard calls the nurse at the desk to phone for help but a visiting doctor intercedes, barks at her that the boy is having an epileptic seizure, she is to stay with them, watching the boy closely so he does not swallow his tongue while he gets someone to help.

"The woman manages to keep the nurse's attention on the child and away from the desk, where the 'doctor' picks up the telephone, ostensibly to call for assistance. We believe in this case he simply used the phone to access the hospital's computer system and enters his own data, writing it to an OAO file."

"Overwrite All Others?"

He nodded. "Then he calmly returns to the group where the child now appears to have recovered. The woman confesses she has run out of the child's medication. The 'doctor' chews her out, then offers to drive her to her pharmacy and they leave."

"It's four days later when the hospital realizes it's been hit. By that time, the little tableau with the child has been forgotten. When they began to experience problems with patient care they called us all right, but this time an examination of their videos showed nothing out of the ordinary. Only when we started asking questions about a woman and a small child did the story come to light."

The implications were clear, though I was having a hard time accepting them. Janus's 'fainting' act was no game. I was beyond speech.

"The point is Sal," he said, taking my hands again. "you can see our interest in your young friend and how damned important it is for us to have her. She may be able to help us find the couple before they strike again."

"You think they'll go ahead now, even without the child?"

"Fraid so. Frankly, we think they've dumped the kid."

"Really?"

He nodded. "You have a better explanation of how she was found?" I couldn't think of one. "Sal look. This may be a whole new dimension in crime with which we're faced, but I believe when we find them we will find they are like any other serial murderers."

"Meaning?"

"Meaning they may not be able to stop now, even if they want to. It's possible they're caught up in all the media attention. Or it may be they want to be caught. The thing is, you can see now I really need the child to go with me."

I thought of what she might be in for. I shook my head. "Look, I can see you need her, but honestly, Andy, legally I cannot let her go. She's PPD's responsibility. I'm sorry, Andy."

"I can get a court order. Why make me do that?"

"Because, as I say, she's my legal responsibility. Show me a paper and I'll be glad to release her," I lied.

He picked up his hat. "Okay Sal. I'll be in touch."

I watched him go. I was shaking. Was I doing the right thing? If this child was involved in this case, which now seemed inevitable, what would happen to her? One thing for sure: in all likelihood her fate would shortly be completely out of my hands.

I felt more tired than I could ever remember being but sleep, I knew, was useless. Then I realized I was hungry. At least about that, I knew what to do.

* * * * *

Honeycutt coughed. "Excuse me, Madam. Chief Warmkessel is on the telephone. Will you take it?"

I told him of course and did.

"Sal? Tom Warmkessel here. Hate to bother you so late, my dear. How are things going for you? All right, I hope."

I assured him everything was all right, moving quickly to what I felt sure was the purpose for his call. "You've heard from Washington about Janus Morgan?"

"Yes," he said, relieved. "Someone high up in the chain. They want the girl."

Dead in Pleasant Company
A Pennsylvania Dutch Mystery

"I know. I just was not willing to let her go without something official. Have they told you why they want her?"

"Not really Your cousin called right after the Central Office. Said he couldn't explain why she was needed. Said you knew."

"What is the order for exactly? They want custody?"

"No. They want you to retain custody but they want you, although 'want'is not the word they use, to bring her to Washington without delay."

"All right. Does their order clear us on this end?"

"It does, yes. And Sal, they said right away."

"Now? It's nearly midnight!"

"I know, but it's official."

"Yes. Yes, of course. All right, Chief."

I hung up, but did not rush right off. How much good would a small child, often uncooperative under the best of circumstances, be after being wakened in the middle of her sleep? In a few hours she would wake on her own. Dare I wait? What if those hours could save lives? Perhaps, but this child would be most helpful if she'd had her rest. Besides, if Mastermind followed his usual time-table, events would already be in motion.

Only later did I remind myself that, sans the child, Mastermind's MO had already changed.

As for now, sleep was out of the question. I sent Honeycutt to bed and sat down with pen and pad to think.

* * * * *

"Hey!"

The voice startled me. A small hand shook my arm.

"What're you doin' down here?"

I mumbled something like 'why ask me' but the eyes were busy examining the remnants of my tray with disapproval. I came back to the world, mumbling some guilty explanations, equally ignored.

"I didn't know where you were," my inquisitor scolded. "What time is it?"

"Don't aks me. You're the one with the watch."

I tried to focus on my wrist, fighting a fog-wrapped brain. "Oh my God!"

Janus' attention turned to the litter of maps, bus and train schedules surrounding me. "Boy have you made a mess! I 'spec Mrs. Honey'll let you have what for!"

I rang for Honeycutt, apologized for the early hour, said I needed Mrs. Honey to get the child ready for a trip while I made myself presentable.

I took a moment to check my night's work, including an analysis of the deductions I'd made and the maps and schedules to support them, all of which I'd faxed to Andy, using our private family numbers, then went to shower and dress.

* * * * *

Wednesday.

As soon as it was light enough to take off, we were in the air, our star witness made malleable by a promise to let her 'help' fly the plane. From the cockpit, I called Andy to give him our ETA, forestalling a reprimand by telling him to check his fax machine.

We were ordered to a landing pad under particularly tight security and, in spite of my having radioed ahead the clearance code I'd been given, a horde of armed Marines waited for us. A suited figure emerged from a small rooftop building as I touched down and I breathed a sigh of relief when I recognized it as one I knew well.

Andy had the door open before the 'copter blades died. A nod to me, a helping hand for Janus, quickly followed by shouted directions to go 'this way,' passed yet more armed Marines, causing Janus to stop in her tracks and yell above the noise, "Hey! They're gonna shoot us!"

We hurried to assure her they were only looking out for bad guys and hustled her along to the banks of elevators.

Security was much heavier than usual with uniformed Marines everywhere and I prayed my young friend would not decide now was a good time to go into her act. Apparently Andy had the same concern for his brow cleared once we closed the door to his quad.

As before, he said nothing about my procrastination in following a direct order to bring the child in at once, attending to the urgent task first, as I would have done. Helping Janus off with her outdoor clothes, he professed himself awed by her 'driving' the plane. She ate it up.

The child's eyes moved slowly around the room, treating each of its contents to a critical survey, much as they had that first morning in my bedroom, it seemed an age ago. For all her diminutive size, she looked like a general come to review the troops. The eyes stopped when they came to a table at the window where several wrapped presents lay next to a laptop computer.

She looked at Andy who was making a show of listening to my limp apology for failing to follow a Federal directive. Rather than the reprimand I deserved, he gave me the same irresistibly compelling smile I remembered from our joint youth. Just so had he transformed the enforced association of the disparate Thaxton cousins from something between moping and mutiny to mirth. I had a sudden clear memory of one of his favorite diversion: some sort of adventurous play featuring knights and duels and swooning maidens. Sam and I had been sure he would follow his mother into the theater, perhaps as actor-cum-director of a small but credible stock company in which his Knute Rockne-like exhortations urged actors to noble efforts, bringing audiences to their feet. I wondered how far off we'd been. Even then we knew, whatever he wound up doing, he would be in charge.

"...know you," he was saying. "I figured you had a reason. In any case you've redeemed yourself with your faxes. Exceptional work Sal. I've turned your conclusions over to our people in the three geographical areas you identified. As you suggested, they're checking short-term rentals in Dundale and Janesville, looking for a pair of adults with a small child who rented within a month or so of the pertinent dates. I agree they wouldn't want to hang around any longer than they had to. Told them to ask, in particular, about a small child who is allowed to eat only every other day. I've got a good feeling about that."

"Really? You think that will turn something?"

"I do. As you said, renters have to have some public contact, no matter how secretive they try to be. They have to eat, go to local stores or get food delivered. There's a good chance the child was along when they went shopping and, as we've learned, she doesn't let herself go unnoticed. Then too, people are always in and out in a rental. Landladies. Maintenance people. The 'eat every other day' business is the sort of thing one remembers. It's so unusual it could be pivotal in making the case against them. Every criminal makes mistakes. Using the kid could be theirs. Excuse me."

One of Andy's 'people' approached. He listened and nodded. "Okay. Get back to me." To me he said, "Could be something."

Janus inched closer to him. "Whose presents are they?"

Andy was ready for her. "You mean those?" He kept it casual. "Oh, they're for my workers."

"Workers? What do you mean workers? What do they do?"

"Oh, different things. You know. Find things. Answer questions. Remember things—things like that."

"Hey! I can do that! Can I be a worker? Please!"

I couldn't believe it! It had taken me, the supposed child expert, days to get this single-minded child to even talk, much less tell me anything substantive and he had her begging to do so in minutes!

"I don't know," he said skeptically. "You're pretty young for this kind of work. You'd have to tell only what is true."

"I could do it!" I reflected there'd been precious little evidence of that so far. "I'm big en I am, too, good at aksering questions. Aks her!" She threw a look at me. "She aks me about a million of 'em!"

"Really?" Andy turned to me. "How about it, Dr. McKnight?"

"She *can*," I tried not to sound petulant, "when she feels like it. Sometimes she makes things up though."

"Oh," he sounded disappointed. "That's too bad. I only pay workers if they stick to what's real." He looked at her. "I don't suppose you can do that."

"Do I get a present if I do?" she asked with Pavlovian eagerness.

"Yes."

The small head bobbed up and down vigorously. "Okay then."

"Okay. We'll give it a shot but, remember, as soon as you begin to make things up the presents stop. Okay?" The head bobbed again. "Let's get started then." He booted up the computer, drawing the girl close. "The first job is to see how many of these people you can name. Okay?"

I watched over his shoulder as faces appeared on the screen, familiar childhood favorites at first, then the faces of men and women clearly taken from police files, these interspersed with photos of members of my household.

Snug on his lap as if she'd know him all her life, she made short work of identifying cartoon characters, Sam and Mrs. Honeycutt, followed by a series of 'don't knows' then by several emphatic but unconvincing statements to the effect she knew the person but couldn't remember the name.

"Okay. That's enough Miss Morgan. Thank you very much."

"Did I do it right? Do I get my present now?"

"You've earned one," he said firmly, adding quietly to me as she dashed off to her reward. "Began to make things up, trying to please me. I'll try it again later.

"What's next?"

"I'd like to..." A ring, so brief and soft I was not sure I'd heard it, stopped him mid-sentence. He produced a phone from a pocket, listened, then, "Good. Great! Give it to me." He scribbled something on a pad. "Yes, yes. She has been a help. Yes, she's here now. I'll tell her. Yes, the girl too." He listened again. "Okay. Buzz you when we touch down."

"Ed Stackowitz," he nodded at the phone. "They think they've found the place the couple rented in Dundale."

"That was quick."

He looked at his watch. "Bit more than six hours since we got your faxes. Ed says it wasn't too hard once they knew what to look for. The hospital's in a part of town where sublets are not allowed and there are not many short-term rentals available. He says to tell you thanks." He called to the girl clutching a doll, but still eying the other wrapped gifts. "Come Miss Morgan. Time for your next job. Get your coat."

From the air, Dundale's airport looked no larger than a good-sized garage, an impression heightened by the handful of cars waiting on the runway. Andy ushered us into one of these and nodded to the driver.

Dead in Pleasant Company
A Pennsylvania Dutch Mystery

"Ed, this is our gal Sal. And Miss Janus Morgan. All right, Ed. Let's do it."

We sped off. Twenty minutes later we pulled up at the curb of a row of small, neat houses, each boasting a small front porch and a patch of snowy lawn.

As soon as we turned the last corner Janus began to bounce about on the seat. Nearing the house itself she became quite lively.

"Hey! There's my house! Oh good! Now I can get my pres..." She was away, up the three steps, across the porch to the door where a woman, well bundled against the cold, waited. Janus dashed past her, shouting, "Hey! Hey!"

"Louise," Andy said to me by way of introduction. He told her, "Okay. Let's go."

She nodded and ushered us inside, reporting without being asked. "We've had some luck, sir. The place has not been rented since they left. Just the three, the landlady said. Except for having the rug shampooed, she hasn't bothered to do much in the way of cleaning. Says she'd only have to do it again when new renters move in."

"Good! Forensics may turn something."

"Landlady's a Mrs. George. Says the couple left the place pretty neat. Says the lady was forever cleaning."

"Damn! Guess we should expect that. There's real brains behind this thing."

"Still could be something. Doesn't take much for DNA to turn something. Prints has already been here. The couple was careful about wiping everything before they left but we've got one clear set of woman's prints from a shelf in the closet, also a partial—a man's—on a bulb over the sink." She looked at the child. "How sure are we this is the kid?"

I was having doubts myself. Since her initial outburst, she had remained in one spot, looking about her, her face a puzzle.

Louise went on. "One thing. Landlady said she's been on to the company that shampooed the rug to come back and put things back where they got them. We've vacuumed the furniture though. Sent the results off to the lab."

We were all watching Janus now, the little face a massive scowl.

Andy turned to me. "What's wrong" he whispered. "She doesn't seem to recognize...I was sure..."

I looked around. "The furniture's been moved."

"Damn!"

"Wait," I said. "Janus, I need to use the bathroom. Where is it?" The child took my hand and led me directly there! Her bona-fides restored, I thanked her, then, faking verisimilitude aimed at maintaining whatever credibility I had with my charge, closed the door behind her.

Inside I pulled on plastic gloves and gave the barren, nondescript room a policeman's once-over. The medicine cabinet was empty save for rusty metal shelves. It looked like it had been empty for a long time. A small plastic wastebasket beside it, also empty. A single metal towel bar, one end left dangling. Sink. Tub. Toilet. Nothing more. No curtains, just a window shade showing the cracks and tiny pin-holes of age and sun. I pulled it down, checked both sides and let it run back up. When I came out Janus was in the adjoining room, a bedroom apparently, fussing at a small chest.

"What are you looking for?"

"Dumbdonna's soda. She hides it here so Raymond can't find it. I bet she...Oh! Here it is!" She pulled out a distinctively shaped bottle of Chambord, empty save for a thin layer of sticky liquid at the bottom. "Oh. It looks yukky."

I grabbed it as she tossed it aside, looked at Andy. He nodded at Louise who took the bottle and disappeared.

Dead in Pleasant Company
A Pennsylvania Dutch Mystery

Janus' head was back in the cabinet. "Where's a new bottle? She always keeps…"

"Never mind," I said, hauling her away. "That is not soda and you can't have it."

"Can too. They give it me sometimes. Tastes like a lollipop. Makes me sleepy though."

The purpose, I thought. Make sure she was asleep while they made love. Or plans for another deadly target. This child, I thought, has certainly had some cosmopolitan experiences for one so young. Chambord after dinner. A pot sandwich on the bus. Before my teaching days I would not have believed it possible.

Andy made a swift, thorough search of the small chest but found nothing. "If she had a back-up, she took it along," he said. "Great help though. May have left prints on this bottle. It's sticky and the shape makes it tricky to wipe clean without a thorough wash and it doesn't look like it's had that." He frowned. "Could help pin-point their present location too."

"How? Oh. Of course. Check liquor stores for Chambord purchasers new to the neighborhood."

He nodded. "Right," adding it was time to go. I stuck my plastic gloves in my pocket and buttoned Janus into her coat. "Are you finished with us then?"

"For now."

"Good. Come Janus. It's time to go home."

"Hold on Sal!" He pulled me a few feet away from the girl, who, once free, began racing about the empty apartment. "I want this child in a safe house."

I objected, citing first grandfather's maxim to the effect that if it isn't broke it's just plain damn foolish to fix it. "Where can she possibly be safer than with Benjam and the Honeycutts?"

In the end he surrendered, escorting us back to his office, making a small but hurried ceremony of letting Janus gather up the remaining gifts and, her arms full, carry them back to the roof.

"You'll be having an escort though," he said, nodding at a second helicopter parked behind mine. He held up a palm at my protest. "Look, I'm going along with you up to a point, but if any word leaks that there's a child in this thing I reserve the right to change my mind." He lifted Janus into her seat and buckled her belt, then came round to my side. "And this time, no going anywhere off on your own. Got it?"

"Yes sir," I said.

He did not bother to tell me to keep my mouth shut. For the Pennsylvania Dutch it goes without saying.

Dead in Pleasant Company
A Pennsylvania Dutch Mystery

CHAPTER 19

On the flight home I called Sam, bringing him up to date on the day's activities. His pat on the back helped to ease my nerves, which were pretty well on edge.

As we flew, I grew increasingly confident that, with any luck now, Mastermind would be caught before he could do any more damage. Moreover, his identity would also provide the name and address of the child, presently fast asleep beside me, one arm holding fast to her gifts, the other resting comfortably on my arm. Somehow neither prospects produced much joy.

For one thing, the thought that I had played a major part in bringing an evil and relentless killer to justice, as Andy repeatedly insisted was unsettling, even frightening. Equally unsettling was the thought of the little girl returning to the home in which she was allowed to eat only every other day.

Only Nature sought to assure me things would get better. Visible from the air as we approached our valley, patches of brown on the southern faces of hill and dale visible from the air, turned my thoughts to home and the promise of Spring: long sessions pouring over seed catalogs with Benjam, weekend trips to the Phillies spring training games, the arrival of foals in Susan's stables.

Unfortunately, such cozy thoughts include some not so cozy and, by the time I'd once again turned Janus over to Mrs. Honey, the part of my brain reserved for worry over family had kicked in.

My few grey hairs bear witness to a perpetual, if transient, concern for the welfare of Joe and Lucienne—forgivable, perhaps, when one has one offspring in the military and another with a penchant for 'going where no girl has gone before.' As for Walt, until now I'd only worried over whether he would ever go out on his own.

Hannah Fairchild

Now that he was apparently doing so, he seemed to be in the gravest trouble of all—another case, I suppose, of being careful of what one wishes.

Where in the devil was he? What was he up to?

I fought off perennial feelings of guilt and booted up my laptop. There were e-mails from Lucienne and Joe as usual, but, sure enough, my last several e-mails to Walt appeared to have gone un-read. It was time to do something about him, always assuming there was something to do.

Munching away at a tray containing at least twice the calories allowed for dinner, I considered the few pitiful ideas which emerged. Replying to Lucienne and Joe's e-mails, I included in each a casual query, which they would no doubt see through, as to whether they'd heard from their brother. Stuck for any other idea, I called Sam, chattered briefly with brother and sister-in-law, declined an invitation to join them for dinner, begging off in favor of an early bedtime.

Gathering my last ounce of energy toward a final effort, I buzzed Walt's rooms. No answer. Barefoot, I made my way there through darkened halls, tapped, got no answer and entered. I looked around for signs he had been there and found none. Closets, drawers, entertainment center, all looked exactly as they had nearly a week ago. The geraniums, left as a subtle message of cheer and support, were reduced to mere spikes, the petals on his nightstand as faded and lifeless as my hopes of his speedy return. Questions repeated themselves endlessly. Where was he? Why had he gone off? Was he somehow, even tangentially, involved in Tunnelson's death? Had Barney Schantz gone berserk and attacked his old enemy and was Walt protecting him? That sounded like Walt all right but not like Barney. For most of us, murder is not an easy thing to do. Some part of one's brain has to be separated from reality, doesn't it?

That's the sort of disjunct my toes usually pick up on and as far as Barney was concerned, they hadn't uttered a peep.

Perhaps a part of *my* brain had lost sight of reality. Surely relying on one's toes could surely not be considered sane. I sat on the edge of my son's bed and thought. Where in the world could he be? What was he doing for food? For clean clothing? Then I remembered the twenty-five thousand dollars deposited in Walt's account and I froze. Twenty five thousand! The same amount Tunnelson had paid in cash to someone. Who?

Not Walt, though, surely. For one thing, it wasn't in him to do business with the man for whom he'd shown every sign of intense dislike. Unless…perhaps he did it to spite him, make a fool of him. Perhaps he wanted to get back at the man who had so injured his friend.

I wished now I'd asked the bank if Walt's deposit had been in cash. I also realized we had not heard if the money Tunnelson had sent to Philadelphia was ever picked up.

A new and horrifying thought occurred. Was it possible Mastermind and Tunnelson were part of the same scenario? Did that mean my son and his friend were also part of it?

A cold chill swept through me. It was too late to check with the bank now. What else could I do?

Inspirationless, I gave in to fatigue, decided to give Walt until morning before taking any desperate action and took myself off to bed.

My last thought was of my toes and the last time they had let me down. * But exhaustion overpowered memories before they could get a foothold and, at last, blessed sleep came.

* * * * *

Thursday.

Hannah Fairchild

Coming downstairs alone, my house seemed oddly quiet. Why odd, I asked myself? A home built of fieldstone and foot-thick beams takes a lot of noise before it is noticed, so why *odd?* It was as if the whole house was holding its breath, waiting for...what? Something happening in the world outside my doors perhaps? Had Mastermind struck again while I slept? Was the news breaking, even now, of a child involved in the Internet terrorist murders? Had a connection been found between Mastermind and Tunnelson's death? Had it something to do with Walt?

Fragments of uneasy dreams floated to the surface forcing a detour to the library. I tuned in the television to an all news channel. Sports. Headlines in five minutes. Enough time to check my messages.

The Fax machine held only the usual bunch. Some half-dozen pale indigo sheets bearing the PC logo lay waiting in the mail basket—the repository for messages coming in after I'd gone to bed. All but one were from Sam, asking where I was (the "hell' missing from Mrs. Sweeney's neat script). The last, from Mrs. Sweeney herself, inquiring if I wanted her to do something about Walt. Nothing from Andy.

I booted up and checked my e-mail. Quite a few entries there but nothing from either Andy or Walt. How long would it take for yesterday's events to find their way to the press? Had the promising trail been lost? Recalling that dismal apartment, the ominously silent and swift comings and goings of Andy's 'people,' seemed more like a dream than a memory. Indeed the whole idea that Mastermind was to be unmasked after so many months began to seem impossible; that a child should be his undoing, implausible.

I shivered. Naturally, I told myself. I was dressed for swimming and the room was cold. I drew my robe more closely around me, wishing I'd taken the time to put something on my bare feet. With icy hands I pulled up e-

Dead in Pleasant Company
A Pennsylvania Dutch Mystery

mail messages from son and daughter. Lucienne's was long: excited reports of her efforts to attach minuscule numbers to sand beetles in order to track their activities. I wished one could do the same with one's children.

Joe's was more to the point, reminding me I had a gun in the house and knew how to use it. For him, there is no danger but physical danger.

I wished it was all that simple. Still, waiting around for the news, I obediently opened my desk drawer, pulled out the police special required by my job, clicked the safety on and off, checked the barrel, re-locked the weapon and returned it, setting the security lock on the drawer.

When the news finally came there was no mention of either Mastermind or Tunnelson, all attention now on yet another disturbance in the Middle East.

I flicked off the set, still feeling at odds. Halfway through my laps it hit me. Ken! I'd not heard from Ken since, when? Monday. Odd, I thought. I did not think he would leave town without saying goodbye. What was up? First Barney, then Walt, now Ken. Was Plainfield developing a Bermudic hole?

An hour later, showered and changed for work, I looked in the old nursery to check on our star witness. Janus was still fast asleep, no surprise after her grueling past few days. I took a raging hunger to breakfast, stopping in the kitchen to bring joy to Mrs. Honey's day by asking for a small omelette with my toast and coffee.

Two envelopes lay at my plate: one small and white, the other thicker and larger. I opened the small one first.

It was undated.

Hannah Fairchild

"Dear Lady Jane,

I am so sorry I missed you yesterday. I most desperately wanted to see you before I left but the time has come and go I must.

My dear Sal, I wish I had the words to describe what meeting you has meant to me. You are one of those rare people who one instinctively knows will leave a hole in one's life.

I had hoped that, once the Tunnelson matter was cleared up, I might persuade you that marriage to one with whom you have so much in common was a good thing. If I thought for a minute there was any vestige of hope you felt the same, I'd stay here, face the devil and be damned! But as things look now, I do not see any resolution to the case, at least none that I like. As it is, it seems incumbent upon me to reduce as much of my angst as possible.

I want you to know I shall be leaving Horizon's employ as well. You are asking "why." I'm afraid I do not feel at liberty to explain as the story is not mine. However, should any suspicion in the Tunnelson matter remain with you or anyone about whom you care, the item in the accompanying envelope will clear you. I did not have the heart to use it myself and I hope and pray you will not have to either, but use it if you must.

Be well, Salome Jane. I'll never forget you!"

Ken

P.S. *Sorry about the Valentine's Day dance. I'll be thinking of you.*
K.

Dead in Pleasant Company
A Pennsylvania Dutch Mystery

PPS. Do me a favor and put that rose colored dress away and never wear it again!
K.

I stared at the flamboyant "K." Had the man lost his mind? I re-read the note, finding a second reading even more astonishing. The message irritated me. True, I had thoroughly enjoyed his company but had I led him to think it was more than that?

I picked up the second envelope as Honeycutt brought my breakfast and Sam with it. I mumbled good morning.

"So's yer ol man," Sam said in greeting. I handed him the note by way of response and dug into my omelette.

My brother accepted coffee. "You okay with all that happened?"

"What...oh, you mean with Janus and Andy. Yes. Up to a point, anyway."

"Anything new since then?"

I said not yet. "I'm on pins and needles waiting. I wish I knew what was actually happening at this moment and what effect this will all have on Janus. My God! What could have been in that man's mind to use a child in that way?"

"Possibly the same set of self-serving convictions which enabled him to indiscriminately kill and maim people he's never met and against whom he has no particular complaint, don't you think? Some of *them* were children too, don't forget."

"Yes. Yes, of course. What a relief it will be to finally unmask him! I admit to wanting to see his face. It always amazes me that our crimes don't show on us. Joy certainly does."

"I hadn't thought of it that way, but yeah. It's almost impossible to conceal happiness from others. It just seems to ooze out, but evil—well." He sat across from me, still holding the notes. "Isn't it your theory that the whole reason people get away with murder and other crimes is our reluctance to believe that criminals walk among us, seemingly normal, even pleasant?"

"Yes. One expects to see the mark of Cain, I suppose. Unfortunately, even believing that as I do, I still get caught up..." Now the memories, so carefully shut out last night, were free to return to the events a few years ago when misplaced trust brought me within a whisper of death.

Sam glanced at me and hurried to change the subject. "Her Majesty still sleeping?"

I said she was. "Actually, it's Walt who is worrying me most right now. What is keeping him away? Where could he be? I swore I'd do something about him today, but what? I know what you're thinking—an occasional pants-warming during his formative years would have helped, but even if I did agree with you, and I don't, it is water over the dam."

"I know. That's why there's no point in worrying about him, Sis. You'll hear from him when he's good and ready. You know how he hates being pushed." He waved the note at me. "So, what's this all about?"

"Read," I said.

Read out loud, Ken's note sounded even more odd.

"Angst!" Sam spluttered. I'll angst him! No resolution he likes?" At the end, Sam tossed it down in disgust. "What the hell is he talking about? What crap! Quitting a job that pays what his does? It just doesn't ring true. Neither does his leaving you like this."

I grinned at him. "Imagine how I feel—the woman scorned! And me still with my back teeth!" I sipped coffee. "Anyway, he's free to do what he wants and what he wants, regardless of what the note says, is obviously not here. As for his job, he doesn't have to work anymore than I do. He's got plenty of money. And family too. Besides," I grinned at him again. "I thought you wanted him out of my life."

Dead in Pleasant Company
A Pennsylvania Dutch Mystery

"I do, but not like this, the phony!" he grimaced at the note. "Valentine dance? What's that about?"

"Oh, I mentioned the church's Valentine's Day dance in passing. He said we should go." It had been, I thought, no more than a perfunctory pleasantry mentioned while we took a few turns around the floor after dinner in New York. "He is a good dancer." I said by way of explanation. My brother knows I love to dance.

He gave me a sharp look. "Well it looks like you're not heartbroken at least, otherwise I'd have to break his damned neck! What the hell's in this other one? If it has something to do with the Tunnelson case, he knows damned well you have to use it. You going to open it?"

"You," I nodded at him. "I'm eating."

A single sheet of stiff, expensive, yellow paper fell out of the envelope.

"What the hell...?" He passed it to me. The Horizon Insurance Company logo spread across the top, the initials RF in bold relief visible just below. It appeared to be a handwritten memo, the same kind I'd seen in the office of Roland Finch.

HORIZON Insurance

R F	*#1*	*#2*
R. Wilson	*unknown*	*30*
T. Starrar	*pneumonia*	*10*
M. Stahl	*heart*	*10*
L. Hysart	*cancer*	*25*
R. Rodriquez	*cancer*	*15*
J. Tunnelson	*heart*	*50*

"What in the hell...! Look!" He waved it at me. "Tunnelson's name's on here. What in all that's holy...?"

The hall clock chimed faintly. I took a final sip of coffee, thrust the list back at him. "I've got to be going."

"Going? Going where? We have a lot to talk about."

"To work. The press has finally called it quits and my cases are really piling up. We can talk later if you have time. How's Roselma?" He said she was expecting me for dinner tonight. I nodded and picked up my bag. "Be there, Lord willing and the crik don't rise."

"Just a minute sister!" He pushed the two papers at me again. "What are you going to do with these damn things?"

"I don't know. Oh, I suppose as Tunnelson's name is on it I better take the list with. I'll turn it over to Peters. Will you be around? I'm a bit concerned about leaving Janus with the Honeys. She's likely to be pretty full of herself after yesterday's excitement."

He said he'd take her home for Roselma to play with. "Want me to do anything about Walt?"

"If you can think of anything. Wish you could take *him* home for Rose to play with!"

He said his wife would love that, she'd always adored Walt. "Listen, don't you think you ought to make a copy of that thing before you turn it over?"

It was a good idea and I did so as soon as I reached my desk, scanning it in and sending it back to my own computer. I was returning it to the envelope when something struck me as odd. I studied it until the increasing chatter announced it was time to report for roll-call. I tucked the envelope in my desk drawer, locked it and went to join the others.

* * * * *

Dead in Pleasant Company
A Pennsylvania Dutch Mystery

My co-workers greeted my return with the Pennsylvania Dutch equivalent of enthusiasm—which is to say their smiles widened, perhaps a quarter of an inch. Still I was glad to be on the receiving end and with Captain Miller in charge, both roll call and workout were dealt with briskly. When the morning roll call included no mention of Mastermind, I couldn't decide whether to be relieved or concerned. One look at the mounting case-load waiting at my desk, however, left no time to worry about either.

I was making a quick survey of the new cases with a view toward prioritizing them when I heard Captain Peters arrive. I tapped on his door and gave him the list. He read it, frowned at me and asked what it meant. I told him I had no idea.

"Really?" He sounded skeptical. "You say Ken left it? Why? I mean why leave it with you?"

I flinched. The personal note, which would have made that question unnecessary, I'd left at home. "Oh. Well I...that is, he...well we had dinner a couple of times."

"Really?" His eyebrows rose to full mast. My reputation as ice-maiden reared its head.

I tried to look as if everything was business as usual. "Yes. He wanted to interview me when he first came here and it just saved time to do it while we ate." I hurried to add supporting data. "This list came with another note telling me goodbye. He said to use the list if the Tunnelson case did not get resolved—which is why I brought them in. He said he didn't have the heart to use them himself, whatever that means. I suppose he thought...I mean I don't think he expected me to turn them in right away."

Peters grunted. "Doesn't know you very well, does he?'

I wanted to say something like 'well enough.' Instead I said, "It isn't, is it? Resolved I mean—if you can tell me."

"There's nothing to tell or not tell," he said with disgust. He frowned at the list, then at me. His face took on the expression of a cop during an interrogation. "The other note?"

"The other...oh, it's...a little personal. I'm afraid he let himself get carried away a bit. Or at least..." I let it hang.

"Really? I would have thought he was the last...well." He stopped, the 'well' speaking volumes. He turned the sheet over, frowning again. "Tunnelson's name is here. What the hell does it mean?"

"I haven't the foggiest." The look on his face made me realize how out of character it was for me. My addiction to looking for facts, for meaning is no secret. I began to wish I'd spent more time looking it over, then wondered why I hadn't. I tried to explain, to him at least. "Actually, they were at my place at breakfast this morning. I was eager to get to work." His look demanded more. "I saw Tunnelson's name there so I figured it had something to do...Look, Bill. I've been doing my best to stay out of your case," I said lamely. "Perhaps I've gone too far."

He grunted. "You say you got them at breakfast? He didn't..." Spend the night. He would have said it to anyone else. He switched tactics as I'd seen him do dozens of time when trying to drag the truth out of a suspect. "That mean they came in yesterday's mail?"

"Well, no," I admitted reluctantly. "Honeycutt said they were left at the gate this morning. In the newspaper box," I said, before he could ask.

"Oh. I see." He looked up at me again. "Well. Thanks. We'll be in touch." He dismissed me with a wave.

I resisted the impulse to explain, to assure him I had only seen Ken a few times, that he had not slept over, but why should I? I collected my reserve and settled down to the new cases.

And a mixed bag they were: two runaways, a couple of shoplifters, three high school boys charged with sexual harassment. First signs of spring, I thought. Once the snow begins to melt, everybody seems to lose focus.

Which was more important? Most urgent?

I set aside the more important runaways for the moment in favor of that which experience taught was more urgent. A few hours could make all the difference in the testimony of a high school student to whom what classmates think is more important than truth.

I arranged to have officers pick up the trio of high school boys reported to have surrounded a female classmate in the school gym, pulling off most of her clothes. I had no doubt that right now they would be full of themselves, keeping each other pumped up by repeated recitals of their 'macho' exploits. Bundled into a single police car and rushed to an interview with me would merely provide them with something more to brag about. To get at the truth, it was advisable to keep them apart. I'd requested the officers use separate squad cars and place them in separate interview rooms. There they could wait until I could get to them. A few hours on their own would not hurt them and would give me time to speak to the girl and advise their parents.

A call to the parents of the girl caught shoplifting, another with the father of the boy who'd punched him and left home, produced appointments for later in the day. The parents of the nine-year-old who'd stolen a doll on a wind-up swing insisted the child be brought in, to 'give her a good scare.' I knew them. The child was one of a large family and perhaps, like Janus, falling between the cracks. I tried, without success, to persuade that returning the swing with an apology was adequate punishment for this shy, chubby child. Punishment which is too harsh often breeds resentment which, in turn, breeds further infractions. I made a note to myself to keep a look-out for her in the future.

I had a talk with the guidance counselor about the other missing student and sat down to think. Then, grabbing coat and hat, I went in search of the runaway.

Peters stopped me on the way out to tell me he had faxed Ken's list to the New York police, asking for help.

"New York?"

"Where Horizon's headquarters are. I sent the list off to NYPD. Let them look into it."

So. He'd passed the buck. I regretted bringing the darned thing in now. I hadn't thought it would get completely out of my hands. Feeling increasingly uneasy, I forced my mind back to my job, and began making the rounds of the places I'd listed as possible havens for a young girl on the lam. My thoughts returned to another little girl far from home. I called Sam.

"She's fine," he said. "Roselma's teaching her how to play gin rummy."

"I hope not for money," I said. "You'll need to take out a mortgage."

By mid-morning I had the runaway in my office, by noon she had agreed to stay with her grandparents while the family met with a counselor. It was a start. My phone rang. What did I want done with the three boys? I asked to have them each in separate interview rooms until I could meet with them. I said, not altogether truthfully, I had yet to speak with their victim. Let them get good and hungry, I thought. They would be more malleable then.

I returned from my interview with the girl, so victimized by her fellow students, and was playing phone tag with one more parent when the Chief called me away from my desk, shutting his door carefully behind me.

"Thought you ought to know. New York's looking into that list you turned over."

"Oh? They're taking it seriously then?" By now I thoroughly regretted my cavalier attitude toward it. I'd put it down merely as puzzling. I said as much. "Into what are they looking?"

Warmkessel lifted massive shoulders and let them drop. "I guess they figured they couldn't just ignore it, not with Tunnelson's name on it and him being murdered and all. Anyway, they decided to check into it. They sent somebody to call on this Finch character and asked for an explanation. Wanted to see Tunnelson's policy. The guy refused. I understand he got pretty hot under the collar. Then they asked to talk to Fowler and were told he wasn't there, that nobody knew where he was. I guess the cops pushed a bit and Finch threw them out. They got a subpoena to see the insurance policies of all the persons named on the list but when the cops got there, there was no record of those six policies to be found."

"But that's ridiculous! Obviously Tunnelson had a policy with them or they wouldn't have come..."

"What New York said too. They're waiting now for a judge to sign a *subpoena duces tecum*."

"So they can take all their records, yes. I suppose that makes sense, but what do they expect to find?"

He shook his head. "No idea. They want to talk to you about just how the list came into your possession."

"Oh? Well, certainly. Shall I telephone them?"

"The sooner the better, I'd say. They sound irritated. Here's the number. Ask for Captain Carderra."

I called NYPP. The Captain was out. I left a message and my extension. So Ken wasn't at work. Had he really quit then? If so, where had he gone?

I returned to the cases about which I *could* do something. I visited the girl, now in the hospital, took her statement, then returned to headquarters where I videotaped each of the meetings with the three boys. I reviewed the tapes with O'Connell, got permission to charge the three boys and did so. I called Juvenile Court and arranged for a hearing. Near the end of the day Captain Peters sent for me.

"Bring you up to date with this thing," he began, shutting the door behind me. "New York's holding that Horizon guy overnight. Looks like some pretty fancy goings-on up there."

"By whom?"

He looked at his notes. "Guy named Finch I take it."

Not Ken then, I thought. "How? I mean what did he do?"

Peters shook his head. "Some kind of insurance fraud, I expect. This Finch guy either can't or won't explain where the missing records are, so they hauled him in while their forensic accountants examine Horizon's files. NYPD expects they'll find some sort of fraud connected with those six names and that includes Tunnelson."

"Fraud connected to Tunnelson's death?"

"Apparently."

"But how?"

"No idea. They said they'd keep in touch. You talk to them yet?"

I said I'd been playing phone tag with Carderra all afternoon and had finally left him my cellphone number.

"Good. Well, let me know if anything develops on your end." I turned to go. "Oh. One more thing, Sal. Almost forgot. They want to see the other note."

I blushed. "Other note? Oh. Yes. Certainly."

"Here." He scribbled a number on a piece of paper. "You can fax it to them directly."

"Right." I turned to go.

"And Sal."

"Yes, Bill?"

"Don't put it off."

I could feel my face flush. "No, Captain Peters."

Dead in Pleasant Company
A Pennsylvania Dutch Mystery

* * * * *

Dinner with Sam and Roselma was pretty much a wash. Janus, apparently elevated to super-star status, had completely conquered my sister-in-law's household. Roselma put her in charge of the little crystal dinner bell which the child put to full use, ringing every few minutes, keeping up a steady stream of orders to a bewildered maid, accustomed to the family's modest needs.

Normally I enjoy Rose's stories of her very large, very Irish family, but tonight I heard myself laughing along with the others more than once with no idea what had been said.

I hadn't fooled my brother for an instant though and as soon as he could do so without offending his much-loved wife, he cited my early work day and, insisting Janus stay with them, chased me home.

Alone, all the disquieting thoughts I'd been fighting to keep at bay began to sort themselves out. At the top of the list was worry over how the mystery of Janus would play itself out. It had been, I checked my watch, nearly thirty-three hours since parting with my cousin. I'd heard nary a word from him and I was growing increasingly apprehensive. What was taking so long? They'd found one place Raymond and the woman had rented so quickly, what was holding things up now? Had they lost the promising trail?

Equally troubling was what the message would be when it finally came. Would it be that they'd caught Raymond and he was not Mastermind or that they caught Raymond and he *was* Mastermind? I was hard put to decide which was the more alarming.

And what about Walt? Why hadn't he shown up? Perhaps he really was in danger. If not, what in the world was he up to?

And then there was Ken. More mystery. Why had he quit his job? Why had he dumped the damn list on me? What did the list mean? What had his boss done? Was there some connection to the supposed fraud and his unexpected attendance at Tunnelson's autopsy? I had put Finch down as a simple, honest man to whom family meant everything. He appeared content with his lot with no sign of the greed and ruthless disregard for the welfare of others which is tantamount to those perpetrating frauds.

I pictured the puzzling list again. What did it mean? Something about the list still bothered me but what?

And finally, why was I not more upset over Ken's cavalier departure? Was I an ice-maiden after all?

I went back to the list. The whole mess surrounding the list seemed to have taken on a life of its own. I was beginning to look back on my days working with juvenile psychopaths at Hawk County[4] as halcyon. A pair of dark eyes stared steadily into mine, a familiar scent seemed to rise out of nowhere. I told myself to knock it off.

What I needed was a nice, long talk with Sam. What I needed was for him to tell me I was letting my imagination run away with me. What I needed was about fourteen hours sleep. What I needed was something to eat.

There was only one, well two, things to do. I donned robe and slippers and went down to the 'porch,' turned on the lights and cut fresh geraniums for my son and took them up, replacing their defunct brethren. Then back to the kitchen and a peanut butter and banana sandwich, a glass of milk, (skim of course—after all, I *am* on a diet) and a handful of sour cherry fritters.

I ate propped up in bed with Robert Barnard providing enough diversion to turn my brain off and let sleep come.

---

[4] *If It's Monday, It Must Be Murder* Hannah Fairchild

Dead in Pleasant Company
A Pennsylvania Dutch Mystery

* * * * *

"But what about the pin-pricks?"

I sat up, knocking book and plate to the floor. "Who's there?"

My reading lamp is programmed to turn itself out if there is no movement in my room for an hour, so the darkened room told me I'd been asleep at least that long.

My heart pounding, I switched the lamp back on and looked around. The room was empty. I struggled to wake fully. What had I heard?

"What about the pin-pricks?"

There was no voice, just the question running around in my brain, looking, I suppose, for a way out.

I turned the lamp off in disgust. I had half a notion to call Sam but I knew he would just say it *was* all in my head. Perhaps, I thought, drifting off, he was right.

CHAPTER 20

Friday.

I had no sooner gotten to my desk next morning when my telephone rang.

"Tom here, Sal. Calling from home. Wanted to let you know. Just heard from New York. They're goin' to arraign this here Roland Finch today."

"Oh?"

"Said they were solving our case for us. Apparently Tunnelson's death was due to natural causes after all."

"Really? Why do they…"

"All I know now. They're sending details as soon as they have 'em together. Peters will be talking to you I'm sure."

"I see. Did that list I gave Peters have anything to do with it?"

"Everything apparently. Opened the whole case up. Thought I'd let you know. By the way, we've canceled the APB on your son and his friend."

"You have? Thanks."

"Don't thank me. Thank your buddy."

I told him thanks again anyway and hung up, waiting for the feelings of relief now that Walt, Barney Schantz and Pleasant Company were no longer involved. No such feeling came.

I stuck my head in Captain Peters' door, "Got a minute?"

"For you, yeah. Headed over in your direction anyway. Chief said he wanted to tell you himself. You hear from him?"

I said I did but what did it all mean?

"Damned if I know," he shook his head. "Seems like the guys at this insurance outfit have found a way to disallow certain large claims. Forensic accountants are expected to find something."

I thought it over. "You said 'they'."

"He, actually. Top guy himself. Looks like he was in it all by his lonely. New York said to tell you thanks. Say you did them a good turn. Say to tell you they owe you one."

Oh yeah, I thought. If it was such a good thing, why were my toes wiggling?

* * * * *

Sue Leiby waved at me, pointing to my ringing phone. I nodded and took it. A woman reporting her grandson's suicede threats. I treat all suicide attempts as genuine. I told O'Connell where I was going and signed out.

Pulling out of the police garage, I was pleased to see nothing remained now of the media invasion save deep tracks of oily snow. Thaxton Park was all but deserted. I breathed a sigh of relief.

A moment later I was where I most love to be—alone, behind the wheel of my car, out and about the countryside. The sun shone brightly. The snow was beginning to melt. The status of my world gradually began to return to quo and, in spite of my grave errand, I felt my spirits lift.

Things were looking up. The threat of our involvement in Judd Tunnelson's death was gone and no doubt Walt would return to the nest. At any moment now I would hear that Mastermind had been caught and I had played a small part in his capture. The rapidly melting snow was a tacit reminder that baseball's spring training camps would be well under way. I turned the radio on to an all-sports station. More good news. Early reports from the Phillies training camp were out and prospects for our team looked good this year. Yup! Spring was just around the corner! I felt ready to turn my full attention to my job.

I considered how to approach the boy. Would I be savvy enough to distinguish a ploy for power from a cry for help? Would I know what to do to keep him safe?

* * * * *

Back again at my desk, I continued to work on my open cases. At the scheduled hour I gathered the necessary papers for a scheduled hearing and headed for the courts.

"But what about those pin-pricks?"

I told myself to put it to music.

"Still," I found myself saying aloud as I rode upward in the glass elevator "what *about* them?"

A check of my watch showed I had just enough time for a quick stop at the coroner's office.

Hal Strauch's face flushed angrily when I asked him if he'd heard the news.

"Oh I heard all right! Wish I knew what the hell it all means!"

"I imagine it means you were right all along, Hal. That Tunnelson's death was natural, I mean."

"Oh yeah?" He sounded belligerent.

"What Peters says New York says," I said soothingly.

"New York! Don't talk to me about New York! Yesterday they were wanting to dig the guy up! Dig 'im up? What the hell do they think this is? Now they say forget it and I say screw that. I'm going to dig him up anyway, damn it! I want an explanation for those damn pin-pricks!"

At last. Someone to join me in la-la land. I said mildly that they had been bothering me as well. "What does NYPD say about them?"

"That's just it, they don't. They're tellin' me they don't mean diddly squat!" His face reddened with anger. "Listen,

Dead in Pleasant Company
A Pennsylvania Dutch Mystery

I saw 'em myself! Are they trying to say now I imagined them?"

I reminded him he was not the only one to have seen them. "Hal, I was wondering what made you notice them in the first place?"

"I didn't notice 'em in the first place! That wise-ass idiot from the insurance company did! I didn't know what the hell to make of 'em then and I sure don't now! Between the Feds and us we've spent a small fortune on tests and they've all come up blank."

I admitted it was tough. "Where exactly were they? The holes, I mean?"

"Back of his neck, right at the base of the hairline."

I wanted to ask him to show me. I wanted to ask how he'd missed them. I reminded myself the Chief had said the medic was on the verge of quitting. I thanked him and left.

The elevator rose and the questions with it. Why *had* Hal missed them initially? It was not like him. Wait! Hadn't Ken said it was Finch who actually found them? Come to think of it, given the new information provided by Finch's list, what was he doing there? Ken, I could understand. Insurance adjustors do attend autopsies. Or do they? The elevator door slid open.

I pushed the first level button again and descended to Strauch's office. I stuck my head in the open doorway. "Just one quick question, if I may, Hal. Was it Mr. Fowler or Mr. Finch who saw them first?"

"How the hell do I know? The two of them were jabbering away and then the older guy just called me over to have a look. Last time I let amateurs in my morgue!"

I repeated my thanks and left, trying to sort it out. If they had not caused the man's death, what were the two pin-pricks doing there? What did they mean? What caused them? Why had Hal missed them? What if Hal *hadn't* missed them? I pushed that thought away making way for my brain to toss me another, equally troubling question.

"What does that darn list mean, anyway? Why was it so important?"

* * * * *

The juvenile hearing over, I pulled out my copy of the list in the now empty courtroom and studied it. I had to start with the one thing on the list I recognized—Tunnelson's name. What could I infer from that?

Assume it was because he held a policy with Horizon. Was it reasonable to assume the 50 represented the face amount of the policy? If so 50 what? Not thousand. Hundred thousand? Million? Yes. Both his income and the fact that his death brought Horizon's CEO to Plainfield supported that. That could also explain why Ken had sent for Finch. Perhaps he wanted to share the responsibility for the enormous pay-out. Ken was no shrinking violet but, it would be a whopper.

Was it reasonable, then, to assume the other names on the list were those of policy holders? I thought so.

I looked at the second column. Across from Tunnelson's name it said 'heart,' in his case the original cause of death. Could one assume that was true in each case?

HORIZON Insurance

R F	*#1*	*#2*
R. Wilson	unknown	30
T. Starrar	pneumonia	10

Dead in Pleasant Company
A Pennsylvania Dutch Mystery

M. Stahl	*heart*	*10*
L. Hysart	*cancer*	*25*
R. Rodriquez	*cancer*	*15*
J. Tunnelson	*heart*	*50*

Heart, pneumonia, cancer. All typically named as cause of death. Was it possible that each of these was later changed to murder as it was in Tunnelson's case? The list was beginning to make sense.

My phone rang and the list was no longer important. A distraught father reported his daughter had not returned home from a school dance the night before. I stuck the list in my pocket and got to work.

* * * * *

I wasted no time in making contact with those who had last seen the missing girl. Anger with her parents coupled with a willful nature and her stated wish to "teach her parents a lesson" gave me an idea.

Come summer, it would be more difficult to find the young girl, but now, with everything snow covered, there were only a handful of places she was likely to be. A few minutes between computer and phone and I'd narrowed it down. Mrs. Gaumer had a big house, a big family and an indulgent heart. Hers was always a reasonable place to look.

The young girl was there. A promise from the girl to stay put until we could meet, another from her parents, and I was on the way back to headquarters.

But back at my desk, questions about the list persisted in popping up, like headless bodies in a Fun House, interfering with my attempts to get back to my job. What was bothering me? The list, I supposed, but why? All we had was a list of Horizon policyholders with rather large face amounts, yet, according to Chief Warmkessel the list had been central to Finch's arrest. Ken must have known or guessed that such would be the outcome, ergo his reluctance to use it himself. But what had Finch actually done?

Ken's note also said the list would clear my family of involvement in Tunnelson's death and so it had. Why? What was the connection? That led to another question. What was so awful that Ken felt he 'had to go,' that he had to quit?

Time and again I pulled the list out of my pocket only to resolutely return it in favor of my work. Finally, I gave in and set it in front of me, trying to piece it all together. Some kind of fraud, Peters had said. Obviously some tactic that would save the company money...I had my hand on the phone when it rang.

"Busy?"

"I was just going to call you. What's up? Janus okay?"

"She's fine. I called about that damned list." I laughed. "Oh. That means you...Natch. Two brains beating as one again. Well, I'm blessed if I know exactly what it means, but it looks like Finch's outfit was set to pay out a bundle."

"One hundred million, give or take. A lot of money. Is that your thinking too?"

"Only thing I can think of. Is that enough to commit fraud?"

"Well, Tom Halloran said it was a small, struggling company until recently and now it's going great guns. But if fraud is involved, they must have found a way to deny these claims. You're the one with the imagination. Any ideas?"

I said not at the moment. "We're missing something but I'm blessed if I can think what." I looked at my watch. "Anyway, I'd better get back to my job."

"Hang on a sec! Can you get away for a bit? We can talk it..."

"I don't know. I'm really busy here. Check with me later."

I struggled to focus on my cases, finding it uphill work. I was relieved when the grandmother phoned to say that all three—father, son and grandmother—had had a sit-down and come up with at least a temporary solution. The boy would be permitted to plan his own sixteenth birthday party. A decision would be made then to see how well he handled the responsibility. Sixteen. Someone else had had a sixteenth birthday party recently too. Oh yes. Finch's daughter. Was it to be a last happy memory for the girl? Had it gone well? Had Finch remembered to pick up the items on the note he'd scribbled then left behind? Was the girl's party over before her father was arrested and charged with fraud. What was he supposed to pick up anyway? I pictured the scribbled list.

Then the pin dropped! I remembered clearly now the reason I stopped to look at it. The scribbles were all too familiar. I'd worked with dozens of people, young and old, who, despite their keen intelligence could not spell a word if their lives depended on it.

I was certain now. The note in the manila envelope could not, in a million years, have been written by Roland Finch!

I buzzed Sam, asked him to pick me up for a quick coffee and, willingly now, got back to the troubles of Plainfield's youth.

CHAPTER 21

SAM

Sal's sudden invite came as no surprise. I knew something was bugging her about those damned memos, meaning she'd pick at it until she got it. Naturally that meant I'd stay on it too. I'd been trying to work it out while I brushed Nimbus.

My only worry was *why* she was on it. If it was because of that damned phony Fowler...! Nimbus warned me not to take it out on him. "Sorry, old friend," I told him, promising him an extra parsnip tonight. He nuzzled my neck. "Only problem is," I told him, "I can't tell how far it's gone."

As it was, Sal's emphasis on 'quick' limited my options but the day, though cold, was brightly sunny and that meant she'd want it to be outdoors.

She began before she had her seat belt fastened.

"Sam, I think I know the problem with that list Mr. Finch is supposed to have written. Oh. You brought lunch?"

I told her of course. "So what is it?"

"Well, it's handwritten and on Finch's personal memo paper, therefore intended to be the sort of note one scribbles to oneself, wouldn't you say?" I said it would appear so. "Well, I don't buy it, Sam. Fact is, I don't believe Mr. Finch could possibly have written it."

I pulled into a secluded section of Thaxton Park where a half circle of evergreens provides protection from the worst of the weather. She explained while I poured thick soup into a cup. Handing it to her, I gave her a good look for signs she was missing the creep. But, in spite of her uniform, she looked much like she had as a kid: chestnut hair swathed in a furry helmet, poking around the hamper in search of a pickled egg.

Dead in Pleasant Company
A Pennsylvania Dutch Mystery

She took a bite and a sip and explained. "Remember the day we were in his office and he took a call from his wife? He scribbled a note then, remember?"

"Yeah. And you picked it up and read it. It's not like you to read other..."

"I wasn't reading it. I was looking at it." I thought it sounded like something Janus would say. She hurried to explain. "The writing, I mean—the spelling in particular. It was the same sort of hen scratch I've seen in students who have learning disabilities in spelling and writing."

"Learning dis...Oh. Like the kids who are great at math or science but can't read. Or those who read well beyond their age but can't get the hang of even basic math."

"Right. Those are the more familiar types of learning disabilities we see, but there are some (always remembering those afflicted are well above average in other ways) who have enormous difficulty in dealing with the interpretation and production of letters. It affects their ability to spell or write, sometimes both."

I thought back. "Oh, right. Like our buddy Jack Coleman, the Physics major who aced all his math and science subjects but couldn't get a college degree until the college dropped its written exit exam."

"Exactly. Well, the problem doesn't disappear once they're out of school. People learn to live with it, work around it so others don't really notice, but it's still there."

"Due to brain damage I think you said."

"One theory, yes. What they used to call minimal brain damage. There are some new understandings and treatments being..."

"You think Finch has that kind of problem?"

"I do. Look at this list." She spread it on the seat between us. "Remember his wife called and asked him to pick up his daughter's birthday cake? Well what he wrote was 'pic up cuk,' Now look at this list." I did as I was told.

"The only way Finch could produce such a perfect list would be to actually *trace* each letter—a laborious task. And why should he with the computer right there? You see what I mean?"

I said I saw. "But wasn't that just because he was in a hurry? Hell, I scribble…"

She was shaking her head. "Not the same thing. You can write it out perfectly if you take a little more time. He can't. Besides, it's the *kind* of spelling errors he makes. Not at all the kind most of us make if we're in a hurry."

"So you're saying…"

"Finch could not have produced this handwritten list if his life depended on it."

* * * * *

I'd no sooner dropped my sister off at work when my phone rang. "Want to do something for me?" I told her to name it. "Thing is, I'm beginning to feel like a three-tailed rat. I turned over that darned list, handing over the evidence on which Mr. Finch was arrested and, always assuming we're right, ought to do something about getting him un-arrested. Problem is, even if I could get off work, and I'm so jammed up with cases that would be difficult, I've promised Andy I'd keep myself available for a trip to Washington with Janus if needed. So…"

"You want me to go where and do what?"

"I don't know. New York Police I guess. Find out what else they have on Finch. If that list is the main thing, they've got to know the truth about it. One way or another, see if you can talk to Finch. Or his attorney if you can't see Finch. Also Finch has a family. They're probably hysterical." I told her I got the idea. "You know Sam, as long as the cops have somebody in custody they're not going to be easy to convince. Nothing says they have to accept what I say. It's puzzling Sam because if Finch didn't write the list, who did? And why?"

So she'd come to the creek but she wasn't ready to drink. Okay. She'd get there.

"Try to find out how far the case is gone. Are they taking it to a grand jury or turning it over to the Feds? Insurance fraud is a federal crime."

I accepted her commission with alacrity. I was feeling magnanimous. Sal was convinced the Finch list was fishy. I was equally sure the note that went with it had the same smell. Not that I wasn't glad to have him out of her life, I just wanted to make sure he stayed that way.

* * * * *

When I need a car in the 'city,' I usually fly in and borrow a company car from among those in the garage of the Manhattan office building we acquired when some of the Thaxton businesses went global. Invariably, however, somebody there nails me, trying to get me to make decisions we pay them to make, so I decided to give it a pass and drive the couple hundred miles.

With mountains of snow still hanging around, some of which had begun melting and was now ice, and Ma Nature deciding whether to treat us to another ten inches of the white stuff or a couple of inches of rain, driving was not without its own hazards. You're thinking I must be completely bonkers to drive in such weather when I don't have to, but driving in bad weather is like anything else— you gotta keep your hand in if you don't want to forget how.

I tallied up the possibilities. If it was rain, we'd have rain on top of snow which meant ice. More than one car had wound up in a ditch recently and, with the possibility of downed ice-laden power lines, you risk being stranded somewhere, pretty much on your own. If it was to be more snow, plowed roads could drift shut and in less than an hour you and your car could be made invisible. There was a lot to do.

I checked the trunk for shovel, sand, tow chain, flashlight, first aid kit, emergency lights, wool blankets and sleeping bag. Knowing when you poke a snake's nest you sometimes get bit, I went back in the house for my gun. I was adding a large thermos of water and a smaller one of hot coffee when my watch beeped. I told it I was listening.

"Me." Sal's voice came. "Where are you?"

"Home. Packing. What's up?"

"Glad I caught you. New York wants me there for a first hand account of events. Want company?"

I told her always. "You're too popular. What about Washington?"

"Chief says to go to New York. Half an hour okay?"

* * * * *

I'd met Captain Carderra of Manhattan's 18th precinct a year or so back in connection with some problems we'd been having in our New York office. I thought him a good cop, tough but rational. He shook hands, waved us to a chair and called in the investigators running the Tunnelson case.

Three detectives came within minutes. They did not offer to shake hands. Sal and I had decided en route that I should try to see Finch while she made her report to the cops, but I didn't like the way they looked at her so I hung around.

They barely listened to her explanation of how the list came to her and things went from bad to worse when she threatened to blow their case against him by telling them the man they'd arrested could not have written the list of names.

Dead in Pleasant Company
A Pennsylvania Dutch Mystery

She laid it on them as concisely as possible, pretty much avoiding educational jargon. Her counterparts listened, hanging on to civility only because they were under orders. They let it be known they did not like some hick cop, especially some high-brow, up-town, do-gooding rookie cop, sticking her nose in.

Sal stuck to the point. Did they, she asked, have any questions.

They turned sarcastic. They saw no good reason not to accept the list as the real skinny and they could not see why she was being so nit-picky. To say they were skeptical is to call an ace-high royal flush a good hand.

Sergeant Mendoza pointedly questioned her real motives, counting out objections on his fingers.

One: The Plainfield cops had sent them the incriminating list and on the basis of the damned list they'd investigated and found Finch with his hand in the cookie jar. Based on that info, they'd hauled Finch in, charged him, properly Mirandized and booked him and he was damned well going to *stay* booked! If Plainfield was looking to get a piece of the collar they could guess again.

Two. This Tunnelson guy had bought the farm in the cop's own damned restaurant! What the hell kind of deal was that?

Three. She'd been withholding evidence. Why had she not been charged?

Four. She was personally involved with this Ken guy and why had he given her the evidence instead of the cops? How involved could you get?

Five. If Plainfield didn't think the list was legit, they shouldna sent it. What was going on? Was the whole Plainfield Police force in on it?

I forbore to point out this was circuitous reasoning and point five was really an addendum to point one.

Mendoza was going on. "Point of fact," he said, "Finch's already been arraigned. Naturally he denied everything. We naturally expected him to deny everything. I don't know how it is in the 'boonies,' but here crooks don't just up and confess. Besides, the 'perp' didn't say anything about a spelling whachaamacallit and what the hell is a spelling watchamacallit anyway? Just another damned excuse to get a guilty guy off. That might work in Hicksville but it's goin' nowhere here."

Apparently unruffled by Mendoza's unyielding hypothesis, Sal appeared to have decided, by whatever osmotic way she has—probably something to do with her damned toes—that Mendoza, rather than his senior officer, was the one to deal with. I held my breath as she began, but once she caught and held his eye, I relaxed. Seldom did that self-effacing, earnest gaze fail. Amused, I watched my sister dig into the same bag of tricks which had coaxed the conservative aunts to vote twice for a Democrat, persuaded some of the world's best chefs to join the PC chain and, most recently, brought a class of adolescent misfits in line. I admit I get a kick out of seeing it work.

Today, interlacing her whole conversation with 'Sergeant Mendoza' this and 'Sergeant Mendoza' that and tossing a bucketful of 'yessirs' and 'nossirs' in his direction, she began by apologizing for getting in the way, said she was only there on orders from her Chief, told the Sergeant he knew what *that* was like, admitted she had only a fraction of the experience he and his men had and would be honored if she could sit at their feet and learn from them. She admitted, with genuine humility, she could be wrong. She confessed she realized she was being a pain but, knowing they had an enviable reputation as honest and competent cops, they would want to do the right thing, and that, that said, she would get out of their hair as soon as possible.

Disingenuous, you might say but it wasn't. She meant every word of it. Well almost every word.

"Look Sergeant Mendoza," she said, coming to the finish, "I promise to go along with whatever you decide. And look, if you're too busy, I can come back later. I just want you to have all the information possible." The low voice dripped with sincerity.

"Whatever," Mendoza said. You could almost hear them say 'We don't need no stinkin' spelling disabilities around here.' What they said was, "So what do you want from us?" He looked sourly at me, "And what the hell do *you* want? You her bodyguard?"

I protested this perceptive charge, insisting I'd hoped to speak to Mr. Finch while they talked. "If that would not interfere with your investigation."

"Look! Our investigation's over," he said firmly. "How come you want to see Finch? You two buddies?"

"Oh no. In fact, I only met him once and then he threw me out of his office."

He grunted. "There's one thing in his favor. Oh hell! I said we owe you one. Go ahead. Be my guest. That it?"

That, we said as one, was it.

They said they had some questions for her. I said if there were no objections, I'd be going. Mendoza picked up the phone and barked for some lesser being to show me the way. He wasted no time starting on Sal. As I left he was asking how she got the list and why the hell this Fowler guy gave them to her.

By the time my guide arrived, one of the officers had pulled her aside and pieces of the conversation floated my way. "...my kid...call him lazy...works like a dog at it...whiz at math...teachers think he ain't tryin' but write a paper...hell breaks loose...wit's end."

Obviously it was not my twin who needed protection.

Hannah Fairchild

* * * * *

They brought Finch in and left him, a sad-looking sack if ever there was one. His round face flushed with embarrassment when he saw me, the liquid blue eyes blinking back angry tears. I dealt him a firm handshake across the bare table and got back the same limp one he'd given me back in his office.

In response to his growled question, I told him neither my sister nor I thought him guilty of anything and wanted to help if he was willing.

"Willing? Oh hell, I'm willing enough! I'd talk to the devil himself if I thought it would help. I suppose I should thank God *anybody* believes me," he said. "My wife's about crazy! They're appointing a receiver for all of Horizon's accounts! She got me a lawyer and the damned idiot wants me to confess! Confess! Hell, I'm not even sure what I'm accused of!"

I asked if he could explain the list Fowler had left with my sister.

"What list?" I showed him my copy. "Oh that! I don't get it! Where did this come from? What the hell does it have to do with anything? Of course I can't explain it. I never saw it before the cops showed it to me." His eyes teared up again. "You say your sister got it from Ken Fowler? Where the hell did he get it? And why did he give it to her? He doesn't even like…" He flushed. "What does it mean?"

"This is your personal stationery, isn't it?"

He squinted. "Yeah, so what?"

"We-el, it's handwritten. I imagine the idea was to make it look like you wrote it. Do you know anyone who might do that?"

"As a joke you mean?"

I shook my head. "No. I don't think it was meant as a joke."

Dead in Pleasant Company
A Pennsylvania Dutch Mystery

"Then who? Or better yet, why? Why would anyone do that, Mr. Thaxton? My people like...My God! I'd tell you to ask Fowler but they're trying to tell me he quit! I don't believe it! I just don't believe it!" I assured him it was true. "Oh my God! Just like that! How could he do that to me? I thought of him as a son! We were friends!" Join the club, I thought. "It's just hopeless."

I told him it was not hopeless, that Sal at this moment was showing the cops he could not have written the list and I was arranging bail.

"You mean it's possible I'll be getting out of here?"

"Depends on what else they have on you. If the list is it, yes, I think you will. Try to relax a little Mr. Finch. It could take a while. Is there anything I can do in the meantime? Would you like me to see your wife?"

Relief flooded his face. "Would you? God, yes! Hell, they've frozen my accounts because of the fraud charge so she hasn't been able to raise money for bail. She can borrow some from my brother to pay the bills and buy groceries but hell, I don't know what she's to do about the business! Yes, Mr. Thaxton. Any advice you can give will be most welcome."

I said I'd help wherever I could and got another shower of thanks. "Forget it. Are you ready to answer some questions?"

He threw me a quick suspicious look, then let it go. He sat back in his chair, the flush fading from his face. "Go ahead! Ask away!"

"To begin with, do you often attend autopsies?"

He looked surprised and pained. "No. Just...in special cases."

"So how was it you attended Mr. Tunnelson's?"

"Fowler asked me to! You can understand that. Hell, when he signed Tunnelson it was an enormous coup. His name alone brought in lots of new policyholders. We had to be careful if the claim was questionable...Besides, he said he had you and your sister in a...," here he had the grace to blush, "...ready to plump for a big policy but you'd insisted on meeting the head man. Had to leave a board meeting, for God's sake!"

"So you came."

"Hell yes! A chance to sell the famous Thaxton twins one of our policies! Hell, I would've walked across hot stones! Just to be seen with you with all the reporters around..."

"I see."

"God! What you must think of me!" He slumped further in his chair. "No worse'n I think of myself, that's for sure."

"Look, forget that. What do you know about these other pin-prick deaths?"

"Huh? Pin-prick deaths? What do you mean?"

"Like Tunnelson. Remember? Fowler told my sister there had been others. Do you remember hearing about them?"

"Fowler said that? Well..." Obviously what Fowler said carried great weight. "Let's see. I've got a good memory but I don't know. Only time I remember hearing about them was when Fowler mentioned 'em that day at the Tunnelson autopsy. He said it was just like the others."

"What others, did he say?"

"No and I didn't think to ask. Frankly, I just wanted to get the hell out of there. Just 'cause I sell insurance don't mean I like morgues!"

"Okay. Let's move on. Do you personally review all large claims?"

He shook his head. "Used to. Not in the last couple of years. Leave it to Fowler. Sign where he tells me to. He loved that kind of detail. What the hell am I going to do if he doesn't come back? I wish to God I knew why he left and where he was. He could save Horizon if anyone could."

Take a brick house to fall on him before he admitted he'd been schnookered, I thought. I told him I would like permission to look at Horizon's records.

"Our records? Oh yeah. Like before." He look chagrined. "Of course. I don't know what you expect to find but why the hell not? At this point there's nothing to lose! I'll give you a note to my secretary. She's still hanging on there, though I'm damned if I know why."

I asked what he knew about the six names on the list he'd supposedly written. He showed some discomfort, but shook his head. "They're familiar now, of course. They would be. For God's sake they were all read off at my arraignment as estates I'd defrauded! Defrauded! Hell, those claims were denied properly! There was not one single thing wrong with 'em!"

"You said you signed all...Hold it. Did you say *denied?* These claims were denied? All six? Tunnelson's too?"

"Yes. Of course! That's what all the damned ruckus is about!"

"But why?"

"Why do you think? Because Tunnelson was murdered! Hell, that's what your damned coroner's jury said! We didn't make it up, for corn's sake!"

I heard the words of my insurance friend when I compared Horizon's progress to Lloyd's. "More like the opposite, he'd said. I'd been a complete idiot! I'd assumed Horizon had to pay double or triple benefits to the names on the list. "So these high-risk policies in which you specialize pay off only in the case of *natural* death?"

"Of course! What most people die of, after all! Even high-risk people like you. It's a great idea. People in the high risk category just can't get the kind of insurance they want. Fowler put it together and we're pretty much alone in the market although I've heard Prudential is thinking..." He drifted off.

"I just assumed..." I'd been a complete ass! No doubt all six policy holders on the list had also been denied payment and who knows how many more there were. No wonder Finch had been arrested.

A guard came, motioned Finch to follow. I went to see about bail. An extra twenty to the clerk secured a promise to see Finch got a cab home as soon as he was released.

I collected Sal and we, too, hailed a cab for the cross town trip. Manhattan traffic on a Friday with snow piled six feet high in every direction is no place for a country boy.

* * * * *

I filled Sal in on the way to Horizon's New York office.

"So you're saying Tunnelson died from a heart attack after all and someone tried to make it look like murder to avoid paying the claim?"

I shrugged. "Looks like."

"Incredible! A risky idea, wouldn't you say. And clever."

"Right. Problem is, whoever came up with it..."

"...wouldn't be so dumb as to leave that incriminating list lying around. Exactly."

"So, you're suggesting the whole list is phony?"

"Well, yes. I suppose I am."

"Okay. I've one more problem for you then because the more I think about it, the more I see that it just does not sound like a square-shooter like Finch. As you said, it's clever and daring."

"I agree."

I decided to throw caution to the winds. "So let's see. Who, connected with the case, does it sound like?"

She looked at me. "Ken," she said softly. "It sounds like Ken Fowler."

CHAPTER 22

SAM

It was half-past one when Horizon's articulated elevator deposited us at the top floor. The place was in an uproar, a sharp contrast to the pristine order of their sister offices in Washington. Of course a lot had happened since then. Today a scattering of men and women sat around listlessly while telephones went pretty much unanswered. We found Finch's secretary in tears. We said we'd come to help.

"Thank God! Somebody's got to help him," she wailed. It is absolutely ludicrous to think Mr. Finch could do anything illegal! I phoned Mrs. Finch for instructions and she said to ask Mr. Fowler what to do, but he's gone too! Can you believe it? Ken gone! Where is he? We rely on him so much! He's so good at fixing things! Everybody knows he'll take over when Mr. Finch retires."

I looked for a nameplate. "Look Miss Ready," I said, tossing a buck's worth of oil, "it's not going to help Mr. Finch if his staff lets him down. Don't they realize that letting the phones go unanswered is likely to trigger panic among your policyholders? Can you get them back to work?"

She wailed again. "That's just it! People are demanding to know what's going on and some are already demanding we cash in their policies. What are we going to tell them? And besides, they're," she nodded at her fellow employees, "all convinced the company will go bankrupt and they won't get paid! I've tried to tell them to hang in until we know something for sure, but..."

I held a palm up to halt the flow. "Okay. Okay. You can tell them not to worry. Horizon is not going under and they will be paid as usual, but not if they let things go to pot.

They can tell callers that the business will be fine, but if policyholders want to cancel, they will get a full refund without delay. Chances are, if folks know they can cash in immediately they'll give it a second thought. I'll talk to your accountants before I go and make sure funds are available. Will the others listen to you?"

She nodded. "I think so. Let me tell them right away. I can't stand to see them all..."

She hurried off, stopping to speak to each of the small groups of laggards in turn. Each reacted the same, turning to look in our direction. I gave Sal a look and she went to offer support. That brought them together. They listened, asked for and got assurance they'd be paid, asked and received instructions regarding what they should say to callers. They cast another look at me before slowly returning to desk, computer and phone.

Finch's secretary took the note from her boss and cringed. "Oh God, try to translate this," she said. "Do you think they would let someone take his small recorder in to him? He always dictates on that."

I told her bail was being arranged for him and he would no doubt be back by tomorrow.

She thanked God, I assume for the news not the note, rolling her eyes heavenward at that, perhaps expecting help from above in translating her boss' scribble. "If I can decipher this," she said. "He can't spell for a da...at all. Can't even look up a word in the dictionary, it's that bad!. Even spell check can't help him. Let's see. I guess that says files. What's that word? Den...something. Oh, denied. Claims denied. Gosh, Mr. Thaxton. The police took all that with them. Said they're evidence." Her voice rose to a wail. "Evidence! Oh my God!"

Sal told her to take it easy. "You store your records on computer though too, don't you?"

*Dead in Pleasant Company
A Pennsylvania Dutch Mystery*

She admitted they did. "For the past two years, yes. When Mr. Fowler joined us he put all our records into a new program. Saves the girls a lot of work."

"And for prior years?" Sal asked.

"Oh, we still have them. Stored on disks. You want them now?"

"Let's just start with the last two years, if you don't mind." We were directed to a couple of monitors and waited while she went to her own, wasting no time in tapping in commands. I asked if she could send the files from last year to Sal and those of the prior year to me.

We spent some time at it before I got up and joined my sister. "Do you see any cause of death in your files?"

"No I don't. That space is blank. Odd, isn't it?"

We called Miss Ready and she came to look. "That's impossible! You're just not looking at the right place. These are just scanned on to the disks from the originals so they are exact duplicates. I'll show you." She began scrolling down my screen. "Everything's here," indicating each line as she scrolled. "insured's name, age, address, the amount and terms of the policy, the date, time and place of the insured's death, the signature of the verifying physician and the legatees identity and manner and amount of pay…huh! That is odd! This one says the claim was denied but the line for cause of death and reason for denial is blank! Let me…" She scrolled to another file. "Here too! You're right! That's odd!"

Yeah, I thought, that was one word for it. "Did the police say when you would get the paper files back?"

"No. I didn't think there was any rush. After all we have them on…At least I thought…" She looked up at me. "Mr. Thaxton, can you tell me what evidence they have against Mr. Finch?"

I explained about the lists Fowler had left with Sal.

She gave my sister a sharp look. "Oh. So it was you he…"

Sal shook her head. "I just met him through my work. It was you on whom he relied, you know."

That threw the woman off balance. "I don't understand…I can't believe…but if Mr. Fowler left it…" She struggled with mixed loyalties. "You mean he's the one who said Mr. Finch…" Then she pulled herself together. "Well! I would sure like to see it."

Sal called up her own computer and faxed a copy into the secretary's system. It did not take the woman long to take in its meaning. The list seemed to blow her away.

"I can't believe Ken would do such a thing! There must be some explanation." She eyed Sal with suspicion. "No way could Mr. Finch have written this."

"What about those names?. Are you familiar with any of them?"

"Not really, but I don't work with policies or claims anymore."

"Oh? Who does?"

"We've got three or four people who work for agents signing up new policies. As for claims, final approval was pretty much Ken…Mr. Fowler's department—the large claims anyway and mostly he did his own work. Likes to save work for the girls. He's so thoughtful! I wish I knew where…"

I told her I saw.

She looked at me. "Mr. Thaxton, what does it all mean?"

I said that's what we were trying to find out. "But one thing seems certain. Someone is trying to make it look as though your boss is defrauding claimants."

"And you think it's Mr. Fowler, don't you?"

I didn't push it. "Well, it has to be someone here, don't you think? So that would make him a candidate. Can you think of anyone else who could have made up this list? Do you recognize the handwriting at all?"

She shook her head vigorously, too vigorously I thought.

I realized my sister had deserted her computer and was wandering around the large office, pausing for a word here or there. She returned to ask if she could have a look at Ken's office.

Fowler had a corner office every bit as big as that of his boss, but without the clutter. Here there were no photos of family, no ash trays made by little hands. One wall was hung with framed awards, another held a single painting, a mass of shades of brown and black with small dabs of red. Something about the picture was disturbing and I wondered who the artist was. Curious, I looked to see if it was signed. It was, with a single flamboyant K.

I turned to show Sal. Her attention was on a small woman struggling with a large carton. It was both too full and too large for her. I moved forward to help, but it spilled nearly half its contents on the floor. Naturally I went to help, but Sal's look told me to back off. She wrapped the girl in a smile and began to help return the mess of papers and disks to the box.

"These men think we have arms and legs of iron, don't they? Let me help you. Where do these go?"

"Down to Recycle. Mr. Fowler was most specific. Said to make sure all this stuff was recycled immediately. If you just stick those damned disks back on top I can manage."

"Look here," Sal said too reasonable to be denied, "we're going right by there. Let my brother take the box. It's right down at the end of the hall, isn't it? I saw the sign on the way here. I'm sure you've got tons of work to do."

I guessed what she wanted and gave the girl a cowed look.

It was Sal she thanked. "Boy, you said it! This whole place is a mess! They're saying by the time Mr. Finch pays everybody back we'll be out of business. Who would've thought nice, kind old Mr. Finch was a crook! I guess it's what they say though, isn't it? I mean about still water running deep. Although, come to think of it, Mr. Finch was never really what you call 'still.' Always moving around, here and there. Cracking jokes. You know the type."

Sal admitted she knew the type. The girl heaved a sigh of relief and parted with the box. Sal said to the girl, "At least Mr. Fowler thought about you. It's lucky you were here when he called. Was that this morning? Did he say where he'd be? I have a book of his I promised to return."

The girl sighed. "Yesterday. That's when he called. He wanted me to do this before I left last night but things got so hectic I forgot. Actually I don't know where he is. He'll be furious if he finds out I'm just getting around to it. You won't tell him, will you?"

"Of course not! Hard to work for, is he?"

"Well, he's fussy. Wants you to do what you're told without making a big deal of it, but then he's always so sweet afterwards..."

Sal told her she understood, assured her the company was being bailed out by a friend of Finch's and that her boss would be back himself shortly. The girl seemed to be divided between disappointment that the excitement might be coming to an end and relief that she'd be getting paid as usual.

"Well, if you don't mind taking those things down..."

Sal nodded her off.

"Gone to tell the others," she said to me.

"And what," I asked, hefting the wobbling load, "is this in aid of?"

Dead in Pleasant Company
A Pennsylvania Dutch Mystery

"Evidence, sir. Evidence! If Ken is the *qui bono*[5] in the case," she said, squinting at me, deep in thought, "we'd better hustle and find out *quando, quomodo* et exactly *quare es bono,* don't you think?"

I turned to look at her. If she was feeling whimsical enough to toss Latin at me, it could only mean Fowler had not broken her heart.

I jumped in. "And, perhaps," I said juggling the heavy box, "of more immediate concern, *quo* the hell *es?*"

I reflected that I could have answered the "why" he did it then and there but the time was not yet right.

We went right past the recycle room, turned and took the stairs to the garage and our car. I stowed the carton in the trunk.

* * * * *

On the way home we called Mrs. Finch and brought her up to date. She got tearfully grateful when she learned her husband would soon be back home and I turned the phone over to Sal to get her calmed down.

I phoned the Horizon board president next to say we would underwrite Horizon until it was back on its feet as long as our name was kept out of it. He said he was not sure the board would go along with it, that it was likely they would insist on selling.

"Fine," I said. "Then you've got a buyer. We'll advance the operating funds in the meantime. Make sure they pay salaries and benefits as usual, including Finch's. I'll have

---

* Roughly translated:

[5] *qui bono* – is this one who benefits; *quando* - how (he benefits); *quomodo* - when (he benefited); *et quare es bono* - and what (exactly) the benefit is

quo es? - where is he?

our people up there first thing in the morning with a check. One condition—we want no press on this. As far as everyone knows, it's business as usual."

"Will you be buying it personally?"

"Can't say at this point. I'll leave that to my people after they see you tomorrow. Ten o'clock suit you?"

Then a call to Mrs. Sweeney, giving her the skinny and telling her to get somebody from The Firm to New York in the morning.

"You don't want New York to handle it?"

"No. Let's keep this quiet."

One more call, even longer, this to a friend in the Insurance Information Group. He promised to have his research department look into the matter of pin-prick deaths.

By the time I dropped Sal off at her place, I had a reply from IIG. They could find no record of any such deaths.

I reported this to Sal. "Why are you so all-fired worried about those damned pin-pricks anyway," I asked, walking her to her door. "They can't possibly have anything to do with Tunnelson's death now. His death was natural."

"That's just the point. What were they doing there?." She turned to go. "Maybe something in that box of Fowler's…"

"Right," I said. "I'll go through it." I looked at her to see why she'd stopped mid-sentence.

"Look!" She pointed to the windows in Walt's rooms. "Lights on! He must be home!" Relief flooded her voice. "Look, can you keep on your own for a bit? I must check on Janus and if Walt's home…"

I told her to go ahead. "Call if you need me," I told her back. She disappeared into the house.

* * * * *

Dead in Pleasant Company
A Pennsylvania Dutch Mystery

SAL

Walt opened the door to my knock. "I was asleep," he said unnecessarily.

I apologized for waking him. "I saw your lights. I just wanted to welcome you home. Are you all right?"

"Yeah. Just tired. We didn't get much sleep."

I wanted to say that being 'on the lam,' running from both police and family will do that. "How is Barney?"

"Fine. Back at work. I'm going in later."

"Good. Will you have dinner with us?"

"No thanks, Mom. We had plenty to eat. I just need some shut-eye."

"All right, Son." I wanted to ask him where in the world he'd been, tell him how thoughtless he'd been to worry us, comment on his recent interest in the restaurant business and bring him up to date on my news. In the end I said, "We missed you. Glad you're all right."

He sat on the edge of his bed and yawned. "See the kid's still here. She moving in?" You been sucked in again his tone said.

I told him not really and explained her status as witness in the case against Mastermind. His eyes flew open at that. "You mean this kid's been hooked up with that nut? Wow!" His eyes blinked and he yawned.

"Wow indeed. Look, why don't you go ahead and get some sleep and I'll fill you in later. That do you?"

"Fine. Okay." I turned to go. "Hey Mom!"

"Yes?"

"That mean you're involved with that Mastermind guy too?"

"Only peripherally." The small boy who worried over the worms cut in half when we dug in the garden returned to his eyes. "Don't worry Son. I probably won't even see him. Cousin Andy's taking care of him."

"Good. And Mom," he looked at me from lowered eyes. "I'm sorry about Tunnelson going off like that. I mean, I gather you and he..."

I shook my head. "No, Son. I had no special feelings for him."

"Good," he said. "Real good," he muttered, yawning widely. "Oh, by the way, Mom, Mrs. Sweeney says you're worried about he 25k I put in my account. It's Barney's dough really, part of the settlement he got from Tunnelson. We're planning to start a small business together marketing Barney's great rhubarb jam, maybe some other rhubarb products he's creating. He wants us to talk it over with you first. Says you're best at that sort of thing and I guess I do too really," he added sheepishly. "That okay?"

"Okay," I said, feeling foolish. It was so like him. Just when I'd worried he was headed for the worst sort of trouble, he's actually making great strides forward. His twenty-five thousand dollars had nothing to do with Judd Tunnelson's twenty-five thousand. This time the coincidence.

Walt was already back in bed, seeming to drift off to sleep before his head touched the pillow.

Unable to resist, I pulled the crumpled comforter out from under him and covered him. I touched his forehead. No fever.

His eyes opened a crack. "Thanks, Mom. Sorry if I worried you."

Kids, I thought.

* * * * *

Honeycutt waited at the foot of the stairs. "Mr. Andrew called, Madam. He says he will be picking you and the young lady up shortly. He says you shall be prepared to stay a day or two."

"Really? Did he say why?"

"No, Madam. Just that it was urgent and private. Mrs. Honey has picked up the child from your sister-in-law and is packing now."

"Thank you, Honeycutt. Do you know where Sam is?"

"In the library, Madam."

I thanked him again and went in search of my brother. He was at my desk, surrounded by floppy disks. I told him I would be leaving for a day or two.

"Leaving? In the middle of this? Going where?"

"Andy. Wants Janus and me. He says it's urgent."

"Oh yeah? That must mean there's a break! I'll just grab a bag and *geht mit*."

"Don't be silly! I'll be safe with Andy." I assured him this was one argument he was not going to win. "You've got your own culprit to track down, haven't you? How's it going?" I nodded at the heap on the table. "Box any help?"

He grunted, pushing the purloined disks with disgust. "Naught but crashed files here."

"They might could be recovered though," I said.

"Yeah but I have a better idea. Okay then. Be off with you. So I know when I'm not wanted. Should you come to your senses, however, and want me, I'll be at my place." He grabbed his coat and ran.

CHAPTER 23

SAL

If you were alive anywhere on the earth at the time of is capture, you know something of the man the media dubbed The Criminal of the Century.

You will have heard techno-jocks describe, in baffling and bewildering detail, how Mastermind manufactured death by simply tapping away on a keyboard, leaving behind no fingerprints, no usable DNA, no voice to be matched. You may have joined the Anti-Internet movement, decrying the insidious spread of a system which not only cloaked a callous murderer, but shielded the deadly path taken to kill and maim.

You would certainly have heard discussions, philosophical, political and psychological, attempting to explain just who should have done what to protect the public from a force that could be neither seen, heard, nor touched yet do such evil from which no man, woman or child was safe. That it happened at all still lingers with us in the certain knowledge it could happen again. It is as if some heretofore prohibition against wickedness had been breached forever.

Yet in the end, it was left to a child and a sticky bottle of Chambord to bring down the infamous cyber-terrorist. As for me, by the time the order finally came through to push ahead with it, my thoughts were less on the world-wide implications of the moment than on the relief I felt that the child, who had become increasingly manipulative, could be reigned in before she had gotten completely out of hand.

As of this writing, only a handful of people have had the full story but Sam says I owe it to you, so here it is, pretty much the way he got it, settled before a fire on my porch, watching rain turn mountains of snow to slush.

After Janus and I left the apartment in Dundale, Andy had turned out the full force of the federal government, sending teams to move quickly from town to town, armed with the collected information about the personal habits of Ohraymond and Dumbdonna. It took two days and the keen eye of a part-time clerk in a state-run liquor store in a small, quiet suburb of Philadelphia to locate them.

But finding them was one thing, conviction another. Take the problem of identification. Andy believed a child's identification of a sketch was not likely to hold up against a clever defense lawyer. On the other hand, identification by the dozens of others who had made contact with the trio, had its own problems. As they had in the hospitals, the couple had adopted subtle and varying disguises: a change of hair color, a variety of vision wear, the representation of the girl as a boy, all these contributed to the difficulty of a certain identification. In one lineup after another, landladies could not reliably pick out this anonymously indistinguishable couple from dozens of other young renters.

It would have to be left to the child.

A reunion between Janus Morgan Alexander and 'Ohraymond' was called for. The couple's daily habit of walking to breakfast at a small restaurant near their current apartment provided the means. Janus would be the bait.

Andy arranged to have the child be seen, seated alone in the window of the self-same restaurant where she was readily visible from the street. With me playing waitress in an impossible blonde wig concealing a small video camera, the family reunion was recorded. Andy himself manned the surveillance equipment from a van parked just outside at the curb.

It was something to see!

The couple's initial shock at seeing the child, sitting alone inside a restaurant hundreds of miles from where they'd last seen her, is clearly visible on the videotape.

The next few moments are touch and go. The couple remain outside, watching the table, apparently waiting to see who was with the child and arguing whether or not to go in.

The way the young lady herself handled it was proof of how readily she'd learned to play the fainting game. Even with me parading back and forth in wig and pink-and-white checked uniform filling cups and glasses, she did not turn a hair. (This particular tape of me, be-wigged and 'trucked out' to beat the band, being ordered about by the child, is to this day, cause for merriment at family occasions.)

Janus was quick enough to recognize she had me at a disadvantage and use it to order one sweet treat after another. 'Oh miss, please bring me another cupcake.' 'Waitress! More chocolate, please.' Small minded as it was, I could not help asking, when my back was turned to the couple outside, if she was sure this was an eating day.

The videotapes show the couple pass the window twice. Finally, apparently convinced she is alone, the two enter.

The woman's voice is heard, saccharin and silky. "Janus dear! What are you doing here, honey?"

"Oh! Hey! Where are my presents? Hey Uncle Raymond. Where's my Barbie?"

That was enough. Andy and his minions closed in, handcuffed them, read them their rights and led them away and the long search was over.

To the public, it seemed right, somehow, that a high-tech terrorist should be brought down by a child and their conviction nailed down by another technology half-a-century old. Credit card receipts for the sales of Chambord, along with the Barbie dolls and other presents bought in Dundale and Janesville were retrieved and these aided

Dead in Pleasant Company
A Pennsylvania Dutch Mystery

investigators in disclosing the bones of the plots. The child is clearly identifiable in the hospital videotapes despite attempts to make her look like a boy. When appearing before a judge in his chambers, she obligingly went into the act she'd been taught to play, staggering around and falling to the ground. Raymond Fargoe saw the end and finally confessed.

The duo's televised arrest produced the phone call for which I'd been waiting. Thirteen days after I was called to the bus terminal to pick up a lost child, Mr. and Mrs. Philip Morgan came to claim their daughter.

Mrs. Morgan's explanation of how the child had been left with the couple also revealed: the motive for the deadly acts. Raymond Fargoe, her younger brother, had been devastated by the death of his own little girl—a death laid at the feet of the hospital and doctor charged with her care. His efforts to proceed against them legally died a-borning when the case was dismissed as 'frivolous' under a new state law prohibiting such cases. Mrs. Morgan said she thought the loan of her child, who was (one could read between the lines) in the way after all, would help him recover.

Under a court 'gag' order prohibiting them from telling their story to anyone until the trial was over, the Morgans were referred to me. I arranged for a meeting giving them a chance to see and talk with their daughter and me a chance to talk with them. I asked why they had never notified the police their child was missing.

"Because she *wasn't* missing! We knew she was with Raymond."

"But didn't your brother leave town without telling you?"

Mrs. Morgan waxed indignant. "Why not? He's a grown man. He don't need to tell me every move he makes! Besides, once we learned the hospital fired him, we figured he'd just gone somewhere else to look for a job, someplace he could forget about losing his kid. I knew he would get work. He can do anything with computers."

And, as it turned out, with a rare specialty as well. As one of the 'techs' hired to put the hospital's records online a decade or so ago, Fargoe had convinced the hospital that records could be updated more readily if computers replaced the traditional bedside charts. Then he'd gone on to write appropriate software which the hospital subsequently sold to other health care units at a substantial profit, none of which came his way.

When his small daughter became ill he took her to the same hospital where she died. When he threatened to file a malpractice suit against the hospital, he was not only fired but blacklisted.

His name had not come up in the FBI search for recently fired employees or those with a grudge against the hospital because, from their standpoint, once the threatened suit was blocked, that was the end of it. Andy, more angry than I've ever seen him, hypothesized another reason: the hospital had not wanted to call attention to the child's death, perhaps a tacit admission there was at least some fault there.

As for the parents themselves, there was no culpability there. Andy cleared them to return home. But not so Janus. Next for her was an appearance before a grand jury where her testimony would be videotaped for use later should Raymond Fargoe change his plea in the future.

Despite her complete 'ho hum' air, I was concerned with what kind of trauma this child might be experiencing. It would be months, perhaps a year or more, until the case was fully closed. It was deemed unwise to permit the star witness to return home.

I suggested she be permitted to stay with Uncle Peter in Newberry. Their stables were enormous, the child would be anonymously happy among the four-legged inhabitants and a small child could run and play freely, yet protected by the scores of lads and trainers. More to the point, it was one place from which she would not want to run away. The only difficulty might come when she had to leave.

Her family appeared glad to have her taken care of, going so far as to drop hints that they receive some benefit for their generosity in letting her go. I had a few hints of my own, including a short course in the law pertaining to child endangerment and neglect. Not nice, but I'm afraid I'd had it with them.

"Anyway, Sam" I said in conclusion, "Cousin Susan and Janus will be off to Uncle Peter's until she's needed." My brother seemed untypically quiet. "What's up?" I said somewhat testily.

"Huh? Oh. I was thinking...Well, truth is, Rose wants to adopt her."

"Really? Rose does?"

"Well...Oh, just forget it! It's not as though the kid's an orphan."

"No," I said quietly. "She's not, but there are plenty of..."

"I said forget it. What kind of parents would we be? For one thing, we're never home."

"You've been a wonderful parent to me," I said gently. "I'm sure I don't know what I'd have done without..."

"Don't be a mutt! Anyhow, I told you to forget it. Besides, after I tell you what I've found out about your 'friend' you'll disown me."

"Oh?"

"I don't like to spoil your good news though. It can wait."

"No it can't. Give."

"Sure you want it all? It's not pretty."

"Quit stalling, Sir Galahad."

"Right. Look, you posed the question of how Fowler benefited, though I'm sure you knew what the answer to that had to be. The fee paid to him on the claims disallowed on the basis of his investigation is typically right around five per cent of the policy's face amount. If we just look at the six names on that list we're talking about, five percent of one hundred and forty million, that's seven million big ones."

"A tidy enough sum," I said.

"Indeed." Sam gave me a steady look. "In those six claims alone, the company saved one hundred and thirty three million dollars, going a long way to explain why the company's bottom line was so black. That was the basis on which Finch's arrest was made. However, it is our contention Finch was innocent, but were we right and how to prove it."

"I asked myself why the forensic accountants found no record of those six names anywhere in Horizon's computerized or paper records. They had to be there somewhere so what happened to them? I went back and took a good look at the list of numbers assigned to policy holders, looking not so much for what *was* there but what wasn't. Sure enough, I found six places where, in assigning a number to a client, a number was skipped. Six, mind you, no more, no less. Significant but just a beginning. I made a note of the missing numbers and checked Horizon's Account Code for the account line indicating commissions paid. Once again there was no record of any commission paid out in connection with those six accounts. I asked Miss Ready for Horizon's copy of the audits for the past three years."

He paused to throw me a look, gauging my willingness to hang in there with him. I was with him, not at all surprised at the way he'd unearthed the six missing files. When it comes to money matters, my brother can out-bird a Labrador Retriever. I told him so.

"Yeah well. Duck soup really. It was simply a matter of matching their assigned account codes to commission checks disbursed by Horizon. There they were. Six commission checks to the tune of seven million dollars paid out and cashed."

I said I saw. "So easy when you know how. I expect," I added thoughtfully, "I don't have to ask to whom those checks were paid."

"I said you wouldn't like it. Anyway, one check was issued under each of those missing numbers. covering a period of a little less than three years, the last being a week ago—the one issued on the Tunnelson policy."

We stared at each other for a moment. Then I let the papers drop to my lap and looked at him.

"So! Who says there's nothing new under the sun?"

He fiddled around putting papers away, trying not to gloat, giving me time to deal with it. "Incredible!" I shivered, then held my hands out to the flames. "Explains why Tunnelson's blood and tissue samples revealed nothing because there was nothing there to find! But hang on! what about the pin-pricks? How do you account..."

He shrugged. "Hey! That's your department. I'm the fiscal expert, remember? What do you think?"

I gave it some thought. "Just how in the world do you suppose he did it? And when?"

"Had to be right there at the second autopsy, don't you think? By golly! We thought it was damned odd for him to insist Hal do it over! He had to do it right then, didn't he?"

"I think so. That doesn't answer how he did it, though." I shook my head. "It took a very clever man to pull it off, you know."

"That a testimonial? Want to throw him a parade?"

I ignored him, still thinking. "I wonder how long he would have gotten away with it. And why, for heaven's sake? It isn't as though he needed the..." I eyed him. "I suppose you've checked him out though, haven't you?"

"Hell, I did that a week ago. I know! I know! You're a big girl and I should mind my own business, but we are each other's business, as, in your more rational moments, you admit. Besides, you shouldn't think 'cuz I let you boss me around I'm a trained seal."

"I don't. Of course I don't. And of course you have a right to...never mind that. Are you saying he doesn't have money? How do you know?"

He shook his head again. "Talked to a banker in New York and a college classmate of Fowler's. As to family, it seems he was cut off from the family pot some five years ago after he conned the life savings from his own grandmother and disappeared. He wrote home to say he knew the family would take care of her. Last they heard of him he was somewhere in New York. As to money, he makes it all right. Two days ago he withdrew everything from his account in New York, nearly sixteen million dollars, took it out in bearer bonds."

After a moment I looked at him again. "A *scuzz-ball*, I believe you said."

"Of major proportions."

I nodded. "So! You were right all along, you old goat. How come you're not gloating?"

"Goats don't gloat. They bleat. Consider yourself bleated." He looked at me. "You don't seem to be terminally wounded."

"No. I've been thinking about that myself. We had a lot of fun but it was all very...I don't know. Kids on a playground kind of I guess." Nothing at all like..." I stopped.

"Maybe for you, but I've seen his face when he looked at you. Anyway, so does that mean you'll listen next time?"

Dead in Pleasant Company
A Pennsylvania Dutch Mystery

I grinned at him. "You know what they say about how well old dogs learn. However, you have my permission to rub it in every so often."

"Every leap year perhaps?"

"Maybe not *that* often, I said absently, thinking of the fleeting friendship I'd formed with one who turned out to be a complete scoundrel. Where were the tell-tale signs? Why had I missed them? My brother hadn't. Had I become one of those women so starved for romance I could not see the truth? And where were my damned toes when I needed them?

"It'll be a lengthy jail term I imagine," I said.

"Don't worry about him! He'll probably talk the judge into letting him go as a youthful offender!"

I laughed. "Well, perhaps not that but I bet he does serve his time in Club Fed."

"If they catch him."

"when *they* catch him." I rose with a sigh. "Okay, Bro'. That's enough about him. Let's go see if our youthful Crime-buster is ready to leave. I'm glad she's going to Uncle Peter's. The lads there will keep her in line. Since she helped Andy out she's been impossible to live with."

"Is that so? You mean she's got everyone in sight dancing to her piping. A lot of that going around."

"Meaning? Oh. Walt?" I turned to look at him. "Oh! You meant..." He dodged but the pillow got him head on. Silly man! He always dodges to the left.

* * * * *

Rarely do I feel depressed, especially in my own home, and when a few days later I finally put my finger on the reason for it, my spirits sank even lower. I was loathe to admit Ken Fowler's perfidy affected me, but it had. His behavior seemed to diminish, not only him, but me as well.

I'd recognized him from the outset as the sort of person who has made charm his *modus operandi*, had expected treachery of him, but not this. Did this depression mean I loved him? I don't know. I never have been able to recognize the depth of my feelings until it's too late.

What he'd done was so short-sighted, so stupid. A good brain, a fine education, a talent for persuasion and what G.G.H.H. would have called 'guts', all bowed to that basest of faults: greed. Or was it that? Perhaps the money was not as driving a force as the need to prove himself. And there, I thought morosely, for the grace of God, went I.

I was certainly in no mood to face my present task. The note to Judd Tunnelson's sister was long overdue. Now with the child gone, the house quiet and the mask of a February evening pulled down around me, I faced my task, struggling to make it genuinely sympathetic.

"Madam?" Honeycutt approached. "Will Mr. Thaxton be dining with us tonight?"

"No, Honeycutt. Not tonight. They have guests."

He stood waiting. "It feels a bit foggy tonight, Madam. Shall I draw the curtains?"

Indeed, fog hung like a fine, grey curtain against the windows. It seemed right somehow. "Looks it as well, Honeycutt but no thanks."

"An extra fire then? In the garden room?"

"That would be lovely. Thank you."

"Madam?"

"Yes?"

"You sound...tired. Perhaps an early night would help. May I set up for you in the alcove? Mrs. Honeycutt's made a pork pot-pie for you and there are some tomatoes from the hydroponic garden."

So I dined alone at a small table in a corner of my 'porch.' I'd put aside the still unfinished note, waiting for...I don't know. Inspiration. Some kind of resolution perhaps. Maybe Honeycutt was right. Maybe I'd be up to it once I caught up on my sleep.

The pork-pie and sweet and sour tomatoes were gone, washed down with a couple of glasses of a new California Cabernet Sauvignon Sam had discovered. I sat over a celebratory piece of rhubarb pie with that familiar blend of guilt and pleasure which always follows such a plethora of forbidden delights. I looked out at the thawing snow. In a few weeks, the violets would be in bloom. I felt my spirits lift.

"Madam? Sorry to disturb you. Are you receiving?"

"Receiving? Whyever should you ask..." I thought he looked odd. "Who is it, Honeycutt?"

"Mr. Ken Fowler, Madam."

CHAPTER 24

"Will you see him?"

I thought I was dreaming there in the dusk.

"Mr. Fowler?"

"Yes, Madam."

"Did he say what...never mind. Yes. But not here. In the library. And you'd better let Mr. Thaxton know."

Ken rose readily to greet me, much as he had that first time. This time, however, he was drink-less. I wondered if that was his decision or Honeycutt passing judgment.

"Thank you for seeing me." His voice was low and penitent.

"Yes well, there are a number of people out there looking for you."

"I know. I'll be turning myself in, in a bit..." Thank God for that, I thought. At least he's not a complete rat. "...but I wanted to see you first. I feel I owe you an explanation."

If he expected a protest he was due to be disappointed. I remained matter-of-fact. "Perhaps you do. Bear in mind, however, that I am a police officer." That startled him. I sat down at my desk and indicated a chair. "Have a seat." I touched the bell. "Would you like a glass of Glen Fiddich? It may be a while before you get a chance again," I said coolly.

He shook his head at that, whether at the truth of the statement or my callous reminder, I could only guess.

"I think I need to stand. Helps me keep my courage up."

Nice try, I thought. "As you wish. Tell me, to what do I owe the pleasure?"

"Oh Sal, don't! Sarcasm doesn't become you."

"No? Sorry to disappoint you."

"Okay, okay. I deserved that. I've no business judging you."

Another attempt to shift ground, to get me to say it was all right. "We agree on that, at least," I replied. "So! Back to the question. What do you want?" One way to keep out of the net of a man who lives off his charm is to keep focused on what he was getting out of the situation, regardless of his declared intention. I had no doubt he wanted something.

He protested. "I don't want anything! As I said, I'm on my way to give myself up," he tilted his head ruefully at me, "but I couldn't do it without seeing you first. I'm trying to explain why I did what I did." I eyed him, waiting. He sat then, dropping to the chair without his usual élan. He sat across from me, shaking his head. "Oh God, Sal! You must think I'm a skunk of the worst order! Coming here, pursuing you and all the time making a total ass of myself!"

"Again we agree," I said. "Your pranks become you not."[6]

"Oh God! Macbeth!" He groaned. I left it entirely to him, surprising him further. He jerked his head a little and smiled sadly at me. "Ball's in my court, that it?"

"I'd say so."

"Well here goes. One thing I want to stress at the outset," he oozed sincerity. "I really meant everything I ever said to you. I mean," he hurried on, *"everything!* As true as anything I've ever...about how wonderful you are and how I feel about you I mean." He appeared to be studying my face. "Oh God! You're not going to believe a word I say, are you?" He looked pained.

"If I may borrow from Shakespeare again, Mr. Fowler, if candor is to be the currency of our discourse, I suspect that what I believe is probably not the most important concern for you at the moment."

---

[6] *Macbeth* William Shakespeare

"To the contrary, my dear! It's the *only* thing that concerns me! If I thought you did not hate me it would go a long way to helping me through this."

My impulse was to be honest: to tell him I regretted losing the fun he'd put back in my life, to say how disappointed I was he'd chosen to use his God-given talents in this way, to say I felt betrayed. I hesitated. What right did I have to judge his choices? And, the greater question, why should I care one way or another? Not understanding it myself, I chose a middle ground.

"I don't hate you," I said.

"Oh God! I hear what you're saying! I'm not important enough to hate! That's even worse!"

I tried to get him back on track. "You said you wanted to explain."

"Yes. Yes I did. I do. That'll give me something to…"

Honeycutt arrived, setting a tray down in front of him. "I took the liberty, Madam."

Fowler rose, took a quick gulp and sat again. Honeycutt remained a few feet away. "Will there be anything else, Madam?" Meaning, shall I throw him out?

"Not now Honeycutt. Perhaps later." Meaning leave but stay nearby. "The explanation then, Mr. Fowler?"

"Ken, for God's sake."

"Ken then."

He took another gulp. "Yes. Well. Where shall I start?"

"The beginning is usually best. I admit to being curious. Whatever gave you this pin-prick idea in the first place and what made you think you'd get away with it in the second?"

"Oh, I hardly know myself. As to why I thought I could get away with it, frankly, I didn't think I would, at first." He looked at me ruefully, seeming to think I'd be satisfied with that.

"You're intelligent," I said, "and perceptive. Surely you've thought about that."

Dead in Pleasant Company
A Pennsylvania Dutch Mystery

"Yes. Some, anyway." I waited for him to go on. "It just sort of happened really. I kept thinking what a blast it would be if the guy had been bumped off instead of just going quietly. It would mean Horizon would save a bunch and that would look good for me. See. I'd talked Finch into offering this new kind of policy to high risk clients that has an exclusionary clause indemnifying us from paying off in case the client died of anything but a natural death. Well. we'd had it going for nearly two years and I'd sold quite a few of them, but so far it had never worked out for us and the board was beginning to nag Finch to drop it.

"Hell Sal, I don't know what put it in my mind," he took another sip and looked at me covertly. He shrugged. "Just wanted some action. And besides, I wanted to get a rise out of the poker-faced coroner. Hell, I felt like I was back in junior high. I'd been fingering this corn cob holder I'd stuck in my pocket at lunch. So, I took advantage of his turning away and just jabbed the dead guy hard with my corn cob holder. Hell! It didn't hurt him. He was dead...Anyway, I pretended I saw them for the first time and I asked the old guy what those holes meant in the back of the dead guy's neck. That brought him down off his high horse, I can tell you! You should have seen his face! So then they had to empanel a coroner's jury and I testified about the two holes." He shook his head, a thin smile playing under the blond moustache. "Nothing they could do but bring in a verdict of death by person or persons unknown. It was fun!" He rose and paced up and down the room. "I couldn't believe I'd gotten away with it! It was so easy!" He sipped his drink. "Getting a check for half a million bucks wasn't too bad either. Pretty heady stuff, in fact." He stared into his glass. "Old Finch treated me like a prince!" Another sip. "But I knew it was stupid and I knew I'd been lucky and I swore I'd never do it again." He sat back down. "Then months later another opportunity presented itself, then another and..." He stopped and turned away. "I was careful, picking deaths where I was pretty sure I could ge..." Get away with it he was going to say. "I mean I stuck to cases where there wasn't any family to speak of to make a big stink. It was almost too easy. I looked respectable and well, people have always trus..." Here he had the grace to blush. He took another sip. "After the fifth one, I decided to quit. I'd quite a nice sum put away. I was just going to find a reason to quit my job and leave town, make a new life somewhere quiet. Like here in Plainfield. Just think! If I'd done that, no one would ever have known. And I bet, if you'd given me half a chance, I'd have made you happy. We did have some great times together, didn't we?"

I wondered if he'd been reading my mind. I said nothing. He got up, walked to the fire and talked to it.

"When the Tunnelson assignment came to me, as all the big ones do...did, I just...I don't know. So many people hated his guts, I just thought it would be a walk in the park! The conceited ass had a policy for fifty million dollars on himself! Who in the hell is worth fifty million dollars, dead or alive? You, possibly." He bowed to me. "Then when I heard he died in one of your restaurants, well...it was just too much of a challenge to pass up. The Thaxton family has always intrigued me. I read everything I could about you, which is not a lot, given your family's skill in avoiding the press. To be honest, for a long time now I've had a yen to probe the Thaxton legend for vulnerable spots. I was sure you had an Achilles heel somewhere. You couldn't possibly be as advertised. I figured, coming from a similar background myself, I was just the guy to expose you and here was a heaven-sent chance! I've had some success penetrating dynasties. I know how to get to the real..." He was looking away, beyond the thawing landscape. "That first day, when I met your brother, I was looking for the soft

Dead in Pleasant Company
A Pennsylvania Dutch Mystery

spot. I'd met your...cousin is it? No, uncle, I guess. The mayor anyway, and he was just a nice, honorable old guy, that was obvious. So he was out. And the only thing I could find wrong with Sam is that he took an immediate dislike to me." His smile was rueful. "I guess I can't blame him for that. My God! We even have the same tailor! So it was down to you." He looked at me quickly and away. "And here you were, with those grey eyes that see right through skin and bones, and that sweet...hell, it was all I could do to restrain myself from wrapping you up and taking you home!"

"It would have been a hefty package," I said dryly, thinking I had certainly not seen through him. Another failing grade for my toes.

"It would have been a perfectly fine package," he said, for a moment all trace of arrogance gone. "I wish to hell I'd met you before..." He looked up at me. "So, Officer McKnight. What happens now?"

"I think you know what happens now. You've defrauded your insurance company and a number of private citizens as well. You'll have to answer to that, but not here. I imagine you'll be arrested here and returned to New York."

He laughed briefly. "Too bad I didn't follow my father into politics as he'd wanted. I'd probably get away with all this. I almost did anyway, what with your Captain Longnecker helping me out." His eyes softened again and he sounded reflective. "You've had quite an effect on me Salome Jane Thaxton McKnight! Would you believe me if I told you that it's because of you that I'm giving myself up?" He didn't wait for an answer. "But," his tone was different now, "you wouldn't want a jail-bird hanging around your neck for the rest of your life, would you?" This time he did wait and I wondered if he seriously expected me to reassure him. "No. I thought not. Nor·should you. You deserve someone super and if I were a bigger man I'd tell you I hope, if it can't be me, you find him, but, well,...After all," he set his glass down carefully, "it's not as though I've *killed* anyone. And I *am* coming forward so the old guy will be in the clear."

"Yes, I suppose you should be thanked for that. Still, I hope you're not trying to persuade yourself these were victimless crimes." He looked at me briefly, then away.

"So," he said, his voice changing abruptly, "half a dozen charges of fraud. Supposing I make restitution?"

"I imagine restitution would help, Mr. Fowler, but that will be up to the victims' families." I wanted to add something about the lives he'd shattered but I did not know how true that was. He *had* selected his victims well.

"Ken, please my dear. I know I don't deserve it, but for the final moments we have together, please make it Ken."

"Ken." I tried to guess where all this was heading. The whole scene seem uncomfortably familiar. I needed to think. I talked to give myself time. "Even if you made full restitution of the funds, the charges would remain. Federal charges. In addition, most likely you'll also have to face a number of damage suits from those whose lives you've ruined. Your boss, for instance."

"Old Finch? He'd never file against me. And if I'm willing to..." My expression must have stopped him. "But I guess that's the problem with all us crooks, isn't it, Officer McKnight?"

His voice took on an odd tone, a familiar tone. It seemed important to put my finger on...then I had it! Tracy Hall. A student at Hawk County, a sociopath, from whom I'd learned the havoc charm and charisma could wreak. The young man had spoken in just such a tone the day he learned I'd the goods on him and he was done for. He, too, had promised to turn himself in. I wondered if they'd ever

Dead in Pleasant Company
A Pennsylvania Dutch Mystery

caught him. But, if this man was not going to give himself up. Quite suddenly, I felt my toes curl.

Without changing my expression, I assessed the danger the man, not twenty feet away, could pose. A subtle tightening behind his eyes said he would not let me stand in his way, regardless of the sweet talk. I recalled now the slight bulge in the perfectly cut suit. I blessed Joe for harassing me about my own weapon. The silence between us deepened.

"Anyway," he said, breaking it, "I suppose you're right." He sighed and stood. "We never plan on having to pay the piper, do we?" I said nothing. "Well," he said, as if coming to the end.

I stalled for time. Did he realize I was on to him? Could I manage to persuade him I still believed him? Possibly. His vanity would not permit him to think anything else. Was it possible to press the concealed button at my desk without his knowing? I fiddled with some files on my desk, pulling them toward me to cover the edge of the middle drawer. I needed time. I made my voice casual. "One question, Mr...Ken. Why?"

A bitter smile came and went. "That the question of a police officer or a friend?" His eyes moved away for a split second. I pushed the button. The drawer slid open without a sound.

"I'd really like to understand," I said truthfully.

"You would ask that. Well my dear, I've been asking myself the same thing." He sounded introspective. That was good. Sociopaths love to convince others their behavior has been justified. I nodded empathetically. He sighed. "I guess," he said with frankness meant to disarm, "the short answer is I did it because I could." His study of the crease of his trouser leg gave me the chance I needed. Concealed by the scattered files, I eased the drawer open a couple of inches and touched cold metal.

He looked up, half entreaty, half self-deprecatory. "I guess this means our date for Valentine's Day is off?"

"I rather imagine you'll be too busy to think about dancing."

"You may be right at that,*" he said, making a decision. "Well, I guess 'if it were done, 'tis best t'were done quickly." The bulge in his suit flattened. His pistol was small too, but business-like.

I wanted to laugh. A short time ago we were dancing and skating. Now we quoted Macbeth and pointed weapons of death at one another. I had the edge as mine was still out of sight and I was certain he was not expecting me to be armed.

Still facing me, he began to back toward the door. "Forgive me for such a crass action, my dear Sal, but perhaps I'll give your police a pass after all. I'll make much better use of the money myself. And if it's any satisfaction to your ethical mind, I will be punished. I'll have lost you! Please don't get up. I would hate to hurt you. Farewell, love of my life!"

My shot rang out. Fowler yelped in pain and jumped as his gun flew out of his hand. I hadn't moved from my desk and he looked down at me in shock and surprise.

"Don't bother reaching for it," I said as he bent to retrieve his gun. "Somehow we never got around to discussing weapons," I said mildly, "or I might have mentioned I'm a fair shot."

He laughed then, a sardonic laugh, a blend of pain and pleasure. "I should have known. Oh Sal McKnight! You are priceless! But I don't really think you'll shoot me."

He tossed a salute at me with his uninjured hand and was gone, slipping through the wide doorway, out into the hall and beyond. I did not rush after him. I'd swum and skated with him and knew he was stronger and faster than I.

Moreover, I was not sure I could actually shoot him. Besides, Sam would be out there waiting.

I notified headquarters, suggesting a road block was called for on the odd chance he got by Sam. Outside my door, all was silent. Sam's voice came in response to the button on my watch.

"I'm on Nimbus, just at the bridge. What's up?

"Okay Lone Ranger. He pulled a gun on me. He's got about a minute's start. My guess is you can catch him when he gets to the gate."

"Cut him off at the pass, eh? Do I take it you want him caught?"

"Of course I want him caught! I'm a police officer!"

But what sort of a police officer? For the first time I realized none of what he said could be used in court. I'd completely forgotten the cop's Golden Rule. Mirandize. Mirandize. Mirandize.

* * * * *

As it turned out, all my efforts to ensure his capture came to naught. I'd assumed, when I heard his car start up and drive away he would head with all possible speed down my drive. I'd assumed my gate-keeper would close said gate, keeping him in. I'd assumed that, on the off-chance he'd get past the gatekeeper, he would head for town and thence to highway or air terminal. Since the only way to Plainfield is through the covered bridge, a scant quarter-mile from the end of my drive and Sam waited there on Nimbus, I was certain we would have him. But even had he gotten by Sam somehow, I reasoned the length of my drive provided enough time for the Plainfield Police force to reach each of the other flight paths.

But he never reached Sam and, though virtually the whole of the PPD turned out to search, spreading out in ever widening circles through the night, there was no sign of him. I misjudged him again. My erstwhile suitor had prepared well.

On into the moonless, pitch black February night they searched. A bevy of officers joined Sam to micro-search the area around my home. In the thick stands of leafless trees, search-lights mounted on police cars, did little more than throw useless shadows on the snow. It was nearly two hours before someone thought to haul out the sensory-imaging equipment and by that time the only images were those of deer, elk and raccoon. Ken Fowler had vanished!

It wasn't until daybreak that they found his car, abandoned in my own wooded driveway, halfway between my front door and the bridge. A few tiny drops of blood at the trunk of his car and the ski tracks leading away told the story. There could be no doubt he'd been prepared for this escape. Followed, the tracks led through Thaxtonville's Main Street and thence through the village park and beyond, three miles further north to Elk Run. There his trail ended. The debate over whether he was the old man, bundled to the teeth that cold night, picked up by the bus to New York, or simply had another car waiting there, continues. They put out an APB for him but to no avail. I've no doubt he's somewhere well out of reach.

Chagrined, my report to the police, first ours, then to New York, was complete and contrite. Fowler had simply escaped following the same path we'd taken a few days earlier. I did not admit I'd even shown him the escape route laid out in my Putz! I had no doubt my career as a police officer would take a stunning, perhaps fatal, blow. The New York cops would have a legitimate reason to belittle 'hick' cops in general and one in particular. It was not a shining moment for any of us and it was all my fault.

* * * * *

Dead in Pleasant Company
A Pennsylvania Dutch Mystery

Mrs. Sweeney was placing an enormous vase of pink roses on my desk next day as I wished her good morning.

"Good morning. Look Sal! You've got a Valentine's Day present! Your admirers certainly have good taste. There are at least two dozen roses here. Aren't they incredible?"

"Indeed," I said. "Who sent them?"

"There's an envelope. There on the table."

The paper was thick, creamy, expensive looking.

"My dear Sal,

I told you I could find better things to do with the money. Having a wonderful time, but sure wish you were here. Yours."

The initials were scribbled, but there was no mystery whose they were.

I almost missed the single red rose on my desk. There was no card with that. I didn't need one.

Hannah Fairchild

CODA

One year later.

Janus and I were seated in a reception room outside the Oval Office awaiting the President of the United States. I should say I was seated. She was all over the place.

We'd had our own reunion and she'd done her best to impress me with her new knowledge of horses and their training and impressed I was. She'd not only grown taller, but had acquired a jockey's 'sass' to go along with the jockey's cap topping off the indigo and silver Thaxton colors of her riding habit. Both seemed to suit her well. I, too, was 'tarted' up in an outfit Markham had sent for the occasion.

We'd been waiting more than an hour, summoned there to receive a commendation for our part in the arrest of Mastermind. Members of the fourth estate waited too, a lot more patiently than either my young friend or I. When the President was delayed for the third time, an aide brought an ice cream cone and gave it to Janus before I could object. She'd just got a good start on it when two uniformed Marines appeared at the door. Janus ran across the room and leapt onto my lap, wrapping small arms, ice cream cone and all, around my head. The door to the Oval Office opened and our nation's leader bustled out, secret service men on both sides and an aide carrying papers trotting behind him.

At the sight before him, the President stopped and with cameras flashing all around, threw his head back and roared.

"Oh Sal Thaxton! You don't change! You look exactly the way you looked all through school! Hair all over the place!" He advanced, hand outstretched, cameras flashing as I struggled to disentangle the child and rise. He grabbed my hand with both of his. "By God, it's good to see you again! Here now, somebody get something to clean this child up and let's get this damned ceremony over with. I want to talk to this woman!"

* * * * *

SAM

Oh, by the way, in case you're curious, or, like my twin, like your ends all tied up neatly, you may be wondering what has happened to my would-be brother-in-law.

If you know me at all, you know Mr. Ken Fowler may have given me the slip that night, but not for long. I'm sure he's patting himself on the back, convinced he's some sort of genius who outwitted both cops and Thaxtons, but I can tell you exactly in which villa on which tropical island he is currently spreading his line of baloney. A phone call to Markham got him. The moron!

You'll know too at some point. You'll hear a story about the natives of this little po-dunk place being stripped down to their skivvies by some slick tourist who ingratiated himself among them, became the town favorite, then ran off with not only the town's cookies, but the jar as well.

I haven't told Sal. She'd insist on turning the information over to the New York cops. They'd insist on spending a lot of time and our tax-payers money trying to catch him and hauling him off to court. That would wind up costing everybody even more money and he'd hire a lawyer who'd get him off with a slapped wrist and he'd be right back at 27 Longmeadow.

Besides, I kind of like the flush on Sal's face every Valentine's Day when the enormous bouquet of pink roses arrives. It's a safe enough spot of romance in her otherwise work-focused life and the blush they produce. (I really think it's embarrassment that she got diddled), takes me back to the time when we were kids together. And, like I said in the beginning, I know in whose custody her heart really lies.

I talked it over with Roselma and she agrees. Wise woman, my wife.

Dead in Pleasant Company
A Pennsylvania Dutch Mystery

GLOSSARY OF PENNSYLVANIA DUTCH PHRASES

Ich weiss nicht - I don't know.
fastnachts – yeast raised powdered sugar donuts, usually square, sometimes made from mashed potatoes.
freundshaft - the entire family
geht mit - go with you
gut genuk - good enough
mach's nicht aus - it makes no difference
nicht vahr? - Is that not so?
Putz- an elaborate village traditionally set under a Christmas tree
schmutzig - dirty
vas gibt - what gives
versteh - do you understand

ABOUT THE AUTHOR

Hannah Fairchild comes to fiction writing after a lifetime as an innovative educator, businesswoman, lecturer and all around button pusher. When failing eyesight prevented her from continuing her chosen profession as supervisor of student teachers, she turned to her other lifetime interest, mystery writing.

Ms. Fairchild sets her stories in the quaint Pennsylvania Dutch (Throw papa down the steps his hat, Ve grow too soon old und too late smart,) town of Plainfield.

She draws on her family tree, resurrecting her own twin brother for her main characters. In their late forties in the first of the Pennsylvania Dutch Mysteries, Sam and Salome, the famous Thaxton twins, turn sleuths when murder threatens their restaurant chain.

Other books by this author:
If It's Monday, It Must Be Murder!
Pennsylvania Dutch Mysteries in the works:
Death on Delivery
So Long at the Fair
Other books by this authors:
Appleby of Iowa Takes the Hill

Printed in the United States
28983LVS00001B/21